SARAH

Also by Joel Gross

BUBBLE'S SHADOW

YOUNG MAN WHO WROTE SOAP OPERAS

1407 BROADWAY

THE BOOKS OF RACHEL

MAURA'S DREAM

HOME OF THE BRAVE

THIS YEAR IN JERUSALEM

THE LIVES OF RACHEL

SPIRIT IN THE FLESH

SARAH

Joel Gross

WILLIAM MORROW AND COMPANY, INC.
New York

Library of Congress Cataloging-in-Publication Data

Gross, Joel
　　Sarah.
　　1. Bernhardt, Sarah, 1844-1923—Fiction.　I. Title.
PS3557.R58S2　1987　　813'.54　　87-7785
ISBN 0-688-06703-4

Printed in the United States of America

First Edition

1 2 3 4 5 6 7 8 9 10

BOOK DESIGN BY SUSAN HOOD

For Linda

Author's Note

What you are about to read is a work of fiction. No one today knows what Sarah Bernhardt felt about her mother, her son, her lovers. She was a public personage, and her statements, her memoirs, her style of life were all directed to that public. She loved the legend that grew around her, and aided and abetted in its construction. But this does not mean that the legend was true. We know that she lived and died, that she performed indefatigably in plays around the world, and that for some reason, more than that of any other actor or actress, her name endures. The novel that follows imagines one route connecting the facts of her life to the strength of her legend.

Contents

CONTENTS

Quand même! ("In spite of everything!")

—Sarah Bernhardt's motto

SARAH

MAMA WOULD COME

Sarah was small, smaller than Nurse, smaller even than the happy children in the market square. And not just small, but delicate; too delicate to run barefoot over the rocky ground, too delicate to play games at the seaside, too delicate to bathe in the frigid coastal water.

"It is cold and damp outside," said Nurse, stirring up the fire. "In here is best."

"Why do the others play outside?" asked Sarah.

"They are fishermen's children."

"And I am a princess?"

"Yes, Sarah."

"My mother is a queen?"

"Your mother is a queen."

"And my father. Tell me about my father."

Nurse hesitated only a moment. There were some lies she would never allow herself to tell, not for any sum of money or act of kindness. But if the poor child needed to believe in an earthly father, it might as well be a king as an accountant from Havre.

"Your father is a king, of course. Who else could be the husband of a queen, silly goose?"

"Where is my mother?"

"You know that she is traveling. Why do you always ask? How am I to know where Madame Julie is? One day Holland, another day Spain. She is very footloose, your mother."

"What is footloose, please?" asked Sarah.

Nurse was losing patience. "Footloose means someone who likes to travel a great deal."

"I would like to travel," said Sarah. "But you do not even let me go outside."

"For your own good," said Nurse.

"Why are the children of fishermen allowed to play outside while I must stay inside?"

"They are hardier. Their skin is thick, and their lungs are strong."

"I am strong," said Sarah. "My skin is thick." She took hold of a smoke-stained chair and pulled herself to her feet. As if to prove her strength, she threw open the clasp holding the south window shutter in place, letting the wind bang it with violence. Unlike the home in which she had been born, this cottage had no window glass. But Sarah could no more imagine windows made of glass than she could conjure streets paved with brick or stone; all she knew of Paris was the grand silks and satins, the powerful scents worn by her beautiful mother. She stood at the open window, letting the winter light suffuse her and every object in the cottage with magic.

"Sarah," said Nurse, taking hold of the child's elbows with proprietary force.

"I am strong," said Sarah, holding on to the window frame, letting the wind from the sea run through her hair and into every nook and cranny of their two shut-up rooms. For a moment she felt immensely powerful, capable of feats of endurance and will. No one could move her, because her feet were rooted through the rough floor planks, through the packed mud, through the frozen soil. In the distance the sinking sun drew colors from the sea, colors too bold and happy to announce anything as sad as the finish of day, another day in which her mother's promise to visit would not be fulfilled. "I am strong," Sarah repeated, so that her eyes would not fill with tears, so that her heart would not beat its fearful rhythm of loss and abandonment, so that she would not question why she alone of all children did not live with her mother.

"Sweet child," said Nurse. Sarah, feeling the love from the woman towering above, could not resist her. The big brown-eyed woman pulled her away from the window as if Sarah had no more strength than a rag doll. She placed her on the filthy woolen throw before the fire, then quickly and efficiently closed and clasped the shutter, banishing along with the cold wind the natural light.

"Nothing would hurt me outside," said Sarah, lapsing without thought into Breton, the language of Nurse and all the people in this part of the world.

"French, please," said Nurse. "You know how cross your mother becomes if you speak anything but French."

"No," said Sarah. "I do not know how cross Mother becomes. I forget Mother." But she spoke the sullen words in French. If Mother would come, she must be ready for her. She must be pretty and polite, she must speak French like a little lady, she must not disappoint her in anything.

Nurse smiled, and pulled Sarah closer to the hearth.

"Sarah, your mother will be here soon."

"I want to play outside with the children."

"Madame Julie would not like you to play with them. They are rough, they are common."

"I want to be common," said Sarah, narrowing her green eyes into angry slits, pulling back her lips over baby teeth like an animal baring fangs. If her mother did not want her to be common, why had she left her forever in this wild place?

"Hush, Sarah," said Nurse, worrying that the child's temper would grow into a fit. She had asked the priest to write to Madame Julie about the terrible tantrums, suggesting that the child be sent to Paris for a brief visit if Madame could not make the trip to Brittany. Nurse knew well the origin of Sarah's wildness, understood the power of the sadness that could not be contained in her little body, the insatiable hunger for an uncaring mother's love. "Hush, and I will sing to you," said Nurse.

"I want to be common!" insisted Sarah, but the words only served to frame the desperation behind them. Nothing about the child was common, and nothing suggested that her desire was to be anything like the sun-browned children who swam in the wild surf without fear. Sarah crawled closer to the hearth, letting the flames redden her pale skin, drawing in the warmth of the fire as if it were a supernatural food. She was ignored, she was abandoned, she was the child no one wanted, but in spite of everything she would be loved.

"Sweet baby," said Nurse. "Don't go so close to the fire."

"I can go wherever I want," said Sarah.

"You don't want to burn," said Nurse.

"I do want to burn," said Sarah.

Nurse grew frightened. The child's profile seemed to vibrate in the firelight as she threw back her head and shook her mass of curls in defiance. "I do want to burn."

"Hush, Sarah. Come close and I shall sing to you. I shall tell you a story, and I shall sing you a song." Nurse reached out to take hold of the child's shoulders, but Sarah moved swiftly two inches closer to the flames.

It was a moment before Nurse realized that the left sleeve of Sarah's sweater was smoldering, and that the hanging velvet ribbons in her hair had burst into flame. "I am burning," said Sarah without any trace of fear. "I am burning."

Nurse jerked the child away from the hearth, and plunged her arm into a pot of milk. The swift movement had already put out the fiery ribbons, but Nurse pulled these out of Sarah's thick curls as if they were the claws of the Devil. She had been forbidden by Madame Julie to strike the girl, but now she could not help herself. What if she had not been there, a half step from where the miserable child played? Nurse took Sarah over her knees, letting the milk-washed arm wet her lap as she beat her with violence. Nurse cried as she struck her, cried until she could barely see the girl, could hardly remember anything but the wild fear of losing her.

But Sarah did not cry. She shut her eyes, feeling the love that drove Nurse's blows, imagining the terrible story of flames that would fly home to Mama. There had been no danger. She had not wanted to die, but only to burn. The fire was already past. In spite of everything she would come. Mama would come and take her to Papa, and they would all go home and be together forever. In spite of everything.

Chapter 1

MAMA WAS THE MOST BEAUTIFUL WOMAN IN THE WORLD

It was not fire that brought Madame Julie to Sarah, but rioting in the streets of Paris. Every ruler of France since the 1789 Revolution feared the narrow alleys and passageways that allowed common people to hurl rocks at soldiers with impunity. In the winter of 1848, nearly four years after Sarah's birth, students and workers were once again setting up barricades in the cramped quarters of the city, readying their artillery of stones to force the abdication of King Louis Philippe. Julie had no interest or understanding in the politics of the moment. She did not care that France, in the space of fifty years, had suffered revolution, gloried in the rise of Napoleon's empire, and despaired in the emperor's final defeat at Waterloo in 1815. What mattered was that she was invited nowhere and no one came to call. Every aristocrat, every man of means was hiding his gold and praying that the reformist spirit would not grow into madness. As the rich held their breaths and prayed for the best, the lights of theaters, cafés, and private clubs all seemed to dim in unison. For a woman of Julie Van Hard's particular interests, this was as dismal as all-out war. What was the point of staying in Paris if she couldn't go out after dark?

So quite naturally, she read the letter Nurse had dictated to the local priest with great attention and feeling.

She remembered that she had a child.

A child she must go to, and at once.

With the impulsive energy that had shaped her young life, she called on a flood of vague memories: Sarah's little hands and little feet, her soft skin and pale eyes, her blond curls. How she loved her baby Sarah, she imagined, until Julie's heart seemed to swell beneath her shapely frame; how she needed to be near this, her only child, she thought, until the fact of the difficult winter stagecoach journey was overwhelmed by sentiment inchoate and urgent. This was her baby, and she missed her, and she needed her, and she made plans to travel to her at once.

That she had not seen Sarah in nearly a year, and then only for an endless hour, did not enter into her thoughts. Julie was not playacting, for her desire to see Sarah was as true and as insistent as her desire to leave Paris; that both these desires would fade and turn about during the long journey to Brittany proved only that Julie was still as much a child as Sarah herself.

Wild to see the lights of the great cities, Julie Van Hard had run off with her first lover at fourteen; her parents, middle-class Dutch Jews, had mourned for her soul as if she had died a terrible death. But Julie, heartbroken at severing relations with her family, recovered handily. It was not surprising that she had no time to pine for home. She fell in and out of love three times in that first year on her own, and by great good fortune, each new lover was richer than the first. But her youthful success was not that of the calculating courtesan; at fifteen, she feigned none of the emotions she showed to the world. Julie had an abounding appetite for love, so long as this love revolved around the worship of her person. This freshness, this obvious joy in being in love, was aided and abetted by her astonishing beauty. Students fought duels over her attentions, imagining in the glow of her spirit a woman they could possess. They were too young to understand the ambition that drove her.

Julie, in or out of love, had absolutely no inclination to bring a child into her passionate world. At fifteen, when she became pregnant with Sarah, her career had hardly begun. Her student friends were not yet great princes, her lodgings still a tenement on the Left Bank, her clothes no richer than a shopgirl's.

And as her belly swelled, her friends grew scarce. Even the man she believed to be Sarah's father took an extended leave from Paris in the middle of his legal studies; Julie was relieved when he shamefacedly returned, unable to offer her the mixed joys of marriage. She knew that he would never amount to much more than a clerk, in spite of some money in his family. All Julie Van Hard took from him was a promise of a dowry for the child, and the occasional use of his surname, Bernard. Even this she learned to find common. Now when she was not calling herself Mlle. Van Hard, it was Mme. Bern*h*ard*t*.

She was sixteen when Sarah was born, and in love with the son of a duke, a man with fierce moustaches and a stable of spirited horses. He supplied the money for the child's wet nurse, and when the baby's screams interrupted Julie's pleasuring of the young aristocrat, wet nurse and child were sent away.

But Julie was determined not to take blame for the child's lonely upbringing. It was her life in Paris that supported the baby in Brittany. If the world was not cruel, she might have married Sarah's father and settled into domestic bliss in Havre. But the world was cruel, and Julie Van Hard had to content herself with conquering Paris—or at least that opulent underside of the city that held her interest—in place of a mother's joyful obligations. It was fortunate that she was partial to riding through the Bois at breakneck speed, that she loved nothing more than being swept into the crush of the rich crowd at the Opéra and the Théâtre Français, and that her enormous ambition was no greater than what her admirers wanted her to be: the richest of ornaments to adorn their lives.

It was no wonder that the bleak weather, the frozen ground, the unfashionable company on the road to Brittany soon eclipsed the yearning for her child. Julie had been a child when she left her parents, remained a child when she bore Sarah, was kept as a child by a succession of rich and powerful lovers. It was as a child that she scolded herself, shivering with distaste at the poor food in the inns, at the hard beds, the rough language. Princes loved her, she reminded herself, and proved their love with gifts. Artists painted her, poets dined at her table, generals begged to be introduced to her in the private dining rooms that welcomed women of her special gifts. What was she doing so far from Paris?

Only a child could have so willfully forgotten the barricades in the streets, the threatening mobs of workers and students; only a child could have imagined that this trip was induced not by a whim, but by a guilty reaction to Nurse's letter.

I do everything for her, thought Julie, bristling with anger, counting on her fingers the gold coins she had sent Nurse these past four years. *I do everything for that little girl,* she thought, *and this is how she makes me suffer!*

Nurse tried to prepare Sarah. The priest had read Madame Julie's letter to her. It might be this week, it might be next, but she was coming, that was absolutely certain. Nurse fussed over the child's wild hair, tried to wash her hands and face, and to scrub away the dirt behind her ears. She grew suddenly ferocious if Sarah used any word in the Breton language. "Is she here?" Sarah would say upon awaking. "Is she coming tonight?" she would say before going asleep. In her dreams Mama was smiling, head and lips growing larger and larger, as if coming close for a kiss. During the day she waited near the door, or stood looking out through the cracks in the window shutters, watching for any break in the bleak landscape, listening for the clatter of wheels and hooves on hard winter ground.

Nurse reminded her that Mama was a refined lady, not used to sloppy hugs and wet kisses. Sarah must not show how very much she cared, or Madame Julie would think her as badly raised as a peasant's girl. Sarah took in this information with trepidation, wanting so much to please her mother; but she was filled too with the glory reflecting from her mother onto herself. Imagine a woman with such fine manners that one couldn't kiss her without asking for permission! So magnificent a woman must surely be her true mother, and not—as she sometimes feared—Nurse, with her mottled skin and sharp tongue.

Not that she didn't love Nurse.

But she preferred to believe that her mother was someone entirely different, a glorious creature who lived far away. After a thousand stories of Madame Julie's distant palace, before the fire in the hearth, a doubt sometimes penetrated: Perhaps the mother she remembered was only a dream after all, and Sarah was nothing more than Nurse's little baby, too frail to go outside and play.

But today she had woken with a start. She had no doubt that her mother would be arriving before dark. Soon she would need no dreams, no memories. Nurse tried to calm her, to get her to play before the fire. "I will tell you a story," said Nurse. "I will tell you what jewels your mother wore when she went to the Opéra, and how every man in the opera house fell in love with her." But Sarah for once refused the gift of a story. Today she wanted no stories, and her eyes would search out no fantastical shapes in the flames. Now her eyes squinted against daylight as she waited for the grand arrival of a queen, her beloved mother. Today Sarah had no need to ask Nurse whether she was truly a princess; waiting for her mother, Sarah felt as radiant as a star against black sky.

"She's here," said Sarah, whispering the words through the shutters, then turning about and running into Nurse's great skirts. "She's here," she said, but she had closed her eyes now, not wanting to be disappointed by the arrival of someone other than her mother, or worse still—by her mother arriving in the shape of someone ugly and coarse.

For it was not a *charabanc* driven by a liveried servant or a sharp little coupé driven by a royal officer that pulled to a halt in front of their cottage, but an ancient wagon driven by a cabbage farmer. Not for nothing had she listened to Nurse's tales; she had expected a carriage and a fanfare. But there was certainly a woman wrapped up in furs sitting on the wagon's hard bench, exposed to the cold air.

"Is it Mama?" asked Sarah, trying to contain her disappointment, but Nurse didn't answer. She simply pushed her away from the door and hurried to let Mme. Julie Bernhardt into the low, smoky habitation.

Sarah stood where she was, her back to the fire, and watched, in a sudden explosion of daylight, as her twenty-year-old mother removed her fur hat and revealed her long and golden hair.

It was true: Mama was the most beautiful woman in the world.

Sarah watched with a child's open-mouthed fascination as this rarest of God's creatures stamped her cold feet on the rough floor boards, beat her gloved hands together, and took a sip of hot wine from Nurse's eager grasp.

If she was not a queen, she must be an angel.

Her furs were ermine, made into a stole, muff, and hat of

dazzling whiteness. Beneath the stole was a shimmering blue silk gown, precisely the color of her imperious eyes. Sarah was afraid to approach her, afraid that the first step she took would wake her from a dream.

"Pack up the child's things, the wagon is waiting," Julie was saying. "We will stay overnight in the inn at Quimperlé."

"Overnight?" asked Nurse, not comprehending.

"I can't very well stay here," said Julie. "The stagecoach will not be back till tomorrow. Why you didn't reserve me a proper carriage is something I will never understand. Do you think I am made like a peasant? What is wrong with the girl? Why does she stand there? Doesn't she know who I am?"

"I know," said Sarah smartly, but not moving a step.

Nurse answered Julie in her kindly fashion, apologizing for Sarah's shyness, and for the lack of a local carriage to meet the stagecoach at Quimperlé.

"Am I to come too, Madame Julie?" asked Nurse.

"Of course you are to come. What do I know about children? Why doesn't she come when she is called? Doesn't she speak?"

"Hello, Mama," whispered Sarah, but a mounting ecstasy left her limbs numb, sent red flashes behind her eyes. No matter what cross words Julie uttered, Sarah fell more and more into a happiness beyond reason. She imagined the wild love Mama kept hidden behind her proud face. Mama had come because Sarah had fallen into a fire; she had been driven through seven days and nights of fierce weather in a warm coach lined with fine furs and soft leather; and until this very moment, until this instant when she looked her child fully in the face and knew that she was unharmed, her love had left her as weak and frail as sun-bleached twigs along the rocky shore.

"Madame Julie, forgive me, but I am still uncertain as to what you mean. Do we stay with you only overnight, or do we go on with you to Paris?"

Julie hesitated only a moment. She had made a great deal of money in the last four years. It gratified her vanity to imagine her child in a suburb of the city, surrounded by bonbons and fine clothes and toys.

"What sort of mother do you think I am? Of course you are coming with me."

"Sarah," said Nurse. "Did you hear that? Do you know where we are going?"

Of course, Sarah heard, but she had known all along that her mother was coming to take her home. She watched as Julie turned to face her, complaining about the cold, and urging Nurse to hurry up with the packing. Then Mama took three weightless steps across the room, so that her face glowed in the firelight.

Sarah didn't stir, and now her mother was upon her, not so tall as Nurse, but still looming above her, her face and form perfect and clean. The face was familiar from previous visits, but the familiarity was strange, like a landscape seen years before from a distant shore, suddenly brought up close. Mama was so beautiful compared to everyone she had ever known, everything she had ever seen. She smelled of Eau d'Ange, a perfume much used in her circle as a palliative against the rigors of travel; the scent was overpoweringly sweet, a sweetness Sarah used to try to recall in the middle of the night, like a bright beacon to which she could bring her dreams.

"Mama, I missed you for a long time," whispered Sarah as her mother placed her gloved hand on top of her tight curls. Sarah looked up lovingly, wanting to bury herself against her mother's powdered face, to wind the gold strands of her mother's hair about her own neck, to envelop all her senses in luxury.

"She's absolutely filthy," said Julie to Nurse. She touched a gloved finger to Sarah's neck as if it were a bit of putrid flesh. "Haven't I told you to bathe her once a week?"

"The weather has been unusually cold, Madame Julie," said Nurse as Sarah turned red with shame. The wild happiness in her heart suddenly stood completely still. If Mama wanted, she would run naked out the door and into the freezing sea. If only Mama wouldn't hate her, if only Mama wouldn't change her mind and decide after all not to take her home.

"It is never too cold to bathe," said the young beauty, pulling her ermine stole closer to her body as if to ward off any roving particles of filth. Sarah's stilled happiness now grew quickly cold and died, like a bright fire extinguished in a tempest.

"I will take a bath, Mama," said Sarah. She could feel in her heart that this urgent promise would not change her mother's mind; somehow she had disappointed her so profoundly that no remedy on earth could fix her black mood. Already her mother had turned her back to her, and moved away, to hiss sharply at Nurse.

"I don't remember the girl's hair so curly. You must brush against the curls or she will look like a Negress."

"I brush her hair," said Nurse. "It's difficult to brush. I don't want to hurt her." Sarah patted her hair, twisted her lips into a smile, and waited like a good little girl for Mama to turn round and see that there was nothing to be angry with. But she did not have Julie's attention. Her mother slapped her gloved hand against the shut door as if she could barely wait to get out.

"I don't know why I came," said Julie. "What am I to do with her in Paris? I ask you, what am I to do with her?"

"I will be good, Mama," said Sarah, but her words were too quiet for anyone but herself to hear. Her heart raced and her breath came fast, as if in a nightmare. She must keep Mama with her, but she did not know how.

"Once she is bathed, I will brush out her hair," said Nurse, but even Sarah understood how silly and insignificant this promise was. "Please, Madame Julie, I am sorry if I have not prepared the child—"

"Yes, yes," interrupted Julie. "You will bathe her at once, and pack up her clothes and yours, and I shall send the wagon back for you."

"You are leaving, Madame Julie?"

"I must have some proper tea. Surely even the inn at Quimperlé will know how to brew a pot of tea."

"I have the tea you sent, Madame Julie. I can make you a steaming pot with honey and spices."

"There is no place to sit here," said Julie.

"But the plan remains the same? You will take us with you to Paris?" asked Nurse.

"Yes, yes, yes," said Julie, slapping her hands together as if to be rid of any and all further questions.

But Sarah knew that once Mama was out that door, she would never see her again. If she did not stop her, no one would. She would have no one but Nurse.

Sarah's voice had been no more than a whisper, but now it rang out like that of a child lost in a fog.

"Mama!" called Sarah, and the plaintive word took hold of Julie's spirit.

Daughter looked at mother, the green eyes wild with love. "You can sit here, before the fire," said Sarah. "Nurse will make you tea." She put her hands on a tiny chair, rough-hewn wood covered with an ancient blanket. "This is my chair."

"Your chair," said Julie.

She found herself staring at her daughter as if seeing her for the first time. She could not have said how and why she was so affected, but Sarah had stopped her as surely as if steel talons held onto the stuff of her soul. Julie felt such an extravagant outpouring of love beyond the simple offer of the chair that tears came to her eyes. No one taller than four feet could have possibly fit on such a seat, but Julie attempted it, half sitting, half kneeling.

"Don't go, Mama," said Sarah, the childish eyes holding on to hers for dear life.

Oblivious of silk gown and ermine stole, Julie got off the chair and down on her knees before the fire and pulled her dear sweet baby against her heart. "Sarah," she said, momentarily conquered.

Chapter 2

A LIE COULD

BE WONDERFUL

Why don't you go outside and play?" said Nurse, for here in suburban Paris the weather was mild, and children were rosy-cheeked and gentle, dressed in fairy-tale clothes.

"No, thank you," said Sarah, raising both eyebrows in a grand gesture copied from her mother. "Today, I want to stay inside." Outside, the children played a game with a bright red hoop, a game punctuated by sharp cries and wild laughter. They were a short stroll from the Seine River; a carriage could follow its twisting banks to the center of Paris in a leisurely hour. It was in the center of Paris that Mama lived in a great house, in magnificent luxury, but Sarah had not yet seen this place. That was because Father had not yet come home. Because Mama was so busy traveling it was best for Sarah to stay safe in the little cottage in Neuilly with Nurse. But when Father returned from his distant travels, then all three of them would live peacefully together in the great city.

"Did you quarrel with the children?" asked Nurse.

"I do not like them," said Sarah, imitating her mother's condescending tone. "They do not like me, and I do not like them."

"But you must learn to play with them," said Nurse. "Don't you want to be like all the other children?" Ten weeks after arriving from Brittany, Sarah's Breton accent was gone, replaced by the staccato song of the Parisian child. As she imitated everything of her mother's that she could, she had imitated the speech of the

26

neighborhood girls and boys. In a time when a fourth of all Frenchmen spoke only regional dialects or—like Breton—a totally foreign languge, Sarah's instant absorption of the local accent was a minor miracle.

But because she had learned to speak like them did not mean that she wanted to be one of them. Never having played with children of her own age, she found these children of Neuilly cruel. They taunted Sarah about her too curly hair, about her lack of knowledge of games, about the fancily dressed young woman whom Sarah claimed to be her mother. No mother, the children swore, would live in Paris while her daughter was raised by a servant in Neuilly.

"Do you want me to go outside with you?" asked Nurse.

"I must wait for my father," said Sarah.

"But your father isn't coming."

"He is coming," said Sarah with violence. Behind her green eyes a terrible hurt lurked, needing only a wrong moment to burst into uncontrollable passion. Nurse had learned to tread lightly whenever Sarah snapped out her words like this.

"Of course he is, darling," said Nurse. "But if you want, before he comes, I would be happy to walk with you to the river."

"I want to stay inside," said Sarah. "Father may come back today from China."

Father had been traveling in China for a long time.

China was distant, across oceans, beyond mountains, on the far side of the world. But he would come home, her mother had explained, home to be with his wife and daughter.

Father was a merchant, a trader in gemstones. There were gems in China. Father was also a banker and an accountant; he also practiced law and medicine. Sometimes Julie mentioned travels to India and Papeete, sometimes to New Orleans and Montreal. Sarah found these stories difficult to follow, because her father seemed to do so many things, act like so many different kinds of men. She wondered if Father did these things so that he would always be too busy to see her.

But Julie assured her that Father wanted nothing so much as to come home, but he was doing what a man must do: Business. One day Sarah would understand this. Her father wanted to see his daughter, of course, but she would have to wait a little longer. Sarah was growing up, Mama told her, and must now understand that Father was not actually a king, and that she was not a queen. The family's royalty was of a special kind, Julie explained. They were unique: beautiful, witty, spirited. If Sarah was not a royal princess, that did not mean that the blood in her veins was not noble, not as good as the blood in any royal body. That is why Sarah must always hold her head high, must always be immaculately groomed, must always act in a superior manner.

"Does Father act that way?" asked Sarah.

"Why must you constantly talk about your father?" said Julie. "Who is it that takes care of you after all is said and done?"

"Nurse takes care of me," said Sarah.

"Nurse!" said Julie. "And how long do you think she would take care of you if I didn't pay her?" Her mother was angry and brought her beautiful face close to the little girl's. "I am your mother. I take care of you, and no one else. Do you understand? I am the one!"

"When is Father coming home?" Sarah had said at that moment, wondering why Mama didn't include him as one who took care of her. She loved her mother and was grateful to her, but she needed to see her father with her own eyes, even if only for a moment.

"He might come back any day," said Julie with sudden sharpness. "Sooner or later, you will see him. The winds from China are quite unreliable. Your father could blow up the Seine River and land on your doorstep tomorrow."

On her next visit, Julie presented her daughter with a small portrait in a standing frame. Sarah recognized him at once. She could see in his face everything she had always dreamed of in a father. He was tall, with dark hair and a distinguished frown. His clothes were black and gray. His hands were long and pale, and his eyes squinted against a bright sun. Surely he loved her and missed her. She could see a pain of longing in those squinting eyes.

Sarah moved the portrait about: One day it rested on a window shelf, the next on a chest of drawers, only to be lovingly placed on the marble-topped night table next to her little bed. The surface of the painting exhibited cracks in the sunlight, but Sarah's mother promised that the portrait was very new. An artist had painted it on board a schooner in the South Seas, and Father had sent it home just for little Sarah's arrival in Neuilly.

"I don't think that your father will come home today," said Nurse carefully. "China is so very far away." She straightened the child's new dress, its skirt puffed out like a bell by three layers of petticoats. Twice a week carriages arrived from Paris bearing gifts for Sarah and a note for Nurse that she could not read. Long before she would have had the two or three scrawled lines read aloud to her—usually some vague explanation why Julie could not visit that week—Nurse would have "read" the imagined contents of the letter to Sarah:

"My dearest Darling Sarah," Nurse would begin, and proceed to "read" of Julie's undying love and devotion for her only daughter. Sarah adored the letters, especially when they would go on and on as Nurse turned pages of past scribblings, looking up from the indecipherable writing to the child's loving eyes.

In two and a half months, mother had visited daughter three times. Madame Julie explained that the political unrest in the city's streets made travel dangerous for a woman. Nurse had heard that the troubles had quieted with the abdication of Louis Philippe and plans for a constituent assembly to rule the nation; she did not know to what extent Madame Julie was involved with the aristocrats trying to bring Louis Napoleon to power.

What she did know was that Madame Julie looked radiantly happy, more beautiful than ever, and that there was an abundance of ready cash at her disposal. Clearly there was a new lover in the life of Sarah's mother.

Madame Julie's personal maid had whispered to Nurse on her last visit that the Duke of Morny had become a frequent visitor in Paris. The Duke of Morny was the half brother of Louis Napoleon.

"Whenever the duke leaves," the maid had said, moving her head slowly up and down so that Nurse could not mistake her meaning, "I must go and immediately change the bedsheets."

"I see," Nurse had said, rather pleased that Madame Julie's latest admirer was of such exalted rank. If Louis Napoleon—the majestic Napoleon Bonaparte's nephew—was to take control of France, the Duke of Morny would be one of the most powerful men in the country. What then could he not do for his beautiful lover, or for his beautiful lover's daughter?

"It is why she is so busy, you understand," the maid had said. "She would like to see the child more often, no doubt."

"Does the duke like children?" Nurse had asked.

"The duke thinks Madame Julie is a child herself," the maid had said. Perhaps, thought Nurse, that was why her employer's visits had become so infrequent. Madame Julie wanted to remain twenty years old forever. And nothing aged a woman in a man's eyes as quickly as the sight of her own fast-growing child. If Sarah had nothing to offer her mother but a reminder of the passing of time, Madame Julie would come to visit no more than she had when they were hidden away in distant Brittany.

Outside, the children's game had been disrupted. A cabriolet had slowed its race into the street from the direction of the Château de Neuilly, where the royal family had once lived. The carriage was small, but exquisitely appointed; its roof and doors had been removed so that its two passengers, an elegant man and a beautiful woman, could revel in the May air. The man, tall and dark, wearing his coat like a cape, stood up before the driver could rein in the horse; his eyes seemed to reach through the bright window glass into Sarah's own.

"Mama said that Father might come," said Sarah, her voice quiet, leavened with an urgent hope. She stepped back from the long, narrow front windows as Nurse looked through them in wonder.

"That is not your father, child," said Nurse gently.

"I will go outside now, Nurse," said Sarah, hurrying to the door.

Nurse took hold of Sarah at the door. "That is not your mother, and the man with her is not your father."

Still, Nurse did not know why the handsome couple was heading for their door, surrounded by a gaggle of curious children, their game momentarily forgotten. The woman's hat was in her hands, as if better to show off her luxuriant red hair. A diamond glittered in the man's cravat, and as he came to the door, he raised his silver-knobbed cane to strike against its freshly painted surface.

Nurse threw open the door before the cane could strike.

Sarah recognized him at once, even before he could take off his hat, revealing a mass of dark curls.

"Father," said Sarah, rushing out the door, and threw herself upon the stranger.

But then a terrible thing happened.

The man did not open his arms for the girl, but rather shielded his elegant clothes from her enthusiastic approach, holding her shoulder with one hand, and preventing her from getting close with the cane held in the other.

"I'm not your father," he laughed as the neighborhood children crowded closer.

But Sarah could not believe this.

This was certainly the man in the picture, certainly the man for whom she had been waiting all her life.

"Father," she said again, as if the name were an incantation, as if the word would make real what her imagination demanded. "Father, you came for me, Father. You came all the way from China."

Now it was the red-haired woman's turn to mock her: "Leave the baron alone," she said. "He's no more your father than the Prince of Wales."

"Now don't be too sure, Rosine," said the baron.

"Sure about the Prince of Wales?" said the red-haired woman. "Or sure about you?"

"About your sister, of course," said the baron. "You must never underestimate your sister."

Nurse came up behind Sarah, protectively placing a little shawl over the child's shoulders. "It's all right, darling," she said.

"Rosine," said Sarah, turning to Nurse. Sarah remembered the name. Her mother's sister was named Rosine. Sarah turned around and looked up at the red-haired woman. Once, very long ago in Brittany, a beautiful red-haired woman had accompanied her mother on a visit to Sarah. Like her mother, her touch was soft, and the scent of her perfume powerfully sweet. It was terribly disappointing to discover that this man was not her father; but a spontaneous surge of happiness rose up in Sarah at the thought that another member of her unknown family had appeared, for except for dear Nurse she was always alone in the world. "Are you Aunt Rosine?"

"What a smart little girl," said Rosine to the baron. "She knows who I am!"

"Aunt Rosine," said Sarah, dimly aware of the impromptu audience of neighborhood children. All these children had mothers, fathers, sisters, brothers; they drove on Sundays to visit aunts, uncles, cousins of every degree and kind. She knew their mean spirits wanted this woman to be proved as much a stranger as her companion. But in spite of them, Sarah opened her arms and ran at the beautiful red-haired woman. What Sarah had attempted to do with the baron, she now accomplished with her aunt. Rosine opened her arms, and let the little girl bury her head in the silk folds of her gown.

"Come, come, that's enough," said Rosine, finally pushing Sarah away. "I'm afraid we don't have all day, child. I am your aunt Rosine, that's quite correct, and I have been sent by your mother."

Younger than Julie by two years, Rosine Van Hard had run away from home much the same way her big sister had, following her first lover out of bleak Amsterdam toward the brighter colors of Paris. Julie's vanity was large enough to embrace her sister, and to claim Rosine's beauty as a further mark of her own pride. In France, where every family longed to be older and greater, it made particular sense that a grand courtesan's reputation would be enhanced by a ravishing, rapacious sibling. Julie introduced Rosine everywhere, and would never tire of reminding her of that kindness. Rosine grew as rich and as sought after as Julie, but what rankled at the heart of her gratitude was that all her life she would be expected to repay Julie's favor by such things as this visit to Neuilly.

Nurse urged the two strangers inside the little cottage. She understood the malicious curiosity of the neighborhood children, and did not want to give them fuel with which to burn poor Sarah alive.

"We don't have much time," said the baron.

"Julie said there would be no need to stay," said Aunt Rosine. "That you would understand at once. She will not be coming to visit for several months." She spoke to Nurse with an arrogance greater even than that of Sarah's mother; and with something worse than pride, something ignoble and small. As Sarah watched and listened to this woman, her joy at discovering a piece of family in the void around her fell away to nothing. "This I am sure you will understand, my dear woman," continued Rosine, extending to Nurse a packet of francs.

"I am sorry, Madame Rosine," said Nurse with what Sarah considered a performance of amazing dignity. "I do not know what you mean." She made no move to accept the money.

"Are you stupid, woman?" said the baron. "The money is from the child's mother, so that you may be able to feed her and yourself until she comes back from her trip."

"What trip, sir?" asked Nurse, her dark eyes burning. Sarah held on to Nurse's thick right thigh as she spoke. Rosine's scent, similar to the sweet heavy fragrance that Sarah so loved on her mother, had become noxious and vile. Sarah wanted to stay close to the only reliable source of love she had ever known. "Madame Julie has sent me no notice of a trip."

"How dare you question the baron," said Rosine. "I'm sure my sister would have written to you if she thought you could read."

"Nurse reads," said Sarah.

"Listen to the child," said the baron. "A regular little hellion."

"Nurse reads to me," said Sarah. "She reads to me from mother's letters." Neither the baron nor Rosine had been warned of the child's tantrums; but they could feel her strength of passionate defiance fill the room. They turned to Sarah, trying to mollify her rising temper with false smiles.

"The point, I believe," said Rosine, "is not whether or not she is capable of reading."

"Nurse reads," said Sarah again, and this time she removed her hands from Nurse's comforting flesh, and began to approach Rosine. "She reads. Nurse reads better than anybody. Nurse reads!" said Sarah. Now her words were clear and sharp, rising up a scale of passion until the final words exploded in Aunt Rosine's face.

"Julie is going on a trip, as I said," said Aunt Rosine with dull fury, her words as much for the child as for Nurse. "She knew we'd be out driving in the Bois, and asked me to take this pleasant little detour. Who knows when my adventurous big sister will be back? Even as sweet a child as this one may be no match for a duke. Do you or do you not want the money?"

"Yes, Madame Rosine," said Nurse.

Sarah backed away from her aunt as Rosine and the baron made for the door. But Sarah need not have feared: Neither stranger made any attempt to give her a farewell embrace, kiss, or word. They left, and before Nurse could shut the door after them, the sound of their nervous high-pitched laughter drifted back into the cottage.

"Listen, sweet child," said Nurse, getting down on one knee and taking hold of Sarah's hands. "You must not worry about a thing. I am sure that your mother has a very good reason for traveling, and that we will soon get a long letter from her, telling all about how she misses you."

"You can read," said Sarah.

It had not been a question, but a statement of fact. Still, Nurse hesitated before forcing her lips into a smile. "Of course I can read, sweet child," she said.

Sarah reached up her hand to sweep away the tears from Nurse's eyes. An overwhelming love for Nurse filled her little body. She understood for the first time that Nurse was lying to her, and that a lie could be wonderful, an expression of devotion. Sarah kissed her, and then let Nurse hold her for a long time.

"Do you want to go out?" asked Nurse.

"Will you come with me?" said Sarah. "Will you walk with me to the river?"

She never again spoke about her mother or her father to the children of Neuilly. There was no talk of noble blood, or of the father who roamed the seven seas. Sarah did not even mention that she was the daughter of the most beautiful woman in the world. For the next year of her life Sarah had no mother and no father, but only Nurse, and Nurse was sufficient for all her childish needs.

Chapter 3

NURSE IS VERY BUSY

One day a very large man with missing teeth came to Neuilly to visit Nurse. Nurse introduced him to Sarah. His name was Monsieur Georges. When he looked at Sarah, his eyes narrowed to little points, and jagged lines creased the rough skin of his face. He was, said Nurse, a concierge in a very fine building in Paris. Sarah asked him what had happened to his teeth, but Nurse answered for him. Nurse said that such questions were not polite. "I am sorry, Monsieur," Sarah said. "It is just that you look so funny."

At the dinner table, Sarah found herself unable to break the general silence. When Madame Julie visited with one or another of her richly dressed friends—bankers, military men, aristocratic idlers—there was always a rush of words, too fast for Sarah to follow. But the visiting men always remembered that Sarah was present and would eventually do tricks: twisting their lips into funny shapes, barking like ferocious dogs, or pretending that they had stolen Sarah's nose and had stuck it into the pudding. She waited politely for the big concierge to do a trick or, failing this, to ask her about her games, her dolls, her friends. But Monsieur Georges ignored her. When he spoke, it was to ask two questions of Nurse: Who had left such a good bottle of wine, and what would they be eating for their main course?

Sarah watched him eat the dinner Nurse had made. He seemed to smell of garlic and sour wine before he had taken his first bite. The little bump in his throat bobbed up and down as he swallowed large, partly chewed quantities of food. Sounds of satisfaction drifted up from his belly, yet his expression displayed no pleasure. Monsieur Georges almost never lifted his eyes from his plate. When he did, it was to glance briefly at Nurse, not with affection or appreciation, but as if to question what she wanted from him in return for this meal. Somehow he had lost the ring finger of his left hand. Sarah would have liked to ask how this mutilation had taken place, but knew that Nurse would have been made uncomfortable by her questioning the visitor. His fingernails, long and dirty, dug into the soft bread he used to push his peas and mop up his sauce.

"That's not polite either," said Sarah with a conspiratorial smile. She said it softly, so that Monsieur Georges would know that she meant no offense. "You must never use the bread to push food," she continued, her voice, now that she had his attention, diminishing into a whisper. "And it is even worse to use the bread to mop up. Bad manners bring you bad friends."

"Bad friends," repeated Monsieur Georges, his eyes turning from his plate to the wild-haired little girl. "And what do bad friends bring you?"

"Georges," cautioned Nurse. Sarah wondered why she was afraid to let the man talk.

"Bad friends bring you worse manners!" said Sarah triumphantly.

"And what do worse manners bring you, smart little girl?" said Monsieur Georges.

Sarah smiled, enjoying the intricacies of the talk. "Worse manners," she said. "Worse manners bring you worst friends!"

"Well then, little girl," said the big concierge, his voice sounding suddenly strange to Sarah. She could not know that he had taken offense at her cleverness. "How do you explain it? I have very good friends, and very honest too. And we're all honest working people with no use for manners at all!"

"Georges," said Nurse. "She is my baby."

"She's bigger than a baby," said Georges with violence. He turned his back to Sarah, as if he could no longer bear the sight of her.

Suddenly Sarah understood that she was hated by Monsieur Georges.

"Besides," he said to Nurse, "baby or not, she is not yours."

"I am too," said Sarah. "I am Nurse's baby!"

The concierge returned his attention to his plate. As his yellow hand brought another hunk of sauce-soaked bread to his mouth, his thin-lipped smile became a monstrous gap-toothed grin. Nurse turned to her, and Sarah waited for her to tell the man that she loved Sarah, that no one could ever come between them, that he had best finish the food in his filthy mouth and get out of their house at once and forever.

"Sarah," said Nurse, placing her thick fingers on Sarah's wrist, "Sarah, darling, you know you are not a baby."

"He said I am not yours," said Sarah.

"Monsieur Georges did not mean that, sweet child."

"She is not yours," said Georges before taking another great swallow. He spat out his words. "I said just what I meant. This spoiled little girl is not yours."

"Tell him," said Sarah. "Tell him that he is lying! Tell him that I am yours. I am yours, so tell him, tell him."

"See what you've done," said Nurse.

"Tell him," she insisted, but already Nurse had gotten up from the table and come around behind her, holding her fast under her arms, afraid that Sarah would have a fit of temper. But Sarah was not yet in tears, not yet shaking from a frustration that would begin in her belly and spread out like fire to every corner of her body; she was not yet heated, not yet howling, not yet in pain. Only Julie could drive her to such frenzy, only her mother's criticism could make her mad enough to spit blood and lose control. But Nurse pulled her up and away from the table anyway, thrusting Sarah's silent face to her breast so as to stifle any screams. Nurse hurried her through the little drawing room, up the unadorned staircase, into the cozy nursery with its plump and narrow bed.

"Of course you're mine, Sarah," said Nurse. She placed her gently on the bed, brushed aside the hair that curled across her brow, and kissed her.

Naturally Sarah would not return the kiss, nor would she later finish the meal brought her on a tray.

Nurse had not told Monsieur Georges that Sarah was hers.

Nurse waited until they were alone, until they were so far away that no whisper, no cry could carry back to Monsieur Georges.

What did it matter what she said to Sarah in the nursery, when she would say anything to quiet her? All Nurse wanted was to return to feeding that terrible man.

It took Nurse a night and a day before Sarah forgave her.

Monsieur Georges left the house the same day he had arrived. Once he was gone, it was almost possible to forget that he had never existed. Nurse loved her, and Sarah felt that love, love that she needed more than bread or air. Nurse hugged and caressed her, and told her fairy tales, and conjured childish visions of glory: How Sarah would marry a prince and become noble and rich, the most famous princess in the world.

"And you will never leave me," said Sarah, for she wanted this too to be part of her dream.

But two weeks later Monsieur Georges returned.

He sat at the dining table, eyes on his plate. The concierge looked like he had spent the past two weeks sitting in his seat. Sarah stared in horror at the spectacle of Nurse hovering over this stranger with a ladle and a pot of soup. Neither followed her as she turned about and fled upstairs.

Nurse made no apology to Sarah, because none would have sufficed. Sarah remained in her room until the big man left, and then she ran out of the house, though darkness had fallen, and sat alone in the garden until Nurse brought her back, kicking and screaming, inside.

During the following week, he came to see Nurse three times. The third time, Sarah emerged from the nursery to join them at dinner. She wanted to look once more at the face of the man who had ruined her life. Though she barely touched her food, said not a word to either of them, and refused Nurse's goodnight kiss, Sarah knew that her coming down to dinner had been a victory for Monsieur Georges. But she had lost her strength for fighting. Nurse wanted the man to stay, or she would have long since told him to leave them in peace. Because Sarah knew that Nurse loved her, she could only imagine that Nurse loved the big concierge more. After that, Monsieur Georges seemed to be with them every other day. Within a month, it seemed that he had been coming to Neuilly forever.

He never attempted to make friends with Sarah; he brought no gifts of candy or little dolls dressed in satin and lace. Whatever he brought was for Nurse alone. When he said hello or good-bye to the child, it was always with a scowl.

"It's just that he's not used to children," said Nurse.

"He hates me," said Sarah.

"He doesn't hate you, sweet child," said Nurse.

"He hates me, and you don't care. He hates me, and he is going to take you away!"

"Child, child," said Nurse, holding her tightly, offering her love. She knew that Sarah detested meat, and so now she ceased offering it to her. Nurse gave her chocolates at every meal, and jugs of milk, and fresh bread with raspberry jam. She knew how Sarah hated the cold, and so she overheated the room, loading log after log on the fire. She knew how Sarah loved to walk along the Seine, and so she took her there, not once reprimanding her for throwing pebbles at the fishing boats. Nurse even let her wander in the nearby Parc de Neuilly, more rough woods than parkland, praying that she would not dump a handful of snakes and frogs into her apron. As long as the too thin child did not catch cold, she was satisfied. Nurse even let Sarah decide when the weather was mild enough for them to traipse about outdoors, as she let Sarah decide when to eat, when to play, when to sleep.

But none of this gave Sarah what she wanted.

Nurse would not say that she had banished Monsieur Georges, that she hated him, that she wished him to fall off a ship in the middle of the sea.

Then one day the carriage came.

Sarah heard the heavy wheels brake, heard the horses stamping feet against the hard-packed ground outside the door. Before she ran to the window, Sarah could see Nurse trying to steel herself. She had the look of someone who had been hit, but did not want to show her pain.

"Who?" asked Sarah.

Nurse feigned surprise. The carefully composed face twisted into a wondering smile. "Who could be coming to call on you so early, sweet child?"

"Monsieur Georges," said Sarah.

"Never so early, dear child," said Nurse.

"Who?" said Sarah.

"Don't you want to guess?"

"You know who it is. Tell me who it is."

"Who would you like it to be, darling? Of all the people in the world, who would you like it to be arriving in the carriage right now?"

"My father," said Sarah.

"You know that your father is out of the country," said Nurse. The child had crawled onto the divan below the front window and pulled at the curtains. For a moment she was silent. Her mother never visited Neuilly so early in the day, and never without a gentleman companion. Whenever she arrived, her dress, voluminous and wild with color, seemed to precede her by several paces, shouting her appearance to the neighborhood. But the woman being helped down from the carriage wore a simple black dress and black bonnet, an outfit so modest that her incompletely concealed torrent of golden hair seemed to belong to another woman altogether. Nurse placed her head next to Sarah's against the glass. "It is your mother," said Nurse.

Sarah's heart began to pound. Carefully she slid off the divan and stood straight and tall on the worn carpet leading to the front door.

"You must be happy, child," said Nurse. "You love your mother, and she has come for you. She has come to take you for a ride."

"I don't want to go," said Sarah.

"Sarah, don't be a silly baby," said Nurse. "You know how Madame Julie likes her own way. She has come all the way from Paris."

"Why?" asked Sarah.

Though there was a bell, Julie's footman knocked on the front door. Sarah and Nurse both started. Nurse said, "I told you, child: to take you for a ride. You will see the horse-chestnut trees in the Bois. You love to go to the Bois." Slowly, keeping her eyes on Sarah, Nurse went to the door.

"No," said Sarah, but Nurse turned her back to the child and pulled the door open wide. "No," said Sarah again. "I won't go to the Bois unless you go too."

The words were loud enough for Julie to hear, but the beautiful young woman made straight for her daughter with an ecstatic assurance.

"Sarah!" said Julie. "Look who's come to see her baby!"

"I don't want to go," said Sarah to her mother. She had not seen Julie for many months, and the unexpected arrival, the unaccompanied entrance in unfamiliar clothes, the rush to greet the forgotten daughter all contributed to Sarah's terror. She shrank away from Julie's touch, the same contact for which she had longed all her life. But her mother, oblivious of Sarah's worries, grasped her wrists and held on to her; still, Julie did not draw her close. It seemed she wanted nothing more than to examine her. "I don't want to go in the carriage," said Sarah. "I want to stay here."

"She's much bigger," said Julie to Nurse. "And prettier, a little bit prettier, don't you think?"

"You must thank your mother when she gives you a compliment, child," said Nurse. "Sarah's a beautiful child, Madame Julie, as her mother is a beautiful lady."

"She doesn't look a bit like me," said Julie, turning Sarah about, pulling at her unruly hair, inspecting her skinny limbs, her tiny waist, her narrow shoulders. But in spite of her mother's peremptory handling of her body, regardless of the thoughtless words, Sarah felt herself bewitched. If she could not forgive her mother for her long absence, only the latest absence in a life of neglect, still she could not resist Julie's spell.

"I want to look like you, Mama," she said, blurting out the words. Moment by moment, the fact of her love for her mother grew in her heart. No one in the world smelled like her mother, sweeter than any flower, cleaner than any perfumed soap. When Julie took off her bonnet, Sarah could not help but reach out for the golden hair, so much softer and shinier than her own.

"Aren't you proud to have such a beautiful mother?" asked Nurse.

"Yes," said Sarah. But Nurse's words and Nurse's strangely fixed expression reminded her that her mother had not come to elicit her love, or to exhibit her beauty. In a wild twisting of memories, Sarah suddenly remembered the ugly shape of the big concierge's mouth, her mother's obvious relief at leaving Sarah behind whenever she ended a visit, Nurse's feigning of surprise at the morning visitation of Madame Julie. Something was coming toward her, quickly and terribly, and she was afraid to look it directly in the face. "I don't want to go to the park," said Sarah.

"We are not going to the park," said Julie, who had still not kissed her only child, who had embraced the little girl only in the process of examining her for physical flaws. "We are going to Paris." Julie pulled her closer, and for the first time, brought her lips to the top of her child's head. If it was not quite a kiss, it was a near facsimile. "I am taking my own little girl to Paris."

"You are taking me?" asked Sarah.

"Of course she is, sweet child," said Nurse. Sarah saw Nurse take several steps away, not wishing to intrude on the closeness of mother and daughter.

"Does she still refuse to eat meat? You cannot give in to a child at every turn. It's no wonder she's all bones and her skin is so sallow." Julie took tighter hold of Sarah's wrists. "With me it won't be so easy. You will eat what I tell you, when I tell you. It's for your own good, do you understand? I will have a well-run house and properly brought-up child."

"Nurse says you are taking me to the Bois," said Sarah. "To the horse-chestnut trees. I would like Nurse to come. Nurse likes the Bois."

"If you will excuse me, Madame Julie," said Nurse suddenly, backing away toward the interior foyer. Nurse was quick, but Sarah could see that her face had changed once again. It was like the smooth surface of an icy pond shattered by a stone. Her fixed smile had collapsed into a hundred sad lines, her gentle forehead had become wrinkled with despair, and her happy eyes were blinking back tears. She had been wearing a mask of taut skin, and that mask had cracked.

"Nurse," said Sarah, wanting to go after her, but Julie held her fast.

"You must not want Nurse when I am here," said Julie.

"Nurse is sad. I want to go to Nurse."

"Your mother comes before Nurse," said Julie sharply.

"Nurse!" said Sarah, calling out to her, because she was not strong enough to break free.

"She will not come."

"I want Nurse," said Sarah. She did not cry, but neither did she let up her struggling against Julie's strong grip.

"You must not fight me, girl. I am your mother, not Nurse. No one loves you so much as your mother, and you must love no one more than you love me."

"I love Father."

"You cannot compare a mother to a father."

"I want to go to Nurse."

"I will be angry with you in another moment if you don't stop your struggling."

"Let me go to Nurse," said Sarah. "I love Nurse! I love Nurse more than anyone!"

Suddenly Julie let go. The child fell back and away from her, tripping over her own feet and onto the floor. "You love Nurse more than your mother?" said Julie quietly.

"Yes," said Sarah, feeling the anger at the center of her beautiful mother's heart.

"But I am the one cares for you," said Julie, spitting out the words. "I am the one who will put food in your mouth and clothes on your back. I am the one who will have you at my table and under my roof. Not Nurse."

"Nurse takes care of me," said Sarah.

"No," said Julie. "Nurse is a servant whom I have paid to take care of you, because I was busy. But now Nurse is busy."

"Nurse isn't busy," said Sarah. Back on her feet, she took a step away from where Julie had taken a seat on the divan.

"Nurse is very busy, girl," said Julie. "Nurse is very busy with her concierge."

"No," said Sarah. A chasm, endless and dark, opened in her heart. Instantly she could see clearly what had been rushing toward her, what vague nightmare had been threatening her for weeks.

"Nurse is getting married," said Julie. "And I am taking you home."

Chapter 4

THE GREATEST ACTRESS
IN THE WORLD

Sarah lived in Paris. In Paris it seemed that only Louis Napoleon lived in a private house, as Sarah and Nurse had lived in Neuilly and Brittany. Sarah lived with her mother in an apartment building. The building was actually a very big house, but different families lived on different floors. Other children lived there, but they played only with their brothers and sisters. Sarah had neither brothers nor sisters. Nurse did not visit, and Father never came. Sarah knew that Nurse would write to her, if she had only known how to write, or if she thought that Sarah had learned how to read.

Mama could read, and so could Aunt Rosine. The two spoke French with a funny accent that Sarah imitated when she was alone with her dolls. Mama could speak German and English. Men came to the apartment from Germany and from England, just to speak with Mama in their own languages. Aunt Rosine and Mama sometimes spoke Dutch to each other. Sarah wished she could speak Dutch because then she would know the secrets that passed between her mother and her aunt, secrets that made them laugh until the tears ran from their black-rimmed eyes to their prettily rouged cheeks.

Mama's apartment was very beautiful. On the ground floor was a confectioner's shop. The houses on either side of their own had ground-floor stores too, but those shops sold hats and boots and cigars and fancy furniture. Inside the confectioner's shop were candies, cakes, ices. From the window of her bedroom Sarah could smell the sweet, comforting scent of chocolate.

Sarah, Mama, Bella, and Titine lived on the very first floor up from the street: Mama said this was the best apartment to live in. Bella was Mama's maid, and Titine was Mama's cook. Sarah liked Titine best, even though Mama thought her ugly and stupid. No man would ever want such a girl, Mama explained, and she did not want Sarah to imitate her oafish ways. Titine often took her for walks along the Seine, and sometimes sat with her on the quay near the Louvre, watching the boats glide toward the ancient Île de la Cité. Mama had other servants as well: a handsome coachman, who had been a soldier and fought in a great war; a footman, who was also a porter and was very proud to wear Mama's blue livery; and the porter's wife, who shuffled around the apartment helping Bella and Titine. They all lived in the house too, but high up, above the highest apartment in tiny rooms under the slanted roof. Titine had promised to show Sarah these rooms when she was not busy with her cooking, but in nearly two years she had never yet found the time. Sarah didn't complain. The other servants paid her no attention at all. Mama said that Titine took Sarah out only because the cook was as simple-minded as Sarah herself. Only an idiot, said Julie, could find pleasure in the goat carts on the Champs-Élysées, the marionettes at Séraphin's, or Robert-Houdin's magic theater at the Palais-Royal.

A banker lived with his wife and daughter on the second floor; a respectable retired lawyer lived on the third. Like Sarah, the banker's daughter was seven years old. Once, the banker's wife had hurried her daughter away from Sarah and her mother as they had all been entering the apartment. Sarah had a hoop in one hand and a stick in the other, a new game given her by a gentleman who had called on Mama the night before. The gentleman had kissed Sarah's hand, and Sarah and the hoop were momentarily inseparable. But Mama had refused to walk with her to the Tuileries Gardens, where Sarah could have tried out the hoop. Instead, she had left Sarah in their carriage for nearly two hours while she searched through the entire contents of a milliner's shop near the Madeleine.

"Hello," Sarah had called out to the banker's little girl, desperate for an opportunity to try out her game. "Do you play hoops?"

The banker's daughter had turned about on the stairwell, looking at Sarah wistfully, but already the red-faced banker's wife was pulling her child faster up the stairwell, not letting her answer.

Mama was furious. She had warned Sarah not to speak to those people. One must never give them the opportunity for a snub. They were stupid bourgeois who imagined themselves very fine. The wives of bankers and lawyers hated them, Mama said, because the first floor was the most expensive. Everyone wanted to live where it was most expensive, but only Mama could afford the expense. This was because Father never forgot to send them money, and because Mama and Aunt Rosine had so many rich friends. They were jealous about this and for other things too, things that Julie told Sarah she could not yet understand.

But Sarah understood why the women hated them. Her mother was young and beautiful, while the respectable wives upstairs were old and drab. Men and women stopped to stare at Julie when she was helped down from her carriage, as the children of Neuilly had stared at her when she had visited in her magnificent clothes. Every day Mama wore a new dress, and every week there were new jewels sparkling on her slender neck. If Mama was not a noblewoman, she was more beautiful than any princess. No one in the house had the right to look down on them, Mama assured her. Barons and counts and dukes visited Mme. Julie Bernhardt, men who would never deign to enter any of the sober drawing rooms on the house's upper floors.

Sarah liked best when these men visited in the late afternoon. The confectioner's shop was open then, and the gentlemen never failed to bring her bonbons in a satin box. "Thank you," Sarah would say. "Bring more, please."

But Mama didn't like them to spoil her with chocolate. Julie scolded her for prompting such gifts. "If they bring you chocolate," said Julie, "they think they can get away without buying me jewels."

Displayed in the confectioner's plate-glass window was a family of dolls. There were a mother, a father, a sister, and her baby brother. The mother was fair, the father dark, just like her own parents. But the sister doll had long straight hair, like the princess in the fairy tale told to her by Titine. Mama did not like Sarah's thick head of red-blond curls. As a joke, which Sarah did not find very funny, Julie called her "my little blond Negress." Sometimes she would try to brush Sarah's hair, but usually gave up with a few angry words that Sarah couldn't understand; they were in Dutch. Sarah could not imagine herself lowering her own wooly hair over the edge of a tower. Neither could she imagine having a baby brother. The family on the fifth floor of her house had two baby brothers, but Mama had told her never to talk to them: The boys' father was nothing more than a tradesman; that was why they lived at the top of the house.

The address of their house was 256 Rue St.-Honoré. Mama warned her that she must never forget this number, because servants, even Titine, were not to be trusted. A servant could let go her hand in the gardens of the Tuileries or the Palais-Royal, and she would be utterly lost forever unless she remembered her address. In the gravity of Mama's warning Sarah found a great and certain joy; above all else, Mama did not want to lose her little girl.

"My name is Sarah Bernhardt, and I live at two hundred and fifty-six Rue Saint-Honoré," Sarah would say, practicing in her bedroom what she would tell people if she were ever lost, adrift in the world. She had many dolls of her own, big ones and small ones, dressed in lace blouses and leather boots, silk bonnets and cashmere shawls, and she moved them around her bed as if they were men and women of Paris, hurrying along the Rue de Rivoli on the way to and from the Tuileries. Though all her dolls were baby girls, Sarah pretended that some were men and some were women.

"Hello, little girl, are you lost?" she would have one of the dolls say in a gruff masculine voice.

"Yes, sir. I am looking for two hundred and fifty-six Rue Saint-Honoré," Sarah would respond.

"But that is quite amazing!" Sarah's doll would say. "That is precisely where I am going! That is where my little daughter lives, my girl whom I have not seen since she was a tiny baby."

Always at this point in her play, Sarah's heart would grow wild. She would look at her pretty doll and see only the face of her father's portrait that rested on the tiny chest of drawers across the room.

"And your little girl," Sarah would say. "How old would she be today?"

"Not quite seven years old. In October she will be seven."

"I will be seven in October, sir," Sarah would say.

"My little girl was born on October 23, 1844. Her name is Sarah. I have come all the way from China."

Then Sarah would kiss the doll, bursting into tears.

It would be all she could do to hold herself back from running to her mother, demanding to know where Father was and why he did not live with them.

But she was never allowed to run to her mother. Her mother sent for her when she wanted her. If Sarah wanted her mother, she must wait patiently until Julie thought of asking for her. Her mother's suite of rooms was a sacrosanct area of the apartment, never entered without special invitation. Mama needed her sleep, needed her privacy. Even when Sarah had a nightmare, she was not allowed to call to her, and absolutely forbidden to go to her. There was a bellpull in her bedroom. In an emergency she could ring, and Titine or Bella would come.

Still, if Sarah wanted her mother's attention, she knew how to get it. Though Sarah's little bedroom was separated from her mother's suite by a lengthy corridor, she had to pass the door to Julie's dressing room to get to the rest of the apartment. This door was always open when Julie was at her morning toilette, and if Sarah ran past it, looking like she was up to some mischief, her mother's temper would break her narcissistic concentration.

That day Sarah woke at dawn and waited for hours for her mother to get up. At eleven, she saw Bella come to prepare the bath, and leave to prepare the coffee. At half-past eleven, Sarah walked quietly out of her own room and looked down the long corridor. She did not know that this was a bad choice of days to catch her mother's attention. Julie, fresh from her bath, sat at her white marble table, examining her twenty-three-year-old face in the sun-drenched dressing glass. She was worried. Yesterday Alice Ozy's blue coupé had nearly sideswiped her landau racing through the Bois, and Julie had to watch the courtesan, older than she by eight years, wave a triumphant glove at her while the Baron Moresco nuzzled her neck like a badly trained dog.

Baron Moresco had been one of Julie's most reliable lovers until Alice Ozy's stupid little "acting" role at the Variétés infatuated him. Julie could not understand the attraction that aristocrats had for courtesans prancing around in flesh-colored tights and a pair of wings; they saw much more than that in the privacy of the boudoir, and didn't have to share the intimacy with a thousand gaping idiots in the galleries. And even worse than courtesans making a name for themselves by appearing onstage were the new applicants to the unofficial ranks of "La Garde"—the ever more competitive circle of beauties who derived their income from the gifts of France's greatest men. Even at twenty-three Julie felt old next to Giulia Beneni, who could not be a day more than fifteen, despite the diamonds glittering from her throat and wrist, at the Café Anglais and the Maison d'Or. What could she, regardless of her creamy skin and thick black mane of hair, possibly know of pleasuring old aristocrats and ancient bankers? Contemplating her beauty, Julie decided that she was far lovelier than any fifteen-year-old Italian trollop. And Frenchmen always preferred blond women. It was absurd to worry about the loss of Baron Moresco when she had the Duke of Morny in thrall. Surely the duke would not stoop so low as to rob the cradle. Hadn't he said more than once how much he admired the way she was bringing up her child? A man who could admire motherhood would not run after little girls. It was one thing to admire motherhood; it was another thing entirely to frequent a mistress with a child in the house. Well, that condition would soon be remedied. It was not her fault that she must send the girl to a boarding school. She would tell Sarah of her decision later that day.

As Julie was assuring herself of her youth and her beauty, insisting that no one would be more successful in the world of men, Sarah ran noisily past the open door.

"What are you doing?" snapped Julie.

Pleased that she had been noticed by her mother, Sarah stopped short and approached the dressing-room threshold.

"Where are you going?" said Julie.

Now she was allowed to speak. "To the magic theater. Do you want to come with me, Mama?" asked Sarah.

Julie turned in exasperation from the mirror. How could the girl not know that her hairdresser, Marcel, was due to arrive in five minutes, as he did every day of the week at this time?

Couldn't the brat let her alone long enough to finish powdering her face?

"No, Sarah," said Julie. "Not today. And I don't want you running like a wild Indian in the hall."

"I am going to see the magic tricks of Monsieur Robert-Houdin, Mama."

"You may go, Sarah." She wished there was more time to spend with her, and that Sarah was more the sort of daughter with whom she would have enjoyed that time. But Julie was occupied with the details of her profession. A bath at eleven, Marcel fixing her hair at half past, a quick breakfast, and a glance at the caricatures and the gossip in *Le Charivari* before visits from her sister, her seamstress, her bootmaker. A jeweler was due at one to look at some ugly gifts she wished to translate into more practical louis d'or. And most important, her lawyer was due, to see to the last details of the boarding-school arrangements at Auteuil.

Before she knew it, it would be three o'clock, time for the second, more serious hairdressing of the day. By five, she must be fully dressed in the layers and yards of silk and lace appropriate to her station; her jewels must be selected to complement her dress, with special attention paid as to which gentleman she would be seeing later that day. Julie was considerate enough to place against her skin the jewels given her by whoever would that night share her bed.

"The magician can tell you what you are thinking, Mama."

"I am not interested in magic tricks," said Julie, trying to keep a trace of kindness in her voice.

"He made a boy float in the air," said Sarah. She had not wanted to gain her mother's attention just to tell her about Robert-Houdin's magic skill; but whenever she mentioned the magician's name, an entire world took shape before her eyes, a world that demanded to be shared. The magician, a tall handsome man in elegant evening clothes, did tricks with cards, with fish, with handkerchiefs and flowers; he made a wild owl do his bidding, he made solid substances disappear with a wave of his hands. But what intrigued Sarah most was not the man's magic, but his manner. At the matinee performances in his little theater, before an audience of two hundred noisy children, he was able to command silence with a single raised finger. When he spoke, his voice was not like an ordinary man's but like a hero's. As he stood on the raised stage, all the children looked up to him, giving him their hearts. This was the real magic to Sarah. That a stranger standing on a stage could inspire love. "Titine is taking me," she said. "I won't let go of her hand. Even in the Theater of Monsieur Robert-Houdin I will not let go of her hand."

Julie, wanting to be rid of the clinging child, would have dismissed her peremptorily if not for the undisclosed news of the boarding school. Certainly, ungrateful Sarah would make a miserable scene when told that she was being sent to the most prestigious school for girls in the country.

Sarah knew that her mother wanted to be alone, but she lingered. On her mother's table were ivory-handled brushes for her hair, silver flasks containing sweet perfumes, bottles and jars holding liquids that softened her pale skin. Sarah came up behind her so that the faces of mother and daughter were side by side in the bright glass. "May I kiss you, Mama?"

"Yes, Sarah," sighed Julie, looking without pleasure at the child's image before her. Her hair was impossible, and the precocious look in her green eyes was decidedly unpleasant. As Sarah turned to kiss her mother's cheek, Julie found herself further dismayed at her profile. She was not growing prettier, and she chattered all the time. With such looks, she would be difficult to marry off. "Thank you, Sarah," said Julie, pushing her away. "A kiss must not last for an hour."

Sarah took a step back from her mother. It was time to tell her. "I think I saw Nurse, Mama," she said.

"Oh, stop this nonsense," said Julie. "Can't you see that I'm busy."

If only Sarah could command her mother's respect the way the magician could command his audience. She raised her voice, and insisted: "I saw her yesterday, Mama. Titine took me to the little Arc de Triomphe. Nurse was walking through the garden. She was carrying a big bread. She didn't hear me, and Titine would not let me chase her."

"Sarah," said Julie, trying to contain her fury by making her lips very tight around a mouth barely opened. "Marcel is going to be here in one moment, and I shall not have finished with my face."

"Nurse could be trusted," said Sarah.

"What? Why do you insist on bringing up Nurse? Again and again it's Nurse, Nurse, Nurse. You'd think it was Nurse who took care of you still, and not your mother."

"You do not trust Titine," said Sarah.

"Sarah, you do not belong in my dressing room unless I call you into my dressing room," said Julie, putting down her powder puff. "I want you out of my dressing room, and I want you out of it right now." She knew that in another moment she would not be able to hold back her indignation at being saddled with a child already so big and old and thankless; in another moment she would tell Sarah that it was her own fault she was being sent away.

"But Mama," insisted Sarah, "you are always afraid that I will be lost. You tell me every time not to let go, and that you do not trust Titine. I know you take care of me now. But you could trust Nurse. She would not let go of my hand, and you would never have to be afraid."

Julie stood up and rang for Bella, but Sarah held her ground. "It is only so that you will not be afraid that I will be lost, Mama. If you know where Nurse is, you can write to her and tell her to come. Not to be here all the time, but only for walks. Only for walks, Mama."

"You still want Nurse, do you?" said Julie.

"She would hold my hand."

"After two years with your own mother, it's still Nurse that you want?"

"Only for walks," said Sarah. She could hear Bella walking quickly their way, the old silk of her black dress rubbing against her crinoline.

"You don't want Nurse only for walks," said Julie. Bella approached her employer with her eyes lowered, seemingly distraught at the pain to which Sarah was putting her mother. "You want her for stories at bedtime. Haven't you told me that you miss Nurse's stories?"

"Yes, Mama."

"And that you miss Nurse's cooking?"

"I liked her food, Mama. Titine is a very good cook, but Nurse made me soups that I liked very much."

Julie turned her back to her child and addressed her maid: "She imagines that she saw her old nurse yesterday. She misses her terribly. Life here with us on the Rue Saint-Honoré just doesn't compare to the great old days in a shack in Brittany."

"If only I could have grown up with such privileges," said Bella. Then she added: "The jeweler is here, Madame."

"The jeweler? He's an hour early. Where is Marcel? What am I supposed to do with my hair? I told Baron Larrey that he might call at noon today."

Sarah slowly sidled away from Julie's reach. "I did not imagine Nurse, Mama." She would find some other way to get to Nurse.

"What?" said Julie, turning abruptly. "Did I dismiss you? Where are you going?"

"I did not imagine Nurse," repeated Sarah. "I go with Titine, to the magic theater. And this time, if I see Nurse, I shall stop her. I don't care what anyone says. I saw Nurse, and I shall stop her." Sarah waited a moment. "May I go now, Mama?"

"Of course you may go, Sarah," said Julie. "And I hope you have a very nice time at the magic theater, because in Auteuil there is no magic theater."

There, she had said it, thought Julie. If the child insisted on a scene, she might as well have one worth Julie's while. "There is only work in Auteuil, hard work that must be done by all the little girls who go there."

Sarah did not like the sound of the place her mother had mentioned, nor did she like the satisfied grin on Bella's hawk-nosed face. "What is Auteuil, Mama?"

"Auteuil is a place very near Paris, Sarah. It is a town. In this town is a school for girls. I shall visit you when you go there."

"But there are schools in Paris, Mama," said Sarah, a wild fear beginning to rise in her belly.

"This school is much better, Sarah. It's full of little girls who work very hard so they can learn all the things they need to learn to grow up. All the little girls live together. It is a boarding school."

"I would like to stay in Paris, Mama," said Sarah, keeping her voice flat and unexcited, as if by stilling the words she could overcome the growing misery in her heart.

"You must let your mother decide what is best for you," said Julie.

The porter's wife appeared to announce Marcel's entrance, and Sarah felt that her fate, already decided, was now being pushed aside, forgotten altogether. A moment later a skinny, yellow-haired man entered the dressing room with his leather satchel.

"Madame, a thousand pardons," he said in a deep, theatrical voice. Acting as though no one else were in the dressing room but himself and Julie, apparently certain that Julie's partially unbuttoned taffeta dressing jacket were sufficient armor for her modesty and virtue, Marcel took hold of her lustrous golden hair and brought it to his lips. "Good morning, beautiful Madame's beautiful hair!"

"I want to stay in Paris," said Sarah, the fear now in her chest, rising higher and higher. "Please, Mama," she said, even as the fear reached her throat and threatened to climb higher still.

Marcel, oblivious, opened his leather satchel and began to take out the tools of his trade. Bella put her cold hand on Sarah's shoulder. "Come on, little girl, your mother is busy."

"I want to stay in Paris. I didn't do anything bad. I saw Nurse and I wanted to tell you. Because I know how you worry when Titine holds my hand. Only because you worry." There was a fire behind her eyes, and the room had grown hot. It seemed that the unlit gas jets about the mirror were suddenly ablaze, that the gentle fire in the grate had been strengthened with a huge load of burning logs.

"Sarah," said Julie, "I am getting my hair done, and you are going to boarding school in Auteuil." As if on a signal, Marcel began to brush the golden hair, but with sudden irritation Julie stopped him. "And I am not at all worried over who holds or does not hold your hand. As far as I'm concerned, you can run down the street all by yourself until you find your old nurse." Julie paused to tap Marcel's wrist. When he resumed his brushing she said: "Do you know how expensive Madame Fressard's School for Girls is? Only the richest girls in the country go there, and still my girl complains. I think it would be nice if you could bring yourself to thank your mother for what she's doing, for the expense she's going to, instead of whining and complaining."

"Thank you, Mama," said Sarah in a voice both small and wild. She could taste blood in her mouth, rising from deep in her throat; the heat in the room enveloped her like monstrous flames. There was no love for her anywhere in the world, except in the memory of Nurse, and she turned about and stumbled down the corridor, past the room where visitors dropped their coats, into the small drawing room where her mother sometimes dined with a single fortunate gentleman. With what strength was left her, she pushed back the shut doors to the larger drawing room, where a score or more strange men and women gathered to smoke and drink and tell loud stories until two and three o'clock in the morning.

Dimly Sarah could hear someone shouting her name, the voice not her mother's but a servant's, not consoling but furious. Her mother did not care who held her hand, her mother did not care if she became lost, did not care if she were gone forever. Pausing to catch her breath, not from the exertion of running but from the sudden burden of sadness, Sarah banged her hand against her mother's favorite Chinese vase. The vase, filled with lilacs, did not fall; and suddenly Sarah wanted it broken. Without fear or hesitation, she knocked the precious thing over, smashing the porcelain into a hundred fragments, wetting the Persian rug with a delicious fragrance.

In the foyer she overturned an unlit oil lamp she had always hated: A bare-breasted nymph bore the glass and wick, lighting the way to a house of shame. The lamp smashed, and into the mess she threw a delicate visiting-card tray, a crystal decanter, a hideous bust of a nameless hero. Sarah knew that her mother loved these things, so she broke them. She only wished there had been time for further destruction, but the servants, running as fast as they dared on polished wood and marble floors, were growing closer. As she left the apartment, and raced down the steps to the ground floor, she heard the porter bellowing as he ran downstairs after her.

But he could not catch her, and neither could Titine nor Bella.

Sarah was hot, and full of fire, and she ran along the Rue St.-Honoré as though a thousand demons chased her.

She was not allowed in the street, had once been slapped by Titine after getting off the sidewalk and been nearly run down by a speeding fiacre.

But now Sarah did not care who or what might strike her down. She needed to get away from her house, from the servants who might chase her, from the mother who would catch her only to send her away.

Without thought, the little girl stepped into the noontime street, and a coachman shouted at her, raising his whip against the bright sun. Sarah ignored him, running across the path of his carriage toward the other side of the Rue St.-Honoré. Only a skillful braking and frenzied turning of horses prevented a tragedy. So ferocious was the coachman's cursing that Sarah ran yet faster, not looking where she placed her steps, turning into an alleyway, running past courtyards where grooms held the reins of horses and tradesmen delivered straw baskets to porters in bright livery. Out of breath, she leaned against a courtyard wall, trying to get her bearings. Two blocks from her house was the Rue de Rivoli. If she could find this great street, she could walk to the little Arc de Triomphe between the two wings of the Louvre; it was here, in the gardens while looking through the triumphal arch toward the Tuileries, where she had last seen Nurse.

"Are you lost, little girl?" asked a tall servant in a red uniform. Sarah looked at him in amazement. How could anyone know that she was lost?

"No, Monsieur," she said, aping her mother's arrogance. "I live in this house." Sarah didn't wait to see if she had convinced the man. For a moment all servants, all adults were equal conspirators in the plot to keep her from Nurse, to catch her and send her to Auteuil. She turned right, then left, then right in a maze of ancient alleys connecting the courtyards of old *hôtels* to the great streets on which they fronted. All about her were men and women in various, glorious livery; brass buttons and bright colors beat back the sun like the costumes of parading soldiers. Emerging from an alley, Sarah found herself on a winding street with broken cobblestones, victim of the massive rebuilding of the city just beginning: Louis Napoleon wanted to replace the revolutionaries' first line of attack—the constricted city streets—with wide boulevards for his soldiers. A little girl her own age picked her way carefully about the exposed underbelly of the street, while a sharp-eyed maid kept watch at her side, preventing Sarah from approaching to ask which way was the Louvre. Everywhere she turned there were maids, and porters, and footmen. The masters of these servants stayed indoors, or were whisked away to the couturier or the Bourse in closed carriages. Yet, after all it was not the masters she sought, but one of their nurses, her own beloved Nurse.

Then, beyond a turn in the winding street, she saw a white bonnet. Sarah hurried after this bonnet, not daring to get too close lest the image evaporate, not daring to call out Nurse's name lest the woman fade into the sun's radiance like any dream exposed to daylight.

The woman had a long unladylike stride, and Sarah was hard pressed to stay at her heels. She was forced to run to keep up, and the woman heard her and stopped. Sarah saw her turn, saw her profile, saw her face. "I'm sorry," said Sarah. "I thought you were Nurse."

The woman only made the mistake worse. She said that she was a nurse, even if she was not Sarah's; she asked if Sarah was lost; and she reached out a powerful hand to take hold of the child.

Sarah twisted out of the woman's grasp and ran.

If she had imagined once, she could have imagined twice. Her mother could have been right after all. Sarah had never seen Nurse, not even near the little Arc de Triomphe. Nurse lived with Monsieur Georges far away. She never visited, she never wrote, and she didn't care a bit about Sarah.

Suddenly the street grew wider and brighter as it opened into a vista at the end of which was the southern façade of the Église St.-Roch. This made no sense to Sarah, for the famous church where the playwright Corneille was buried was at the other end of the Rue St.-Honoré from her home; this was a landmark, but it was in the wrong place. Her heart began to race. She had thought she had gone in the opposite direction, toward the Vendôme Column, built from a thousand enemy cannons and topped by the emperor Napoleon's majestic statue. At this hour the bronze twisting about the column's stone core was at its brightest, and Sarah often urged Titine to take her there, and to tell her once again tales of the vanished empire.

Now there was no Titine to tell her a story.

The glorious church stood there silently, and Sarah didn't know which way to turn.

She was alone, and lost, and growing afraid.

She approached the great church, but turned sharply about when she saw two elderly gentlemen looking at her with concern from the entrance. Quickly she marched along the street, until she was swallowed from the men's view by a conglomeration of handcarts and wagons of a construction gang. Sarah followed the red-faced workers as they strained to push their loads and control their horses through badly paved streets, toward the beginning of the great new thoroughfare then under construction, the Avenue de l'Opéra. The shouts of the sweaty men and the groaning weight of their heavy equipment distracted her from her fear; she slowed her pace to follow them through a torn-up square dominated by a huge edifice where a crowd had gathered. From in front of this great building one could look up the growing avenue.

But the crowd had not gathered to observe a miracle of road engineering. They were waiting for something, and so anxious was their collective mood that Sarah threw caution away and tapped a young lady's back with her finger.

"Why does everyone wait?" asked Sarah.

The young lady looked down in surprise at the size of her questioner. Sarah could sense in her an agonizing loss. She seemed in the process of swallowing some inevitable, atrocious sorrow. Slowly, in a melancholy voice, she spoke the name that would stay with Sarah all her life.

"Rachel," she said. "She's going away."

"Who is Rachel?" asked Sarah.

The young lady blinked back tears. "You have never heard of the greatest actress in the world?"

Sarah thought for a moment and responded truthfully. "My mother does not like actresses," she said.

"Rachel is more a goddess than an actress," said the young lady. "And I pity anyone who has not seen her, because she will not be with us forever."

At that moment the crowd pressed forward, and through the space between the massed bodies Sarah saw that one of the entrances to the great building—the Théâtre Français—was cordoned off by policemen. One of these policemen signaled to a coachman across the square. Sarah watched the magnificent carriage approach the theater with the slow gravity of a hearse. Spontaneously, a tormented shout rose from the grieving adults around her.

"Rachel!" they cried again and again, their voices wild with adulation, frenzied with worship. Dimly Sarah could see a thin, very pale, dark-haired woman emerge from the theater and look out at the crowd. Rachel's face, very serious, seemed to be searching for a friend among her admirers. She smiled and raised her white gloved hand before being helped into the carriage and driven away at speed.

The lady with whom Sarah had spoken cried freely, like many others in the crowd. If six-year-old Sarah did not know that Rachel Félix was the greatest tragedienne in the history of France, she could still feel the force of that young woman's power in the love that went out to her from every corner of the crowd. The actress was leaving France for an extended tour, and many of her admirers feared for her delicate health. They loved her and wanted her to perform for them, to stay with them always.

Sarah did not understand how one person could be worth so much love, yet knew at that moment that she must find a way to gain what Rachel possessed.

"Please, Miss," said Sarah, once again tapping the young lady from behind. "My name is Sarah Bernhardt and I am looking for two hundred and fifty-six, Rue Saint-Honoré."

The young lady, shaken once more from her obsession, placed her hand on Sarah's shoulder. "Are you lost, little girl?"

"Yes, Miss," said Sarah politely. She took the young lady's hand, and walked with her toward the Église St.-Roch, along the Rue St.-Honoré until all the shopfronts and houses and trees had become familiar. Soon enough, Sarah could see the sun-dashed Emperor Napoleon, uncle of their own less glamorous ruler, Louis Napoleon, in the distance atop the Vendôme Column. "I am almost home, Miss," said Sarah. "I must only go one more block and I know the way."

As they walked, she had filled Sarah's head with all of Rachel's triumphs: No one before or since could ever perform onstage without standing in her shadow. The exalted dead poets of France lived once more on her lips, not only in Paris, but in every country where she deigned to perform. No woman was ever more glorious in France; no woman ever did more for her country's pride.

Sarah hurried through the entrance to her apartment building, running up the stairs with speed. She ignored the fact that she had run away. The boarding school in Auteuil was no longer a threat, the need to see Nurse was less urgent than to share with her mother this revelation, this discovery.

The porter, grinning with malice, opened the door and called to his wife in a dialect Sarah did not understand. Titine hurried out of the kitchen, white flour sticking to her nose. "You had best not go to your mother, Sarah," said Titine gently.

But Sarah ran through the drawing rooms, in the larger of which two strange men waited with their hats on their laps, and approached the bedroom corridor, calling to her: "Mama! Mama, may I see you?"

The door to Julie's dressing room was closed, so Sarah broke yet another rule that day, beating on the door as if her life depended on it. "Mama, Mama, please come, please come!"

There was a sudden hacking cough from a masculine throat, followed by a sharp, tapping sound: her mother's heels on the wood floor. Julie, her hair in disarray, opened the door a crack and looked down at her only child with hatred. "Go to your room and stay there. You will get your spanking later, when I have the time to give it to you."

"Mama, I saw Rachel."

"Go to your room!" said Julie, amazed at her daughter's lack of fear or remorse. Sarah had forgotten the expensive things she had smashed, as she had forgotten her anger at her mother.

"Rachel is the greatest actress who ever lived, Mama." Sarah held both her hands against the open door so that Julie could not shut it without violently throwing her over. The sound of the great actress's name always infuriated Julie, for Rachel was as renowned for the quality and quantity of her lovers as she was for her *Phèdre*. More than once, Julie had shared her bed with a man in love with Rachel, a man in love with a legend. Julie believed that it was only the Comédie Française that kept Rachel from being thought of as one of the courtesans of La Garde. Certainly Rachel's wealth, far greater than Julie's, was as much a product of the gifts of her lovers as it was of her triumphant theatrical tours. What maddened Julie most of all was Rachel's famous pride at her Jewish birth. This could hardly endear her to Julie, who pointedly ignored her own Jewish ancestry as a hindrance to her career. Julie had never told Sarah that she was the daughter of a Jewish mother; and therefore, by the ancient law of her people, a Jewess herself.

"Rachel is the most important woman in France," continued Sarah. "The whole world loves her."

"Get away from this door," said Julie.

"Mama, I will be an actress," said Sarah. "I will be like Rachel."

Julie, white with rage, pulled wide the dressing-room door. Behind her, at the entrance to the bedroom, a man without a frock coat smoked a black cigar. "You will go to your room," said Julie. Sarah was about to speak when Julie stopped her with a slap across the face. Her whole body ringing in pain, Sarah heard her mother's wild words:

"Rachel is three things: a consumptive, a Jewess, and a whore," said Julie. "You will never be an actress, and you will never again mention her name."

Sarah stepped away from her mother, too far away to be struck again. She did not understand her mother's words, but knew them to be terrible. Her mother hated Rachel, hated who and what she was. But Sarah knew that this hatred could make no difference to her, no difference at all.

"I will so be like Rachel," said Sarah, her words not loud, but sharp and insolent in the little space separating her from her mother. "In spite of everything, I will be an actress!"

Chapter 5

A MEMBER OF
THE JEWISH RACE

They were words Sarah would hear again: consumptive, Jewess, whore.

Appollonie, anemic and wan, was her best friend. She was often sent to the infirmary for a few days of rest. The other girls in the dormitory at Mme. Fressard's School for Girls whispered that Appollonie was consumptive and would die before her tenth birthday. Such whispering enraged Sarah. Slender and delicate, Sarah was an unlikely champion. Yet when she lost her temper, she was capable of anything. The genteel schoolgirls could not defend themselves against her biting and clawing, against a fury that could not be met. When Sarah struck at them, they no longer fought back, they simply ran.

Upon Sarah's arrival at Mme. Fressard's nearly two years before, Appollonie was the only girl who had shown her kindness. She had not mocked Sarah for being unable to read, for being ignorant of the songs and games with which all the other girls had grown up. At four o'clock the children were given bread and butter and hot milk; they were allowed to load the bread with jam and chocolate left them by visitors. Sarah had few visits and fewer visitors, and Julie always forgot to bring jam or chocolate. But Appollonie shared her own rich hoard with the new girl.

More than this, Appollonie introduced her to the customs of polite society. It was never correct to criticize one's father or mother, no matter how long they stayed away. Both boys and girls had to submit to, obey, and love their parents. Yet while boys could shape the future course of their lives through choice of a career, girls had no choice. Grown-up girls, Appollonie taught her, were meant to run the households of their husbands. To train for such a career, one must learn politeness, modesty, and dignity. Such things pleased great men. Appollonie's mother ran not one but three households; besides the town house in the Faubourg St.-Germain, there were two country villas.

"Why do you have *two* villas?" Sarah had asked. When Sarah pined for home or refused to eat the school food, kindly Mme. Fressard never failed to bring her to tears with accounts of the daily fate of less fortunate children: the failure of the Irish potato crop stunting the growth of a generation, the cruel conditions in the Welsh mines crippling children who never saw the light of day, the offspring of black slaves in barbaric America separated from their families by the whim of a vicious master. Sarah had never understood that there was so much injustice and inequity in the world. When Mme. Fressard spoke of hunger and deprivation, it did not make her want to finish the food on her plate, but to send it directly to starving India. She did not feel lucky that she had enough clothes to keep her warm; she felt guilty at her excessive wardrobe. Perhaps Julie had a reason that Sarah could not understand for living so luxuriously in Paris, but she could not imagine any justification for one family to have three separate homes.

"It is because we are an old family," said Appollonie, though she knew this was no answer, and loved Sarah for the question. It was not fair, said Sarah, just as it was not fair that girls could only grow up to be wives and nothing else. Appollonie tried to make Sarah accept the world. That the lives of women were circumscribed was simply a rule to be followed, like the laws of the Church, like the rules of etiquette. Appollonie followed all these rules.

Such obedience did not make her dull, Sarah found, but tranquil. In spite of her ill health, Appollonie was steadfast. She knew who were her friends, who were her enemies. She knew how she wanted to live her life. Appollonie was loved by four sisters and three brothers. Her mother visited every week, and though her father rarely visited, when he came he was there in the flesh and not just as a painting on canvas. When Sarah saw her friend walking between her father and mother, it seemed like a golden glow bathed the three of them, as though celestial trumpets shouted their admiration of such family joy.

Sarah wanted such a life. It was possible to forget about the less fortunate in the contemplation of Appollonie's serenity. She found herself imitating Appollonie's silvery speech, her exquisite table manners, the regal way she held her head. She wanted to be so much like her that no one would be able to tell the two of them apart.

When Appollonie asked a question of Sarah, it was always with a sincere willingness to drop the subject if it was at all uncomfortable. Sarah imagined that all aristocrats were born this way. But she wanted to hold back nothing from her friend. She explained to Appollonie about her father, showing her his portrait, telling her of his distant travels. If her mother did not visit, it was because Julie had been blessed by God with another daughter, Jeanne, and the new baby kept her at home. Jeanne had such a sweet disposition, her mother had explained to Sarah, that there was no need to send her off to be raised by a nurse.

"Do you mean that you were raised by a servant?" Appollonie said, failing to cover her surprise. Sarah told her about Nurse. So as not to disappoint her friend, she left out some things and added others. Julie was very busy, traveling to many places, and Nurse had a wonderful cottage with a thatched roof on which gillyflowers grew.

"Do you mean like the cottage in the story Madame Fressard told us last week?"

"Yes, exactly like that one," said Sarah.

"I suppose gillyflowers grow on many thatched roofs," said Appollonie with a gentle smile. And she let Sarah go on, spinning vivid tales of the coast of Brittany, of the extent to which she was loved by Nurse, of the terrible man Nurse married after Sarah went back to live with Julie. She was too kind to ask why Nurse never visited the boarding school, why Sarah was kept from living in Paris until she was five years old, whether her disposition at birth could have been so much worse than her newborn sister Jeanne's. But aristocratic Appollonie could not conceal her curiosity about Sarah's absent father.

"Sarah," she said. "Surely your father must have been home sometime in all these years."

"No, silly," said Sarah. "Do you think he would come home and not say hello to his own daughter?"

"Of course not," said Appollonie. "You're certainly right." With great delicacy, she added: "It's just that you have a baby sister. A mother never gets a new baby when her husband is away."

"You don't understand," said Sarah. "He could not come home so easily. China is so very, very far."

And Appollonie, not simply discreet but unsure of the subject, dropped it at once.

Sarah missed her when she had to go to the infirmary. Sighing and groaning, she would convince dear Mme. Fressard that she was in need of the same sort of care. Mademoiselle Caroline, who taught the girls arithmetic, was neither as dear nor so easily convinced. When Appollonie took sick again, Sarah had to work hard to prove her case to Mademoiselle Caroline. It was not enough to make her voice very small and let her mouth hang slack; Sarah had to take hold of a real terror of illness, and let it loose under her skin. At this she had a natural facility. Even after a good night's sleep and a breakfast of hot croissants and tea, Sarah could make a heat rise from inside her body that would bring fever to her eyes and forehead, that would whiten her skin and leave her shaking with fatigue.

"If you act the consumptive," warned Mademoiselle Caroline, "you will become a consumptive as well." Still, she allowed Sarah to take the bed next to Appollonie in the infirmary. There would be castor oil to swallow, and early bedtimes, but she would have her friend. Besides, here the sheets were fresh, changed with every patient, and one was not forced to finish the hideous meat brought in on trays.

Sarah didn't disturb her friend. She watched Appollonie sleep deeply, though sunlight filled the room, and one could clearly hear the laughter and chatter of girls from the garden outside the windows. She wondered if her friend would die. When Appollonie stirred and slowly opened her eyes, she smiled at seeing Sarah.

"Have you come to visit?"

"No, I'm staying here," said Sarah. Appollonie didn't like her to fib, so Sarah twisted her face into a suitable frame of agony. "My head aches terribly. Mademoiselle Caroline made me come."

"I'm sorry," said Appollonie. "Does it hurt very much?" She had moved to a sitting position, and suddenly let loose a round of hacking coughs. Sarah could not hold back the terrible question.

"Are you a consumptive?" she said. Sarah knew that last year a girl had been removed from the school, victim of the dread disease. Apparently her parents had wanted her to be with them at home at the time of her death. She wondered if she were to fall deathly sick whether her father would return; or even whether her mother would let her come home to die.

"I don't know," said Appollonie.

"I don't want you to die."

"My aunt died of the consumption, and they say that it runs in families."

"Rachel is a consumptive," said Sarah.

Appollonie knew all about Sarah's preoccupation with the great actress, as she knew so many things about Sarah: She had never learned to read until she came to Mme. Fressard's, nearly two years ago, yet she could memorize a hymn or a poem faster than any other girl; she wore the best clothes and was mastering perfect manners, yet Appollonie's mother warned her away from becoming her friend. Appollonie did not want to mention her mother's conviction that Sarah's family was of bad blood.

"You must not always talk about Rachel," said Appollonie. "Madame Fressard says she is not a nice woman. And my mother says the same thing."

"You asked your mother?" wondered Sarah.

"Yes." Appollonie was blue-eyed and long-limbed and lovely; her mother short and squat and homely. Still, Sarah thought the woman very dignified. Mme. Fressard seemed to give her more respect than any other visiting parent. Julie was much more elegant and beautiful and proud. Yet Sarah would have treasured walking about Auteuil with Appollonie and her mother, to be thought a part of so happy a family. "Mother says that an actress is a bad woman."

"Why?" said Sarah.

"It doesn't matter why, it is so," she said. Appollonie paused, as if consulting some interior book of etiquette for what she must now say. "Sarah, I asked my mother if you could visit us this summer, at our country house near Orléans."

"I want to come."

"I want you to come," said Appollonie. "But Mother did not say that you could."

"She does not want me to visit you?"

"Maybe."

"Did she say that you must not invite me?"

"You must not talk about Rachel," said Appollonie, as though this might explain everything. Sarah did not understand, and told her so. "Or the way you lived with Nurse for so long," said Appollonie. "Especially in my mother's hearing."

"Why?"

"Because I want so much for you to come, Sarah. We have an orchard, and a pond, and it is so much cooler than in Paris." Suddenly Appollonie was struck by another fit of coughing, more violent than before. The little girl's upper torso was jerked up with force, like a marionette inexpertly handled. She tried to stop, to settle her body, but the forces that plagued her would not let go. Sarah hurried out of bed to pour her water from the heavy pitcher across the room. After the coughing had subsided for a moment, she brought a glass to her friend's lips. As the color drained from Appollonie's face, Sarah's green eyes filled with tears.

"I want to be with you too, Appollonie," said Sarah. "I will do whatever you say. Don't talk. Only drink. I should not have come to the infirmary at all. I should have let you rest instead of upsetting you."

"You do not upset me," said Appollonie.

"Please do not talk."

"Don't worry," said Appollonie. "I am not coughing now. I am fine."

"I will talk for both of us," said Sarah. "If I am wrong to talk about actresses or servants, I will not talk about them."

"It is more than that, Sarah. It is not just what you talk about." A cough threatened to rise up in her throat, but this time Appollonie stopped it. She did not want to continue, but as Sarah's best friend, she had no other choice. "Mother says that you are a heathen."

Sarah did not know the meaning of this word. But she could sense a violent hatred in its two ugly syllables, no matter how sweetly and regretfully expressed by her friend. "What is a heathen?"

"Heathens do not go to church," Appollonie said.

"I go to church."

"I know," said Appollonie, for they sat next to each other at Mass. "But they do not believe in the Father, the Son, and the Holy Ghost."

Sarah took the glass from her friend's hand and banged it down on the washstand. For a moment she forgot how sick Appollonie was. "I do believe in the Father, the Son, and the Holy Ghost."

"But you are a Jewess, Sarah," said Appollonie.

"What?" said Sarah. She could not have been more surprised if her friend had called her a Japanese.

"A Jewess. You are a member of the Jewish race."

"I am not," said Sarah. "I am French like you. I am a good Christian. I know my prayers better than anyone."

"Prayers have nothing to do with it. You were born a Jewess."

"What do you mean?" asked Sarah.

"A Jewess, you know what a Jewess is!" said Appollonie. Abashed at the pain she was giving her friend, she grew uncharacteristically angry. "Don't tell me that you don't know what it means. You mother is a Jewess, so you must be one too."

"My mother," said Sarah. "How do you know that my mother is a Jewess?"

"Because she is!" said Appollonie.

"Who said so?"

"My mother told me."

"Then she is lying," said Sarah.

"My mother does not lie. If you do not know, you must ask your mother if it is true. My mother would never tell a lie, not for any reason." The friends had never had a fight, not in nearly two years. Every word landed like a violent blow.

"I will ask her," said Sarah. "Since you do not believe me, I will ask my mother."

"Perhaps you were never told. After all, your father has not been at home."

"Do not talk about my father. I suppose you think he's a Jew too!"

"I don't know," said Appollonie. "My mother only spoke about your mother. She said that it was not right that Jewish girls be sent to the school." Though feeling poorly, Appollonie sat up and swung her legs off the bed. "I don't think she's right. In this one case, I think she's wrong. It does not matter to me."

"I am not Jewish," said Sarah. But her whole world of memories had suddenly begun to turn about in her heart as she searched in vain for a moment with her mother in church.

"Maybe you will be able to come. I told Mother that you are my best friend, and I don't care what you are."

"I don't want to come anymore," said Sarah. "You're not my friend." Of course, this was not true. Even as she said it, Sarah poured out another glass of water and placed it within Appollonie's reach. "If my mother said anything bad about you, do you think I would believe it? If I say someone is my best friend, I don't call them terrible names." Sarah put on her shoes.

"Where are you going?" said Appollonie. "You are not allowed to leave. You are supposed to be ill."

"I am not ill. I pretended to be ill, just to be with you. I lied so I could stay with my best friend. Perhaps that is something only a Jewess would do." Sarah gave Appollonie a last look at her tor-- mented face and swept out of the infirmary as though she were about to leap off a cliff.

Once out of her friend's view, Sarah's histrionic misery dissolved. Misery was weak, and she must be strong. She felt strength enter her body, a strength born of purpose. The little girl's body seemed driven now by her grim lips and clenched fists. There were things about her life that she did not know and was suddenly on the verge of understanding: why she had never gone to church with her mother, but only with Nurse or Titine; why the other mothers shied away from Julie on visiting days at school; why Mademoiselle Caroline said that her hair couldn't be brushed because it was "Jewish hair." The only Jews she had ever seen were the peddlers in old black coats hurrying along the streets of Paris. The single time she had heard the word "Jewess' on her mother's lips was when it was hurled about Rachel as an epithet. If Julie hated Jews, how could she be one herself? If she were a Jewess, why hadn't she told Sarah?

All she had ever known of her mother's origins was that she was Dutch, and had lived in many places. Sarah had been told that she had a grandmother, yet she had never met her, had never even seen her portrait. Julie had mentioned other sisters besides beautiful Aunt Rosine, but Sarah had never seen them. They were all in Holland. Perhaps there were many Jews in Holland. Maybe when her mother and Aunt Rosine spoke in Dutch, their secrets were Jewish secrets, and they spoke about the Jewish family they had left behind. If Sarah's red-blond curls were Jewish hair, why couldn't Julie's smooth and golden waves be Jewish hair as well?

Sarah ran to the deserted dining hall, to the chapel, to the study room, searching for Mme. Fressard, whom she finally found in the garden. Here she was not alone, but closely watching a half-dozen girls at their game of jumping rope. As Sarah called to her from across the garden, the game ceased while the girls and Mme. Fressard stared at the vision of the patient in her bedclothes. Sarah remembered the hostility of the schoolgirls, feeling it now with special force. If Appollonie had thought her Jewish, perhaps all these girls thought the same.

"I must see you, Madame," said Sarah. "It is a matter of the utmost urgency." The words were so loud and clear, so much like the opening speech of a children's melodrama, that a few of the girls laughed out loud. Mme. Fressard did not laugh. She hurried Sarah back inside, holding her tightly about the waist. Even from across the garden, she had felt Sarah's pain.

Mme. Fressard said nothing until she had sat Sarah down in her office, putting a thick lap rug over the child's half-bare legs. She waited for the outrage to subside, then she patted Sarah's wild mop of hair.

"What is it, darling? What is so terrible that you must run outside without your clothes?"

"Am I a Jewess?" asked Sarah.

The question took Mme. Fressard by surprise. Walking around the desk, she sat down in the high desk chair, elevated from and opposite the child, and placed her hands under her chin. The weight of the question seemed suddenly to make it difficult for her to keep her head high without support.

"Appollonie's mother says that I am," continued Sarah. "I think she is lying. Is she lying? I always say my prayers."

"Surely," began Mme. Fressard, "in your own home, your mother has explained certain things to you."

"What things?"

"The normal things, Sarah." Mme. Fressard picked up a sheaf of papers on the desk. Perhaps somewhere in the pile was a solution to the child's dilemma.

"She didn't tell me normal things," said Sarah. "I don't know. What normal things? Am I a Jewess?"

"This school," said Mme. Fressard slowly, "is run along strict and proper lines. As long as one is decent we do not care what religion they follow."

"Please tell me, please just tell me."

Mme. Fressard could no longer hesitate. "You are a Jewess," she said.

Sarah stared at her. Perhaps Mme. Fressard was wrong, as wrong as Appollonie, as misinformed as Appollonie's mother. But Mme. Fressard continued, driving home the point once and for all: "That is what I was given to understand. When you were first registered. Nothing wrong, of course. Baron de Rothschild is a Jew." Mme. Fressard smiled and clapped her hands together. "It's quite extraordinary that you did not know."

"Is my mother a Jewess?"

"Yes, Sarah," said Mme. Fressard. "Of course she is. That is why you are."

"I don't understand," said Sarah. "She doesn't like Jews. She hates them. She hates Rachel." Sarah tried to make sense of what she had been told, but the knowledge of what she had suddenly become overwhelmed her. She could never be like Appollonie, never be like a sister to her, never go to the country home near Orléans, so cool, so shady, so much better than Paris. No wonder Mademoiselle Caroline called her hair "Jewish hair." Mademoiselle Caroline hated her because she was Jewish, as Appollonie's mother hated her, as Appollonie herself would hate her too. Perhaps even her own Jewish mother hated her for nothing more than the fact of her Jewish birth.

"I am sure your mother likes Jews," said Mme. Fressard. "In France, everyone likes Jews."

"Appollonie's mother said that I am a heathen. I cannot go to their house."

"Child, we do not think you are bad because of it."

"Appollonie said that it did not matter to her, but her mother did not say that I could come. So I am a heathen too?"

"Well, I suppose since you are not baptized—" began Mme. Fressard. But she stopped herself, stood up, and came around her desk close to Sarah. "Look here, you're a Jewish girl, but you're very sweet and good and kind."

"Mademoiselle Caroline says I am wild and bad-tempered."

"She only says that to improve you, my dear."

"Mademoiselle Caroline says that I am the daughter of my mother. She says that we come from a tribe."

"I will speak to Mademoiselle Caroline."

"Does she mean that we are both Jewesses? Why does she say that we are from a tribe?"

"Sarah, please," said Mme. Fressard. "You are not from a tribe, but you are Jewish. Your mother is Jewish, and you are a Jewish girl."

Once again the memory of her mother's hatred wracked Sarah's body. It seemed that nothing could be worse than being a consumptive, a Jewess, and a whore. But Appollonie was a consumptive and Sarah was a Jewess, and the actress Rachel was both.

"Rachel is a Jewish girl," said Sarah.

"But there are many Jewish girls in France," said Mme. Fressard, who knew this to be far from the truth: The nation's population of thirty-three million contained less than seventy thousand Jews, most of them in Alsace and Lorraine. Friends and enemies of the Jews knew them more from hearsay or legend than from real relationships. Jews were Moses and Abraham, the nameless pawn-broker on a grimy street, and the most famous actress of France. "Madame Rachel is only one among many. You may be sure there are very few of your race who would want to have anything to do with the theater. Jews are a religious people. You must not be unhappy that you are Jewish."

Sarah put aside the lap rug, and got to her feet so that she stood in Mme. Fressard's ample shadow. "Please answer me one more thing," said Sarah. "What is a whore?"

Suddenly all the goodwill in Mme. Fressard vanished. For a moment it seemed to Sarah that the old woman might faint, so rapidly did she pale at this question. She backed away from the little girl, as though afraid to come into contact with her skin. Gripping the edge of her desk, she said: "You must never say that word."

"Why?" asked Sarah.

"You needn't know, just do not use it!" All the kindliness, all the patience was gone from her brown eyes.

"My mother said that Rachel was one," said Sarah. "She said that Rachel was a whore."

Mme. Fressard's breath came in short, shallow gulps. "For the last time," she said. "You must not discuss Rachel, and you must never use that filthy word."

"I will use it," said Sarah. "Tell me what it means! A whore!"

Without thought, Mme. Fressard slapped Sarah's face.

For a moment Sarah stood stock-still, experiencing the stinging pain like the beginning of an answer.

"I'm sorry," said Mme. Fressard. She looked at the child in astonishment, for the blow had not led to tears, or to fear.

"Whore," said Sarah, whispering the word. "Whore, whore, whore."

"Stop it, child," said Mme. Fressard. But she knew that she could not prevent Sarah from having her way. "I am sorry I hit you. You do not understand what you are asking."

"I understand," said Sarah. There were three words, three secrets, and she must know them all. "My mother said that Rachel is a consumptive, like they say Appollonie is. And that she is a Jewess, like you say I am. And that she is a whore, and you must tell me what that word means." Sarah seemed to be growing in size, as if the urgency of her anger were filling out and swelling her delicate frame. Mme. Fressard tentatively touched the child's face where she had struck her, and looked into her feverish eyes. "I will find out," said the little girl.

"I will tell you, but then you must go back to the infirmary. It is just that it is such a bad word, a word that decent girls never use." She whispered, stroking Sarah's cheek with her smooth and plump old hands. "It means a bad woman," she said. "A very bad woman. A woman who is bad with men."

"A bad woman," said Sarah, stepping away from the touch of Mme. Fressard's hands. "How is Rachel a bad woman?"

"That is all you have to know about it."

"No," said Sarah. "That is not all I have to know." She did not understand how Rachel could be a "bad woman." She could not imagine what it meant to be "bad with men."

She remembered a night of whispering when one of the girls, just back from visiting her parents, had thrilled the dormitory with news of Rachel. The actress was in Russia, where even the czar had fallen in love with her. But this was not all. The girl had learned from an older sister why Rachel was so sick. It was because she was a "bad woman," she had said.

Sarah had grown angry when the girl said that Rachel was bad. But she remained in her narrow bed, and listened so that she might hear more about the great actress. Rachel was bad, the schoolgirl said, because she had two children without ever having a husband. She was bad because she still had the name she had been given at birth. No decent woman could have a child without first being married, without changing the name given to her by her father to the one given to her by her husband.

Sarah for once hadn't challenged this attack on her heroine. Appollonie was older than Sarah by nearly a year, and the whispering girl was older even than Appollonie. There were things about men and women that they knew, and that she did not. There were things that she would soon understand, and about which she had not wished to ask.

But now she had no patience.

If Rachel was "bad with men," perhaps that would explain her mother's hatred. But if a woman was "bad" by not having a husband, what did it mean if one had a husband who never appeared?

It seemed her very life depended on the answers that she could wring from her best friend.

Sarah ran outside and across the garden, ignoring the stares of the girls playing their games, and entered the dormitory building, turning left to the steep staircase, running up the one flight to the infirmary. "Tell me," said Sarah to Appollonie, coming up to where she was lying asleep on the bed. "What did you mean when you said that about my father coming home? What did you mean when you said that you can't get a baby when your husband is away?" Sarah shook her friend, but she had already woken, had already heard the torrent of words. Yet Appollonie could not help her. She looked at Sarah through glassy eyes.

"Do you hate me?" asked Appollonie.

"Of course I don't hate you," said Sarah, suddenly overcome with terror. No longer did her life depend on the answers to these questions or any other. Sarah knew that no words, no revelations would ever be strong enough to kill her. Before her now was a true life-and-death struggle. Beyond the pain in Appollonie's eyes she could sense an utter and complete weariness, an exhaustion with trying to hold on to life.

"You are right," said Appollonie. "I should not have listened to Mother. I will always believe you. I will believe you before I believe anyone."

"You must not talk," said Sarah.

"I don't feel very well," she said. "I think you should please call Madame Fressard."

"Of course," said Sarah, trying to smooth the pain from her friend's forehead, trying to heal her with the force of her love.

"And please tell me that you don't hate me."

"Appollonie," said Sarah. "I told you. I don't hate you. Appollonie, you must not talk, you must close your eyes." She turned about, shouting for help, praying that in her haste to wake her friend she had not killed her. Mme. Fressard brought the doctor, and on the following day, Appollonie's mother arrived to take her home.

Even this calamity could not stop up the questions in Sarah's heart.

She wrote to Appollonie, hoping not only to hear that she was well but that she was well enough to correspond. Sarah's wishes were not answered. Her friend was too sick to do more than scrawl her name on the bottom of a little letter dictated to one of her sisters.

Sarah wrote a rambling, incoherent letter to her mother, demanding to know the whereabouts of her father. Julie was too busy to respond. And Mme. Fressard positively avoided her.

Sarah's questions burned inside her, and each day the contained fire grew hotter. When the summer holiday arrived, Sarah fairly leaped into her mother's carriage, her questions pouring out all at once.

"Am I Jewish? If Father is in China, how could I have a new sister? How can you get a baby when your husband is away? Why is Rachel a bad woman? Why does Father never come home?"

That day Sarah wore a becoming blue velvet frock, and the wind had blown a pretty blush into her wild face, and the long green eyes glowed with such intensity that Julie thought her child almost pretty. This pleased her. For a brief moment she could fancy Sarah an accessory to her own beauty, like a striking gown or a handsome coach.

And Julie was happy on other counts too: Though the Duke of Morny was following the court to Fontainebleau for the season, he had left Julie a diamond broach so fabulous that it was almost unimaginable that he would not be returning to her bed in September. While the duke was away, there would be other compensations: The old Alexandre Dumas and his young illegitimate son were both infatuated with her, each eager to outshine the other with gifts and public displays of emotion. Last night she had sat between the two at the theater. There were few things Julie enjoyed more than displaying her beauty to the Tuesday night crowd at the Théâtre Français from Dumas *père*'s box, while Dumas *fils* kept filling her glass with champagne.

So Sarah's fervent questions did not give rise to anger or indifference. Julie, at twenty-five years of age, with a lovely new baby at home, and becoming so rich that she was about to buy the entire building in which her apartment was located, felt her heart swell with the noble travails of motherhood.

"First kiss me," said Julie. She turned her cheek, redolent of rice powder and perfume, and Sarah, taken aback by this unexpected closeness, nearly forgot her overwhelming need to know who and what she was. She kissed her mother, and as she moved her lips away, Julie said: "No, I want a big kiss. I want ten big kisses."

Sarah gave them to her, counting them down in her mind.

This was enough for Julie. "Not so wet, please," she said. "You kiss like a sloppy dog."

"Mama, please tell me," said Sarah.

For a moment Julie almost lost the little patience she had. Why couldn't the child close her eyes and enjoy the first days of summer without a hundred questions? She had half a mind to hit Sarah's knuckles with the bejeweled Chinese fan in her hand. But Sarah's adoration assuaged Julie's selfish heart.

"I only want to be what you are," said Sarah. "But you must tell me. I don't know, and you must tell me."

"I will tell you," said Julie, struggling to come up with a speech appropriate to Sarah's nearly nine years. "I never told you that we are Jewish, because I don't care a fig about religion."

"We are Jewish?" asked Sarah.

"Yes," said Julie. "Now that you know, you may forget about it completely."

"Aunt Rosine? Is she?"

"Yes."

"And Titine and Bella—"

"No, you stupid girl! They are not family."

"We are a Jewish family then, Mama?"

"Only if you tell people," snapped Julie. "Only if you insiston it."

So it was true, thought Sarah. Though her mother looked no less lovely, there was shame in her words. "And Father?"

"Father?" said Julie. "Your father is not Jewish. No, he's French and a Christian, and of a very old and very important family. Don't let these stuck-up little girls try to tell you you're not as good as any of them. One day a very rich and important man will want to marry you."

"I don't understand about Father," said Sarah. "The girls say that if he was not here, it is impossible for you to have a baby."

At this Julie laughed, a long, relieving laugh. Sarah wanted to know so many things, and all of these urgent questions had been prompted by the spoiled brats of the aristocracy. "Oh, yes. You go to school with such smart little girls. It's quite true about your father. It is not possible to get a baby without a husband." Julie smiled at her daughter, for all the world looking like she were about to offer her an unexpected treat. "So I got myself a new husband," she said. "Just so that I could get you a new sister." Julie opened her fan and waved it mightily across her lovely, sensuous face. But just when she thought she had answered every question, Sarah returned to the main point.

"A new husband, Mama? But you have a husband. What about Father? Why doesn't he come home?"

"Sarah," said Julie, thinking as quickly as she could, "the truth is very sad."

"I want to know the truth, Mama," said Sarah. "I only want to know the truth."

"I'm sorry, Sarah." After all, if the child was never going to see the man who fathered her, there was no point in keeping him alive. "Your father never came back from China," said Julie. "You see, child, your father is dead."

Chapter 6

I HAVE DESTROYED
MY FATHER'S PORTRAIT

ppollonie died a month later, and in her perfect grief
Sarah believed that she must surely join her.

In Julie's home, and in the rich neighborhood surrounding it, the mood was contrastingly joyous. President Louis Napoleon, responding to the 1852 plebiscite changing
the nation from a republic to an empire, had proclaimed himself
Emperor Napoleon III. Appropriately, in this summer of 1853 he
was spending the nation's money on imperial-sized enterprises:
railroads, international fairs, telegraph lines. For every new millionaire spawned by these projects, there were a thousand laborers
receiving two francs for a twelve-hour day. Yet it was the million-
aires who lit up Paris with their flamboyant displays of carriages,
jewels, and costumes bright enough to eclipse—for some—the
beggars, the ragpickers, the diseased.

In January of 1853, Napoleon III had married the exquisite
Spanish countess Eugénie de Montijo, dazzling the fashionable
world with her beauty and her delight in ostentatious display. The
new rich aped the majestic couple. Intimates and advocates of the
emperor copied his goatee—calling the little beard an "imperial."
Jealous followers of the court called Empress Eugénie frivolous,
but parroted her sentiments and imitated the brown silks and black
velvets of her extravagant gowns. Men with sources of information
grew much richer, speculating in railroad shares and land sales in
France, in the French and English colonies, even in distant America, where Franklin Pierce was the president of twenty million free

people and three million black slaves. The France of revolutionary ideals was replaced by the France of the Industrial Revolution; the country of the first Napoleon's vision of conquest was replaced by the county of Napoleon III's vision of great public works and grand progress.

For the privileged this vision became one of delight. The emperor's first cousin, Napoleon Joseph, officially known as Prince Napoleon—unofficially as "Plon-Plon" by his numerous mistresses—was building himself a replica of a Roman villa in the Avenue Montaigne, only one of many pleasure palaces built by the wealthy. Every night that summer there were parties, private and public, as the worlds of aristocracy, power, and money came together in a mad mix of ambition and greed. It was to the private parties that the prominent courtesans were invited. Julie had her pick of diversions, had her choice of prestigious men of means. Sarah was as oblivious to the fact that her mother was a frequent guest at Plon-Plon's lecherous festivities as she was to the rumors of his love affair with the actress Rachel. She did not see the splendor of this new epoch. The gold that grew at a thousand percent a month as men invested in the first railroad through the Alps, in the price of American cotton, in outfitting the British soldiers preparing to fight in the Crimea held no fascination for her. The medical miracles being touted throughout the Western world—a compulsory smallpox vaccine, the use of chloroform in surgery, the first hypodermic syringe—had not saved Appollonie. And she did not believe anything would save herself.

Sarah shivered throughout the hot Parisian summer, waiting for death to strike. She looked for death in the rats crawling out from under the rubble of ancient buildings torn down to make way for new streets, squares, houses. She saw death in the clouds of pulverized brick and stone and earth drifting through humid skies. Death was in the hot flesh of overworked horses, collapsing under heavy loads, waiting for the horse butchers to carve them into paupers' meat.

Death was everywhere. The little son of her mother's hall porter had died of pleurisy, as Appollonie had died of consumption, as her father had died from some mysterious ailment that Julie refused to name. Everyone, even the servants, knew that it was only a matter of time before the great actress Rachel would die as well. Every day Sarah searched her own burning eyes in the drawing-room cheval glass for the signs of death.

Sarah was not alone in believing herself a candidate for consumption. When she had been enrolled at the school of the Grand-Champs Convent, Sarah was placed in the dormitory for delicate children; here there was a rug to warm the floor, and the infirmary was the adjacent room. But she remained frighteningly thin and pale for all the years she was there. No rug, no medicine could take away the chill that left her trembling beneath Julie's discarded shawls.

The change of schools was the inspiration of her mother's admirer, the Duke of Morny: He imagined that Julie's temperamental daughter would benefit from iron discipline in an atmosphere both religious and aristocratic. Indeed, the Grand-Champs Convent at Versailles was so exclusive that the duke had to use his imperial authority to arrange for Sarah's admission. Sarah didn't fight this plan. She never wanted to return to Mme. Fressard's, the scene of Appollonie's suffering. And it was obvious how Julie felt: Busy with baby Jeanne and importunate gentlemen, her mother did not want Sarah's gloom or violence interfering with the apartment's atmosphere of cigar smoke, baby powder, and Eau d'Ange.

And Sarah did interfere. The questions that had burned in her heart with so bright a flame festered. She had become as afraid of the truth as she was of lies. She began to doubt everything ever told her by Julie. Perhaps even the framed portrait of her father was a fake; perhaps she had no father, and no mother. Perhaps she was neither Jewish nor Christian, neither French nor Dutch.

Every new frock bought for baby Jeanne, every strange gentleman who came to call on Julie, every phrase uttered in Dutch or German sent wild suspicions through her credulous soul: Julie loved Jeanne and hated her; Julie would find a new husband as terrible as Nurse's Monsieur Georges; Julie would return to the foreign place from which she had come, and never see Sarah again. It was not startling that the slightest demand or complaint put Sarah in a rage.

Only Mme. Guérard, a kindly young widow who lived in a small apartment above theirs, offered any solace. "I wish you were my daughter," she said. "If you were mine, I would keep you home, all to myself."

"What would you do with me?" Sarah asked, never tiring of this stranger's outpouring of affection.

"I would read you your favorite stories. I would give you chocolates round the clock. I would never make you brush your hair or study your lessons or stand up straight. I would spoil you so terribly that you would not be fit for anything."

"I would be fit," Sarah said. "I would still be fit."

Mme. Guérard gave her a copy of La Fontaine's *Fables,* believing in instruction by moral example rather than by autocratic decree. Sarah's favorite fable was "The Wolf, the Mother, and the Child." In it, a voracious wolf hears a furious mother's promise to hand her baby over to the wolves if it does not quit crying. The wolf waits for the mother to fulfill her promise, but is itself attacked by dogs and men with pitchforks. After the wolf is killed, its pelt is nailed to the town hall's wall. Sarah would read the fable to Mme. Guérard with great feeling, particularly when she got to the powerful warning at the end: "Wolves: Do not believe everything told you by a mother when her child cries!" Mme. Guérard said she would rather listen to Sarah read aloud than attend the theater.

"Would you rather listen to me than listen to Rachel?" Sarah asked.

"Rachel is rather a special case," said Mme. Guérard. "I hope she gets well, so that one day you can see her in a great play."

"I hope she gets well too," said Sarah.

It was Mme. Guérard who took Sarah to enroll at the convent school. Julie did not have the time, she said, to waste on a round trip by bumpy diligence to Versailles. Besides, Sarah had once again gone into a rage the day before the trip, and Julie remained violently angry with her. Somehow she had managed to forget the source of her daughter's rage: Julie laughed in her face at a request to know where Jeanne's father lived, and whether he was now Sarah's father too.

"What is his name?" Sarah had asked, her silvery voice threatening to rise into an insistent shout. "If I am to have a stepfather, can't I at least know his name?"

"He is not your stepfather," Julie had answered. "Jeanne has one father, and you have another. That is why you are not sisters, but half sisters. That is why you look nothing alike. That is why she acts like an angel, and you act like a devil!"

It wasn't fair not to know who your mother's husband was, not right that every other little girl was free of terrible questions to take alone to bed every night. Perhaps her mother loved baby Jeanne so much more than Sarah that Julie refused to share even the name of her new husband with her unwanted daughter. With Julie, so unlike the staid and sober mothers who had visited Mme. Fressard's, there was no way to know which man she loved best. There were so many men, so many admirers, and her mother seemed to love and be loved by each and every one.

Sarah had noticed that one very august gentleman made Julie nervous. Of all her visitors, she was especially anxious to please this one. Before he arrived, Sarah would see her beautiful mother go back to her dressing table again and again, reaching for a powder puff, or the rouge brush, or a bottle of scent.

"Mama," Sarah had speculated, "did you marry the Duke of Morny?"

It was then that her mother had slapped her face.

"You and your stupid questions," Julie had said. "I won't have your stupid questions. Who are you to be even mentioning the duke's name? Don't you know what it means to be a duke? Are you really so stupid that you think a duke is going to marry your mother?"

"I am not stupid, Mama," Sarah had said, and turned about so quickly that the sleeve of her dress knocked a bottle of lotion from Julie's dressing table.

"You clumsy little fool!" Julie had said. This time Sarah avoided her slap and deliberately swept her hand across the marble tabletop. Bottles, boxes, brushes crashed to the floor; still Sarah was not finished. Julie had grabbed at her wrists to stop further damage, and Sarah kicked her mother's shin, then bit the hands that held her.

"I am not clumsy," Sarah had said, the rage beating against the walls of her body.

Then Julie's words had flown out in Dutch: harsh, guttural sounds to Sarah's French ears, foreign words of loathing. But Julie backed away from her child, even as her maid Bella took hold of Sarah from behind.

"I am not stupid," Sarah had said, straining in Bella's brutish grip. "I am not clumsy. I think the Duke of Morny is old and ugly. And if I want, I will marry a prince!"

Despite the slap and the broken toilet articles, despite the insults and the anger, when the next day arrived, Julie had demanded a kiss before her daughter's departure to Versailles. Sarah hadn't hesitated. She had rushed into her arms, buried her wet eyes and nose against her mother's powdered cheek.

"If you're a good girl, I will visit," her mother had said, pulling away from Sarah. "You must learn to hold your tongue, or you will see nothing of me, nothing at all."

"I will be good, Mama," Sarah had said, her love for Julie buffeting her body like ocean waves at the shore. Even Mme. Guérard's cheery talk could not erase Sarah's misery. No love from the little widow could compensate for her mother's indifference. If only Julie could find her beautiful, talented, worthy, Sarah would do anything. Even the terrible understanding that threatened to flood into her heart might be pushed aside.

"We are here, child," Mme. Guérard said as the driver abruptly stopped his horses at the entrance to the convent. "It's very imposing. You're a lucky girl."

Because the child was quiet, looking along the enormous walls hiding the convent's buildings from the street, up at the cross on the tall iron gates, Mme. Guérard imagined she was frightened. Julie had told Mme. Guérard of her decision to baptize Sarah. "When she's no longer a Jewess, it will be easier for her to marry a rich man," Julie had said. "Besides, it will be one less question for her to plague me with."

"I am not lucky," said Sarah.

"You will be all right here, darling," Mme. Guérard answered. "Now that you're going to be baptized, no one can call you a heathen. And the sisters always love a little girl as smart and pretty as you."

"Madame Guérard," said Sarah, taking the sweet woman's hands in her own, "is my mother a bad woman?"

"Of course not, child," she said.

"She does not answer my questions, and I must know," said Sarah, imagining that if she could convince Mme. Guérard of the justness of her desire for information, she would surely give it to her. "I never knew my father, and my mother has a new husband, because Jeanne is my half sister. And she won't tell me where the new husband is. Please, I want to know· if she's bad, the way the girls said Rachel was bad. I want to know if my mother is a bad woman."

Mme. Guérard tried to assure Sarah that neither Julie nor Rachel was a bad woman. About Sarah's father, or baby Jeanne's, she said nothing. As far as Mme. Guérard could see, if, as Julie had told her privately, a real Édouard Bernard existed in Havre, this still meant little in the way of fatherhood. Even if Julie had taken his name— only slightly improved to Bernhardt—and the promise of a hundred-thousand-franc dowry for the child, he would never appear when Sarah needed him. Besides, unless he was very, very stupid, or very, very blind, thought Mme. Guérard, he could not imagine himself the only candidate for Sarah's father. In the case of little Jeanne, Julie hadn't even bothered to fabricate a definitive father: The possibilities, glittering though they might be, were endless.

"You must never listen to what silly girls say about your mother," Mme. Guérard said. "They are mean, because they are jealous. Your mother loves you very much and she is a very good woman."

"But you say that Rachel isn't bad, and even Mama says that Rachel is a bad woman."

"Rachel is a great actress, and I am sure that your mother has nothing but respect for her," said Mme. Guérard.

These assurances did not help. Apparently no one would answer her questions. She told herself that the answer would make no difference. She let herself be swallowed up by the Grand-Champs Convent. Certainly she would not live very long in this place, she imagined at first, taking a certain satisfaction in every grim aspect of convent life. The huge crowd of strange girls in the refectory, the frightening black-veiled nuns, the sober religious engravings looking down from the classroom walls at squinting schoolgirls doing endless needlework: All this seemed a fitting background against which to die.

In the wall above her dormitory bed was a niche for a statue of the Virgin Mary. Here a tiny lamp burned day and night, the oil replaced by donations from the children. In this light Sarah found a thousand spectral shapes. Everyone from Nurse's Monsieur Georges to Mama's maid, Bella, everything from Rachel's grand carriage to Julie's bejeweled fan, every memory from her mother's arrival in Brittany to Appollonie's departure from the world swirled in the unsteady flame, in the dancing shadows.

After she was baptized, educated about the convent's enclosed world, she imagined herself a novice taking the veil for the first time. Clothing herself in this sacred image, she would fall asleep, directly into a dream she herself had prompted.

As Sarah grew older, her childish body maturing to uneasy adolescence, the novice in her dream remained a very little girl. Always the little novice's moment of ecstasy thrilled her. This bliss Sarah found only in the contemplation of death.

Lying prone on the hard flat stones of the chapel floor, the heavy ceremonial black cloth would be held over her by four of the sisters: Sister Marie, Sister Séraphine, Sister Catherine, and Mother Ste.-Sophie. Sister Marie hated her, always castigating her for impiety, wildness, and for leading other girls into rebelliousness. Sister Séraphine liked her and protected her as though she were another girl than the one known to Sister Marie. This Sarah was shy, obedient, afraid to speak to anyone but César, the convent dog. Sister Catherine pitied her because she knew her to be both timid and full of pride. This Sarah, too retiring to sing loud her hymns, had insisted on being given a part in the tiny pageant put on for a visiting monseigneur, and had then boomed out her little speech loud enough for a thousand people to have heard every word.

Only Mother Ste.-Sophie, the convent's superior, loved her. She knew Sarah's wildness, timidity, and pride were all of a piece. She knew that Sarah was good, she knew that Sarah was loving, she knew that Sarah wanted only love in return.

Mother Ste.-Sophie was as beautiful as her own mother. In the nun's blue-eyed face, framed by white cambric, Sarah found another Julie, one separated from the evil world by a film of goodness. Sarah wanted to take the black barège veil that covered the Mother Superior's face and wrap it about herself. She wanted to

smell Mother Ste.-Sophie's holiness the way she smelled her mother's rice powder and perfume. She wanted to love Mother Ste.-
Sophie as much as she loved Mama, and that love was wild,
possessive, full of pain. In return she wanted only to be loved by
them, adored by them. Sarah wanted them to long for her when
she died, as she mourned for Appollonie.

In her dream, as the four nuns lowered the heavy black cloth
across her body, she could feel its emblazoned white cross burn
through the fabric directly into the skin of her back. The heat was
scorching, made bearable only by the damp cold of the stones
against which her forehead rested. She felt a suffocating relief
when the nuns placed an enormous candlestick at each of the four
corners of the cloth, anchoring it to the ground as surely as six feet
of shoveled dirt rooted a corpse in its coffin to the earth.

As she proceeded through the ceremony, going from novice to
nun, a miracle occurred: The white cross passed through her skin
and skeleton and vital organs and emerged bloodlessly on the other
side of her unblemished belly, a cross made no longer of fabric but
of Sarah's bones.

That was but half the miracle.

The rest of the miracle was that the novice, in the act of wedding
the Lord Jesus, died.

The realization that she was dead always left her in a state of
bliss. In the dream Sarah would be dead, but dead and beatified all
in the same breath. The black cloth that had made her a nun now
served as holy grave clothes. The nuns would turn her about,
open-mouthed at the miracle of the cross. Mother Ste.-Sophie, her
serene eyes filled with tears, would lead them in making the sign
of the cross, in praising God's name. They would kiss Sarah's pale
lips and sprinkle her with holy water, they would anoint her with
oil and put burning tapers in a circle about her naked, guiltless
body. On her breast would be the cross of bone. Over her eyes
would be flower petals. They would bury her at the convent so that
Mother Ste.-Sophie could pray at the gravesite every day, so that
Julie would have to make the trip to Versailles, over and over
again, all the rest of her life.

This dream was neither a nightmare nor an accident. Sarah
wanted it every night, and she made it come to her through the

strength of her imagination, finding inspiration in the radiance lighting the Virgin Mary's face. Only in the dream was her heart quiet, only in the dream was she completely safe.

Because slowly and irreversibly Sarah had begun to understand who she was, and from where she had come.

She was French, but not as French as those born to two French parents. She was Christian, but not as Christian as those born to the faith. She was Jewish, but not as Jewish as those raised to pray to the God of Moses. She had the pale, slender look of the consumptive, but in her bones were fibers of steel. Even as she dreamed of death, she knew that she would somehow live forever. She was the daughter of a father who had never come home, who had never married her mother. The mother who raised her had powerful, famous friends, yet these men had families, wives and children, who thought Julie a bad woman.

Sarah understood this badness because it called from within her body's innocent frame.

Sarah had begun menstrual bleeding at the age of twelve, much earlier than any of the other convent girls. Sister Catherine had counseled her, explaining that the monthly bleeding was a sign of awakening sinful lust. Jewesses and Negresses always began to bleed earlier than Catholic girls of the French race. This was because the lesser races were more inclined to lust. Prayer, however, could vanquish this natural predilection. Sister Catherine had stopped bleeding completely when she had taken her novitiate's vows. Since Sarah was no longer Jewish but a baptized Catholic, she need only root out what was left of her sinful heritage.

But nothing stopped Sarah's monthly bleeding. She could not speak to her mother about such things because she knew that Julie would laugh at her. A year before, Julie had given birth to a third daughter, Regina, and Sarah was told that this dark-complexioned, blue-eyed hellion was yet another half sister, with yet another father whose name her mother refused to reveal. Apparently her mother thought nothing of sin. If Sarah had told her that she feared the lust stirring in her body, that she feared for her own immortal soul, Julie might have slapped her face. She did not like it when her daughter "played the saint" with her.

But what Sarah most feared was that she was nothing like a

saint. The soldiers quartered at Versailles were too timid to stare at the convent girls who went on excursion, outside the Grand-Champs gates. But Sarah stared at the soldiers. She found herself enthralled by their broad shoulders, manly strides, unfettered smiles, flashing white teeth. She knew the feelings stirring within her were temptations placed there by the Devil, and that outside the convent these temptations were everywhere, and overwhelming. Sarah tried to repent for this and other crimes, refraining from sleep, slipping into the chapel for hours of prayer before the dawn. Mother Ste.-Sophie found her there once, blue-lipped and shaking from the cold, on her knes before the altar on which Sarah had lit two dozen tapers.

"I have destroyed my father's portrait," she said.

"Are you praying for forgiveness?" asked the Mother Superior.

"No," said Sarah. "I have done nothing wrong. I never knew my father. I don't know what he looked like. I don't even know if the portrait was of him."

Mother Ste.-Sophie was not surprised at this, for Sarah confessed everything to her. "If you are not praying for forgiveness, child, what are you doing?"

"I am praying for my mother's soul," Sarah said. "She doesn't believe, and she doesn't care, but I must pray for her soul, I must pray even harder than if she were a nun and a holy woman like you."

Mother Ste.-Sophie brushed back the thick red-gold hair from Sarah's brow and kissed her tenderly. "You are a very dear girl, Sarah," she said.

"I want to be a nun," said Sarah. "I want never to leave you."

Mother Ste.-Sophie held back her smile. "It is not necessary to light so many candles," she said. "We are not as extravagant as you Parisians. The Lord sees perfectly well in the dark." Then she got down on her knees next to the child and joined her in prayer.

When Sarah was thirteen, in 1857, a famous poet named Alfred de Musset died, and even Julie admitted that the fleshly sins he had committed had hastened his death. A terrible book called *Madame Bovary* was published that same year, and though the writer was prosecuted, as was another one, even more depraved, named Baudelaire, the nuns all shook their heads at the state of sin outside the convent. Sarah decided that she must never leave Grand-Champs. Somehow the dowry promised her by the father in whom she no longer believed must be paid to the Church. Surely her mother would have no objection to seeing her eldest daughter locked away from the world.

Even to visit Julie's apartment for a day became an agony. Paris was a terrible place. Every man had a mistress, every mistress measured her worth by what her man paid her. Sarah did not know what to call her mother, for a woman with more men than she could number on her fingers was not a mistress but something worse.

Sarah's mother was famous, and she was beautiful, and she had property worth a half-million francs. Aristocratic women recognized at a glance her carriage in the Bois, men dissipated ancient fortunes in pursuit of her love, couturiers begged her to wear their designs, her image was painted and sculpted by the great artists of her day. Julie was golden-haired and terribly young to be an adolescent's mother. Sarah was fourteen, and Julie was thirty, and looked not a day older than twenty-one. They could have been sisters: Sarah the younger, of course, intensely bright, burning with a passion that could not yet be expressed; and Julie, older, more beautiful by far, and despite her profession, devoid of passion of any kind.

Sarah learned the grand word "courtesan" as she learned words less grand for women and girls who took gifts from men: A "grisette" was a working girl who let a student or a middle-class man buy her body for a few extra francs to supplement starvation wages. A "lorette" had left the ranks of wage earners to work full time at her specialized trade. These girls lived near Notre Dame de Lorette, on the wrong side of the Boulevard Haussmann, a far less fashionable part of Paris than Julie's First Arrondissement. Lorettes were prettier, more practiced, and more expensive than grisettes; still, they were as far removed from the ranks of the courtesans as foot soldiers are from the generals who lead them.

But Sarah knew that money or social status had little bearing on sin. What was committed between a duke and a courtesan was no different than what was committed between a clerk and his lorette, between a Left Bank student and his grisette.

They were each and every one what her mother had long ago called the actress Rachel: a whore.

Her mother was a bad woman, living in a bad world.

Late on a cold January morning in 1858, Sarah decided to approach Julie with the news of her faith and her calling. With a calmness born of fervor, Sarah came close to where her mother sat at her dressing table. The fashionable *Figaro,* now in its fourth year of publication, was spread clumsily about the usually neatly arrayed tools of her beauty.

"I must talk to you, Mama," said Sarah.

"Not now," said Julie.

"I have to, Mama," said Sarah, her silvery voice rising up the scale. "You never let me talk to you, but now you must listen to me." For a moment Sarah had been too preoccupied with the speech she had prepared for this occasion to notice her mother's reflection in the dressing mirror, lit by the harsh gaslights. Julie was crying, and the paint she had applied to her beautiful face ran carelessly along her cheeks. "What's wrong, Mama?"

"Look," said Julie, turning about and pulling Sarah close to the marble table. Sarah looked down in amazement at the surface of the *Figaro,* marked with drops and smudged lines of rouge.

"Why are you crying?"

"Rachel is dead," said Julie, even as Sarah looked wildly across the columns of print, the facts and figures, the famous roles she had played, the infamous affairs. But Sarah knew little of plays and players. She could not be touched by a description of the home near Cannes of the playwright Sardou, where Rachel had finally succumbed. Tributes from dignitaries, poets, theater folk meant nothing to her. The fact that Prince Napoleon, Plon-Plon, had been at her deathbed, did not arouse admiration. Yet, for a moment the fact of Rachel's death nearly swept her off her feet. Sarah stumbled back from the dressing table, and slammed her back against the far wall, near the fire in the grate. She was as sad as when she had heard of the death of Appollonie.

"I can't believe it," said Julie. "She was thirty-six. Only six years older than I."

"I will pray for her, Mama," said Sarah, coming back to where Julie sat, disheveled and distraught. For years she had expected the death of this famous actress, ever since she glimpsed her getting into a carriage in front of the Théâtre Français. Despite her new understanding of sin and lust and corruption, Sarah had remained drawn to Rachel's name and legend. Even when the nuns had warned their pupils about the moral dangers inherent in going to a theater, and the absolute depravity of the life of an actress, Sarah exempted Rachel from such condemnation. Ever since she had felt the adoration that Rachel drew from the crowd about her, Sarah wanted to learn what Rachel knew; and in that desire, she had joined the multitudes who loved the actress.

"He left a warship, to be at her side. The prince. Prince Napoleon left his sworn duty to be at her side," said Julie. "They were lovers, you understand. They were true lovers. It makes no difference how they were born. They were lovers, and that is all that matters."

Sarah did not understand why the death of a woman whom she had believed her mother despised had brought Julie to such a state. She did not know that her mother's hatred of the actress had stemmed from violent jealousy, for Prince Napoleon had been Julie's lover too. While the prince had paid Julie the courtesan for their nights with lavish gifts of jewels and cash, he had paid Rachel the artist with his love. Rachel's fame, Rachel's glory were nothing less than a magnificent rendering of Julie's dreams. Only one woman in the world had risen from the gutter to gain wealth and status and the love of princes without being a whore: Rachel, the greatest actress who ever lived.

Superstitious and guilt-ridden Julie, in reading of the actress's beatific demise, had finally understood why Rachel had been blessed while she was cursed. She had never turned her back on her people. Julie's tears were less for Rachel than for herself, the blackest descendant of her ancient family, the source of her dead father's humiliation, her mother's eternal disgrace.

It was the worst time for Sarah to place her hands on her mother's shoulders and finish the thought ringing in her mind: "I will pray for her when I am a nun."

Julie pushed back her chair, knocking it over as she got to her feet, her mouth open with horror. "What did you say?"

"Mama," said Sarah, speaking slowly and with great conviction, "I have discovered what God wants from me. I will be a nun."

"You dare tell me this?"

"I will dare anything for the love of the Lord."

In the last year Sarah had grown so tall that at fourteen she towered over her diminutive mother. But it was not the disparity in height that prevented Julie from striking her. It was hatred. She could not bear to touch her. She had discovered a hideous monster had taken the form of her daughter's body. "You are a traitor to your people," said Julie, who until that day could have said the same words about herself. Her daughter's inopportune revelation was an opportunity for her to cleanse herself in wild, whimsical sentiment. Irrationally she was suddenly furious at living without respect. Julie could almost blame Sarah for taking her from the bosom of her Dutch family, from her seat on her mother's lap in the women's gallery of the synagogue she had not visited since she was twelve years old. "You are cowardly. You are despicable."

"Mama, I do nothing out of cowardice, but only out of love."

"Shut your stupid mouth. On the day after Rachel's death you dare speak of becoming a nun? Do you know the rewards Rachel turned down when she refused baptism? Do you know the pride she brought every Jew in the world?" Julie pulled the *Figaro* from the dressing table, punching at it with her left fist. "Do you know what this means? Have your holy nuns educated you enough to know how good Jews die?" As her mother shook the crumpled paper in Sarah's face, the smeared ink and marks of rouge looked like a mess of bloody bandages.

"Mama," said Sarah, not understanding her mother's violent reaction, knowing only that it was manifestly unfair, "I thought you hated Rachel. You wanted me to be baptized. You had Jeanne baptized, and Regina too. Why do you hate me so much for being what you told me to be?"

"I never told you to be a Christian, I only told you to be baptized," said Julie. "Baptized so you can live in this miserable world." It was this world that had made her a whore, and Rachel a saint, this world that had given her three bastards, and Rachel the true love of a prince. She threw down the *Figaro* with its dreadful news and left Sarah alone before the dressing mirror.

Sarah had never felt so turned against, rejected. Long ago, when she had asked her mother whether she was indeed a Jew, she made it clear that she wanted only to be what Julie was. In wanting to be a nun, Sarah had failed her. Her mother was right to loathe her. Instead of coming together in mutual sorrow over the death of Rachel, Sarah had brought her pain. She turned away from her miserable image in the glass and picked up the newspaper in her shaking hand. Julie wanted her to know how good Jews died. With wonder, Sarah read the ancient words said by Rachel, her last great speech before leaving this earth: "Hear O Israel, the Lord is God, the Lord is One."

Chapter 7

DESTINED FOR
BETTER THINGS

As she approached her fifteenth birthday, Sarah grew beautiful.

A tall child, she shot up two inches in half a year, becoming a tall young woman. Always thin, she grew thinner, the bones of her cheeks lifting higher in the soft pale flesh. Sarah's green eyes and red lips were suddenly fired by an almost preternatural sensitivity; her face changed from moment to moment, reflecting every thought, every impression, every emotion. Unkempt, childish hair had become sensuous and wild, a red-gold womanly crown for her long-boned, tiny-waisted body. Out of her convent uniform, forced to wear the light spring dresses made by her mother's couturier, Sarah felt the new shape of her breasts and shoulders and neck outlined against luxurious silk. Her beauty was part innocence, artlessness, part immaturity, the promise of what was to come. But the promise was not all of nubile curves and a yielding heart. There was something assertive in her future, something formidable and strong. She was like an unfinished painting, outlined with shockingly vibrant colors, but encompassing empty spaces, blurred and indistinct sections. Standing from far, one could imagine her full-grown, experienced; up close, one saw the convent girl, blinking against the garish lights of the world.

This was not beauty to everyone's taste.

Julie had found Sarah an unattractive baby, and considered her a plain young woman. Sarah's mother knew what beauty was: a voluptuous figure matched with an obliging face. Beauty was soft lines, not hard edges. Beauty was ingratiating, charming, cheerful. Even at eight years old, Sarah's sister Jeanne was more enticing: languid, with long eyelashes, eager to offer her pink cheek for a kiss. Julie thought that Jeanne would grow up to be wooed by rich, respectable men who would ignore the facts of her birth. She worried far more about Sarah: Almost fifteen, it was time to contract her to a husband who would ignore her faults. Such a man had been found in the person of M. Berentz, a thirty-eight-year-old merchant from Amsterdam.

Sarah had refused even to meet with him a second time.

She had found him revolting: too old, too hairy, too eager. Mama had insisted that all bearded men appeared that way at first; because she had no experience with men, Sarah was unable to see M. Berentz's sterling qualities.

But Sarah did not want to see any man's qualities. Couldn't Mama see that she was still a child? No one from the Grand-Champs convent school married at fifteen. Of course, no one else had a mother who so despised her presence at home.

It was no wonder that Sarah walked into Julie's drawing room late in the spring of 1859 like a criminal waiting to hear the sentence of the court. The Duke of Morny, just returned from business in England, caught her eye with his false cheer.

"Mademoiselle Sarah, I've brought you a present," he said. An Anglophile like so many Frenchmen, the duke frequently returned from England with Charles Dickens's latest novel. He had brought her *Little Dorrit* two years before, but Sarah's English was poor. She had to wait until last month to read it in French translation. Besides the duke and Julie, a solemn Mme. Guérard and a brash Aunt Rosine sat side by side on the divan, their pretty faces framed by a dozen exotic pillows. Morny sat across the room on a First Empire armchair, as square and uncomfortable as any throne. Julie had perched on an ottoman at her admirer's feet, but at Sarah's entrance she jumped up.

"You're too sweet to the girl," said Julie.

"Not at all," said the duke. "She gives me great pleasure every time I see her."

Julie gave no credence to this gallantry. M. Berentz was not very handsome, not very young, and not at all sophisticated. He had made an offer for the child's hand because she was the best young girl available to a man of his limited qualities. Julie had no idea that men stared at Sarah wherever she went. What she saw as awkward, they found fresh; what she found backward, they saw as evidence of someone waiting to be formed. There were many men, M. Berentz included, who could imagine the joy of shaping the child into their image of a woman.

Sarah understood only a little of this.

All her life she had thought herself ugly. Mama detested her hair, her nose, her torso. If she stooped, it was to make herself shorter to suit Mama's taste, if she brushed her curls for an hour each day, it was to make her coiffure more presentable to Mama.

But wild hair became abruptly fashionable, and height had become an asset to wearing voluminous clothes. Shedding her convent uniform, Sarah let her curls alone, walked tall, allowed the wind to blow the folds of shawls and dresses against her slender frame. Once, Mme. Guérard had told her that Rachel did not need to wear greasepaint onstage, so strong was the power of her imagination: The great actress had only to will a blush or a pallor into being. Sarah tried to imagine that she was not ugly at all but beautiful, as if, like Rachel, she had the power to make visible what was in her heart.

Sarah wanted this beauty to be noble and good, not alluring and sinful.

In the bleak months since leaving the convent, she had felt the eyes of strangers on her, men and women both, watching her lift a chocolate to her lips, smell a flower, take a walk. She was not complimented by this attention, did not feel that it gave her any merit. On the contrary, she felt cheapened by some of the men who looked at her. Sarah wanted beauty, but she did not want it at the cost of her soul. She wanted to be admired, not desired, and realized that the strangers looking at her were sinful, that they were attracted to what was pure in her so that they could destroy it.

She hoped that she had not collaborated in the sin of their lust. If Sarah's hesitant walk titillated, it was because she walked in constricted shoes, on suddenly longer legs. Beyond the confused stride there was a clumsiness in all her movements. All of a sudden Sarah did not know how to sit, how to lift a fork to her lips, how to drink from a crystal goblet. Even her silvery voice trembled and shook, was too loud or too soft. A few months earlier she had been a schoolgirl, trying to beat back the changes in her body with prayer. But the changes had come, and she no longer prayed with any fervor. Now these changes in her body were celebrated with embroidered drawers, bare shoulders, a strand of pearls choking her neck.

Like her mother, Sarah knew that she had been put on display.

"Don't you say thank you to the duke?" said Julie to Sarah. "He has given you a compliment, and you must acknowledge it like a young lady."

"Thank you, sir," said Sarah, looking from Morny and her mother to Aunt Rosine and Mme. Guérard. All of them stared at her, waiting for her to speak. She had been commanded to appear where she was usually not wanted. There was little love for her in these drawing-room faces. Only in the eyes of the diminutive Mme. Guérard did Sarah find sympathy. Already late afternoon, the "absinthe hour," only tea was evident in the drawing room. Further evidence of the seriousness of this gathering was the absence of little Jeanne. Her mother would never choose Sarah over Jeanne for company unless she had something special in mind for her eldest daughter: to use the authority of the duke and the support of her sister to insist on Sarah's marriage and be rid of her forever.

"Don't you want to know what the duke's brought you?" asked Aunt Rosine. Her red-haired young aunt was even more rapacious than Julie. Rosine insisted on rich gifts from her admirers, but unlike her sister, she seldom sold them. There was too much joy in exhibiting these prizes, symbols of her great worth in the eyes of men. She wore so many bejeweled rings, raising her hands was an arduous task.

"What did you bring me, sir?" asked Sarah, staring at the duke without enthusiam.

The Duke of Morny, half brother of Emperor Napoleon III, had lost status in Sarah's eyes. He had often taken time with her: When he had met with Lionel de Rothschild, since last year the first Jewish member of the British Parliament, he answered all her queries about the man's manners, appearance, and character. After a trip to distant Moscow, he had acquainted Sarah with Czar Alexander II's difficulties in emancipating his huge population of serfs as though she were one of his political cronies. The duke admired intelligence as much as beauty, and he spoke to Sarah as one who could follow his accounts of intrigue in high places.

None of these genuine attempts at befriending her could change the fact that his impeccable frock coat and immaculate linen shirtfront were the same as those of any other rich admirer of her mother's. When the duke had had enough to drink, Sarah might find his crumpled coat outside Julie's dressing-room door on the way to her solitary early-morning breakfast. She took care to tramp on this, as she tramped on the discarded clothes of the other eminent men who shared her mother's bed. For all his English tweeds, manicured hands, and elegant speech, he did not have enough decency to make Julie his mistress. In the orgiastic spirit of the times, the duke blithely shared her with the nameless, numberless men who bought her jewels, left envelopes stuffed with cash on her bureau, and fathered her bastard children.

"Only a comb," said the duke, reaching inside his coat for a small object wrapped in bright paper. "I hope you won't be disappointed."

Rosine launched herself out of the divan and joined Julie in reaching for the present, but the duke pulled it away from them. "Ladies, this is for Mademoiselle Sarah."

Sarah walked closer to the duke and took the gift from his hands. This was a bribe to ensure her goodwill as the impromptu "family" of mother, aunt, neighbor, and stand-in father prepared to explain why she must marry the industrious M. Berentz. An hour before, she had been reading of the exploits of Blondin, France's greatest acrobat, who had just crossed an eleven-hundred-foot tightrope over Niagara Falls blindfolded, and who had plans to repeat the performance on stilts. She was certain that no marriage would ever be arranged for M. Blondin; and that M. Berentz would neither want to walk a tightrope nor marry a girl who aspired to adventures of any kind.

"Will you look at her dawdle," said Julie. "Let's have a look."

Sarah removed the wrapping. The comb was of thick ivory,

elegantly carved. Without a word, she gathered a handful of hair at the back of her head and stuck the comb into the knot with violence.

"What a charming hairstyle," said Aunt Rosine.

"She does it to annoy me," said Julie.

"Turn around, Sarah," said the duke. "I can't see the comb."

Sarah turned about once, and rapidly. Then she retreated from where her mother and aunt flanked Morny, sidling closer to Mme. Guérard, huddled into the overstuffed pillows of the divan.

"I do not want to get married," said Sarah. "I thank you for this beautiful comb, and for taking an interest in me, but I will not marry Monsieur Berentz."

Julie fanned herself in the still drawing-room air.

"You see what I must put up with," said Julie.

"Yes, my dear," said the duke. "Your child anticipates you."

"It is not funny," said Julie. "Would you stop pulling up your bodice, Sarah? You'd think you were trying to cover mountains."

"I do not like this dress, Mama," said Sarah.

"If you'd eat a little meat it would do wonders for your dress," said Julie. "No dress will hang properly on a skeleton."

"Mother Sainte-Sophie says that dresses must not be so low-cut," said Sarah.

"If it were any duller, you might as well be wearing her nun's habit altogether," said Julie. She left the duke and crossed the drawing room, taking dainty steps over the Persian rugs. "Is that why you say you won't marry? Do you still imagine that I shall let you enter a convent?"

"No, Mama," said Sarah. Looking over her mother's golden head, she saw the duke frankly examining her as if measuring her worth. In the room only Mme. Guérard was her friend, and the duke's august presence was sure to leave her tongue-tied. "I am not good enough to become a nun. But I am too good to marry a man that I do not love." In response to her own words, Sarah felt a rising indignation, a swelling of sadness mixed with rage.

"Perhaps," said Aunt Rosine, "you might tell her the details of Monsieur Berentz's offer."

"No, Rosine," said Julie. "You have heard my sweet child. She is too good. A mother may try to bring a daughter to happiness, but if the daughter is too good, what can one do? Obviously my beautiful, talented daughter is destined for far better things."

"You can have the money," said Sarah.

"What money?" asked Julie.

"I *am* destined for better things, Mama."

"What money are you talking about?" insisted Julie.

"One hundred thousand francs," said Sarah. "My dowry from Father."

"Her dowry from Father!" said Rosine, her painted lips opened wide. "How very sweet of Sarah to offer you so much money, Julie. Just think what you can buy with one hundred thousand francs."

"Don't make fun of me," said Sarah.

"And after you've given me all your money, I suppose I should have done worrying about you," said Julie. "I suppose with all your talents and wisdom, you will quickly find a place for yourself in society."

Sarah could feel her heart begin to pound, and knew she was on the verge of a fit worse than any produced by a taunting school-mate.

"You hate me," said Sarah.

"Now listen to me," said Julie. "I want none of this. You're not a baby anymore, and it's time you understood the world."

The rage grew larger, filling every part of her body. "You've always hated me," said Sarah, but quickly she shut her mouth, trying not to breathe, because the fit was ready to break free, even as Julie's words fed the madness.

"You are not an aristocrat, despite your airs," her mother snapped. "So any plans to marry above your station, even if you were as beautiful as your sister Jeanne, are stupid dreams. You will find that your Grand-Champs Convent will not welcome you into their midst because I will never give them the princely sum they will insist on to make you a nun. As for your father's famous dowry: Collecting it will be as difficult as getting him home for a visit from China."

Julie paused for a moment, gathering scornful arrows from her memory. She had not asked to bring Sarah into the world, yet she had given her life, had paid to feed and educate her. Sarah was old enough to marry, and once she did so, Julie would be free of her once and for all. "Your needlework is embarrassing, you don't know how to launder, and your breasts will never be big enough to wet-nurse. There is nothing you can do except marry, and you will marry Monsieur Berentz."

"No," whispered Sarah, very aware of the attention centered on her but no longer fearing it, no longer self-conscious. She did not have to shout because a sudden madness lived in her, she did not have to think of words to say because they arrived directly from her heart. "You hate me," she said, her eyes burning with the full force of truth. Each quiet word was clear, as if ringed by fire, blazing in the hot air. "You've always hated me, Mama. You gave me away to Nurse and hoped that I would die. You forced me to go to Madame Fressard's because you couldn't stand to look at my ugly face. You sent me away to the convent and hoped that I would die just like Appollonie. You wish I were dead, and if that's what you wish, that's what you'll get!"

Sarah paused, not for a breath of air, but to batten on the feelings she had stirred in the drawing room. Where a moment before had been hatred and contempt were now the beginnings of love and pity. This had not been her intention, for in the moments of her rage, she was bereft of reason. Still, she could not be oblivious to the emotional change she had created. In the heart of her pain, she had discovered a great power. She took hold of this power, letting it overwhelm her spirit. In spite of everything, they would love her.

"If you want me to die, I'll pray to the Virgin," said Sarah, the whispered words threatening to become a shout, her agonized spirit evident in every breath. She was suddenly sick, suddenly fading before their eyes. "That's what you'll get, I swear before everything that's holy, I'll die here, I'll die right now!"

"Oh my God," said Mme. Guérard, "she's bleeding."

Sarah felt the blood come, but did not start at the sensation; more than once she had spit up blood during a fit of anger at school. And this fit was far greater than any she had ever experienced, because she relished it, she absorbed it, she blew into it every memory of pain in her life. She was unloved, she was dying, and she would show them all who was responsible. She had never expressed herself so fully, never before understood how deeply she missed her mother's love. As Mme. Guérard pushed her plump little body off the divan and onto her feet, as Rosine and Julie hurried to her side, Sarah felt a climax to all her miseries. The blood on her lips tasted sweet, like a sacrament.

The three women were in a frenzy over the child.

Though there was not much blood, and in the wild moment it was impossible to tell if it came from a bitten lip or from deep within her throat, Sarah was deathly pale. She was as pale as Rachel had been playing Marguerite Gauthier dying in the arms of Armand Duval. Blood collected at the right corner of her mouth, blood stained the low-cut silk dress that her mother had told her to wear for this family conference. Yet more than blood had shocked Rosine out of her cynicism, more than Sarah's pallor had brought tears of horror to Julie's eyes.

"Sweetheart," said Julie.

"Dear child," said Rosine.

"Poor dear girl," said Mme. Guérard.

Before they could take hold of her, Sarah's knees collapsed under her paltry weight, and no one could stop her open palms from slamming into the hard polished floor between two rugs. She wished to keep her head up, to say one more thing before it would be too late. She opened her mouth, where the flow of blood had already stopped, but all that came out was an exhausted sigh. Slowly, against her will, she let her forehead lower gently, meeting the thick rug in a caress. Before they could touch her, she was already turning slowly over onto her side, her wide-open pitiable eyes seeing nothing. If not for her vigorous breathing, it could have been a death scene.

"Call the doctor," said Julie, ringing the servants' bell, pushing past Mme. Guérard and Rosine, placing her little white hands on Sarah's feverish forehead. "Water, smelling salts! Are you getting the doctor? Would you please give the poor child some room?"

But even in the midst of all this attention, Sarah could hear a single ludicrous sound: a slow clapping of hands.

The Duke of Morny was up from his throne, giving Sarah Bernhardt a standing ovation.

"Brava, brava," he said.

"What on earth do you mean?" began Julie, but she quieted as the duke came close to where Sarah, dazed but out of her faint, could hear him speak.

"The child does not have to marry, Julie," said the duke. "She is very talented. I have never seen such acting in my life."

There was a flurry of protest from Julie, Rosine, and Mme. Guérard, but Sarah raised her eyes to meet the duke's. "I was not acting," she said.

"Don't talk just yet," said Julie. "You must rest. The duke is being very naughty. I won't allow anyone to talk to my Sarah that way."

"What do you think acting is, child?" said the duke. He did not deign to kneel before her as the women did, but there was something in the man's voice that inspired Sarah more than her mother's unfamiliar caresses. "What do you think they do at the Théâtre Français but wring tears from sentimental old fools?"

"The child was not acting," said Julie, taking a glass of water from a servant and bringing it to Sarah's lips. "Do you call this acting?" she said, exhibiting her handkerchief of Venetian lace stained with her daughter's blood.

"I have the smelling salts, Madame," said Mme. Guérard, nodding her head and blinking her eyes apologetically for getting in the duke's way. Rosine took the bottle from her hand and began to bring it close to Sarah, but Morny took hold of Rosine's wrist.

"She does not need smelling salts," he said. "She is perfectly fine. The performance is over."

"Nonsense," said Julie, allowing herself to grow angry with her most important protector. Sarah raised her head a bit more and then pushed herself to a sitting position on the floor.

"I do not need the smelling salts," she said.

"Listen to that voice," said the Duke of Morny. "Not a bit of laziness in that tongue. Didn't you ever notice the music in your own child's voice?"

"I have, sir," said Mme. Guérard impulsively.

"You never said it was like music," said Sarah.

"This is all nonsense," said Julie. "If anyone has a musical voice in this family it is Jeanne. Sarah and Regina both sing like a couple of frogs."

"How about if your aunt pours you a nice cup of tea?" suggested Rosine.

"Yes, tea is a good idea," said Julie, answering for her daughter. "Lots of sugar is what she needs." Her mother stroked her wild hair, and though Sarah adored her touch, her attention was turned elsewhere. "Sarah, if you feel better, you should try to get up. But only if you feel better."

"I feel better," said Sarah, but she did not move. She wanted to remain rooted to this moment when everyone loved her. The Duke of Morny had said that she was talented. That she had been acting. That he had never seen such acting in his life.

Mme. Guérard dared to continue speaking to the duke: "It is true what you say, sir," she said. "About the music. I don't know why no one else has noticed, but you can ask the girl. I've often said so myself. I've told her that I'd rather listen to her read a fable of La Fontaine's than go to the theater."

"Quite so," said the duke, clapping his hands one more time. He had an idea, a project, and as always he insisted on carrying it through at once. "Up, Sarah, up, up, up," he said. The half brother of the emperor of France brushed past his favorite courtesan, and bent down to help raise her daughter to a standing position.

"Not so fast, please," said Julie. "She's bleeding."

"The bleeding has stopped," said Morny, examining the young girl. "How do you feel? You feel all right, don't you? You feel well enough to go to the theater, don't you?"

"I feel all right," said Sarah.

The duke turned about and snapped at Rosine: "Where's that tea? Give her some pastries, chocolate pastries. That's what you like, isn't it, Sarah? We'll all go to the Français tonight."

"That's absurd," said Julie.

Rosine, pouring the tea, was suddenly all for it. "Tuesday night, Julie," she said. "Everyone will be there."

"I feel all right," repeated Sarah quietly. Now there was no talk of marriage, of ungrateful daughters, of a body too thin for beauty. Sarah had made them love her, but only the Duke of Morny admired her. He wanted to take her to the theater and she wanted to go.

But her mother would have none of it. "My daughter has just fainted and coughed up blood and you want to drag her to be bored out of her mind by the Comédie Française?" Julie rang the servants' bell with violence. "It's too hot this time of year. Every time I'm there someone passes out from the heat of the gaslamps."

"One must never forget to bring a fan," said Mme. Guérard, lining up on the side of the duke.

"It's very exciting, Sarah," said Rosine, giving the dazed girl her tea. "I don't know why we've never thought of taking you before. Tuesday night is *the* night for the Français. And sitting in the private box of the Duke of Morny drinking champagne, a thousand people eat you alive with their eyes. It's wonderful."

Julie's footman appeared and she barked at him: "Bring in the absinthe."

"And of course you must come too, Madame Guérard," said the duke, bowing in her direction.

"Oh, no," said Mme. Guérard. "That's so kind of you, sir, but I could not possibly impose."

"Please do not force me to get down on my old knees to beg you, Madame," said Morny, winking slyly at a more and more astonished Sarah.

"Oh, no, sir," said Mme. Guérard.

"You must come," said Sarah. "I am not going to go unless you do too!"

"You will go if I tell you to go," said Julie. "What in the world are you trying to do to my household, my dear sir?"

"My carriage will pick you up at eight. I will meet you at the theater." Morny chuckled to himself, delighted with the life he was about to change. "I must see that Dumas comes by to pay his respects. I must call on Monsieur Auber, tell him all about his new pupil."

"I have not agreed to any of this," said Julie. She gestured to the footman, returning with a crystal decanter of absinthe, to pour out a drink at once. "Who is Monsieur Auber?"

The duke smiled. "The director of the Conservatoire," he said. He turned to Sarah once more, answering her look of non-comprehension. "The Conservatoire is where they teach you to act. Very difficult to get into without the proper connections." The duke paused, his smile reminding Sarah that few men in Paris had connections better than he. "Everyone at the Français trained there, everyone. And if Madame Julie's little girl is going to be an actress, she might as well be an actress of the Comédie Française."

"Like Rachel?" said Sarah.

Everyone laughed, except for Julie. "Just like Rachel, of course," said Morny. "Eight o'clock. My coachman is never late." He took hold of Sarah's hand and raised it briefly to his lips. "My God, Julie, how can you not see what a beauty your daughter is becoming?"

"Thank you, sir," said Sarah. She knew from the nuns that acting was an immoral profession, and that actresses died young and full of sin. Yet she felt beautiful under the duke's approbation, as though her world had turned on its axis; after an eternity of eclipse, Sarah might find herself in the sun. "I would love to go. I would love to go to the theater."

Chapter 8

BEAUTY IN THE LIMELIGHT

I'm not tired," said Sarah to Mme. Guérard. "I'm not hungry."

How could she be anything but wide awake, all her senses opened outward? Sarah was on her way to see the place where Rachel had triumphed: the Théâtre Français, home of the Comédie Française, since its founding by Louis XIV in 1680 the greatest company of actors in the nation. The core of the acting company was formed earlier still, in 1658, under the leadership of the playwright-actor-manager Molière, the most revered comic writer ever produced in France.

Molière's plays were often presented at the Français, and the playwright's seminal contribution to the troupe was honored in an annual ceremony of homage; nonetheless the Comédie Française was better known for its presentation of drama. In the France of 1859, as in most of Europe, a comedy was loosely defined as any play with a happy ending; moreover, the company "comedians" customarily retricted their comedies to Molière's two-hundred-year-old masterpieces, and made their reputations performing the poetic dramas of Corneille and Racine. This often confused visitors from England and America, where the term "comedy" usually referred to a farce, and the designation "comedian" was reserved for actors who made fools of themselves in disreputable music halls. They could not understand how Rachel, the greatest actress in tragic plays of her day, was known as a "comedienne" during her tenure with the Comédie Française and, though performing the same repertoire of plays, a "tragedienne" thereafter.

Sarah didn't trouble herself with these distinctions. To her the name "Comédie Française" was glorious and meant nothing other than a group of brilliant actors who could do anything required of them onstage. What they actually did, what acting looked like, was as yet unknown to her. Having seen Rachel, she fancied that acting was something that demanded genius and sacrifice, a labor for which the audience paid out their adoration. Sarah was flattered that the Duke of Morny imagined that she had talent, that she could be trained for the world that these actors inhabited.

Mme. Guérard had brought sweetmeats in a bag and pressed these upon Sarah in the duke's plushly upholstered charabanc, much to the annoyance of Julie and Rosine. Though the carriage had room for six passengers, the voluminous dresses of the two grand courtesans took up most of the interior space, and neither beauty wanted sticky candy staining her taffeta creation.

"There will be supper waiting for her when Sarah goes home, Madame Guérard," said Julie. "If you would like to join her, I'm sure that Titine will be only too happy to give you a bowl of soup too."

"Perhaps Madame Guérard would like to join us," said Rosine, pulling apart the leather curtains that shielded the three rear windows. "If you've never been to the Café Anglais, it will be quite an experience."

The little widow blushed at the mention of this restaurant. Like the equally famous Maison d'Or, the Café Anglais had public rooms and private rooms, but the reputation of these restaurants was based primarily on the latter. In the private rooms, a gentleman, no matter how well known, could dine in absolute discretion with his mistress. Some private rooms were small, furnished with only a table and chairs. Others were more elaborate, as large as a small drawing room, with divans large enough to recline on in comfort. Mme. Guérard did not want to imagine what took place in those extravagantly appointed chambers, deliberately shut off from the eyes of society. She would have had to be deaf and blind not to have heard the stories: aristocrats and courtesans in all-night debauches, champagne drunk out of evening slippers, chocolate bonbons wrapped in thousand-franc notes for those ladies who would eat them without the protection of their clothes. All of Paris had heard the rumor that when the Prince of Wales had last year visited the famous "Grand Seize" room of the Café Anglais, he was served a naked courtesan on a silver platter. But Mme. Guérard had been alone in wondering whether that could be the reason why her beautiful neighbor caught so frightful a cold last year.

"Leave Madame Guérard alone," said Julie. "She is much too high-minded for your jokes. And don't forget that we are accompanying a young girl to the theater."

"When I was her age—" began Rosine.

"You were not a good young girl educated in a convent," snapped Julie.

"I know some young convent girls who didn't turn out to be particularly holy," teased Rosine. "A few of them even went into the theater. One or two might even be at the Café Anglais tonight. One or two convent girls just about your daughter's age." Rosine addressed Mme. Guérard in a stage whisper: "I suppose Julie's sensitive, now that she's the mother of a grown woman."

"I am not a relic, even if Sarah is fourteen," said Julie.

"Nearly fifteen, in fact," said Rosine. "Thank God I'm your younger sister. I'm young even to be an aunt. I wonder if anyone will mistake me for your daughter tonight?"

"You are not funny," said Julie. "You do not amuse Madame Guérard, who knows that I am only twenty-eight." The little widow took no joy in knowing that Julie, who looked no older than twenty-one, was in fact thirty-one years old.

"If you're going to be twenty-eight," said Rosine, "I think I'd like to be twenty-five. How old does Sarah think you are? Maybe it's not too late to tell her that she's really twelve. Shave a few more years off her mother."

"I look exactly as young as the girls who go onstage right now," said Julie. "Marguerite Bellanger, Léonide Leblanc, Blanche d'Antigny. If I wanted to parade around in my tights like they do . . ."

"You can't blame them for showing their legs," said Rosine. "They've got great legs, those three. No wonder they're making fortunes. Gives the men a chance to look over the merchandise under the lamps before they even pay out a franc."

"We are not putting Sarah onstage," said Julie. "We're taking her to a private box at the Français, where she will sit among respectable people."

"I beg both your pardons," said Mme. Guérard, who fancied herself something of a theatrical expert, "but I would like to point out that the ladies you have mentioned, beautiful as they may be, have merely performed vaudeville. The Duke of Morny believes that Sarah can aspire to higher things."

Rosine winked at her sister, holding herself back from telling the little widow a bit more about the vaudeville players than she'd probably like to hear. "How are Sarah's legs anyway?" asked Rosine. "Do you think she's got the legs for the *acting* life?"

"Will you shut up about Sarah?" said Julie.

"Your convent girl is in a world of her own," said Rosine. She moved her head closer to Julie's, to exclude Mme. Guérard from her comment: "I don't think she knows what happens to little girls who show their legs onstage. She probably doesn't know why all those bouquets get sent backstage."

Indeed, Sarah was not listening to her aunt's jibes.

She was on her way to the Théâtre Français, and she concentrated on the waves of people rushing alongside them. Surely this too was part of the show. There was much to hear in the noise of adjacent carriage wheels, the opening and shutting of doors as ladies and gentlemen escaped from the crush of vehicles on the boulevards to merge with the crowds of pedestrians on the paved walkways. The drivers cursed their horses and each other; their passengers shouted that they would be late. Sarah battened on the general enthusiasm. All these people, varied in class and age, were drawn by the same goal. Like Mme. Guérard, they loved the theater, they loved the actors and actresses—like the departed Rachel—who brought forth magic on the stage and drew adulation from the audience.

Sarah couldn't know that most of the theatergoers were going to gawk at the celebrated, and to parade about in their finery. The magnificent Rachel had been an anomaly, an actress who forced the audience to face forward in their seats. Since her death, the Comédie Française played in the shadow of the greater attraction in the boxes, reduced to a background function, performing venerable tragedies in poetry written by men long dead. The words, gestures, costumes, and sets were so familiar to the audience that they had become like tunes played at an open-air ball, much less important than the beer for sale, the pretty girls one might meet. The recent agitation among English actors to further dim the lights in the house during the performance so that only they would be visible once the curtain was raised, would have been met with astonishment in France. The audience, and not the play, was "the thing."

Julie and Rosine prepared for the society they might see by beginning to gossip about them: Was it possible that Dumas *père* and Dumas *fils* were again chasing after the same courtesan, as they had once—all too briefly—competed for Julie's favors? Would the ugly wife of Prince Metternich, the new Austrian ambassador to Paris, appear? Would the emperor's mistress appear on the arm of another man while Napoleon III was away with his empress Eugénie? Who would snub them and whom would they snub?

"Just a few more moments," said Mme. Guérard, patting Sarah's hand. "Then you shall see beauty in the limelight, you will hear voices that will make you cry."

If not for the impending curtain time, Sarah would have wished the Théâtre Français to be even farther, the traffic heavier, and that they be surrounded all night by the brightly lit joyous cacophony of the city. She had never been out after dark before, not in a grand carriage, not wearing white gloves and drenched in her mother's perfume, on the way to the most important theater in the world. From her window at home, gaslights were visible along the Rue St.-Honoré, but these had long ago become familiar, a gloomy background of the hours passed alone in her room.

Tonight through the side windows of the carriage, slid down against her mother's wishes, Sarah saw a different, fabulous illumination: rows of unevenly burning gas jets lighting up elegant outdoor cafés; gaslamps shining inside shop windows, reflecting everything that was glass or gold or gilt; gas illuminating lanterns, globes, streetlamps. Up and down the broad boulevards were dots and patches and broad swatches of light. Every carriage was lit, every storefront, every street corner. A gigantic fan, delicately outlined with flaming gas jets, advertised a shop selling women's fashions. Two huge cylinders in the shape of golden pens glowed above a stationer's broad, bright window. An enormous representation of a pocket watch, composed of brass wire and gaslights, hung over a watchmaker's like a flaming fragment of a childish dream.

The lights were irregularly spaced, of varying intensity and size and shape. As they approached the queue of carriages near the Théâtre Français, Sarah felt as if all the lights were merging, all running downhill toward their natural destination. It was brighter than day here; so many lamps were burning about the exterior of the theater where years before she had seen Rachel wave to a crowd of well-wishers.

"As the emperor and empress will not be there," said Julie, "you might be a bit disappointed. We will miss a good many people. They take the whole court with them when they go off to Saint-Cloud." Julie was talking for the benefit of Sarah and Mme. Guérard. Rosine, with her own admirers at court, knew the royal family's annual schedule as well as any chamberlain: from the Tuileries to Saint-Cloud in May, to Fontainebleau in June, to Biarritz in September, to Compiègne in October. Not till November were the rich courtesans of La Garde satisfied with the man-hunting in Paris. "They will remain in Saint-Cloud for another week, then go directly to Fontainebleau."

"But there is Princess Mathilde," said Rosine sharply, looking past Sarah's head out the window at the emperor's cousin, famous for her refusal to marry him and for her intense devotion to the arts. Although she was the sister of rakish Prince Napoleon, who had been the lover of Rachel and patronized many of La Garde's most flamboyant courtesans, Princess Mathilde was stately, dignified. Her salon was open to painters, journalists, musicians, men of achievement who were often intimates of Julie's; still, no courtesan had anything else in common with Princess Mathilde, who looked through them at any public place—like the theater—as though they were of no more substance than air. Julie much preferred the look of horror and the deliberate snub of an aristocratic lady, mortified at being so close to an expensive harlot.

"She appears to be suffering from delusions," said Julie. "She imagines herself the empress of the French instead of the little princess who feeds unwashed artists."

Sarah couldn't distinguish the princess in the mob of fashionably dressed theatergoers. Twisting and gaping in the close space, she recognized few names and no faces. Every time Julie or Rosine announced another fashionable theatergoer, Sarah would swivel about, hoping to catch a glimpse of someone out of the ordinary. Yet it made no difference, for everything was extraordinary, every moment was charged with a first-time glamour. Men's tall black silk hats and women's carefully curled heads bobbed and turned, their owners looking for people they knew or people they would like to recognize. Three open gates led to the theater entrance. Here the lines of gas jets were so numerous that one could read the small print on the posters as though it were midday. White evening scarves and pale complexions looked yellow in this light, but a radiance softened every sharp feature, lent a beauty to every plain face.

"Hold me tight," said Mme. Guérard to Sarah. The two were helped down from the carriage and swallowed up at once by the crowd surging up the steps. Julie and Rosine had no difficulty following Sarah and the little widow; the brilliance of the courtesans' jewels, the whiteness of their teeth, the bravado of the colors painted onto the proud planes of their faces gave them an ersatz majesty that caused the mob to give way. There were some who moved aside so they could have a better look as the courtesans passed. There were others who got out of the way so as not to be sullied by their touch.

"What are they playing anyway?" Julie asked Rosine in a loud and bored voice.

"Whatever it is," said one of the cigar-smoking men huddled beside the entranceway and staring directly at Julie, "it won't be nearly as much fun to look at as the audience."

Sarah, turning about to keep her mother in sight, saw Julie give a sly smile and half a bow at the man who had complimented her.

Smitten, the man dropped his cigar to the pavement, forced himself into the flow of bodies so that he could get closer to Julie and hand her his card. "Hurry, Mama," said Sarah, urging her mother forward.

"Mama?" said the gentleman, looking from tall Sarah to little

Julie in amazement. He let go of the card and retreated, letting the crowd separate him from Julie.

"Yes, Mama." Rosine laughed at Julie. "Come along now like a good dear old lady."

"One play is called *Britannicus,*" said Sarah. "It is by Racine. And there is another short one by Molière. Madame Guérard has seen them both, and told me."

When they were ushered through the crowd to where the Duke of Morny awaited them in his private box facing the stage, the little widow told her more: Down below them were the stalls, where all the beautifully dressed men and women remained standing so that they could look up at the boxes, at the faces of aristocracy, celebrity, and riches. Boxes hung all about the stage, to the left and right of them, with the women sitting up front, the gentlemen at their rear. High above them were the rows of gallery seats. The higher one went, the less expensive were the tickets, the rougher the dress of the crowd. These theatergoers were young and old, students and workers, and just as noisy with each other as their social betters were in the seats below. Mme. Guérard insisted that in these poor seats were the true friends of the theater: They would become silent once the curtain rose, no matter how many times they had seen this same play. Like Mme. Guérard, they wanted the magic to happen, the god to appear in their midst. The galleries had been the first to champion Rachel, because they were always there to watch the stage.

"This is where Rachel could make her face turn pale?" asked Sarah, looking way from the audience to the awesome red curtain of the stage, washed in yellow and red gaslight from the largest chandelier she had ever seen.

"Yes," said Mme. Guérard. "This is where Rachel performed. This is where she was Phèdre."

"You won't see anyone as good as Rachel tonight," said the duke, addressing her from the back of the box. Earlier, a tall young man had entered the box and was now being pushed toward them by the duke. "And *Britannicus* is not Racine's greatest play. But you will get the idea."

"What idea?" asked Sarah, trying to keep her heart from

pounding. Surely the duke was about to introduce her, and she felt suddenly clumsy, her limbs awkward, her tongue fat.

The duke only smiled at her, convinced that she would understand soon enough. "May I introduce Prince Henri de Luyen?" he said. "This is Mademoiselle Sarah Bernhardt. I have only just discovered that Mademoiselle Sarah has the makings of a great actress."

The young man was as handsome as a prince in a painting. He wore a very low-cut waistcoat, a large gardenia in his buttonhole. How could so appealing an aristocrat take seriously the duke's claims? Behind her she could hear her mother and aunt continue to exchange double-edged witticisms with a stream of visitors.

"I am honored to make your acquaintance, Mademoiselle Bernhardt," said Prince Henri. She did not know why his pale skin was blushing before her eyes.

"Prince Henri is a great lover of Racine," said the duke. "Perhaps one day he shall see you perform in one of his plays. Perhaps right here."

"I am certain to come anywhere Mademoiselle Bernhardt chooses to perform," said the prince.

"I am not an actress, sir," said Sarah. "I have never even been to the theater before tonight. The duke does me too much honor."

"I beg to differ with you, Mademoiselle Bernhardt," said the prince. "If you will forgive me for saying so, the duke does not honor you enough. You will assuredly perform in great plays in this very theater, and I shall certainly be there. If you will forgive me for saying so."

"I forgive you, sir," said Sarah, totally dazzled. He had blond hair in short tight curls, and a high, intelligent forehead. His accent was not Parisian, and she wondered if he might be Belgian, and if so, whether he lived in Brussels or had come to Paris to stay. But she could not, in politeness, ask him any of this. Indeed, she could think of nothing else to say at that moment and only wished that the curtain would rise to hide her ignorance of witty talk. Prince Henri de Luyen mumbled a few quick words, indicating that he must join his party, and that he would look forward to following her career.

"What a handsome young man," whispered Mme. Guérard.

"And a real prince. I've never met a real prince. Your mother looks very jealous."

Sarah became even more impatient then. She wanted the curtain to rise at once, so that she would comprehend what stage acting was. A prince as well as a duke had insisted on the fact of her talent, an insistence that might have no more basis than a desire to charm her mother. Yet the prince had blushed not for Julie but for herself. Perhaps she had some power of which she was not yet aware. She remembered the magician Robert-Houdin, whose powerful personality could hold captive an audience of two hundred gaping children: That was a talent. Sarah wondered if she would ever learn to hold even one person captive with her personality. Perhaps the Conservatoire would teach her this. There must be a secret to the way one stood, or spoke or gestured. Perhaps attractiveness was dependent on the plays in which one appeared. Prince Henri loved Racine, and if she had a part in one of Racine's plays, her personality would vanish, to be replaced by something irresistible, magnetic.

She hoped that the prince was interested in her, that he imagined her something a thousand times finer than what she was in real life. If he had any regard for her, it must be because he had believed what the duke said to be true: that she had the makings of a great actress. For what other reason would she have been noticed, flattered; under what other circumstances could she have been the cause of a prince's embarrassed blush?

Perhaps, thought Sarah, she did have a talent after all.

Maybe her prayers for love had been answered with a gift that she could not yet recognize. Maybe the solace she had found in the devotions of the Church could be found in the rites of the theater; her long fascination with Rachel must be the sign of a kindred spirit.

"Are you all right?" asked Mme. Guérard. "You look pale." Though the bell in the foyer had rung and rung, the velvet seats in the stalls below remained empty as stragglers continued to enter noisily. Those who found their seats took their time about sitting down. Sarah saw pretty women train opera glasses on their box, and handsome men adjust the flowers in their lapels. Seated behind her and Mme. Guérard, Julie and Rosine said good-bye to the last of the visitors to the duke's box, and began to scan the stalls with their own shared pair of opera glasses.

"It's just that I wish it would start," said Sarah.

"There, you see?" said the duke, standing over her. "The foot-lights are coming up. And now the chandelier will slowly rise. Watch it. It's finally getting a little darker in the house."

"Why don't they quiet and sit down?" asked Sarah.

"That is exactly what the actors are asking at this very moment," said the duke.

Sarah was struck by this remark. She had a vision of a frail figure, shivering in heavy robes in the wings, waiting to come alive. A tiny stab of fear penetrated, as if by some miracle she were not in the audience but behind the curtain, waiting for it to rise. She tried to imagine what it must be like to prepare yourself to be the focus of a thousand and more men and women; the lights would shine on your face, and the audience would quiet their last few whispers, waiting for your words to break the expectant silence. Sarah shut her eyes, wondering if the frail, frightened figure in her imagination was herself, a warning of the fear she would have to face in choosing this future.

"Did you like Prince Henri?" asked the duke.

Sarah opened her eyes, and turned to him. "Yes, sir," she said.

"I am quite certain that he liked you," said the duke.

"Only because of what you said to him about me," said Sarah.

"No," said the duke. "I think it had something to do with your hair."

"My hair?"

"He asked me to introduce him. He asked me who was the girl in my box with the beautiful hair." The duke smiled. "What do you say to that?"

The noise from the stalls was lessening. At last everyone hurried to take their seats. "He is very complimentary," said Sarah. It required a superhuman effort for her to keep from touching her hair. Apparently the prince liked more about her than she had realized, more than she had thought possible.

The footlights brightened the curtain's deep red, shot yellow streaks through the purple drapery that framed it. As the chandelier moved higher, the elaborately painted domed ceiling gleamed in a false dawn of pink and crimson and violet. Sarah found herself in a self-enclosed heaven, warm and close enough to be touched by mortal men. She wondered if the prince could see her from where he sat; if even as her heart pounded in anticipation of the magic to come, he could study her face in the muted light.

The chandelier reached its highest point, leaving the house darker but never so dark that the audience would not have the joy of looking at each other. Sarah looked straight ahead, aware of her mother's knees pressing through the velvet back of her chair, her aunt Rosine's clearing her throat. There were whispers still, there were titters and sneezes, there was heat rising up from the masses of human bodies below. She felt the fear of the assembled company of actors, waiting for the curtain to rise. All these sensations were suspended as the curtain rose. Suddenly the silence was absolute. The curtain was up, and at that glorious instant even thoughts of Prince Henri de Luyen were banished.

There was a grand stage, bathed in light.

There were columns of a palace, blue Italian skies, vivid costumes of ancient Rome.

There were actors and actresses, men and women who had slipped into characters of another world, another time. The fear that Sarah had felt coming from behind the curtain vanished. In place of fear was power. The actors moved up and down on a raked stage, and her eyes followed them wherever they went. A smile could flash through a hundred rows of packed seats. A threat could bring foreboding to a thousand hearts. Every emotion was magnified, every moment was filled with a great event.

Downstage, the footlights washed the painted faces in an ethereal glow. It seemed that every actor wore the mask of a god. Sarah wanted such a mask, she wanted her face to be bathed in stage light, she wanted to move with the certainty of an actor following the dictates of a play.

When they spoke, their words were full and proud, beautifully paced, elegant. The words were not invented by these actors, but when they recited the verses, the words were fresh on their lips, never before imagined until that moment. Sarah was thrilled. It was a privilege to witness and share such emotion. She listened carefully, profoundly, trying to bring every utterance directly into her heart.

Junia, played by an actress more beautiful than any human being Sarah had ever seen, loves the noble Britannicus, and remains devoted to him despite the evil machinations of the emperor Nero. Villainous Nero poisons Britannicus, though they are half brothers. The moon appears in a cone of limelight, gentler than gaslight, but so bright it seemed capable of lifting Britannicus from the stage floor directly into the heavens above.

Sarah knew that Britannicus was going to die, and that beautiful Junia would never be his bride. Her entire spirit wanted to leap out of her body and descend onto the stage to embrace the lovers. Sarah had a kinship with sadness, a background in treachery. Her lonely childhood had prompted such wild feelings, but she had been trained to keep her passions to herself, locked behind a smile. Here emotions were vividly exposed; anyone who sat under the theater's great dome would be privy to what could be seen in the world outside. Surely nothing was more lamentable than this, that true lovers would be separated by murder, that evil men could triumph over virtue.

"Hush, child," whispered Mme. Guérard, pressing her warm fingers into Sarah's hand. Sarah was crying, and her sobs were loud and growing louder. But she barely responded to the admonition, understanding only dimly that the little widow was passing on an order from Julie that Sarah had not heard. "You must try not to cry," whispered Mme. Guérard, bringing her face protectively close to Sarah's. In the adjacent box, there were already a few titters, and from the stalls below, theatergoers, less entranced with Racine than with Sarah's tears, were staring up at her with amusement.

Sarah could not stop crying.

Knowing that Britannicus would die did not make his death scene any less emotionally exhausting to witness. She could not understand why her mother and Mme. Guérard were prodding her, why anyone's attention could be anywhere except on the scene below. Watching the hero die, Sarah felt herself overcome by an ecstatic sadness. She could feel the horror building in Junia's breast as though it were her own lover who had been poisoned, as though she too lived among the columns and palaces on the broad stage.

"Tell her if she doesn't stop, we'll take her out before the curtain," said Julie.

When the despondent Junia escaped from Nero to become a vestal, Sarah's heartfelt sobbing could be heard throughout the front of the house. Junia was going to shut herself away from life as Sarah had wanted to do in the convent. So beautiful was the despair, so perfect the tragedy, Sarah wondered if any happiness could be as fine. If only a prince might die for her! Sarah rode the crests and troughs of Racine's poetry, so close to the spirit of the play that when the on stage mob turned on the poisoner of Britannicus, she felt the impulse to violence and murder in her own soul.

When the curtain came down, there was scattered applause, and quite a bit of head turning directed at Sarah. The young actress-to-be was oblivious of the attention. When the actors took their bows, Sarah beat her hands together like a madwoman. Even if she'd had an inkling of the sophisticates smugly looking up at her from the stalls, she couldn't have stopped her applause. She had been moved, and the emotions that had been stirred up in her were still being released. The Duke of Morny had brought her to the theater to see actors at work, and she had been drawn to them with an ineluctable power. She could not imagine anything more touching than the moment when Junia and Britannicus came far downstage to acknowledge the applause. In the glare of the footlights, Sarah could see their painted faces change. The godlike masks fell away, replaced by modest wonder, by an immense relief in being able to resume life on a human scale. The two who had walked the stage as hero and heroine, approached the house as actor and actress, a man and a woman stepping from behind the guise of art. Sarah watched them bow again and again, joyously devouring the love coming their way.

"It's so beautiful," said Sarah, feeling that the sorrow discovered in her by the play might be tapped again and again, every tear releasing a promise of joy. She was so swollen with tragedy that she could spend a lifetime crying, an eternity waiting for happiness.

"Do you know that they're laughing?" asked her mother, gripping her shoulder. "They're actually laughing out loud and looking at you in this box." As the huge chandelier grew quickly brighter and was lowered for the interval, Julie urged her to her feet. "Would you please come to the back? Everyone is staring."

"I am sorry," said Sarah, unable to stand, still unable to stop her tears.

"At least she kept the audience awake," said Rosine. "Now for once everyone knows we're here tonight."

Mme. Guérard stood up, shielding Sarah from the view of the stalls. "It's just that the play is so sad for a young girl," she said. She was sure that there had been crying in the galleries too.

"I have never been so embarrassed in my life," said Julie.

"Nonsense," said the duke, giving Sarah his handkerchief. "The child is highly emotional, which is quite naturally what she must be in order to go on the stage herself."

"You must stop saying that," said Julie. "You fill her silly head with impossible things. You know perfectly well the child can never be an actress."

"You don't know a thing about it, my dear," said the duke. "If I say she will be an actress, she will be an actress."

"Will you please stop your idiotic sniffling," said Julie to Sarah. "If you are going to be an actress, let me see you act happy. Everyone in the world thinks we are with an absolute fool."

"Not everyone," said the duke. As Rosine swung open the door of the box to escape for the intermission, they saw that Prince Henri de Luyen had already returned, very much out of breath. Two servants followed carrying champagne in a silver bucket and crystal glasses that glittered in the light of the great chandelier.

"If you'll forgive me for the presumption, sir," said the prince to the Duke of Morny. The duke readily forgave him, as did Julie and Rosine, eager to drink the rich wine, lifting their glasses against the raised eyes of the audience.

Sarah, on the other hand, kept her eyes straight ahead on the closed curtain shining in the gaslight. She could not bring herself to speak to the prince, and he could not think of anything to say to her once she had refused his offer of champagne.

The play had so aroused her passions that she dared dream that the prince's timely entrance confirmed a mutual infatuation: He had liked her hair, she had thought him handsome; together they had seen Britannicus expire for love, Junia defy an emperor for the sake of her lover. She understood now why the nuns disliked the theater, distrusted actors, thought Rachel a victim of her sins. Here, under the theater's great domed ceiling, anything was possible. Love, lust, murderous desire could be brought to fruition in an instant. Sarah knew that she could love the prince, that, if he wanted to, he could take her away at once and forever.

When the bell in the foyer began to ring the approach of the second play of the evening, *Amphytrion,* Molière's comedy of confusions, the duke invited Prince Henri to remain in their box.

"I don't want to intrude," said the prince, looking directly at Sarah.

Mme. Guérard moved quickly to the back of the box, saying in a surprised little voice that there was a seat up front, next to Sarah.

The prince nodded at Mme. Guérard, bowed to the duke and Julie, smiled at Rosine, and sidled quickly up to the seat and sat down.

"This play is safer," he said, turning his handsome face from the curtain to look into her green eyes. "Nobody cries at Molière."

"I want to cry," said Sarah.

"Yes, of course," said the prince.

He didn't understand that to experience so much pain and then have it be released at the close of the play was magical, as liberating as removing hands that are strangling your throat. She would have liked to explain that the tears had cleansed her, that the tragedy had exalted her so that every fiber in her body yearned to sing. Before words could come to her, the house lights dimmed and the curtain began to rise.

This time the columns were Grecian, a palace in ancient Thebes. In the play a god assumes the form of a man in order to make love to his wife; another god forestalls this by assuming the shape of the wronged man's servant. The audience began to laugh almost at the rise of the curtain, and as confusion begat confusion, the laughter grew and grew.

But Sarah didn't laugh.

Prince Henri could see that though her tears had stopped, the young girl was in pain.

"Are you all right, Mademoiselle Bernhardt?" whispered Prince Henri.

"No, sir," said Sarah.

"How may I help you, Mademoiselle?"

"Please take me out of here, sir."

The prince, who was all of nineteen, was nonplussed by this request. Taking a deep breath, he stood up abruptly and helped her out of her chair.

"Now what?" whispered Julie.

"I must leave, Mama," said Sarah.

The duke placed his hand firmly over that of his mistress. "Go ahead, Sarah," he said. "Perhaps the prince will escort you home."

"It would be an honor," said Prince Henri.

"Just one minute," said Julie.

"I understand, Sarah," said the duke. He did not get a chance to explain to Julie that her daughter did not want to spoil the emotions exposed by Racine by viewing the twists and turns of Molière's comedy. Julie followed Sarah out of the box, and in the corridor she took hold of her arm. The prince excused himself, and waited for Sarah at a discreet distance.

"I'm sorry, Mama," said Sarah.

"First you cry like an idiot when everyone is half asleep, and now when everyone is laughing, you can't stand to look at the stage." Julie quieted, then brought her head close to her daughter's. "Two things. First, if you are old enough to be taken home by a young man, you had better stop calling me Mama."

"What do you want me to call you?"

"Julie," said her mother. "Call me what Rosine calls me. I'm not an old woman, you know. I was a baby myself when I gave birth to you. Every stranger in Paris does not have to imagine that I have one foot in the grave."

"What is the second thing you wish to tell me?" asked Sarah. "You said there were two things."

"Be careful," said Julie. "He is very handsome and young, and you do not know anything."

"What do you mean?"

"I mean do not let him kiss you, do not let him touch you, and most of all do not believe a word he says." Julie looked up at her tall daughter. "There is not much that I can do for you, child, but

I can tell you about men. Do not believe a word he says. Not a word."

The prince had to support Sarah at the elbow as they descended the stairs, so wildly did her head reel from the evening's revelations. She had a calling, she had an unending need for love, and like her mother, she had a lust as big as the world.

Chapter 9

THE AUDIENCE WAITED

Sarah opened her eyes, saw what she wanted, and leaped wholeheartedly into a new world.

Discovering the vast fields of the published works of Racine, Corneille, Molière, and Casimir Delavigne, she pressed to explore them, play by play, and part by part. After months of lassitude away from the convent school, Sarah found that she needed little sleep. Reading did not weary her, for it brought her to a joyful place she had never known. In the old scripts she could be anyone, do anything. The boundaries of her life expanded each time she slipped beneath another character's skin. Except for occasional blissful outings to the Comédie Française, accompanied by Mme. Guérard, she had no diversions, no other interests. Her diligence was obsessive and rewarded with self-confidence. Sarah ignored Julie's cynicism and sister Jeanne's mocking of her zeal; even baby Regina's wailing did not penetrate. She shut out everything but the poetry of the plays, the fact of her ambition.

France, without Sarah's help, persisted in its Second Empire revelries, while the world continued taking heroic steps into the modern age. In distant Egypt, construction, directed by the Frenchman Ferdinand de Lesseps, was beginning on the canal that would connect the Mediterranean and Red seas across the Isthmus of Suez. British and American lighthouses were being illuminated with electricity. A telegraph cable was making its third year of progress across the Atlantic Ocean. Steam had powered a boat in

1803, a locomotive in 1814, and, in this year of 1859, a steamroller. Steamships were crossing the Atlantic in nine or ten days, racing past sailing ships still carrying the bulk of the world's cargoes. Fortunes were being made by those who paid attention to the shifting fates of American cotton planters, owners of slaves who would surely one day be set free. And more than cotton was being wrested from American earth. Eighteen fifty-nine was the year of the first oil well, drilled in Titusville, Pennsylvania.

As Sarah's dreams focused on the stage, her mother's generation narrowed their concerns to the building of financial security. War no longer made sense. National honor could better be served around the diplomatic table than on the battlefield. Even contentious, un-civilized Americans would surely make peace between their con-flicting states rather than risk ruinous civil war. The cotton crop was more important than the struggle over slavery. Rich Parisians believed in the brotherhood of business, the international camara-derie of traders in commodities, the peaceful harmony of a thou-sand species of new machines.

Prince Metternich, who had been instrumental in humbling Napoleon and restoring conservative order to Europe at the Con-gress of Vienna forty-five years before, had just died at eighty-six. No one took it amiss that his son, the current Prince Metternich, was the Austrian ambassador to Paris; few took any more notice of this even after a brief outbreak of hostilities between France and Austria over the uninteresting question of Sardinian autonomy. Business was being done with Austrians, Italians, Prussians, Ba-varians. Frenchmen of influence, particularly those who patron-ized Julie and her circle, were more interested in the money to be made in German steamship companies than in the movement to unite Germany under the rule of Prussia. Few paid attention to the zealous rebuilding of the Prussian Army by the state's war min-ister, Albrecht von Roon. Fewer still followed the career of the new Prussian ambassador to St. Petersburg, Otto von Bismarck, who would three years later become the prime minister.

Sarah had to wait until the fall of 1860 to matriculate at the Conservatoire National de Musique et de Déclamation. After four-teen months of immersion in the literature of the French stage, Sarah entered the school eager to devour the curriculum whole.

She had just turned sixteen. Despite her thin body and pale complexion, she exhibited the energy of a robust peasant. She never missed a class, never caught cold, never omitted a session with her acting coach. The dedication that had once drawn her to prayer in the convent's deserted chapel before dawn drew her to herculean tasks, memorizing the transcendent roles of the French theater long before anyone asked her to perform.

She aspired to be taught what Rachel had been taught, she yearned to follow in the line of the generations of actors who had passed through this school since 1786 and gone on to glory. What had overwhelmed her as a member of the audience watching *Britannicus* overwhelmed her again as a student craving to appear one day in that very same play: the desire to drive her emotions to their full force, into a frenzy. Sarah wanted to love and to hate, to revel in fury and to grovel in despair; she wanted to be exalted by a thousand feelings whose potency would inescapably arouse the acclaim of the crowd.

Sarah took long classes in declamation three times a week with the prominent melodramatic actor Jean-Baptiste Provost, as well as auditing the classes of his colleagues Léon Beauvallet, Pierre Régnier, and Augustin Brohan. She thought Provost grand, and Beauvallet an idiot; Régnier an insightful, helpful teacher, and Brohan a hateful and jealous one. All of them were members of the Comédie Française. This lent an authority to every lesson: These were more than teachers helping to train unsophisticated actors for a life they themselves had never known; Sarah was being educated by actors of legendary consequence, firmly ensconced in the company into which all their students longed to be admitted. Sarah, alone of her class, regularly attended the deportment lectures of the absurd Georges Antoine Élie, who spent futile hours instructing fledgling actors how to rise from chairs and how to gesture gracefully with their arms. She regarded M. Élie, despite his severe pedagogical shortcomings, as worthy of respect. He was an actor too, an actor first; someone who had stood onstage and braved the expectant faces on the other side of the footlights. Even if the other students laughed at him, Sarah listened. There might be a single simple virtue embedded in all the elaborate twistings of his technique, and she could not afford to miss it.

Still, she spent as much time fighting the training at the Conservatoire as taking it in. The professors who labored over her clenched teeth, who insisted on exercises to open up the "o" and roll the "r," were easier to ignore than others who told her to raise her voice when her heart told her she must whisper. M. Auber, the white-haired, kindly director of the Conservatoire, often spoke about the beauty and uniqueness of Sarah's voice. Whenever he heard her recite Racine, he declared that her voice was so melodious that it sang the poetry.

This praise from the director did not impress everyone. All the students knew that Sarah had been admitted to the Conservatoire without playing a scene for the examining professors. Instead, she had simply recited a favorite fable of La Fontaine's, and been admitted on the spot. Either this indicated a talent so vast that the professors could discern it without having to judge the future actress in a conventional audition, or the question of her talent was irrelevant: The director would have been forced to admit the daughter of the mistress of the Duke of Morny under any circumstances.

Nearly every day she was coached by Provost's assistant, Denis-Stanislas Talbot, one of the youngest members of the Comédie Française. Talbot told her how lucky she was to be studying with such men, all of them brilliant actors. If she were fortunate enough to be admitted into the Comédie Française after graduation, she might have the honor of working on the same stage with her own professors. Even if she were not admitted, as most graduates of the Conservatoire were not, she would have stories to tell her grandchildren.

"You can tell them that you learned to declaim *Phèdre* from the man who taught Rachel," said Talbot.

"And you can tell your grandchildren," said Sarah to Talbot, "that you are the man who taught Sarah Bernhardt."

Talbot did not laugh at this, for Sarah had not intended to be funny. Sarah wanted more than tales to save up for grandchildren. She had entered a world rarefied and unique, the world of the theater, and she needed to stay there forever. Here, anything was possible, any wish could be granted as long as one believed with a truthful heart. Belief was evident in the way one embraced the mystery of a part; and every new student swallowed his or her role with searing faith. But there was not room enough in this world for everyone who burned to be in it. Few could get into the Conservatoire, and even selectivity did not guarantee the graduates their longings. There was not room for all of them in the Comédie Française.

Despite her work, her energy, her dedication, she was not a professor's delight. She made it only too clear to students and faculty that she was special. Her wild red-blond hair and frail frame had become advantages, dramatic marks of her difference. Some thought her beautiful, some judged her grotesque; everyone noticed her. Sarah saved the sous Julie gave her for the omnibus to school, trudging back and forth to her classes so that she could occasionally arrive gloriously at the Conservatoire in open-top fiacre. Her clothes were castoffs from her mother, but no other student had a mother like Julie Bernhardt. Only Sarah had school dresses of blue velvet and ribbed black silk, frocks short enough to exhibit exquisitely embroidered drawers.

Her reputation at school could have survived this ostentatious manner. But there was a greater sin than arriving in a rented fiacre or wearing a courtesan's clothes. The girl who had once burst into tears when her mother criticized her curly hair insisted on her talent. She might not have a father, might not be as welcomed at home as her sister Jeanne, might not be a member of a family as old and aristocratic as that of poor Appollonie, but she did claim one thing: That she would be a great actress.

Her best friend at the Conservatoire, Marie Lloyd, defended Sarah's vainglory, attributing it to a terrible shyness, an attempt by a quiet convent-school girl to fit in with a crowd of flamboyant acting students. No one else could see Sarah's conduct as anything but a manifestation of ludicrous conceit.

"You are too thin and too Jewish-looking to be an actress," her mother told her, advising her that a suitable, profitable marriage could still be arranged. "I will know that you are grown up when you have let go of this nonsense that the duke has put into your head." When Sarah recited one of Junia's heartfelt speeches from *Britannicus* before an audience of Mme. Guérard, Julie, and the Duke of Morny, the duke's enthusiastic applause was vitiated by her mother's response. "Anyone can learn to memorize a pretty speech," she said. "If any of my daughters has a chance for a career on the stage it is Jeanne. It will take more than a wild stubbornness to succeed in the theater. Don't forget that at sixteen, Rachel was already a sensation."

Sarah couldn't forget this, even if her mother hadn't rubbed it in her face. Everyone at the Conservatoire idolized the memory of Rachel. All the young women were made to feel old, knowing that by their age Rachel had made a spectacular debut at the Théâtre du Gymnase in *La Vendéene,* and that by the age of twenty she had already performed before Queen Victoria, bringing London as well as Paris to her feet. If Sarah insisted on her greatness, it was only partially to combat her mother's lack of encouragement. She knew that despite her conversion to the Catholic faith, the fact of her Jewish birth, coupled with her ambition to perform in the same dramatic roles that Rachel had already defined for a generation, would lead to animosity. Rachel had died so young that her reputation had become something sacred, despite her Jewishness, despite her lower-class birth. No one, particularly another Jewess, would be welcome to compete with her memory.

But Sarah had no choice.

Every time she recited in class, every time she argued with a teacher, every time she dreamed aloud among her peers, someone would raise the specter of the dead actress. "Who do you think you are," they would ask, "Rachel?"

Joking about Sarah's thinness, they would bring up Rachel's poetically consumptive appearance. Listening to Sarah tell about meeting Prince Henri de Luyen—in the absence of the prince the story had assumed legendary proportions—some doubting wit would remember Prince Napoleon's great love for Rachel.

There were reminders from the professors as well. Augustin Brohan, who had little use for Sarah, held the Conservatoire professorship that, had she lived, would have been taken by Rachel. Joseph-Isidore Samson, who encouraged Sarah and fueled her dreams with talk of her talent, had also brought Rachel into the Conservatoire and guided her career. Samson taught Sarah's dramatic-literature class, and eventually took over her course in declamation. How could she not hope to see in Samson's criticism and praise a continuation of what he had begun and never completed with Rachel?

It was clear to Sarah that in order to have a career onstage, she would have to become a great actress; and if she attempted greatness, she would be compared with Rachel. No wonder that she manufactured confidence, that she pulled over a frame of lifelong fears a fabric of intransigent glory.

Even had Brohan been a hundred times meaner, or Beauvallet a thousand times as boorish, she would have suffered through their classes. Sarah imagined herself a blade being tempered by fire, hammered into shape with powerful blows. No insult, no hatred directed at her could do anything but make her stronger. According to the legends of Rachel's early career, she had been discovered as a little girl singing songs in the street for pennies, while other girls her age were long since tucked into their beds. Such early hardships had steeled Rachel, Sarah believed, had opened her heart to the pain that she must have expressed onstage.

Sarah didn't want to sleep, because she lusted after adventure, experience. To be an infallible instrument for transmitting the words of the playwright to the stage, she must allow life's events to flow into her. Even the great Rachel had been limited in her repertoire, more successful at the classical works of Racine and Corneille than at the modern plays of Dumas and Hugo. Rachel's spectacular triumph in *Adrienne Lecouvreur* was her only one in a contemporary play. Sarah swore that she would attempt modern plays and classics, she would not shy from anything that might have merit onstage. While the other girls did what they could to avoid the fencing lessons required by the Conservatoire, Sarah swallowed her antipathy to the sport and practiced with a vengeance. It was a short leap of the imagination to dream of playing Hamlet, since she fenced as well as any male actor. Rachel had never attempted *Hamlet;* all the more reason why Sarah could aspire to the role. Her *Hamlet* fantasy drove her fencing lessons, compelled her body to crave physical exercise on those days that other classes kept her from her foil. Sarah was convinced that no other student could want what she wanted with the same intensity of desire, the same irresistible need. What she did not understand was why, despite the mask of strength and confidence, she could not rid herself of her debilitating stage fright.

After a year of study, fear had crippled her performance in the school's annual contest. Sarah told everyone who would listen that she had failed to win the Conservatoire's First Prize for Tragedy only because that honor always went to a second-year student. But she knew that was completely untrue. She did not win because she had not been the best. Her ability remained, and the strength of her will, but at the crucial time her ability had failed her, her strength had been stifled by her own hand.

Suddenly Sarah had lost confidence.

Nothing seemed more terrifying than having to go onstage in the school's recital hall. Her mother had been there, and the mothers of all the competing students, and every professor, and every student who was not backstage waiting to go on. She had tried to believe in her own powers at that moment, tried to ignore the feeling that to walk out from the wings into full view of the audience was to expose herself to ridicule and humiliation.

But the *trac,* the terrifying stage fright that her teacher Samson claimed afflicted every great actor, took hold of Sarah and would not let go. She felt ugly, tongue-tied, and she feared that once she said her first line, all the others would vanish from her head. Sarah tried to beat back these fears, remembering the praise from her teachers and coach, remembering the envy of the other students, remembering her need to succeed at any cost.

Yet when she had gone onstage, the scene she had chosen and labored on from Voltaire's *Zaïre* had no poetry, no shape, no fire. Instantly she knew she was not being true to the character or the play. All she could think of was the prize she would not win. So clearly did Sarah know she had failed during the competition, she might as well have been sitting next to her bored mother in the recital hall; in watching herself perform, she had vanished from the scene, made herself insignificant onstage.

When M. Auber announced the winner of the First Prize for Tragedy, Sarah swore to herself that she would win next year's prize. In that moment she wondered whether the entire legend she had built around herself at the Conservatoire was nothing more than a fantasy made up of wishes no more likely than a visit from her father.

A year passed, her second and final year at the celebrated school, and the competition loomed.

There would never be another chance to compete at the Conservatoire. Only the competition separated her from graduation. There was one First Prize for Tragedy, one First Prize for Comedy. There were second prizes too, but Sarah did not imagine that these would guarantee admission to the Comédie Française. She had prepared her scenes well, had worked with Samson, had been coached by Talbot. Sarah did not know what would happen to those scenes when they were moved from the classroom to the stage of the recital hall. She did not know if she would be struck again by incapacitating fear.

On the day before the competition, she invited Marie Lloyd—who was in the competition too—to sleep at her house, less to rehearse than to afford each other company during an interminable night. Marie was a tall brunette with enormous brown eyes and conventionally beautiful. Sarah's friend was an orphan, raised by a series of impoverished relations. Before the miracle of entrance into—then the introduction to the rigors of—the Conservatoire, Marie had been taught, like Sarah, that her lot in the world was limited to marriage or poverty. As with Sarah, the school had exposed Marie to additional, more brilliant possibilities.

Sarah loved Marie because Marie listened and looked up to her. Marie allowed Sarah her dreams, her ambitions. So secure was her future in Marie's eyes, that it was only in her presence that Sarah could relax her aloof posture. This love was not like what she had felt for the departed Appollonie. That love had been unselfish and admiring. She did not admire Marie, and she knew that her love was limited, confined to a sphere that would not intrude on her own needs. Sarah was too conscious of Marie's faults, too aware of Marie's unqualified praise to glory in it for more than a moment. She wanted Marie to be happy and well, but she did not wish to sacrifice anything of herself—as she would have gladly done for Appollonie—to ensure this. And surely, Sarah did not want Marie to have a greater success as an actress than she. Her own selfishness pained Sarah. Perhaps in forsaking the life of the convent, she had given up the chance for true friendship. Perhaps all artists were self-enclosed in this fashion, their desires not to serve others, but to succeed. No matter what little favors she did for Marie, Sarah felt as if she were a traitor, an incomplete friend. No matter how much she loved her, she could not respect her talent. Worst of all, Sarah would never tell her this to her face.

Marie understood well how to walk, how to hold up her head, how to present to the world a coquette's slyly innocent smile. Yet Sarah believed that her acting was almost worthless. Any effect she created was related to the gentle curves of her body, the full sensual bow of her mouth.

Rather than tell her this, Sarah bathed her in kind words. Perhaps if she had a theory of acting with which to help Marie improve, she might have spoken her mind. But it was hard to imagine how Marie could read her lines any differently; she chose to play simple coquettes, and she inhabited these dull parts with heartbreaking verisimilitude.

Marie had no such guilt about her feelings for Sarah.

Sarah Bernhardt was both her friend and her idol, and the idea that she might be needed to bolster Sarah's confidence would ordinarily have been laughable. Still, she remembered the unhappy results of the last competition, and Sarah's insistence on her sleeping over the night before today's contest. When Sarah dragged Marie out of bed before dawn, even she couldn't be oblivious to Sarah's fear. Sarah spilled the coffee she brought to Marie's bed, twice asked whether the neck of her dress was too low, and three times demanded to know whether she really believed that Sarah had any chance to win at all.

"Sarah," said Marie, sitting up higher in bed with the bowl of coffee in her white hands, "it's not possible for you to be nervous. You are the only one who got admitted into the school without a proper audition."

"Which is why everyone says that I should have never been admitted in the first place."

Marie put down the coffee and threw off her blanket. Suddenly she had been given a great responsibility, and she resolved to settle Sarah's worries promptly. "You're the only one who was asked by her own professor to take a role in his new play," said Marie, reminding her of what she had never forgotten!

That Sarah's teacher Régnier had wanted her to take a small role outside the Théâtre Français meant little more than that he liked very young, very thin girls. "At the Vaudeville Theater," said Sarah, "because of my red hair. Besides, the minister of fine arts would not allow me to take the role."

"Because the ministry wants you for the Théâtre Français," said Marie Lloyd. She had become peremptory, demanding that Sarah accept the logic before her: "Everyone knows that you will win First Prize for Tragedy. Everyone knows that you will have your debut at the Français a few months after you graduate."

"Let's go," said Sarah, unable to listen to the words that she wanted too much to believe. She hurried Marie into dressing, though half the morning must pass before it was time to arrive at the Conservatoire. "We will go look at the posters at the corner of the Rue Duphot. Just for the fun of it. Just for the confidence it will bring."

"Yes," said Marie, "just for the confidence." It would be a roundabout route from Sarah's home to the Conservatoire, but Marie was as glad as Sarah of the chance to kill the hours in this way. Though unhappy to learn of Sarah's fear, she had been immensely complimented at being asked, after a fashion, to help assuage it. Such an unfamiliar task had relaxed Marie. Whatever fears she had herself at the coming competition fell away under the greater interest of her paragon's insecurities. They dressed with speed and were out of doors before any of Julie's servants had awakened, and hurried down the deserted Rue St.-Honoré with a wild enthusiasm that for the moment calmed even Sarah.

At the intersection of the Rue St.-Honoré and the Rue Duphot a score of theaters advertised their attractions on large posters. What could be more inspiring than to surround themselves with these printed bills from the Odéon, the Gymnase, the Variétés and of course, the Théâtre Français? Let the other Conservatoire students toss and turn, Sarah had said earlier, trying to get a few more moments of sleep before the omnibus ride to the most important examination of their life. They knew their lines, they had each prepared for her role as though life and death hung in the balance. They had only to rid themselves of the *trac*.

"I don't have the *trac,*" said Marie.

Sarah stopped short, dropping her hold on Marie's arm. "No, of course not," said Sarah. "You have nothing to fear." She looked straight down the Rue St.-Honoré, wanting nothing less than to be able to fly down the elegant street, past the Vendôme Column, past the Café de la Régence, all the way into the sacred foyer of the Théâtre Français itself.

"Of course I have something to fear," said Marie, hoping that she had not wounded Sarah's pride. The last thing she wanted to suggest was that she was more prepared or more able than her friend. "Samson thinks me untalented, Brohan told me that my accent will never be suited to the classics, and Beauvallet called me hopeless, right to my face. Hopeless."

"I was not good last year, Marie," said Sarah.

"That's not true."

"It is true. I have never admitted it to anyone but you. How can I be good, if I can hardly bear to walk out onstage?" Sarah took hold of her friend's arm again, and Marie could feel the fear shivering through Sarah's pale skin. The posters grew larger as they walked toward them, close enough so they could touch the famous names. "Perhaps my mother is right. Perhaps all I do well is dream."

"Sarah," said Marie, "you know that you are the best actress in school. You know that everyone feels that way, and that it is not just you who dreams it."

"It will make no difference, if I have the *trac.*"

"You will not have it."

"How do you know?" said Sarah. "You've never had stage fright. You don't know a thing about it. I would have won last year if not for the *trac.* If I get the *trac* today, I am finished. I might as well paint my face and show my legs at the Variétés."

Last year Léonide Leblanc, a completely untrained eighteen-year-old actress, had another in a series of enormous successes at the Variétés. Despite atrocious reviews, she was back again, her name on the poster in letters larger than those of the theater in which she performed. Blanche d'Antigny, like Léonide Leblanc a courtesan aspiring to Julie Bernhardt's own exalted circle, was now appearing at the Gymnase. Sarah knew that if she did not succeed in jumping directly into the sober, serious company of the Comédie Française, if she had to accept being employed by any other theater, every graduate of the Conservatoire would say that she was joining a company that suited her family background: a company of whores.

"I have no luck," said Sarah

"What do you mean?" asked Marie, pulling Sarah closer to her as they finished their walk through the gauntlet of posters. "Who is luckier than you at school? Who else has a real prince in love with them?"

"Perhaps no one," said Sarah, though she had never before suggested any such negative possibility. Just as she had let Marie believe that her mother's glittering household came from something more than a courtesan's bed, she had allowed her to believe that Prince Henri de Luyen was an integral part of her life. No other student would have so readily accepted either fantasy. The truth was that Sarah had not seen Prince Henri since the night he had taken her home from her first visit to the Comédie Française more than three years before.

"Is he very handsome, your prince?" asked Marie.

"Why do you bother with such questions?" said Sarah. "Haven't I told you about him a hundred times?" Almost as soon as she snapped at Marie, Sarah felt a wave of remorse. Marie had slept at her house, had woken early, had taken this walk only to comfort her. She had tried to quiet Sarah's fears by complimenting her skills; now she tried to bolster her worries by reminding her of a love that did not exist. "I'm sorry, I didn't mean to shout at you."

"I like to hear, Sarah," explained Marie. "I have never met a prince, or a duke, or a count."

"I had rather he be Constant Coquelin, the son of a baker," said Sarah, intoning the name of one of last year's Conservatoire graduates who had already made a spectacular debut at the Française.

"But I had rather be loved by a prince," said Marie. "The way Rachel was loved."

"Yes," said Sarah. "Of course. A prince's love is a great thing." They had turned away from the array of posters, heading north into the duller streets of the Ninth Arrondissement. An elderly early-morning street sweeper, his broom on his shoulder, crossed their path, the only disturbance in an otherwise still vista down a street of old houses, lined with older horse-chestnut trees. "To answer your question, Prince Henri is as handsome as a god."

"What sort of god?" asked Marie, instantly slowing her pace, feeling Sarah's fear begin to fade.

"A blond god," said Sarah. "With broad shoulders and white teeth and elegant hands."

"What color are his eyes?"

"Blue," said Sarah, enjoying and embellishing the memory. "But not ordinary blue. They are dark and hard about the edges, but clear and light at the middle, like the light blue of the country sky."

"And his voice, Sarah? What sort of voice does the prince have?"

"He has a deep voice," said Sarah. "As deep as Beauvallet's when he shows off a piece of his acting for the class." Sarah smiled, and picked up the pace. A pair of washerwomen, their petticoats dragging along the muddy street, stared at the two young women as they passed, surprised to see anyone wearing new straw hats and polished shoes up so early in the morning. Sarah imagined that they must think the two fine gentlewomen were en route to something urgent and grave.

And they were going to an important place, to a significant event, and Sarah would go there without fear.

For in answering Marie's questions, Sarah had begun to perform. She was acting for an audience of one, and there was no *trac,* only the acclaim in Marie's enraptured face.

The truth was that Sarah's only recollection of Prince Henri's speech was that it was accented by his native Belgium. But she did not feel as though she were lying to Marie, or even tampering with the truth. All her life, she had a tendency to imagine things to be what she hoped they might be. Her father too had been "handsome as a god." A deep voice was preferable to a shrill, high-pitched one. Prince Henri's eyes were almost certainly blue; if they turned out, on reexamination, to be green or brown or black, what difference would it make? When Marie asked her how old he was, she remembered that she had been nearly fifteen when they met, and he had looked to her like a man of eighteen or nineteen. Now that she was approaching eighteen herself, she preferred that he be at least twenty-five. Of course, the Conservatoire training was too thorough to allow her imagination to respond without details.

"The prince is twenty-five," said Sarah, "and will be twenty-six in October. His birthday is the twenty-second, only a day before mine."

"You must not get married too soon," said Marie.

"He has not asked me, you understand," said Sarah.

"I'm sure that if you want him to, he will," said Marie. "How could he resist you?" She held her friend's arm a bit tighter as they walked past a policeman, beaming under his helmet, his breeches dazzling white under the early-morning summer sun. "After today's competition, you will certainly be asked to join the Français. You must not get married until you have had a chance to show them what you can do."

"You are a very good friend to me, Marie," said Sarah. She remembered at the last moment to return the compliment. "And surely you will get a prize too. We shall be asked to join the Comédie Française together."

"If you did not help me with my scenes, they would laugh at me. If you had not asked me to sleep at your house last night, I would have gone insane. You are the best friend in the world."

"Stop it," said Sarah. "I have done nothing but talk about stage fright."

"That's not true," said Marie. "You have given me confidence. You have let me believe it is possible, anything is possible. 'In spite of everything,' right?"

"In spite of everything," said Sarah, repeating her own motto. Walking on in silence, she knew that the fear had left her body. As the ugly weatherwashed four-story structure of the Conservatoire finally appeared before them, she felt ashamed, unworthy of Marie's friendship.

"Look," said Sarah, "do not thank me for your confidence. You must get your own confidence. Today and every day you must try to rely on yourself. You are in competition with me, and I am in competition with you."

"Oh, no," said Marie. "I am not in competition with you. I am not even competing in tragedy anyway."

"I am entered in both competitions."

"If you take the First Prize for Comedy, I shall be happy if I get a second prize."

"Don't be an idiot," said Sarah. "We are all in competition. Every one of us at the Conservatoire is in a race, and only the fastest wins."

"But you are the fastest," said Marie, speaking slowly and carefully, craving her friend's good temper. "You will win a first prize in tragedy and in comedy. I do not want to compete with you, but only with the others."

"You must try to beat me, Marie," insisted Sarah. She felt if she could only get Marie to understand the nature of the contest ahead of them, she would have repaid her for helping her lose her fear. "I will try to beat you. You must understand that the only way you get a chance to go on the stage is by being judged better than your peers. You must bring those judges to their feet, shouting your name. You must do it, you must do it this morning."

Because she was not competing for the tragedy prize, Marie was able to watch Sarah perform her tragic scene from Casimir Delavigne's *La Fille du Cid*. Sitting in the recital hall, crowded with tense relatives, Marie thought Sarah's entrance elegant. Yet a moment later she knew that her friend would not win the prize. Sarah's voice, always silvery smooth, her poetry reading as clear and liquid as a song, was too high, too tight.

In the wings Sarah had longed for the moment of her entrance. The *trac* was banished, her lines ready to be declaimed. She wanted to go out, conquer the audience, and win her prize before she lost her nerve. Once onstage, Sarah found herself drawn to the white faces looking up at her from the stalls, and down at her from the modest little boxes. Somewhere among them was her mother, and Mme. Guérard, and the Duke of Morny. They wanted so much from her, and she wanted so much to be able to give it to them. She could not help but think about them: the mother who would love her only if she had a spectacular success; the little widow who believed she, Sarah, could be as great as Rachel; the duke, whose whim had made the chance of a life in the theater possible.

Even as she played out the scene, following the stage movements with perfect accuracy, remembering her memorized gestures, re-creating every tragic pose, she was aware of the audience, watching them as they watched her. Despite this, the performance was not terrible. There were some who were moved by her green eyes in the gaslight, by the pale face surrounded by a romantic thicket of hair. When she clutched her throat, when she held her hands to her chest, some of the professors wrote commendations in their competition notebooks.

Then her beautiful voice betrayed her.

Just like the year before, Sarah could feel the poetry die in her throat; no speech can simply be remembered but must always arise with a spontaneous magic, as if being spoken for the first time. And there could be no magic onstage when an actress was busier with the stalls than with the life of her scene. When it was finished, she took a half bow, knowing it was more than she deserved. She left her astonished scene partner alone to embrace the applause on an empty stage.

Sarah ran through the wings and up the shabby staircase to the communal dressing room. She spoke to no one, not even to answer a question or respond to a compliment. The tragedy scenes were finished, and in a moment the comedy scenes would begin. She did not need to hear M. Auber read out the names of the four prize-winners for tragedy, a first and second prize in the male and female divisions. Sarah knew that she had lost, that her world was collapsing about her.

Not for a minute did she think of giving it all up.

The attraction to the theater was too great, too certain. She had not been good, but she could be good, she could be great. She had lost the tragedy competition; therefore, the only chance to salvage her life was to win the First Prize for Comedy. She did not think of herself as naturally funny, nor did she particularly like the play that had been chosen for her comic scene. But she had no choice. To get into the Comédie Française she must win a first prize. In spite of everything, she would win the First Prize for Comedy.

Very carefully, she dipped a brush into a pot of kohl and slowly drew it between her eyelashes. Through the open door of the dressing room came the intermittent sounds of laughter, the sharp, poorly distributed handclapping of a partisan crowd. Putting her nose close to the mirror, she shut out the faces of the students about her, and with a wet finger added carmine to her lips, rouge to her cheeks, powder to her forehead.

Marie Lloyd came up behind her and pressed her shoulders, her beautiful face smiling in the mirror. Sarah didn't respond. She did not remember to wish Marie well when she left to do her scene, nor did she congratulate her friend when she returned. Sarah could not take notice of her or anyone else. She was drawing herself deeper and deeper into the scene she was about to do from another Delavigne play, *L'École des vieillards,* until there was no reality for her other than the one she was about to create onstage.

After a half hour, the first-year student functioning as callboy shouted her name through the open door. When she did not respond, one of the students shook her roughly. Sarah smiled, understood that her scene partner was waiting in the wings, that it was time. She stood, only a little lightheaded. There was a strength in her thin legs now, a desire to go out and confront mother, fellow students, judges. The audience waited, and she would show them of what stuff she was made.

In the wings she felt washed by the vivid colors of the filtered lights. A former Conservatoire student hired for the day sat at an intricate table of levers and cocks; from here he regulated the flow of gas to the lamps that hung from battens and flies and crossbars. Other students, looking out from the wings onto the stage, turned as she approached, her eyes cold, steady, obsessed. She was beautiful in her heavy makeup, animated in that impromptu ephemeral backstage world. Marie waited for her at the upstage left entrance; she wished her luck. Sarah stopped for a moment, her hands flat on the ramshackle walls of the wing, and looked out at the stage where two students from the previous scene were taking their bows to a scattering of applause. The curtain boy, sitting on a high stool, his calloused hands about a thick rope, lowered the heavy curtain with awkward, unintentional speed.

"Go," said the stage manager, and Sarah's scene partner ran out of the wings onto the stage, finding his position at center, clearing his throat, and looking with dread at the closed curtain.

Sarah's entrance would be a moment after the curtain rose. In the wings she felt her voice waiting to grow from her belly. She closed her eyes, shutting out the strange effect of red and blue lights washing the inner curtain, and imagined only the drawing room she would enter when her character's name would be called.

"Hortense," said the man onstage, and Sarah felt a push from behind. She saw that the curtain was up, that her scene partner waited frantically for her to appear.

Yet Sarah was not frantic.

Hortense took her time. She was not for the moment living at Sarah's pace, but rather at the pace of the character she had brought inside her skin. Slowly, with a languid pose, Sarah walked onstage. She saw none of the white faces behind the footlights; her eyes saw only the face of the man who had called to her. When she began to speak Delavigne's comic lines, a laugh came quickly from the middle of the house, sending a vague pleasure through her body. The laughing did not confuse her. She lost nothing of the sense of the scene, instinctively keeping the rhythm of the poetry alive. Her scene partner moved downstage, speaking directly over the footlights. From where Sarah stood upstage, a yellow haze hung over his head, but she saw in this only the sun shining through glass doors. She cajoled him, her voice sweet and full of flirtatious charm. He turned around, threw up his hands in a histrionic gesture, and someone in the front row clapped his hands. A sense of cheer and well-being came from the house, a sense of fun. People laughed, taking care not to do so with volume. They wanted to hear every word.

This was Sarah's scene, not her partner's, chosen so that she would have center stage, the large speech, the long minute under the full glare of the lamps. She watched her scene partner move stage left, near the exit; he faded into the background as Sarah held the stage.

Suddenly there was absolute silence.

Sarah let a thin smile raise the corners of her mouth, knowing that her carmined lips would be visible to everyone in the house. She touched a finger to her left eye, she allowed a sigh to rise from her belly out of her throat and into the glow of the stagelight. Everyone listened, everyone watched. Then words came to her lips, syllable by golden syllable, so beautifully spoken that many in the audience were afraid to laugh at all. Sarah took no notice of the laughter or the lack of it. She was an instrument, playing a song; a spirit romped through her body like a divine wind, and nothing was more effortless, more joyful. There was no fear, only jubilation. She could have stayed there under the lights forever, but the scene was short, and the curtain was suddenly lowered, and muffled applause reached her almost at once through the heavy fabric wall. Her scene partner took hold of her elbow, and with great force, moved her downstage as the curtain rose for them to take their bows.

Now she saw the white faces, blurred by her tears.

She bowed and bowed, as though she had performed five acts of Racine at the Français instead of a single scene of Delavigne in her school's recital hall. When the curtain came down, Marie ran up to her from the wings. She told Sarah how wonderful she had been, how funny, how truthful, how beautiful.

"Thank you, Marie," said Sarah. "I could not have done it without you."

Marie had not performed as Sarah had demanded. She had thought nothing of competition, of whom she must beat, but only of the scene she had prepared from Molière's *Le Misanthrope*. Marie had been interesting as Célimène, a heartless coquette with a contrastingly delicate manner. A half hour later, when the awards for comedy were announced, the first prize for girls went not to Sarah's Hortense but to Marie's Célimène.

M. Auber announced her friend's name with great relish. He predicted a great future for Marie Lloyd. The director said that the prize had been awarded unanimously. There was no talk of any such unanimity about the Second Prize for Comedy. This was awarded to Sarah Bernhardt. When she walked up from the house and onto the stage, Sarah forced herself to smile. She had not seen Marie perform before the crowd, but she had coached her performance a hundred times. There was not a chance in the world that Marie had been better than she, Sarah thought. Still, Marie would be offered a chance to join the Comédie Française, and she would be reduced to begging for a chance in a boulevard theater.

"Congratulations, Mademoiselle Bernhardt," said M. Auber. Sarah smiled up at him, smiled at the boxes, felt a strength rise into her soul from the aged boards of the stage. It was not fair, but she would survive, she would get her chance to perform.

Until then, she would remember the feeling she'd had onstage when everything worked, when everything was easy and sure and joy descended on her like a gift from God.

Chapter 10

HE HOPED THAT SHE
REMEMBERED HIM

There were worse things in the spring of 1862 than Sarah's failure to win a first prize, the Duke of Morny said. King Otto I of Greece had just been forced to resign after a revolt by the military. Abraham Lincoln, whose inauguration last year as American president had brought the smoldering conflict between the states to war, was about to issue the Emancipation Proclamation. The Union forces, twice defeated at Bull Run, had this year captured Fort Henry, Roanoke Island, Jacksonville, and New Orleans. "Just think," said Morny. "You could be the King of Greece without a throne. Or a slaveowner losing all his slaves."

"I don't care," said Sarah. All she had was her misery, and for the moment she wanted it intact.

"You were wonderful, darling," said Julie Bernhardt, astonishing her daughter with these words of tribute. "You deserved first prize. They are idiots. I hardly knew you up there, you were so pretty and so fine."

For the first time in her life, Sarah did not take any pleasure in a compliment from her mother. There was no room for satisfaction in a carriage filled with gloom. As she rode home with Mme. Guérard, the Duke of Morny, and her mother, Sarah knew that the gloom was her responsibility. If she had won the Conservatoire's First Prize for Comedy, they would all be gilded with light and splendor. The duke, glad of his decision to put Sarah on the stage, would be laughing out loud, reaching out to pinch the prizewinner's cheeks. Mme. Guérard would be altogether too full of joy to move or to speak. And Julie would be taking wild pride in the highly cultured accomplishments of the daughter of a poor, uneducated Dutch immigrant girl.

As it was, she was knee to knee with Julie in the cramped four-passenger compartment, listening to her words of consolation. Nestled against a perspiring Mme. Guérard, Sarah did not quite recognize her mother in this role of comforter. Julie, pressed against the duke's bright linen shirt front, seemed faded, somehow less than her usual golden self. No one could have looked alive, thought Sarah, when forced to utter such sympathetic, clichéd phrases about courage and perseverance. She would have expected Julie to dredge up poor M. Berentz, hopefully ready to assume the burdens of matrimony after three years of anticipation. In the confined space of the carriage, the hot ride through dusty, heavy traffic was interminable, made worse by the distinct possibility that poor Mme. Guérard might suddenly burst into tears. When they finally reached their destination on the Rue St.-Honoré, Sarah was the first out of the carriage. She excused herself and ran upstairs to her room and threw herself into her bed.

She barely stirred for eighteen hours.

Her sleep was fitful at first; she would wake to agonize over Marie Lloyd's abilities, wondering if there might be some lesson to be learned from her friend's first-prize triumph. Perhaps, she thought, there was such a closeness between Marie's own simple, coquettish character and that of the role she had played that what the judges had awarded was not a prize for an actress but an accolade to Marie's personality.

Even if this were true, the knowledge was of no use to Sarah.

She couldn't imagine finding a role that would fit the character she herself possessed. Sarah was not drawn to acting so that she might parade a facsimile of her own life before strangers. Besides, she had little idea what that facsimile would look like to an audience, either onstage or off. Her fellow students thought her wildly ostentatious, given to grand gestures and wild affectations; everything from her hair to her clothes to her manner of speech was self-consciously histrionic. At the convent, only a few short years ago, she had been considered quite the opposite: painfully shy, reclusive. Sarah knew that there was a measure of her true self in both these images. When her aunt Rosine brought the famous composer Rossini to their home, Sarah had insisted that he accompany her recital of a poem on Julie's out-of-tune piano. A week later, when Julie was visited by a celebrity of far lesser reputation, a minor official in the Ministry of Arts, Sarah could do nothing but blush and stammer in the face of his attentions.

One day she was forthcoming and outgoing, another she was quiet and introverted. In the presence of her Dutch-born mother and aunt, Sarah's education, innocence, and youth might allow her to feel vastly superior to these high priestesses of the demimonde. Just as often, being around the resplendently beautiful Julie and Rosine left her feeling homely, undistinguished. Abruptly Sarah's disciplined, mellifluous voice might—in her own mind—sound coarse compared with the courtesans' sharp-witted, charmingly accented speech.

Walking the streets of the city with pretty Marie Lloyd, she sometimes felt that the eyes of the men of Paris were on her friend alone; at other times Sarah believed that the strength of her own great passions must overshadow her friend's childish posturing. One day the mirror would find her hideous, the next day nothing less than a goddess of rare beauty. In the morning she would imagine herself capable of winning any man's heart; by evening she would despair of ever marrying at all.

If Sarah did not know which image was the one she presented to the world, she did know that she yearned to play greater parts than the one she was playing at the moment: a seventeen-year-old aspiring actress. Sarah wanted to put on the guise of a princess, of a siren, of women capable of overwhelming lust, of hideous murder, of wild vengeance.

No, she would not learn anything from Marie Lloyd's triumph, she decided, other than a life in the theater did not promise to be fair.

Vaguely, drifting between wakefulness and sleep, she sensed Mme. Guérard's presence in her bedroom. Sarah was not certain whether it was in a dream or at the threshold to sleep that she imagined the young widow worrying over her, her soft hands pressed to her closed lips. Much later that night, she thought she could hear Julie's soft steps, and smell her sweet perfume; someone was gently calling her through a web of gossamer. She longed to speak to Julie, to thank her for coming to the Conservatoire that day, to express gratitude for trying to console her. But before she could find a way to speak, her mother's presence diminished, slowly at first, and then with nightmarish rapidity; it was like watching a figure dwindle to nothing from the window of a runaway coach. Sarah understood that sleep prevented her from speaking; some kind spirit drew her more and more deeply into a blissful, peaceful state until she was enclosed by something strong enough to shut out the world.

"Sarah," said Julie. She knew that her mother spoke to her not from in her room but from a dream. The dream explained the love in her mother's blue eyes, the gentle tone, the tentative touch of her hands on her child's feverish forehead.

In this dream Sarah embellished Julie's words of solace during the carriage ride home: "You deserved that prize. It was not your fault that they did not give it to you, but my fault and mine alone. If the Duke of Morny was not my lover, they would not always think of you as the girl who was forced into their great school. You were the best, better than all the boys, and better than any girl, no matter how pretty."

"It is not your fault, Mama," said Sarah nobly. "It does not matter."

"But if not for me, you would be accepted into the Comédie Française," said Julie.

"I do not care about the Comédie Française."

"If not for me, you would be accepted into society."

"I do not care about society."

"If not for me, your Prince Henri would have long ago offered you his hand in marriage."

"I do not care about marriage, Mama. An actress does not need a husband. And I shall go on the stage without any help from anyone. I shall succeed on the strength of my own merits."

"It is your own merits that are not being judged on my account," said the Julie of her dreams. "I am holding back your career. I am responsible for your failure to win a first prize."

"I forgive you, Mama."

"Sarah, I love you. I love you more than Regina, I love you even more than Jeanne."

Sarah woke with this dream curled in her heart. She smiled at the morning light that flooded through the curtains and drapes over tall east-facing windows. When she took to her bed at three in the afternoon, she had not thought to lower the wooden shutters for the night. On the commode across from the bed was the Swiss clock given her by the Duke of Morny as a graduation present. Squinting against the light, she could just make out the sun-dazzled golden hands against the white face and black numerals. It was nine o'clock, and she had not yet changed from the clothes she had worn to the Conservatoire the day before.

"In spite of everything," she whispered, stretching her arms toward the sun, revitalized from the long sleep, feeling loved from the residue of her dream. Getting out of bed, she pulled off her crumpled clothes until she stood naked against the windows, basking in the diffused warmth of the sun. If she ever had a husband, she thought, he would be more jealous of the morning sun than of any man. The passions it aroused in her body were deliciously real. She turned about, her neck stretching luxuriously, as if under a lover's caress, allowing the sun to flow onto her back, letting it penetrate her famished, shivering body.

It was then, with the light at her back, and her body alive with lust, that she saw the silver tray on her night table.

It had not been there when she went to bed.

In this tray were two items: a visiting card and an envelope. From across the room she could see that the envelope, which was a familiar pale blue, stood propped on its side against a crystal paperweight. Under the crystal was a long white visiting card. Someone had taken the extraordinary step of creeping into her room while she slept, to place this tray where she would see it upon awaking. Slowly she approached the tray, recognizing at the corner of the blue envelope the embossed crown of the Duke of Morny.

It was not surprising that she forgot the visiting card, reaching first for the envelope from the man who had facilitated her entry to the Conservatoire, the man who could make almost anything possible in the country where his half brother was emperor. She tore it open with speed.

"My dear Sarah," the duke had written in his crabbed hand. "Though it was probably not at all necessary, I have taken the precaution of speaking with my dear friend M. Camille Doucet. He assured me, in his capacity as the minister of arts, that M. Thierry, the director of the Comédie Française, will ask you to join the Comédie as a *pensionnaire.* You will make your debut at the Théâtre Français in a matter of months, perhaps in time for your eighteenth birthday. I hope you will forgive me for speaking on your behalf, but I could not bear to think of you suffering any unhappiness as a result of the stupidity of inferior judges. You will learn that the best judges of those onstage are the people who pay for their tickets in the audience. I am certain that they will find you entirely as enchanting as I do."

The letter did not end here, but Sarah needed to sit down, and begin it over again. Yes, she thought, accepting everything, taking help from any quarter, allowing influence to achieve what her own performance could not. She was not dreaming, and what she had just read was not a fantasy but a real letter written by a real man in a real world. In spite of everything, she was to be engaged by the Comédie Française. Her heart beat wildly against the walls of her chest, and she needed to place the notepaper flat on the tray to still it in her shaking hands. Once again, the man whose money and power were her mother's greatest source of support had changed her life. A man whom she had hated for sharing her mother's bed had proved himself her greatest protector. As she read the letter, she heard behind the words on the page her own ecstatic commentary, thanking the duke, thanking the minister of arts, thanking her mother for her connection to the powerful. The world had been dark and cruel, but the duke had waved his magic scepter and she had been granted her greatest wish.

Still, she did not need more than a minute to allow herself to believe that what the duke had written in kindness was perhaps no more than true: that even without his help, she would have been asked to join the greatest acting company in France.

The First Prize in Comedy was not everything, apparently.

Tragedy was her true calling, after all, and the actor-professors of the Conservatoire must surely have rallied to her cause. She would have won the First Prize in Tragedy if not for the *trac.* She was not meant to suffer all her life to pay for a single silly experience with stage fright. She had after all been an exemplary student, had bewitched Samson, Provost, Régnier. All of them believed in her charm, her talent, her seductive voice. That she would be barred from practicing her art at the Théâtre Français because of an unfortunate contest was unthinkable. She had fire in her heart, she would dare anything for the stage, and the Comédie had recognized this, the Comédie wanted to engage her because she had within her the ability to be a great actress.

Sarah, her naked body glistening with sweat, turned left and right in front of the light-drenched, draped windows, taking bow after bow to an imaginary crowd, all of them on their feet and shouting her name.

Suddenly a real clapping of hands stopped her.

"You're looking pretty pleased with yourself," said Julie, standing in the open doorway to Sarah's room. "Apparently you are too in love with yourself to hear my knock."

"I'm sorry, Mama," said Sarah, unable to get the overweening smile off her face. "It's just that my good luck—"

"You're about to become a member of a respectable society," said Julie, stopping to preen before Sarah's miniature cheval glass. "Don't you think it might be a good idea to put some clothes on?"

"Yes, Mama," said Sarah, hurrying to throw on her blue flannel bathing wrap.

Julie walked past her to the windows, taking care not to touch Sarah as they passed. She pulled back the drapes and curtains, and let in some of the close morning air. "Aren't you wondering why I am up so early?" she said.

"Oh, yes, Mama, why?"

"You can't think of anything now but your two letters, I suppose," said Julie. "Your two admirers." The number of letters had been one, and not two; she would have questioned her mother about this mistake, or at least picked up the unread visiting card, but Julie's manner, so different from the day before, arrested her. She turned from the windows, and Sarah could see behind her thirty-four-year-old mother's rice-powdered face, a world of vexation.

"Is something wrong, Mama?"

"Yes," said Julie. "Your selfishness for one thing."

"I am sorry if I am selfish."

"Why do you not thank me?"

"I thank you," said Sarah, not knowing exactly for what she was expected to be thankful.

"You think it is all the duke, of course. I suppose you think it is you that charms him, that your old mother has nothing to do with it anymore. Yesterday, at the Conservatoire, one of your professors mistook me for a student. There are some who think I look even younger than you!"

"You are the most beautiful woman in Paris."

"That is my profession, Sarah," said Julie. "It is not just the duke who must think I am beautiful, because the duke alone cannot be depended on, regardless of the good he has just done you today. I make myself beautiful so that we may all live, you and Jeanne and Regina, not for myself alone. We are all alone in the world, believe me, except for our family, our true family. You must remember."

"I will, Mama," said Sarah. She did not understand what made her mother so sentimental this morning, so close to a declaration that she was living as a whore to support her daughters. "And I am very glad that you have influenced the duke to help me—"

Julie interrupted. "Are you too blind to see that it is nine o'clock and I am up and already dressed for traveling?"

"I see," said Sarah, trying to fathom her mother's mood. She drew closer to her, wondering what she could possibly do to help ease her mother's pain. "I know that it is early. Where are you going?"

"I am tired. I was awakened at six-thirty. A messenger came, very dramatically you may be sure. He woke up the whole house, except for you. A private, secret message for me from the Duke of Morny. About a slight change of plans." Julie paused and smiled. "Have you ever seen his wife?"

"No, Mama," said Sarah. She had never even known that the duke was married until this moment. Of course, that hardly surprised her. Most aristocrats who made the circuit of the Café Anglais, the Maison d'Or, and the expensive boudoirs of women like Julie Bernhardt were married, their great names linked to those of their respectable wives.

"Winterhalter has painted her portrait. She is very beautiful. One of the empress's best friends. I am going to Saint-Cloud." Julie spat out the words as though they tasted of dirt. "You are not the only one with admirers, you know."

"I don't have admirers, Mama."

Julie shook her head at this modest protestation. "The duke admires me too. He is taking me to Saint-Cloud. As he has promised me for six months and more. I was to have my hand kissed by royal lips." Julie brought her head close to Sarah's. "Saint-Cloud is very respectable, you know. The emperor will be there with his boring empress, as the duke will be there with his even more boring duchess."

"I don't understand, Mama."

"The Duke of Morny will be at Saint-Cloud with the Duchess of Morny. A last-minute change of plans. The duchess was originally planning to remain behind, but apparently could not abide being left in Paris this season. Your mother will be nearby, you understand. Very comfortably set up, you may be sure. I shall be treated with all due respect by the servants who wait on me. And when the duke gets away from his wife, I am sure he will be able to give me his full attention. It will be just like Paris, only I shall be slightly more shut in. They are not accustomed to grand courtesans in the countryside, and I must not flaunt myself among all the narrow-minded respectable friends of the court."

"You are better than any of them," said Sarah.

"We shall see how long you feel that way, my dear child," said Julie. "You are entering the Comédie Française, and that is very dignified. And you have an aristocrat waiting to call upon you as an honorable young woman, and not as your client."

"What do you mean?"

"I mean that he does not think you a harlot."

"Who is the aristocrat who wants to call upon me?"

"You really can be very pretty," said Julie, shaking her head at Sarah, as if her question was no more than a rhetorical flourish. "In a most unusual way, of course, but I can see it, I can understand why there are some men who might absolutely lose their heads over my oldest daughter."

Sarah interrupted: "I do not know any such man."

"Any more than you do not have a place at the Comédie Française," snapped Julie. "Why do you think he wrote you?"

"The duke was merely being polite," said Sarah.

"Are you stupid?" said Julie. "Where is the card?"

The visiting card was where she had left it under the crystal paperweight, forgotten in the wild joy of the letter from Morny. Sarah reached it before her mother could, removing the paperweight with one hand and picking up the heavily embossed card with the other.

"You have not seen it?" asked Julie.

"No," said Sarah, looking down in speechless wonder at the regal crest of Prince Henri de Luyen's family. For a moment she had difficulty separating the prince she had woven into her fantasies for three years from the memory of the prince she had actually met on a single magnificent occasion: that first night in the audience at the Théâtre Français. "He was here?"

"Well, of course he was here, and if you have the strength to turn over the card you'll see that he is coming back."

"Coming back," said Sarah. Indeed, there was writing on the card, a deep blue ink in a tiny, meticulous hand. One by one she deciphered the words: He hoped that she remembered him, he congratulated her on graduating from the Conservatoire, he regretted that he would be in Paris for only a short while, and would therefore take the liberty of calling again the next day.

"I do not mean to persecute you," he wrote. "You have only to leave word that you are too busy to see me, and I shall understand."

"He was here yesterday?"

"At five o'clock," said Julie.

"What did he look like?"

"I didn't see him. He called on you, not me. He asked Bella to wait while he wrote you this interminably long message. The letters are almost too small to read."

"Then he will be back today."

"I would expect so," said Julie, her eyes cold and distant. "You are to be congratulated in any case. A prince, even if he is from Belgium."

"What is wrong, Mama?" asked Sarah.

"And congratulations on your acceptance by the Comédie Française. I shall look forward to your debut. As for me, I must hurry. I am going to Saint-Cloud." Julie turned about and would have left if Sarah had not stopped her, placing her hands on her mother's shoulders and turning her about. She had suddenly understood that what her mother needed was her touch.

"You are better than any of them," said Sarah for the second time that morning, drawing her diminutive mother into her arms. "Better than any duchess, better even than the empress." Sarah held her close, feeling her mother's sobs like stabs directed into her own heart. This was not simply because she sympathized with her mother's humiliation. It was because Sarah understood that what her mother had said before held the awful possibility of truth: that she, Sarah, might grow to be ungrateful.

From the glorious revelations of this morning—she would be a member of the Comédie and a real-life prince would come to call upon her—came a further greedy kernel of desire: that her talent might transcend her origins, that her name would be linked not with courtesans but with princes, that her fame would overshadow the shameful mother who gave her life.

Even as she held her mother, becoming a source of comfort to her for the first time, Sarah could not help imagining the adoration that was to come: the ride through the Bois with Prince Henri de Luyen, the debut at the Français. She would be famous, she would be rich, men would love her with the obsessive passion only artists could inspire. Even as she clutched Julie, she sensed herself drifting away from the mother who had never loved her enough, who had never needed her until this very moment.

There was another, greater source of love that beckoned to her, a bottomless well of adoration that she could reach only from the stage. It was toward this source to which she was about to travel. Sarah knew that the embrace for which she had longed all her life had become nothing less than a way of bidding her childhood good-bye.

Chapter 11

TELL ME THAT
YOU LOVE ME

During the following two weeks, Sarah met with M. Thierry, the director of the Théâtre Français, was officially made a *pensionnaire* of the company, and assigned her first role: Iphigénie in Racine's great tragedy *Iphigénie en Aulide.* A month after her graduation from the Conservatoire, she would begin rehearsals with the Comédie Française. She would make her debut on September 1, 1862, six weeks before her eighteenth birthday.

But all of these marvelous events, the culmination of her fervent dreams, were overshadowed by something far more powerful: first love.

Sarah Bernhardt, new *pensionnaire* of the Comédie Française, had fallen in love with Prince Henri de Luyen of Brussels. This was nothing like the unrequited adoration she had felt for her mother, or the intensely possessive attachment she had had for Nurse; neither was it like the tender affection she had given Appollonie. Least of all was it anything like her idealized devotion for Mother Ste.-Sophie.

Though she had been attracted to the soldiers billeted near her convent school—and shamed by the lust that their handsome figures prompted in her nubile body—that attraction, and that lust, were childish and inconsequential weighed against the feelings that moved her now.

Her love was jealous and insistent and blind. She wanted Prince Henri to want her, and to want her alone. Every other woman in the world became a potential enemy, to be watched, to be criticized and ridiculed. The prince must see that Sarah was uniquely worthy to be his wife. Because she was obsessed, she wanted her desires to be met at once. She could not see what frustration she caused herself, what fantasies she built on a few slender words from the young man she adored. If he complimented her voice when she recited a poem, she imagined that he heard it in his sleep. If he said that he did not like to think of returning to Brussels, she imagined that he could not live without her. If he spoke disparagingly of his father's staidness, she imagined that he was already gathering the fury he would need to defy his family for her sake.

But not all her imaginings were so optimistic.

When the prince was a minute late, she worried that he had decided never to see her again. If he did not speak rapturously of her beauty, she imagined that he was searching for someone prettier. When he did not demand every moment of her time, she was sure that he had found someone else to fill his hours.

In this way, she thought of him constantly.

Every action she performed was dedicated to him. Selecting her clothes, she hoped that they would please him. Biting into a fruit, she imagined that he was there, entranced by the movements of her sensuous lips. Sarah could barely study her lines in *Iphigénie* without including Prince Henri in the process: She did not think of the all-important debut audience at the Français; all that mattered was that he be impressed when they read the lines together on the morrow.

She had fallen in love, and nothing in the world mattered save that the prince would love her in return. Because she wanted him, she thought anything was possible, that despite being the illegitimate daughter of a Jewish courtesan, he would learn to love her so much that he would force his family to accept her. Blood and alliances would not be of concern. Only desire mattered. He had only to want her as much as she wanted him. She could become a princess.

"You're mad," said her aunt Rosine, when Sarah shared this ecstatic possibility with her. "A prince never marries for love." She had come to call on her niece at the absent Julie's request, and did not relish the task at hand. Mme. Guérard had written Julie at

Saint-Cloud, saying that it was impossible not to notice Sarah's happiness. Then Julie had written Rosine: There was certain information that Sarah must have at once if her life were not to be ruined.

At least, thought Rosine, it would not be her job to tell Sarah that princes were always swine.

"He is kind, and he is handsome, and he takes me everywhere," said Sarah. She looked at Rosine with shining eyes. Rosine knew nothing would penetrate except what Sarah wanted to hear.

"Does he touch you everywhere too?" asked Rosine.

This was the wrong approach to use on her convent-educated niece, but Rosine was in a hurry. A British earl—who on his last visit to Paris had given Rosine an emerald brooch—was back in town. Naturally she had invited him to her house for a glass of afternoon absinthe; if she did not get a nap in before much longer, it was unlikely she would get any sleep until the following day.

"I will not allow anyone to speak of Prince Henri in a disrespectful fashion," said Sarah.

"I don't mean any disrespect, my dear," said Rosine. "I am simply concerned that you do not get pregnant."

"That is impossible!" said Sarah.

"Only if he is not a man," said Rosine.

"I am a virgin and he treats me with courtesy," said Sarah.

"Stop it, you sound like a little fool," said Rosine. "And you're not a little fool, are you? You know that if he hasn't touched you, he wants to. And that if you plan to resist, you will lose him. Sit down, and I will show you what you must do when the time comes."

"The time will come when he marries me," said Sarah. After a moment's thought, she sat down. "I don't know what Mama imagines."

"That you will fall in love, that you will get pregnant, that he will leave you, and that you will be unable to perform with the Comédie Française," said Rosine. "And worst of all, of course, is that Julie will be a grandmother." Rosine removed a small square piece of sponge wrapped in a cloth from her bag. Sarah was horrified by this pale tool of harlotry. A double twisted red ribbon was affixed to one corner. She watched Rosine's painted lips move as she explained that the ribbon facilitated withdrawal of the sponge from the vagina after lovemaking. "This does not interfere with pleasure," said Rosine. "Neither yours nor his. It is far superior to a wool plug. The most comfortable way is to wet it first in warm water, then just put it in. And take care to wash it. Wash it well every time."

Sarah didn't comprehend what the horrible object was suddenly doing in her hand. She let it fall onto the divan and said: "I don't need it."

"It is an unpleasant thing to force a miscarriage," said Rosine, attempting a conspiring tone.

"He does not intend to use me indecently."

"If he practices withdrawing at the last moment, neither of you will leave the bed with a smile. If he uses a sheath, you will feel next to nothing, and he will spend the whole time wondering whether his cock is wrapped in a pig's bladder or a sheep's intestine. Jumping up and down after sex doesn't prevent pregnancy. Douching yourself with cayenne pepper in water will only irritate you. Your mother was pregnant when she was two years younger than you are right now. Don't think it can't happen. I have no more time, Sarah. This is yours, it is very clean, and it will work."

Rosine stood, finished with her mission. Whether Sarah would heed her advice or not was no longer her concern.

"I am not like you," said Sarah. "I am not like my mother. Prince Henri does not expect anything from me other than the love that I already give him and gladly. Take this disgusting thing and leave me in peace." She could barely bring herself to pick up the sponge from the divan. She let go of it a moment too soon, and it missed Rosine's heavily ringed hand and dropped to the floor.

"I suppose, like your mother, you insist on having a bastard to call your own," said Rosine. She didn't stop to retrieve what Sarah had dropped. An abortion Rosine had suffered at nineteen had made it impossible for her to have children, though she hardly envied Julie her three daughters. "A bastard just like yourself," said Rosine and left.

Sarah picked up the sponge and hurried with it to the kitchen, where she buried it in a mess of scraps. Then she ran downstairs and outside, where the gray sky was letting in a tantalizing line of sunlight. Rosine's carriage was already gone and with it, all fleshly affairs. Sarah took a deep breath, closed her eyes, and remembered her dreams: He loved her, he respected her, he would never expose her to dishonor.

But she had only to open her eyes to see that they were not two lovers separated from happiness by the prejudices of an aristocratic family. She had only to remember his words, his actions, the look on his face to see how right her aunt was.

Though the young Prince Henri de Luyen had found Sarah awaiting him the second time he called on her, he did not get to his knees and explain that only a magical spell had kept him from seeing or writing her in three years. And though he had been calling on her every day since, there was nothing about his well-dressed figure that suggested the enervation of the obsessed lover.

At first he took her about town like the Belgian visitor he was. They visited the Tuileries, the Panthéon, and would have gone so far as to trek through the famous sewers of Paris if Sarah, disdaining to be a complete tourist in her own city, had not finally put her foot down. Instead, they climbed to the top of the Arc de Triomphe, where Sarah took the ivory comb out of her hair to let it blow wildly in the wind.

Then Sarah saw him looking away from the sight of the roofs of Paris. He stared at her, his twenty-two-year-old sophistication suddenly inadequate for the passions she had stirred in him. The wind was so strong that he had to shout the words:

"You have beautiful hair, Sarah," said the prince.

This was wonderful to hear, but it was not a proposal of marriage. Indeed, the gentle compliment prompted in her a sudden sense of the immense emotional distance that he must cross before wanting to fight the world to make her his wife. Sarah turned away from him. Neither had spoken a word of love. She could demand from him neither fidelity nor commitment. She could reveal nothing of her love, for the prince had exhibited nothing of his. Hurrying down the steps from the top of the great arch, he stopped her, squeezing her arm with great force. Sarah faced him, the wind howling down the stairs. At that moment he reached down from his higher step and gathered a great mass of her red-blond hair into his hands.

"Why do you do that?" asked Sarah.

"Forgive me," said the prince. "The wind was blowing hair into your eyes." She didn't move as he brushed her hair back from her forehead with his fingers spread wide.

"Thank you," said Sarah, though there was no reason for him to do her this service; through his touch he had revealed nothing of love, only desire.

"I must tell you," said the prince, "that is not the reason. I wanted to feel your hair in my hands. I'm sorry. But I must always tell you what is in my heart."

She did not answer. His phrase was like a great expanse of the thinnest glass, exposed at every point to the possibility of fracture. Either he did not know what was in his heart, or he was prevaricating. What was true was that his touch thrilled Sarah. What was true was that he wanted her. But she knew from her mother's life that desire was quickly spent, that the prince must want more from her than the freedom of her body before she could believe it was possible he would give her what she wanted: his hand, his name, his life forever.

Indeed, had her mother been home, instead of waiting for the Duke of Morny to sneak away from the court at Saint-Cloud to visit her bedroom, she would have told Sarah at once what the prince was: a dilettante, a ne'er-do-well, a rich young rogue. Sending Rosine to talk about contraceptive sponges did not have the same effect.

There was no one better equipped than herself to know what the prince was, but she refused to believe the evidence he spread out before her, a detailed map of useless accomplishments. He was made for carnal pleasures, for superficial feelings, for friendships as friable as ancient clay.

He had traveled in Greece and Italy, remembering nothing of those places other than the balls he had attended. Sent to London to study English, after twelve months of student life he could barely ask for a glass of water in that language. Spain was a current preoccupation. He had heard that Madrid was the capital of romance and intrigue. And because, as the prince frequently explained to Sarah, he had been born too late to enjoy the romance and intrigue of Napoleon's time, he needed to search for its remnants in the modern world.

He had never been a soldier, though he was tall and broad-shouldered. A music lover, he could play no instrument. Possessing a connoisseur's eye for fine paintings and sculpture, he had never tried his hand at painting or sculpting. Most of all he loved the art of acting, though he could not, because of his family, even dream about a career on the stage. In those first weeks, Sarah often thought that he was selecting her, an actress for his budding collection, the way his father might buy an oil painting or a marble bust.

The truth was, thought Sarah, that Rosine hadn't had to tell her a thing about his motives. Prince Henri had made it clear enough. Nowhere today could one be a glorious soldier fighting for honor; instead, he would fight another battle. He would find romance and intrigue in sweeping her off her feet.

Now Sarah went back inside her mother's house, found a copy of her playscript, and waited for Bella to announce his arrival. She would be grim, she would be demanding, she would put him to the test the moment that he arrived. He must tell her that his intentions were honorable.

This was not the first time she had steeled herself for his presence. Yet it was difficult to be grim when he arrived at her door with two footmen bearing six dozen roses. It was impossible to call him to task when he brought her a gift of stationery engraved with what she had told him was her motto —"In Spite of Everything"— enclosed in a shield at the top of every sheet. Even when she was convinced of his selfishness, knew that his gifts came from money that he had never earned and that his attentions were simply boyish measures of seduction, everything went to her head. She slept with his roses all about her bed, she kept a sheet of the stationery under her pillow.

"Prince Henri de Luyen, Mademoiselle," said Bella, enjoying the grandeur of the name as much as Sarah. Even after two weeks, even after Rosine's visit, it was not possible to keep the ecstasy from Sarah's face.

"How very good of you to take the time to see me," said Prince

Henri, removing his straw hat and performing a little bow. Today his politeness was not enchanting. She was confused by her love, eager for joy, and she was furious at the prospect that joy might be denied her. In his hurried attempt to kiss her hand, she discovered a possible insult. What would Julie think, or Rosine? Perhaps too much courtesy was more than a mockery of her great love. She was so unsure of his feelings that suddenly every compliment contained the possibility of sarcasm or, worse, condescension.

"Do not make fun of me," said Sarah.

"I do not make fun," he said. "I know that you are busy. That you must have time to study your play."

"I will always have time for you, Henri." Looking at him in his white flannel suit, his dandy's red cravat, his patent-leather side-buttoned shoes, she didn't know whether to strike him or jump into his arms. "You know perfectly well that I want you never to stop calling on me," she said sharply.

"Then come away with me, Sarah," he said. "Come away with me to Spain."

"And you know that I do not like it when you say things like that," said Sarah.

"So many things that I know," said Prince Henri de Luyen, taking her hand and briefly pressing it to his warm lips.

"I only want you to say what you mean," she said.

"I mean it, Sarah," said Henri. "You have only to agree and we can set off immediately." Sarah pulled her hand from his grasp with no great gentleness.

"Shall we go into the drawing room?" she asked.

"You look thinner," said the prince, stepping closely behind her, so close that his breath blew against the nape of her neck. "I shall have to feed you ices and ice cream at Tortoni's. I shall have to watch you swallow every drop."

She took him into the small drawing room, trying to still the fear shaking inside her. "It's very simple, really," said the prince, standing next to where she sat on the small divan. "We go to Marseilles, and book passage on a wonderful boat, very clean and safe and comfortable. You must always have beautiful memories of your first sea voyage, because a great actress like you will surely one day tour the world."

"Please sit down, Henri," said Sarah. A pounding rose from her heart into the back of her head. He stood over her like a giant, pulling at his cravat as if they were already in the blinding white heat of Spain.

"How can I sit when I am declaiming, Mademoiselle Bernhardt?" he asked, going away from her rapidly, his arms extended, like a tragedian onstage. When he turned about, his blue eyes were wild with desire. "From Marseilles we sail to Alicante, where the fishermen will sing to us. Our boat will be too big for the little dock. We will anchor at the entrance to the crowded harbor, and to get to shore we will have to walk across wide planks, extending from one boat to the next, all the way to dry land. The fishermen will watch, amazed at your red hair, at our servants hurrying after us, trying not to drop our bags into the sea. We will drink the local wine and watch the sun set over the Atlantic Ocean. Then it will be night. It will grow cool, and through the windows we will hear the sea."

The prince came closer, and got down on one knee before her. She felt his nearness to her legs, to her thighs, separated by only a single petticoat, and by a skirt of the thinnest taffeta. It was absurd what he was saying, impossible, but her body grew weak from desire. Rosine had asked if he touched her all over, and she had not answered her, had not told her how much she hungered for him. "From Alicante," he said, "we go to Madrid, where everyone will know at once of our love. Every day we shall see bullfights, and every night there will be another ball. It never rains, and the sky is blue and green and gold, and we shall hire magnificent horses and drive about like the king and queen."

She could barely talk, she could barely look at him half-kneeling before her. Rosine was right. A prince never married for love. And this particular prince might not feel love even at this moment of fabricated passion at her feet. Sarah said: "What love?"

"What?" said the prince, with the petulance of an amateur actor unhappy with paltry applause. He stood up and came close, so that she had to raise her head to look into his beautiful eyes.

"Do not speak of love, if you only do so to torment me." Her love made her angry, and she stood up, too, forcing him to step back. "Please," she said, pointing imperiously to the square formal armchair across the room. Henri sat down, and Sarah returned to the divan.

"Why do you speak of torment?" asked the prince mildly.

Sarah snapped back at him. "They will not know of our love in Madrid," she said, "until I know of it here in Paris."

"I do not understand why you are angry."

"Because you are not serious."

"I am completely serious, my dear Sarah," said the prince, pretending that he had abruptly discovered what troubled the young woman. Certainly he would make it right: "I am not trifling with you when I speak of my love."

"Why drive about in Spain like the king and queen," said Sarah, "when we can stay here and drive about like the prince and princess?"

"I am already a prince, my dear Sarah, so I am afraid that your joke is a bit lost on me," he said. But the sudden coldness in his eyes made it clear that nothing was lost on him. Usually, when Sarah spoke he didn't seem to listen with any great care; he was more intent on staring at her, looking for an opportunity to take hold of her hand, either to put into the crook of his arm while walking or bring to his lips to say hello or good-bye. This time he had heard every word. She wanted more than pretty words of assurance, more than flowers and ice cream. For a moment his anger broke the forward rush of his desire. What had he been doing for two weeks if not giving her everything within his power that she could want? Now it was time for her to give him what he wanted.

"Please don't look at me like that," said Sarah. "I do not deserve your anger for speaking the truth."

"I can't bear it when you are so unfair to me," said the prince. He could not take Sarah back to his family's little Paris apartment, with servants incapable of keeping a secret for more than a day at a time. And Sarah's mother would not remain in Saint-Cloud forever. "You know that I myself care nothing for social distinctions. Yet I am forced to fulfill certain duties to my family. If because of this you do not wish to associate with me, I will understand, even if it will break my heart."

"It won't break your heart, Henri," said Sarah. "Nothing could break your heart."

"That is a fine way to answer a compliment. If you do not want me here, you need only ask me to leave."

Sarah would have liked to shout that it was no compliment for him to invent what he didn't feel. Those words did not come, for she wanted desperately not to believe them. Instead, she told him the truth, the only truth that mattered: "I can't ask you to leave!"

She remembered what her mother, vastly experienced with princes, had warned her after Sarah first met him at the Théâtre Français: He is very handsome and very young, and Sarah must therefore not believe a word that he tells her. Julie had warned her further: not to let him touch her, not to let him kiss her. But how could Sarah prevent this? Rosine, if she knew nothing else, knew very well that she could not resist a mutual urging. Sarah's body ached for his touch. Every time he brought his lips to her hand, she wanted to pull his face to hers and kiss him with the full passion of her heart.

Imagining that he had earned the right to stand again, he got up from the armchair and crossed to where she sat, her elbows pressed against her thin frame, her eyes looking at the carpeted floor.

"I don't want you to leave," whispered Sarah. "I never want you to leave."

"Then you must please be a little nicer, Sarah," said the prince. "You must not act like I am a monster because I want to touch your hand." He could see the defeat in her love-struck face. "You must not accuse me of heartlessness because I want to take the young woman I love to Spain."

"You still say it," whispered Sarah. They both understood that she was talking not about Spain, but about his frivolous declaration of love.

He bent over her and brushed a wild strand of hair from her warm forehead. She shut her eyes and imagined that everything he said, everything he did was nothing less than true.

He sat down next to her, and she could feel his eyes on her still profile. "The young woman I love," said Prince Henri. He took her hand, and brought it to his lips. She allowed him to do this, as she had so many times before. She knew that it was suddenly more dangerous, that the feelings this kiss prompted would not be stopped by letting go of her hand.

"May I offer you something?" she asked, desperate to regain her balance, to be able to be bold enough to think, strong enough to look steadily into his hungry eyes.

"Nothing to drink," he said, twisting his smile into something rakish.

"You may smoke if you like," said Sarah.

He moved his fingers from her hand to her wrist. "Don't think that I don't find thin young women attractive," said the prince. "I think it quite suits you, with your great pile of hair, your magic green eyes, your pale skin."

"My arms are too thin," said Sarah rapidly. She opened her eyes, and looked at his long and elegant fingers wrapped about her delicate wrist. "For the tragic roles," she added, no longer sure of what she was saying. She was terribly frightened, knowing that she was capable of giving herself to him, knowing that her hopeless prattle would last only until he shut her up with a wild embrace. "I will have to wear a tunic. As Iphigénie my arms will be bare. I am afraid someone might laugh."

She looked up at him at that moment, and shivered. She wanted him to touch her. As in the role she had not yet adequately prepared, she imagined she was like Iphigénie, daughter of Agamemnon and Clytemnestra, being led to the marriage altar. Her betrothed was the hero Achilles, handsome and noble and good. Only at the last moment did she understand that her father had tricked her and was obeying the stern decree of the gods: The altar was not for a marriage but for a sacrifice, the price that must be paid to allow her father's fleet to go off to war. But still, Iphigénie did not defy her father's order. If death was what the gods required of her, she would grant it without complaint.

"Are you all right?" asked the prince.

The desire was unmistakable in her eyes. For a moment innocence was lost in a siren's voracious pose. "Yes," she said, her lips open, her head inclined as though at the beginning of sexual ecstasy. He had only to drop her wrist and bring his lips to hers.

But the prince did not let go.

"Your arms are beautiful," he said. Suddenly his smile, his confidence, his urgency were all gone. Romantic and impulsive, he frequently talked himself into a position where he had no wish to be. The look he directed at Sarah was full of fear: that passion might lead to love, and love to obligation. She could see that he had to avert his eyes; as he had on the first night he met her, he blushed. Quickly he let go of her wrist, but instead of bringing his hands to her cheeks, he reached inside his jacket and extracted an exquisite lacquered tobacco box.

Just as she was ready to surrender herself to him, he had decided to smoke.

"Every part of you is beautiful, Sarah," he said, his voice going up half a register.

"There are many parts of me that I would be happy to improve," said Sarah.

"No. You must stay as you are. Exactly as you are." She watched him open the box and stir with an elegant finger the golden tobacco within. "I would like to tell you something, Sarah," he said, his voice returning to its normal range. "I would like to tell you something that you must believe."

"I will believe anything you tell me, Henri." She looked at him, and suddenly found a reason to imagine that her wishes might be answered after all. If he had not taken the opportunity to embrace her, it was only because he respected her virtue. If he had taken hold of the tobacco box instead of pulling her into his arms, it was to treat her with the regard due to the young woman he would marry.

"I know that you are not like other women," he said.

"What do you mean?"

"That you are special, that you are daring, that you are not like a hopeless bourgeoise." He was too busy with his tobacco to take hold of her arm, but desire was returning to his eyes.

"Thank you," she said, for he had complimented her. She stared at him frankly, fearlessly, trying to understand what he wanted from her. She was ready to accept anything, as long as he would lead her away from this terrible uncertainty, as long as he would make it plain what she must do to take firm hold of his love.

"I would like to offer you something extraordinary," said the prince. "I will make you a cigarette."

"I am sorry, that is not a polite offer," said Sarah, getting to her feet. She was absolutely dizzy. It was impossible to remain in this position, being seduced by his words and his beauty and his gestures, and then to be dashed with cold water. Suddenly to talk about cigarettes, instead of finishing their talk of love, was infuriating. Besides, she knew of only two or three women who smoked, and all belonged to her mother's circle of gaudy coutesans. Maybe he needed to insult her further before he would try to treat her the way her mother was treated by her paying admirers.

"I beg your pardon, my dear. Because you are an actress, I thought you might dare it."

"What on earth does acting have to do with that filthy habit?" said Sarah.

"Please sit down," he said. "I truly meant no harm. It's just that I have heard that George Sand smokes, and naturally, knowing what I do about your fearlessness, I thought you might want to try."

She watched as he tore off a sheet of cigarette paper from its pad and began to place tobacco on it. All his movements were sure and exact. She did not know how to interpret this comparison to the great writer who had taken a man's name, wore men's clothes, and had male and female lovers. Perhaps next he would ask her to dress up in a jacket and breeches. George Sand was not alone in dressing like a man; she had seen her own aunt Rosine in trousers. Other courtesans often appeared at costume balls in the guise of men. It was just another way of shocking, of being enticing to gentlemen by daring what no decent woman would.

Yet she could not remain angry at his request as he rolled the cigarette and licked it closed. "In spite of everything," said Prince Henri, offering it to her. "For the one who dares everything always."

Perhaps, she thought, he needed her to have a cigarette dangling from her lips to complete the portrait of her in his mind. Certainly this would be a minor addition to an entire world of imagined feats and events she had created on his behalf. She did not know why she was impelled to fabricate so much about herself to the man she loved. Already she half-believed the fabrication she had told him to justify her motto: She alone of all the girls at Mme. Fressard's school had dared to jump across a shallow creek filled with sharp rocks. Though she had fallen into the creek half a dozen times, she had tried again and again, each time declaring, "In spite of every-thing." When she finally succeeded, Sarah told the prince, the phrase was acknowledged by the other girls to belong to her and her alone.

"I knew you were special the first moment I saw you," the prince had said, and Sarah responded to the praise with other tales, from unspeakable hardships in Brittany to marks of her courage, integrity, and artistry onstage. She did not think of herself as a liar, of course, only as someone given license to embellish the truth. If she had not actually jumped across a dangerous creek when she was a child of nine, perhaps she would have, she told herself, had such a creek existed.

She knew she possessed the will of which the tales were used as examples. After all, Sarah had learned about the artifices of love and beauty in watching her mother employ stage makeup for use in her boudoir and heroic compliments for use with her flaccid admirers. It was not false of Julie to paint her beautiful face or make fantastic conversation; the essence of her character was to be more beautiful than was naturally possible, more clever than any woman had a right to be. If Sarah needed to aggrandize the character of her prince to make possible the fantasy that he would one day insist on marrying her and force his family to yield to his wishes, it was sensible to aggrandize her character in the same breath. She might as well be worthy of the dream she was creating about the two of them.

Still, nothing appealed to her less than the sight of that paper-wrapped weed. "For the one who dares everything," repeated Sarah, taking the cigarette and putting it daintily between her teeth.

"You must hold it with your lips," said the prince. "And very gently." He lit a match and brought the flame close to Sarah. "Just breathe in through the cigarette. And you mustn't cough like the beginners do. You must be better than that."

Sarah sucked on the paper tube, bringing smoke deep into her throat. The impulse to cough was immediate and wild, but she forced it down with the smoke she swallowed.

"You look absolutely ravishing," he said, placing the spent match into a dainty porcelain dish. "I doubt if George Sand did as well the first time. Wait until we go off to Spain. Wait until they see the two of us smoking in their fancy cafés." He smiled as she struggled to keep down the cough, holding the cigarette at arm's length. "Aren't you going to try another puff?"

Sarah didn't speak. She smiled over her discomfort and extended the cigarette to him.

"What do you mean?" asked the prince. "Have you had enough?"

"Yes," said Sarah through pursed lips, wisps of smoke still escaping from her tortured throat. "Share it with me."

"Delighted," said the prince at once, as if he had been dared to strike at convention. He took the cigarette, wet from Sarah's mouth, tapped a minuscule bit of ash in the dish into which he had dropped his match, and drew deeply and pleasurably on the slow-burning tobacco. "Like the Indians," he said, handing it back to her. "Like a peace pipe."

She took it again, very seriously, still refusing to give into the impulse to cough. This time she took a greater gulp of smoke, imitating the prince; handing back the cigarette, she spewed forth the smoke with even more alacrity than before.

"Thank you," he said, taking another breath; but as he did so, the cough she had been holding back finally exploded. The prince smiled at this evidence of a female frailty in which he needed to believe. Sarah continued to cough until the tears came to her eyes. With patronizing sympathy he stubbed the cigarette into the porcelain dish and took hold of her hands.

Sarah pulled her hands away, turned her back to him. She was wild with anger. She could not stop coughing, and her nose was beginning to run, and her throat felt raw, and it was all because she would do anything to please this stupid boy, this prince who was incapable of love. He had gotten to his feet, and was saying, with infinite stupidity, "Try to relax your throat. Try to breathe normally, try to allow your lungs to fill with fresh air."

She stood up and followed him. He was throwing wide open the long windows overlooking the morning traffic on the Rue St.-Honoré. Stepping out of her way, he let her cough into the golden light, let her breathe in the scent of flowers and fresh bread along with the summer's dust raised by a thousand clattering wheels below.

173

Finally the smoke was gone from her throat, and the terrible coughing ceased. She kept her back to him until she had wiped away her tears, until she had brought her wrist to her runny nose like a peasant girl, oblivious to all manners. Then she turned, the light and the breeze from the windows running through her tangled hair. "I hate you," she said.

"Sarah," he said, coming toward her tentatively. "I certainly did not mean—"

"Get out," she said.

"I can't leave you like this," he said. "Not over a silly misunderstanding." He was close enough to reach out and touch her yearning neck, exposed in her vanilla-colored taffeta frock. But he kept his hands at his side and looked at her with tenderness, with longing. She remembered with what beautiful courtesy he had taken her home from the theater the first night they had met, with what elegant manners he had treated her in the first days he had come back into her life after more than three years.

"You treat me without respect," said Sarah. She brought her hands to her pale throat, as if the spirit within her wanted to strangle any last vestige of love. Gently, the prince placed his hands over hers. Then he brought them from her throat to his lips. She shut her eyes, and allowed the kiss.

Unexpectedly she tore away from his grasp and slapped his face with great force. "I am not like that," said Sarah. "Despite what you think, I am not a whore."

The prince, red-faced and still, waited. He had no part in the decision that Sarah must make at that moment. Were she to tell him to go, he decided, he would leave at once.

Sarah made a decision of her own: Were he allowed to stay, she must yield to her love. So what if Rosine was right, that her infatuation must end in bed? Sarah's mother being a courtesan did not mean that love for a man must be denied Sarah; that her aunt Rosine sold her passion like apples from a grocer's cart did not mean that all love was false, base, founded only in lust.

"Swear that what you tell me is true," said Sarah. "Swear that when you say you love me, it is not just to get me to fall in love with you."

The prince, stung by the blow she had given him, knew he must not hesitate. No woman had ever dared slap him, yet his anger was tempered by desire. This sort of seduction was entirely new to him. The girl was not a prostitute, even if she was about to become a professional actress. That she was the daughter of a courtesan was likewise irrelevant. This was not a business, but a romance. He wanted her, and she wanted him; what was exciting was that this would be the first time he would make love to a woman without having to leave an envelope stuffed with cash.

"I swear it," said Prince Henri de Luyen, and Sarah let out a cry of pain worthy of Iphigénie discovering that she is about to be offered as a sacrifice to the gods. She shut her eyes and brought her open mouth to his, and when they kissed, the young prince felt all the restraints to his desire fall away. He brought his lips from her mouth to her neck, he pressed her waist and wrists and shoulders, he brought the heels of his hands against the taffeta covering her small breasts.

Sarah opened her eyes and saw the joy in his eyes, the flush of happiness in his cheeks. "A moment," she said, breaking away from him and walking first to the heavy doors leading to the larger drawing room, then to those leading to the anteroom. While she closed the doors, Prince Henri de Luyen pulled on a heavy chain, which brought down the exterior wooden window shutters with an enormous crash.

"Tell me," she said, sitting down once more on the little divan, scene of thousands of Julie's seductions.

"Will the servants come?"

"No."

"You are so beautiful," he said.

"Tell me that you love me," said Sarah, and he did, over and over again, saying the words, sitting next to her, removing his cravat, pulling the ivory comb from her luxuriant hair.

Chapter 12

YOU ARE A
GREAT ACTRESS

The summer of 1862 was hot. The heat added fuel to fiery uprisings against authority in Warsaw, Russia, and Greece, and contributed to the misery of the troops fighting in the American Civil War. Responding to that war, the American Richard Jordan Gatling patented a crank-operated, .58-caliber ten-barrel gun—the Gatling gun—that would change the tactics of battle for fifty years. That same summer, the Swiss humanist Jean Henri Dunant responded to war in another way, proposing the creation of an international aid society to relieve the sick and wounded in war and peace; two years later his work would lead to the formation of the Red Cross.

In Paris there was little talk of war. The rich ran off to the country, and those left behind complained about the weather, which grew particularly torrid in August. The heat and humidity added to the discomfort caused by the dust and debris of citywide demolition and construction. Baron Haussmann, architect of the emperor's reconstruction of the city, had accelerated and enlarged the scope of his master plan for Paris. Napoleon III's admiration of London's parks had encouraged Haussmann to attack the wasteland of the Bois de Boulogne, transforming the natural forest to a manicured version of paradise. The Champs Élysées, in Sarah's childhood a disgraceful strip of dull gravel through patchy grassland, was landscaped and brightened with the largest display of flowers in the city.

These were relatively modest tasks for the indefatigable Baron

Haussmann. Wide avenues were more important than flowers, for from these roadways Napoleon III would derive power: Soldiers, with rifles ready, could march in wide rows without danger of being waylaid in alleyways by pitchfork-wielding rabble. Some Parisians, fond of their revolutionary traditions, feared this new power. Others complained about the loss of so many familiar streets and buildings, even if those streets had led into dead-end mazes, and the buildings, crawling with vermin, were crumbling on antique foundations.

The vast majority, however, were pleased with the grand plan: Paris annexed its suburbs, expanding from twelve to twenty arrondissements, spiraling out from its ancient core on the Île de la Cité. These districts were filled with new squares, churches, parks, and connected by roads that even one who hadn't spent a lifetime driving a fiacre could navigate. On every corner were new excavation sites, demolished old *hôtels,* piles of brick, blocks of limestone, and mountains of earth. The frequent rain brought thick mud, which stuck to boots and petticoat hems; and when the heat baked the mud to dust, the traffic blew it into the steamy air. Still, the results were not in the distant future, but around the corner. The glorious sewer system was already open to tourists, the work being done on the Grand Opéra, the Hôtel-Dieu, the Palais de Justice was nearly complete. New roads and railways brought in one hundred thousand pilgrims a day to gape at the city's developing secular majesty. Visitors from around the world craned their necks at the blocks of apartment houses, each an astounding six stories high. Eventually the summer heat would vanish, the construction crews would go away, and the Second Empire would have a city more glorious than any in the world, a city of parks and monuments, of fresh air and wide boulevards, of gaslights and flowers.

Neither Prince Henri nor Sarah worried about the weather or the dust. For them the city was already perfect, glowing and glamorous at night, fragrant and free during the day. They were young, infatuated, emancipated. The twenty-two-year-old prince had extended his stay in Paris and had the use of the empty family apartment.

All he and Sarah could think about was making love.

Sarah's mother remained sulking near Saint-Cloud, receiving the Duke of Morny with a pout that, had she been a better actress, might have been tragic.

The duke was not fooled, and Julie was not as sad as she pretended. For one thing, Sarah's half sister Jeanne, now an ivory-skinned, dimple-cheeked beauty of ten years, trailed her mother about the rented villa's garden, picking flowers and strawberries, and providing her with uncritical, adulatory companionship. And she had other company, men who expressed their appreciation for the largesse of Julie's loving in businesslike fashion. More than the gifts of one admirer had been required for Julie to purchase the entire apartment building in which her richly furnished Paris residence was situated. Before leaving the city, Julie had decided not to take along her scrawny, least pretty child, Regina. Mme. Guérard, now a tenant as well as a friend, was supervising the child in her own flat until September. Always mindful of justice, Julie insisted on not collecting any rent from the little widow while Regina was in her care. She didn't bother to tell her to keep an eye on Sarah. Mme. Guérard, loving Sarah like a daughter, would do that in any case.

So Julie, unhappy at being neglected by the duke, was happy in the company of Jeanne and without the annoying presence of her less favored daughters.

Bella had joined Julie at Saint-Cloud, lingering in Paris just long enough to finish household chores and spy on the beginnings of Sarah's romance with Prince Henri. Only Julie's cook, Titine, remained to look after Sarah in the mostly shut-up rooms in the house on Rue St.-Honoré. Her mother's other servants made themselves scarce, simply taking care to feed the horses and sweep the outer hallways in case Mme. Bernhardt made a surprise return.

Aunt Rosine, after the single visit demanded of her by Julie, successfully put her niece out of her mind. Mme. Guérard, looking after Regina in her small upstairs apartment, kept herself from intruding on Sarah's privacy with a hundred questions. The little widow knew that Sarah was hopelessly in love, and hoped that she slept alone in her own bed every night. Mme. Guérard believed she was fulfilling her duty by offering the young actress a place to have tea every evening and a shoulder to cry on at any time of the day or night.

Thus far, Sarah had nothing to cry about.

The prince waited for her in a landau outside the Théâtre Français after every rehearsal, and always made a great show of getting up from his seat and helping her inside. Theirs, he believed, was not a clandestine romance. Let the theater doorman, let her fellow actors, let the leering stagehands have a good look at the cut of his clothes, at the family crest on the side of his carriage; Prince Henri de Luyen did not care who knew that he was in love with Sarah Bernhardt.

This was not a very daring sentiment: During the summer nobody the prince knew was in Paris.

The court had gone to Fontainebleau, and the prince's family had scattered from Brussels to various summer homes at the shore, in the wine country, in the mountains.

"How were rehearsals today?" he asked, five weeks after the beginning of their affair. She didn't answer except to squeeze the hand he offered her to step up into the carriage and, once inside, to bring that hand against her heart. Sarah had never had the freedom to explore such a masculine hand, had never had the chance to trace the path of golden hairs reaching from the wrist to an inch above the knuckles. He had long thin fingers, as tapered and fine as the composer Rossini's; when she saw them resting on the silver handle of his walking stick, she felt an intense pride of possession. Because those long fingers had caressed her skin, they must belong to her forever.

"You've come to take me away," said Sarah.

"Go!" he said to the liveried driver, and as they lurched forward, he looked into her hungry green eyes, moved by how very much she wanted him. He brought his hand out of her grasp and placed it against the soft fabric of her summer dress, enjoying the soft curve of her breasts, the hard edge of the corset, the sweet scent of the Eau d'Ange she had rubbed along her neck. Sarah shut her eyes, thrilled by the sweet beginnings of an ecstasy lusted for all day.

"You're my prince," she said finally.

"And you are my actress," he said, answering her fantasy with one of his own. What he thought would end after he took her on the divan in her mother's home had proven to be the beginning of

179

an obsession without end. They were lovers, and the passion that ran between them overwhelmed all his puerile plans. He did not understand how he had allowed this, his first affair of the heart, to get so out of control. No influence, no power could stop his coming to pick her up at the theater. He could not bear to spend an entire day without her, he could not imagine a time when he would no longer be able to make love to her.

"It was terrible today," said Sarah. Already her hands were on his chest, tearing past the fresh linen of his shirt, rubbing into the soft cotton lisle undershirt that covered his hot, damp flesh. They kissed, teeth and lips savage with hunger, their tongues wild, insistent, her knee behind her skirt, behind the steel hoops of her crinoline, behind embroidered drawers, behind silk stockings, moving up and against his narrow trousered legs, until he spread those legs wide, letting her knee bend into his groin, against his swollen sex.

"It was terrible today," repeated Sarah. "I missed you every minute. Did you miss me?"

"What do you think?"

"Tell me," said Sarah, biting so heedlessly, so urgently into his lip that she drew blood.

Prince Henri made no protest. The blood was a mark of passion, and tasting it he was pleased. She could do with him what she liked. She was wild because she was an artist, and he loved her because of it; to love someone who was reckless, who was an actress at the Comédie Française, who was the daughter of a famous courtesan, all reflected on himself. He was not just the son of an ancient family, born into staid respectability and landed wealth; he was romantic, lustful, passionate. He was brave enough to ignore convention. Through passion the prince had fallen in love, and through passion he took the measure of his own worth.

"I missed you," he said, his eyes looking past her beautiful hair at the silent driver, at the sober streets of the Ninth Arrondissement, where all the aristocratic town houses seemed to have had their shutters down for a century or more. Within those carefully preserved relics was no furniture built later than the Revolution, no love but of King and Church, no desire other than to exclude anyone and anything that was not a part of a lifeless circle.

"Tell me that you love me," she demanded, and he had a brief, crazy fantasy of the young wild-haired actress coming into his parents' drawing room in their mansion in Brussels.

"I love you," he said, and the vision of his father's furious eyes, his mother's incredulous face, faded as Sarah placed her girlish hand on his swollen penis, straining against his trousers. All he could see was Sarah's glorious head, held high and framed by red-gold hair, her powerful eyes taking fearless delight in everything before her. His parents would not have to be told who her mother was, what manner of appetite Sarah had inherited from the famous courtesan. Nothing could be more obvious than that she and their son were lovers, that they could not keep their hands from each other, that they had no desire to fulfill the sickening moral restraints of his class.

"You're so big," she said. "So big and so wet." It didn't matter to her if she acted like a courtesan, if she sounded like a whore. She had stopped worrying about what part she was playing with her real-life prince. When she touched his penis, it was not because she was her mother's child, forced to follow in her shameful footsteps. No poverty, no longing for a master who would provide for her every need fired her lust. Sarah was not a ruined convent girl or a scheming adventuress. She could feel the delicious wetness in her private parts, she could smell the rising scent of her womanly fluids only because she loved this man. She did not care how this made her look in the eyes of the world. All she cared for was the chance to love him, to keep loving him. She could taste his mounting ecstasy in the sweat running under his handsome jaw, and she wanted his ecstasy as much as she wanted hers. Since the commencement of their affair, he had been growing a manly imperial, the fashionable little beard covering lower lip and chin in the manner of the present emperor of France; she clasped the entire area of blond stubble in her strong right hand, pressing the fledgling beard roughly into his boyish face.

"Tell me again," she said.

"I love you," he said, removing her hand from his beard and placing it sideways into his open mouth. "I love you," he repeated, not questioning the words, but only the madness of the situation. He wanted to eat and drink her, he wanted to swallow up her hand, and then her breasts, and then the soft inner part of her thighs. He wanted to devour her, so that she would be his forever, and so that she would no longer exist on her own, a constant threat to everything in his future.

"Tell me what you always tell me," said Sarah.

"I love you more than a kingdom," he said, smiling. "I love you more than great riches. I love you more than life."

"Why does he drive so slowly?" asked Sarah. "After all this time doesn't he know what a hurry we're in?"

"There is traffic, my darling," said the prince with a logic entirely too calm for her ardor. Sarah brought her hot forehead against his and ran her tongue along his shut eyes. "My God," he said.

"We must get there," she said. "At once."

"Drive faster, you idiot!" shouted the prince.

The prince had long since decided not to worry about the servants in the apartment his family kept in this respectable quarter of Paris. The responsibility of finding a bed for the two of them must be his. He would never again risk letting Sarah be embarrassed in front of her mother's servants. It was different, after all, for a man. In his parents' apartment, the servants were his to command. No one dared disturb them once he had ordered them to stay away.

"Now try and behave like a gentleman," said Sarah as the landau pulled into the courtyard behind the apartment house. But she made this difficult for him by pulling him back into her arms as he attempted to jump down from his seat in the slowing carriage. "Try to pretend you've just invited your ancient aunt for an afternoon cup of tea."

"No one in my family has red hair," said the prince.

"Then we shall have to risk the scandal," said Sarah, jumping down before he did, pretending to assist him from his high seat.

Like Julie's, the apartment was one flight up. They ran, hand in hand, laughing like schoolchildren. The prince used his key to get inside, though a liveried servant stood at stone-faced attention next to the entrance. Sarah had long since grown immune to the sight of the dark lofty rooms, wooden shutters over huge windows keeping the sun from ancient oils, hideous old velvet-covered furniture, and tapestries that must have blinded a hundred needleworkers half a millennium ago. Despite the bright afternoon, a single lamp covered with a greenish lace lampshade burned over the mantelpiece so that the servants wouldn't bang into each other in the dark. Prince Henri threw the footman his silver-headed walking stick and his straw hat, without saying a word. The servants understood their orders. Once the prince returned at fifteen minutes past five o'clock, they must not stare at his mistress, they must not speak.

Arriving at the open door to his bedroom, he picked her up in his arms, as he did every time, and carried her across the threshold like a bride.

But Sarah no longer mentioned marriage, nor did she grow angry when he spun fantasies about taking her to Spain. It was enough, more than enough, for her to believe in the fact of his love.

"I'm so hot," he said, carrying her to the First Empire mahogany bed.

"Perhaps you shouldn't be carrying around so much weight," said Sarah as he deposited her gracefully on the dear, familiar mattress. "Besides, I think you're dressed too warmly for the weather. I think you had better get out of some of those clothes."

"Even in darkest Africa, a gentleman never removes his jacket," said the prince, helping her take off her high-heeled shoes while she extracted the pins from the tiny porkpie straw hat that sat on the piled-high twists and curls of her voluptuous hair.

She had lost any modesty around her lover the first day he had made love to her. When they were naked in each other's arms, the ground hadn't split open to send them both to damnation. She had felt no guilt or remorse or pain. When she was younger, her mother had sometimes permitted Sarah to watch Bella dress her. The child had been fascinated by the sensuous curves of her mother's body, by the dark blond hair under her arms and the reddish-blond hair that lay in a mysterious triangle over her private parts. She had relished the way Julie accepted the ministrations of her maid, completely at rest with her revealed body. This was not because her mother was a courtesan, thought Sarah, but because Julie enjoyed her physical self.

Sarah discovered the same enjoyment.

Nothing was more natural, more wonderful than to be with the prince, out of one's clothes and away from the heat and the dust of the street, removed from the petty excitations of the rehearsal to the true excitement of lovemaking.

When Sarah studied the prince's body with the tips of her fingers, drawing a line from nipple to nipple across his manly chest, following his breastbone to his navel to his waist; when she felt the skin of his neck with her gentle tongue; when she buried her nose and her forehead into the small of his back, or stroked the flat of her hands against the inside of his thighs, or moved her pelvis against his, feeling the unique sensation of pubic hair scratching against pubic hair, all her senses were filled with bliss.

There could be no possibility of sin when there was this much rapture.

Sarah had learned the contours of a man's body, she had begun to understand the limitless pleasures a man and a woman could draw from each other's flesh. What the Church said about carnal sin, what her mother said about untrustworthy men, what her own fears warned her about the obligations a prince would have to his ancient family were all ignored. She believed there was no pretense between them, no lies, no expectations other than that this ecstatic madness would continue forever; all that mattered to each of them was the fact of their love, their desire.

If the prince's servants had been instructed to be silent and out of the way, they still managed to prepare the master's bedroom for this afternoon ritual: A gentle light penetrated the room's open, lace-curtained windows; the bed was turned down, as it was every day at this time. These were preparations made for their tryst; just as the fresh flowers in three Chinese vases, the sponge sitting in Eau d'Ange in a gold scent box on his commode, the chilled champagne and two glasses in a silver bowl filled with melting ice were more than afternoon necessities for a young man's repose. They were explicit accessories for his lovemaking.

There was no shame in this.

She didn't care if servants knew she was the mistress of Prince Henri. She didn't wonder if Marie Lloyd—like herself, a new *pensionnaire* at the Français—thought she was stupid to throw away her innocence on a man who would never marry her. She didn't worry about what her mother would say about her first lover, a rich aristocrat who gave her no jewels, cash or gold.

Sarah was here to make love, the purpose for which the prince had brought her to his mansion. This did not make her a slut or a trollop or a whore. How could their lovemaking cheapen her, she wondered, when it was nothing but exalting? If all it took was one "fall" to ruin a woman, why was each time they made love more poignant, more delicious than the time before? If it was wrong, why did she dream of it all day, why did the anticipation of it make her weak with joy?

Indeed, the enchantment of her love contrasted bitterly with her introduction to the world of the Comédie Française. No one had welcomed her to her first rehearsal. She had barely been able to locate a boy to show her to the dirty dressing room she had to share with three other *pensionnaires*. Clearly, few expected all the novitiates to be well received, and none expected them all to remain in their august company. The experienced cast was bored with the rehearsals, content to drone out Racine's poetry as though it were little more than a laundry list; they had all done *Iphigénie* before, and none of them, unlike Prince Henri, were in love with the debuting actress. The famous actors snubbed her, the stage manager restricted his suggestions to telling her how the great Rachel had raised her arms to the galleries in the same role. It was no wonder that the declaration of the prince's love had become more important than a silly play, and sexual ecstasy more satisfying than the vague promise of applause.

"If only you weren't an actress," said Prince Henri suddenly. "Think of all the time we would have. All the time in the world."

"I have all the time in the world, darling," said Sarah, wondering whether this comment was any more than a gallantry. She could not tell what part his attraction to her was based on the fact that she was an actress, not like other girls, but an artist who dared to face the crowd with her talent. Conversely, she did not know how deeply ran his aversion to her being on the stage at all, his lover becoming a part of the dreams of every man in the audience. "If you ever want me any more than you have me, you need only ask."

"I would never ask you to give up a rehearsal," said the prince.

"If you did, I would," said Sarah.

"But you must not," said the prince, suddenly adamant. "You have a great talent. You don't think Rachel would have quit rehearsing only to be with one of her lovers."

"I don't have more than one lover," snapped Sarah.

"That is not the point," said the prince, "You have an obligation to your art."

"I have a greater obligation to what I feel about you," said Sarah.

"No," said the prince. "I don't believe that. No great actress feels that way, and I wouldn't want you to feel that way either. Prince Napoleon would never have compromised Rachel's talent—"

Sarah interrupted sharply: "I don't want to talk about my talent. I don't want to do anything more or less than what we were about to do half a minute ago. And above all, I don't want to be compared to Rachel."

Every day at the theater, on the way to her fourth-floor dressing room, she had to pass Gérôme's famous portrait of that great actress; every time she tried to inject some excitement into the tedium of the *Iphigénie* rehearsals, one or another company member would ask sarcastically whether she imagined herself taking Rachel's place. Sarah loved the childhood memory she had of the tragedienne, but she was tired of hearing her name as a universal symbol of excellence. No one could imagine a healthy young girl to be as talented as their dear, departed icon. Even to mention Sarah Bernhardt in the same breath as Rachel was dangerous; in a comparison Sarah would always be found lacking.

"We must discuss this, darling," said the prince. "I won't have you so upset."

"I will not be upset if we stop talking about it at once." She wanted his hands on her body, and though she was angry, she continued to hurry out of her clothes. She was determined not to let the prince's silly talk about the theater threaten the beauty of the late afternoon. "Talk about anything else. Talk about Spain if you like."

The prince hesitated for a moment. He could not explain to her what he barely understood himself: That as glamorous as their affair already was, it would burn a thousand times brighter if his mistress was not just a *pensionnaire,* but a true star of the Comédie

Française. If Sarah was as famous as Rachel, his glory would be limitless. Even his father, discovering the fact of the liaison, would have to give pause and wonder, despite his piety, what it must be like to be with a woman who lived without moral bounds and, because of her great fame, without real moral censure. Rachel, lover of princes, had been beloved by the entire French-speaking world. Sarah must not give up her dream to be a great actress. The prince wanted it for himself as much as he did for her.

Yet he did not want to anger her. He knew he loved her, he wanted her, and when the time was right, he could bend her to his will.

As Sarah began to work on the first of a score of buttons, the prince was just as quick. The fact that they were in love did not lessen the travail of disrobing. He tore off his cravat, his sack coat, his white summer waistcoat, and sat down on the edge of the bed to unlace his newly fashionable patent-leather shoes.

"In Spain I will keep you naked all the time," said the prince.

"And you will supply slaves to fan me?"

"And ice buckets, and cold champagne," he said, dropping his shoes to the floor. "And Russian game birds in wicker baskets. We will visit the Alhambra, and we will ride white Arab horses along the shore."

"I think the biggest advantage of running off to Spain," said Sarah, trying to forgive him his outburst about Rachel, "is that we could have servants to help undress us."

"Not at the same time, my dear," said the prince, tearing off his starched shirt cuffs and collar. "I'm still a little too properly brought up for that."

Sarah, nearly out of breath with the exertion of unbuttoning her cone-shaped dress from the top of her neck to well past her waist, said: "The Greeks had the right idea. Tunics. You're practically naked all the time."

"Don't remind me," said the prince, confusing her once again. "I am not looking forward to sharing the shape of your arms and legs with every man-about-town on the first of September."

"They will be too appalled at my acting to notice a thing about how I look," she said.

"You must not say anything bad about your acting," said the

prince sharply. "You will be a great actress, but only if you are the first one to believe it."

Sarah stopped undressing, feeling a sense of dread at the outer reaches of her joy, some poisonous substance vitiating the purity of their love. "Then why," she said with great care, "do you say that you are not looking forward to sharing me with the audience?"

"That is entirely different," said the prince abruptly, as loath to discuss the issue as she. "There were many duels fought over Rachel, fought because men did not properly respect her. I will fight any man who dares not treat you with the proper dignity."

"I don't understand, Henri. On the one hand you want me to be on that stage, on the other hand you do not."

"There is nothing to understand, other than you must do what you were born to, my darling." His beautiful hands stroked her face. "Naturally when you are onstage, I shall be jealous of the men who stare at you. But just as naturally I want you to have the glory that is yours by right of your talent. I am very proud of you."

"I have not done anything."

"You are at seventeen a member of the Comédie Française."

"I will be eighteen in October, and nobody knows my name. Your Rachel was famous at sixteen."

"She is your Rachel too," said the prince. "More yours than mine."

"What is that supposed to mean?"

The prince had stopped stroking her face. He did not like being challenged at the very center of everything that he held dear: "That you were born to fill her place on the French stage."

"That is ridiculous," said Sarah, feeling the passion drain away from her heart. "I was not born to be anyone but myself."

"Sarah, the reason that I love you is that I am so proud of you," said the prince. "Like Rachel, you are a tragedienne, like Rachel, you were born into the Jewish faith—"

"I was baptized into the Catholic faith, Henri," said Sarah. "And I have never won any prizes for tragedy, and regardless of your pride, the fact remains that I am only a *pensionnaire*."

"I am very proud of you," insisted the prince. "You have told me what you have dreamed, and naturally I share those dreams. You will bring the world to your feet."

"Come on and help me," said Sarah with flat tones, dismissing the conversation. She raised her arms, and he jumped off the bed, his two red silk socks in his hand. Now she needed every bit of self-control even to remain in this room; she did not know if she would be able to make love at all today. She watched his face in the cheval glass, trying not to hate him. Very carefully he helped pull her dress over her head, and just as carefully placed its nearly five yards of material over an adjacent chair. Yes, her dreams were grandiose, and she had once imagined herself so famous that her picture would be on posters in every capital in Europe, that before she said her first speech the entire audience would be already overcome with love.

She did not, however, want his love for her to be based on those dreams. She wanted it to exist without prerequisites, without conditions. If she were to quit the Français tomorrow, she wanted to believe that nothing of his love would be changed, nothing would be diminished.

"You must love me, Henri," she whispered. "No matter what."

"No matter what," he agreed, nearly crushing her corset with his rush to bring her against his chest. Clearly he wanted to gloss over the sentiments he had just revealed, he wanted to manufacture a passion even if it could no longer exist on its own.

"Whether or not I am ever famous," said Sarah.

"Of course," said the prince, pulling back the hair from her eyes. "I will love you no matter what. Even if you become addicted to absinthe and opium. Even if you become a spy for Prussia. Even if you are forced to make a command performance before the Queen of England, I will still love you."

"Don't say that," said Sarah, becoming angry again. She had told him of the glory the twenty-year-old Rachel had won for the French stage by appearing, with astonishing success, before Queen Victoria. "I think that you will not love me unless I become a great actress."

"But Sarah, this is silly. You are a great actress."

"Stop it."

"You are just a bit worried about your debut performance."

"I am not worried about any performance. I am only worried about you." Sarah crossed the room, very upset, and pulled a rose from the smallest of the Chinese vases. She remembered a time, years ago, when she had smashed a Chinese vase, one of her mother's favorites. It had been filled with bright lilies, and she had hurled it to the floor, breaking it quite deliberately, wanting to destroy something that was loved by her mother.

"There is nothing to worry about," said the prince. "I am not going to be onstage."

"That is not what I mean," said Sarah, tearing away the rose petals and letting them drop to the carpeted floor. For a moment she wondered if there was any truth at all to what the prince said: that her debut worried her. The memory of the *trac* was still fresh; and stepping out onto the Français's stage during her first rehearsal, she had scanned with trepidation the absent audience's seats. In the spill of poor stage light—an otherworldly mixture of daylight from high backstage windows filtered through battens and partly hung drops, and gas work lights from which the actors could consult their lines—the dark house had seemed populated by monstrous forms. "I mean that I worry about whether you love me."

"You are such an actress," he laughed. "Look at you, dropping rose petals, arching your beautiful neck, talking of love in that amazing voice."

"I want you to love me," said Sarah.

"That is a wish that I may just be able to fulfill," said the prince, trying to joke away the madness in her eyes. "In Spain we will each have separate rooms. Separate servants, who wait to strip us the moment we walk in. Two minutes later, we eject the servants, and we open the connecting door." He smiled broadly at his wit, and then shook his head to indicate sadness at her lack of response. "I love you, Sarah," he said, the words as cold and dead as a fish on ice in the market square.

"Please stop joking," said Sarah. As she said these words, she knew she was pleading for far more than he was capable of giving her.

"Only if you take off your clothes," said the prince, oblivious of the change in her mood. She watched while he pulled off his shirt and undershirt, and then stretched flat on the bed to remove his trousers. For the first time, despite his youth and his beauty, he looked ridiculous to her in his long white underpants.

"All right," said Sarah, trying to understand how a love so overwhelming could die with such speed. He watched her critically as she removed her small cagelike crinoline, which gave her dress its conical shape. The crinoline's steel hoops began at her knees and ran as far as the long dress's hem, unlike the ones in fashion a few years before, which had extended all the way from the waist. "I will take off my clothes."

"I don't want you to take off anything if you're going to have a long face."

Sarah understood: He wanted her naked, and he wanted her smiling, and he wanted her to be a great actress. He had a fantasy, and she must fulfill it for him.

Sarah removed her petticoat, sensing that every moment took her one definite step farther from her love for him. The girls who shared her dressing room thought her insufficiently dressed because she did not use additional petticoats to build up her shape. She watched him stare at her in the embroidered drawers, her stiff corset, her gray silk stockings. The desire in his eyes had always pleased her, but unexpectedly she saw the desire as something less than an expression of love. She could see herself through his eyes as a sexual plaything, a young girl of questionable parentage, in a profession that bred promiscuity, that promised tawdry adventures. He took pleasure in the sight of her thin body in its elegant lingerie because he imagined that the strength of his will had brought her to this place, this position. Henri's smile was more arrogant than loving, she thought. He believed that he had fashioned her into his mistress, and that the creation was less worthy than its creator.

"All right then," said Sarah. "I will change my face." She lifted her serious lips, and narrowed her green eyes.

"You still don't look happy," said the prince. "You have to be happy. The way you are always happy with me."

"The point of all these petticoats and steel hoops and whalebone is to make my outer shape," said Sarah, turning her back so he could unhook her corset while she detached her stockings from their garters, "as much unlike my skinny naked shape as possible." He finished the unhooking, and Sarah removed the corset and turned to face him, her breasts at the level of his mouth. "But this is my real shape, Henri."

He had no comprehension of her words. "I like your real shape," he said. Before he could claim her naked skin, she stepped away from him.

"I am not Rachel," said Sarah.

"Of course you're not."

"I want my love for you to be the greatest thing in my life, not my love for the stage."

For a moment it seemed he would disagree, but then his impatience with argument changed his mind. "I am very flattered to hear that," said the prince. He pulled her close and kissed her breasts gently. Sarah did not fight this, nor did she resist when he more urgently brought his tongue and teeth to her nipples. Her anger was not directed at the desire in his body, but at the emptiness in his heart. She felt so far removed from her body that she was surprised at the sudden rush of pleasure that ran through her, that nearly brought tears to her eyes. Her nipples were erect, she could feel the weakness in her legs. She was like a disembodied creature floating in space, watching her separate physical self sink onto his bed. Despite the deadness in her soul, her body was shaking with excitement.

"This is how I like you," said the prince, pulling down his underpants. "This is how I love my beautiful actress to be."

Save for her silk stockings, which clung to her hot legs, and for his long white underpants, which were bunched about his ankles like manacles, they were naked. She did not know what demon had returned lust to her body: whether it was anger or fear or hatred. But when he brought his hand to her vagina, she was wet, and when she opened her mouth, it was not to shout imprecations into his face but to swallow his fingers, to kiss his chest. Her prince would not release her private parts, holding her with a clumsy strength, with an insistency that her body recognized as desire. A wild rhythm began to beat once again in her blood, an insistent, violent interior sound that overwhelmed all thought.

She tried to remember why she was so miserable, to recall what she had learned only a moment before; she tried to bring back the anger at what had been revealed to her. But all she could see before her was pale flesh and golden hair bathed in the gentle light of the dying afternoon.

She wanted love, and love was all around her, and she forgot everything but the urge to passion. Her hands stroked his neck, they squeezed his buttocks, and as he arched his powerful back, she took hold of his penis and opened her mouth to caress its surface with her teeth and tongue. "Oh my God, Sarah," he said, swinging about over her bent knees, and she squinted up at him just as he began to penetrate her, sensing the joy behind his shut-eyed face. In that instant she remembered.

All her life she had wanted love, and all her life she had been disappointed by those who had promised to give her love. She had never been loved by a mother, or by a father, and everyone else from whom she had wanted love had disillusioned her: Nurse had deserted her for a husband, Appollonie had abandoned her through death, Mother Ste.-Sophie had lost interest in her from the day Sarah had left the convent.

And she had loved none of them so well as she had loved Prince Henri.

For no one else had she so completely denied her own vision of life. She had no past, no future, no wants or needs except to be held in his arms, to be loved by him, and by him alone. "You're so beautiful," he said, and Sarah knew that he could not even see her. The prince had wanted an affair, he had wanted an actress, he had wanted to be famous in his tiny set of spoiled young aristocrats. Now he was inside her, his hands gripping just below her waist with hurtful force, his sex pumping within her with as much love as a ramrod experiences for its gunbarrel. Even as his passion grew wilder, she could sense all her muscles constrict, could feel every part of her desire turn to disgust.

"I love you," he said; and Sarah knew then that the prince loved nothing and no one in the world. "I love you," he said again and again, until he could no longer speak, until his childish dreams brought him to consummate his passion, until an automatic, mindless smile crossed his beautiful face. "Sarah," he said, "darling."

Long before he finally withdrew from her body, she knew that the love she sought must be found elsewhere, must be found where it could not be touched, not be spoiled by vanity or arrogance or greed. The love she needed must be pure, like a fresh current from a swollen river, like an inchoate force of nature, far too vast for anyone to know its limits; and despite such strength, it must be desperate, yearning, it must have a need as great as her own.

Chapter 13

A RESPECTABLE HOUSE

Sarah was pregnant.

Perhaps as much as ten weeks, or as little as six. Often, she counted back on her fingers the number of days since she had last seen Prince Henri de Luyen, the number of weeks since they had last made love. Despite the changes in her body, she remained thin, without the nausea or fainting fits of popular fiction. And if her mood was wild that October, only a fool would blame that on the pregnancy.

After all, that summer Sarah had lost both her prince and her chance for a great career at the Comédie Française.

These were not small matters, not even when weighed against the doctor's confirmation of the pregnancy in early October, two weeks prior to her eighteenth birthday. Just as Julie had been, she was unmarried, without protector or profession, and soon to bring a baby into the world.

Like mother, like daughter, she thought. They would call her a whore.

Sarah lusted after men, and men lusted after her. Actors great and small made sure to brush against her body at every rehearsal, and to speak their lines within an inch of her sensuous lips. Sarah imagined that they could tell at a glance that passion burned not only in her heart but in her loins. She had adored her prince, and surely that first, true love had fired her lust. Loathing his weakness, his greed, his selfishness, she still missed his slender hands, his muscular thighs, his searching tongue. Sarah longed for the ecstasy he had given her, late every afternoon, an ecstasy of sweat and Eau d'Ange and sexual fluids. She missed his hands on her breasts, she missed his head resting on her belly, she missed his penis thrusting inside her. Backstage, behind a drop, on the creeking narrow staircases to the dressing rooms, fixing her rouge in the green room, she had to steel herself not to return the actors' stray touches, not to answer their insulting jokes with a direct request to take her to their beds.

"You think everyone wants to make love with you," said Julie in the luxurious confines of her new carriage, an English charabanc, its back wheels nearly a third larger than the two in front. Sarah enjoyed the smell of the pristine leather upholstery, was encouraged by the sun flooding through the clear rear-window glass. The carriage was large enough to seat Julie and her three daughters, attended by a nurse or a maid, and whatever size gentleman might be offering his devotion at the same time.

For the moment Sarah was alone with Julie. She was enjoying a long spell of her mother's favor, and in that rare period of grace had taken to sharing confidences: how she had suffered during her first menstrual periods, believing them the product of sinful thoughts; how all her life she had felt proud of Julie's sensuous beauty, and coveted her mother's curves and pale and fragrant flesh. Now that she was herself a young woman, she explained, an object of attention, she found herself disliking this scrutiny; she did not enjoy the fact that every actor in the company, every man on the street could not look at her without leering. But her mother did not like listening to boasting about anyone's allure but her own. She never suspected that Sarah hoped to make this conversation a prelude to that much greater unvoiced subject: her pregnancy.

"It's only that I had never noticed it before, Mama," she said. "All the men who look all the time."

"Do you suppose that every man in Paris who looks at you is a maniac who will be satisfied only by your young body?"

Perhaps not every man, thought Sarah. Yet she did not think it imagination that the young policeman in his tight white breeches who took off his gleaming helmet every time he saw her cross the Rue Rohan on the way to the Théâtre Français wanted to make love with her. She did not believe it a fantasy that M. Thierry, the florid-faced, hostile director of the company, wanted to take his least favorite *pensionnaire* into his office and make love with her. And there were so many others: the printer's apprentice who stared up at her from the street into Julie's carriage; the middle-aged gentleman in an adjacent carriage holding up a large eyeglass mounted in gold, the better to examine the object of his desire; the rickety-limbed doorman of the theater, who could not resist a crooked, insinuating smile every time she passed.

Not surprisingly, the most flamboyant Bohemian in Paris also wanted to make love to Sarah. His name was Nadar, and it was to his studio that Julie was taking her that day. When she dropped her in front of the new four-story building on the Boulevard des Capucines, where Nadar's name hung in huge red letters—gas-lit at night—from the top floor, she cautioned Sarah not to believe a word he said.

Yet the first thing that Nadar had told her was true: She had the look of someone who had been cruelly disappointed in love.

And then he had said more outrageous things, mentioning what must either have shown in her face or have been astonishingly intuited by him on the spot: That she would soon forget that disappointment because she would have a greater love, an over-whelming one that no man in the world could experience.

What else could he be speaking about but a newborn child?

"And another thing," said Nadar. "Even though every man in Paris will desire you, no man can ever desire you more than I do myself at this moment."

"You must want to take my photograph very badly, Monsieur Nadar," said Sarah. He looked at her a half moment before pulling her to him in a great, fatherly hug, laughing so hard that her chin bounced off his chest.

Nadar was very tall and thin, with a thick gray-specked red moustache. His hair was red, his scarf was red, and the walls all about him had been painted red too. "You are the mate of my soul," he said, taking her hand and bringing it to his lips. "I am only twenty-four years older than you, hardly worth mentioning, it's such an irrelevance. I can't marry you because I already am married, though I can take you to my country house, spread out a blanket near the lake, and feed you strawberries and cream until you're nice and fat all over."

Sarah liked this vision, as she liked this man. She decided that he was wise, and that he was capable. He wore a dozen rich rings, yet his fingers were as rough as a laborer's. Julie had many times pointed him out to her at Tortoni's—the man with the crimson cape, the flashing teeth, the crowd of followers. Nadar was a cartoonist, a journalist, a dabbler in the sciences. He had loved many actresses, and had kept more than one of them in this famous studio. The entire demimonde knew that he was madly in love with his wife; they also knew the names of his many mistresses.

For an hour and more he never stopped stroking Sarah's shoulders and caressing her hair, explaining why he needed to know her before he could hope to capture the essence of her soul: an actress burning with ambition.

Sarah was not one soul now but two, she would have liked to say. She was no longer a girl carrying a dream of greatness, but a young woman carrying a child. Perhaps he would understand; he would explain to Julie, and he would make everything all right. Yet she could not find an opportunity to tell him this. Nadar never stopped talking, even as he rubbed powder onto her forehead, even as he lifted a mirror under her chin and brought his nose to within an inch of her own. And suddenly he was taking her photograph: She was forbidden speech or movement, proscribed from so much as following him with her eyes.

Her immobility grew more and more uncomfortable, but Sarah was glad of the chance to be rid of the possibility of speech, of the responsibility of moving her body. The locked pose was a kind of freedom. She need not react physically because any movement would destroy the image-in-the-making. She let her entire physical self assume the frozen moment that the photograph would duplicate, while her mind, beyond the mask of the body, was free to imagine what she dared not do.

She would tell her mother that she was pregnant, she thought, as Nadar chattered on, bathing her in his admiration and goodwill. *I am pregnant, Mama. I have had a lover, a prince, and he has left me.*

Julie must surely understand; neither Sarah nor her two half sisters were legitimate.

Marie Lloyd, her admiring friend from the Conservatoire and fellow *pensionnaire* at the Français, had sworn that it was possible to miss two or even three menstrual periods without being pregnant. There was no reliable test so early in a pregnancy, she had insisted, though Sarah did not need the evidence of a swollen belly to believe that inside her womb a new and purer creature was being readied for life. Marie Lloyd had whispered further female secrets to her: An abortion cleaned away whatever life was growing inside the womb. The dangerous part was getting past the cervix, the womb's narrow opening, with a scraping tool called a "curette" without puncturing or infecting its soft walls. Marie had heard of an ingenious method used by a Dr. Wendell, originally from London, currently practicing from a basement in the Latin Quarter. In awed tones she detailed the doctor's methods to a disgusted Sarah. Asparagus steeped in alcohol was packed tightly in the cervix so that it might slowly absorb moisture from the surrounding tissue, thereby swelling and slowly dilating the opening. After twenty-four hours, the curette could be inserted with the only danger being the possibility of infection from the asparagus.

"Why asparagus?" Sarah had asked. "Why not broccoli?" She allowed herself a joke at her Belgian lover's expense. "Why not Brussels sprouts?"

Sarah was terrified by the changes a baby would bring to her life, but even if some painless trick could take away this result of her lust, she would never ask for this magic, never refuse what heaven had sent. She did not think of the baby growing within her as a product of the love she had shared with Prince Henri; nor did she imagine that a son or daughter would bring him back to her. She knew that the baby was his only because she had no other lover. It would belong only to Sarah. Only she would bear it, she would nurture it, she would love it as she had never loved anyone else in the world.

"You are the most beautiful woman in the world," Nadar was saying. "Eighteen is the perfect age, and you are the perfect eighteen. Don't move and the world will worship you."

Possibly Julie would not be so angry. The new life might even become a bond between them. How funny to imagine Julie a grandmother at thirty-five! Sarah must be careful to remind her mother that she looked no older than twenty-two, that everyone thought Julie was her sister.

Only a single doctor and Marie Lloyd knew that Sarah was pregnant. If Nadar understood that there was something roiling beneath the surface of her face, he had not voiced it save in the vaguest terms. All that the actors at the Français discerned was that her prince was no longer to be seen picking her up after rehearsals, and that, a month after her series of disastrous debuts, she remained sullen and insolent at being assigned the small parts her talents merited. She knew that she was disliked by the company. Sarah did not fit in with the bright-eyed *pensionnaires,* eager to sit at the feet of the established company members. She yearned to shine in her own right, she wanted her star to be so bright as to bewilder, to make all of theirs invisible.

"You will be the most famous woman on earth," continued Nadar, coming closer to her, waving his hands as if he were pulling strings attached to her motionless body. "I am glad that your eyes are almond-shaped. I am glad that your hair is wild. I gave George Sand a wig to wear when I photographed her. You I will give nothing but what is yours."

For the occasion Julie had bought Sarah a dress and lent her the emerald necklace she had received from the Duke of Morny at the end of the summer. Nadar dismissed Julie's contribution to his photograph's immortality. He insisted that Sarah disrobe, that she remove all jewels from her neck, her ears, her fingers. She sat on a stool, a coarse, ancient cloak draped over her right shoulder and pulled slightly askew, baring her neck and all of her left shoulder. Under her right arm, partially hidden by the smock, was another, higher stool on which she could rest her elbow while holding her hand frozen to her cheek.

"You are an actress, so you must pretend. Pretend that this is your very last picture," said Nadar. "Pretend that you will never have another opportunity to be photographed. Pretend that what you present me with now is the only face you will be able to show a hundred future generations."

She knew that she was not supposed to change the lines she had already drawn into her face, and imagined that his words were a kind of encouragement to keep those lines in place. It was not difficult to do as he asked; she wondered if the picture already in the process of forming in the mysterious chemicals on his plate would expose the joy and fear in her heart. Conceivably she never would be photographed again. Maybe there would be no more work for her in the theater; her mother might prove to be a doting grandmother, insisting that Sarah stay home with the baby, Julie's first and only grandchild.

While the red-haired man spoke, he padded about on soft-soled Indian moccasins, a gift, so he said, from the writer Balzac before his death more than ten years ago, just as the paint-spattered artist's smock he wore was a gift from France's most famous living painter, Eugène Delacroix. Nadar's speech was filled with many extravagant claims of friendship with the celebrated, living and dead: bon-vivant writers like Alexandre Dumas and Alfred de Vigny, dissipated poets like the suicide Gérard de Nerval, painters as different as Ingres and Courbet, actresses like the departed Rachel and the current leading tragedienne of the Comédie Française, Mme. Devoyod.

"You are gloriously happy," demanded Nadar, performing a psychological adjustment on his subject's face. Perhaps her musing was carrying her too far toward gloom, she thought. Nadar, a consummate artist, could sense the change. "Imagine that all the world is waiting for you to come out from behind the curtain and make your bows. Make believe that you are in love, and that you are loved in return."

Nadar's words did not have their desired effect.

She was suddenly so frightened that she had to focus all her strength on her right elbow, to keep it firmly in place on its steadying stool. Sarah understood that Nadar's crazy patter was for her benefit, to keep her entertained and immobile while he performed minute adjustments to a dozen mirrors and reflectors, shining the daylight into and about the serious features of her face. Yet there was nothing to enjoy in pretending that the world was waiting for her to come out from behind a curtain, when no one in the world cared if she ever graced a stage again. There was nothing amusing about imagining that she was loved, because that was what she had been forced to do all her life.

"That is fine, that is very beautiful, just the right touch of gravity, just that little bit of melancholy," said Nadar, twisting his face comically from across the room.

How could anyone keep her entertained, she thought suddenly, with Prince Henri gone from her life? In place of her prince's coldness and vanity, she remembered his perfect posture, his white teeth and blue eyes: more than an ordinary mortal, a prince. Just as the Comédie Française was more than a place to act, it was a shrine to the Theater. What could anyone discover in the image that Nadar would freeze forever on his magical plates save sadness, desperation, failure? Even if the prince had not entered her life, only to exit with such bad grace, what delight could show in her face? She had been given a chance in the greatest theatrical company in the world, and she had failed. How could she be amused at the photographer's litany of great names when she knew her own could never be among them?

"You must keep your eyes on fire," said Nadar, trying to adjust her mood once more. "A few sad thoughts, but nothing horribly sad. Remember the glory due you, remember your gorgeous white shoulders, your heavy golden hair."

She wondered if Nadar had been at any of her debuts, if the small note of desperation in his voice exhibited his knowledge of why her tranquillity might collapse at any moment.

Sarah, like every *pensionnaire* of the Comédie Française, had been given three debut roles in rapid succession: Iphigénie in Racine's *Iphigénie en Aulide* on September 1, 1862; Valérie in Scribe and Mélesville's melodrama of the same name on September 8; and Henriette in Molière's *Les Femmes savantes* on September 11. These were the sort of pivotal, attention-grabbing roles that would not be offered again until the *pensionnaire* had weathered several theatrical seasons playing servants, minor soldiers, messengers. Critics attended debut performances to decide whether the fledgling artist, usually freshly snatched from the boughs of the Conservatoire, was worthy of present or future fame. The roles were chosen by the director of the company, M. Thierry, in concert with the older members, the *sociétaires*. Plays were selected from the enormous classic repertoire of the company, a repertoire that the veteran actors could recite—and often did—in their sleep. The *sociétaires* swallowed with grace the indignity of allowing unknowns to act major parts; the debuts marked the beginning of the season, with the summer heat not yet banished. Other than critics, few leaders of fashion would brave the sticky warmth of early September to sit through a heavy evening of Racine or even a lighter evening of Molière. Besides, the fresh-faced actors were usually good for a few extra rows of ticket buyers, packing in relatives and friends for what might be the only moment of glory in their lives. After all, every *sociétaire* was a profit-sharing stockholder in the company, with an interest in getting as many seats sold as possible.

"I know what you're thinking, Sarah," Nadar continued, pulling at a shade in the glass roof to let in an additional sliver of light to compensate for what his precise eye saw as a sudden darkening. Maybe a low-lying cloud had stuck a flimsy arm between the sun and Nadar's glass-roofed studio, or a silent flock of birds might have scattered the sun's rays only for a moment, so that in another second he would have to pull the shade back to prevent his plate from being overexposed. "You're thinking what a perfect occupation I've chosen for myself. I can talk all day, and you can't say a word back to me. I can stare at your pretty face all I like and you can't so much as sneeze at mine."

Sarah's elbow remained in place, her serious smile held, the contemplation of her bleak future momentarily faded. She forced herself to concentrate on the elaborate displays of flowers in the romantic studio, cluttered with bizarre paintings, fine porcelain, and a hundred costumes. Nadar had gathered the flowers—mostly late-season yellow and white roses—into haphazard bouquets. Some were in Chinese vases, like those in the prince's bedroom. Others were crammed into cheap vases of purple glass; these reminded her of the type actors had to use at the Français when flowers arrived for them backstage. Prince Henri had sent Sarah roses to honor her debut nights. Before the curtain rose and between the acts, the callboy would rush up the actors' staircase, arms filled with rich and fragrant displays. Actresses receiving flowers in their dressing rooms always had to send a few pennies to the porter to bring up a vase or two. On her third debut night, her worst public performance yet, she had not bothered to send for a vase. Smiling at the three actresses with whom she shared her dressing room, she had crammed the last gift from her prince into the wastebasket beneath their dressing table.

"It's not worth the penny to send for the vase," Sarah had said, holding back her tears.

Nadar crossed her line of vision, and she could see that he was losing patience with her. Though he was well paid for his services, his subjects considered it an honor to be favored by the master's attentions. Sarah was not properly receptive. He was about to tell her that a Nadar photograph would immortalize her more than any role she would ever attempt onstage. She could sense more than annoyance from him; he was insulted.

Quickly she tried to shut out all thoughts of crying, tried to retain the boundaries of the image into which he had posed her. She had cried enough after her first debut when the prince took her home, barely touching her hand, scarcely saying a word on the short drive from the theater to the Rue St.-Honoré. Earlier, he had promised to take her to the Café de Paris on the Boulevard des Italiens, or to one of the newer cafés, their trees laced with little electric lights, on the Rue Royale. Sarah had wanted ice cream or oysters or just a little champagne. "Something to make me feel special again," she had said. "In spite of everything."

The prince had reneged on his promise. He had other concerns than assuaging Sarah's mood in a glittering café. All he did was take her home. While his driver waited, he walked her to the front door of the apartment building. She turned away from him to look into the window of the ground-floor confectioner's shop, where miniature gaslamps illuminated a toy train made entirely of chocolate. "I wish I were small enough to take this train," she said.

"You must not be upset," he answered in a flat tone. Sarah had hated him for treating her like a stranger. Yet despite their physical intimacy, despite the lust that had pretended to be love, he had never known her. How could he know what memories of childhood were conjured for her by the scent of chocolate, the promise of spun sugar and candies and ices? Standing before the display window, Sarah became dizzy trying to remember the names of men who had brought her bonbons from this very shop on their way to a paid place in her mother's bed.

"About my performance in the play, or about you?" she asked, though he had not yet told her that he was leaving Paris, that he was returning to Brussels, that his father had found a proper wife for him, an heiress with huge estates in the French colonies. The prince would save this for a letter in his careful, elegant hand.

"You must not be upset about anything, my dear," he had said, disappointment clear in his voice, and clearer in the deadness of his touch. "You looked very beautiful under the stage lights."

Indeed, Francisque Sarcey, the all-powerful drama critic of *L'Opinion* thought her "remarkably beautiful" in the next day's edition. He admired her carriage, her enunciation, the tilt of her head; but he also wrote that it was impossible to praise anything else about her performance. He could discern no special voice, no unique talent. For her second debut a week later, the same critic found her "fetching," but faulted her characterization. She was not natural, she was not relaxed, she was amateurish. By the time this opinion was in print, Prince Henri was on his way to Brussels, having brought his flowers to the porter's lodge, having stayed for the performance and kissed her hand without any passion at all as they said goodnight for the last time in front of her door.

Late that night, she had lain in bed, the Rue St.-Honoré outside her windows absolutely still; in the distance, like the promise of a future existence, she could hear the murmurings of life from the direction of the Rue Royale, where the prince would not take her, an indistinct rumbling of music and laughter. She loved the way cafés glowed at night: Gaslights and, in a few places, far brighter electric lamps burned so brightly that women opened parasols to protect their skins. There the new streets were paved with macadam, deadening the sound of the carriage wheels so that artists could enjoy the brilliant talk, so that lovers could hear each other whisper against the rush of music and the gently melting ice in tall summer glasses. Sarah heard it all, and imagined herself in a great café, across from the tall, elegant prince, waited on by the proud and eager owner of the establishment.

How very nice of you to grace us with your presence, she heard in her dreams. A real-life prince with his famous actress.

That Sarah was no longer in love with him made it no better. The fact was that he had left her. There had been no scene where she confronted him with her indifference, with her knowledge that he could never love anyone but himself. He had never understood what had suddenly left her bereft of joy, aimless; in his great egotism, he probably imagined that it was her fear of being deserted by the man she adored. And there was truth in this vision. For someone who had been neglected and abandoned all her life, the prince's desertion was one more mark of her worthlessness. His pulling away from her coming at the same time as her disappointing series of debuts could only reinforce her feelings of being undeserving of anyone's love. Sarah believed that if her first debut had been a spectacular success, the prince would have toasted her achievements in every grand café in the city. If her second and third debuts had made her name great, he would never have contemplated returning to Brussels.

But she had had no success.

As Nadar continued adjusting his camera and his mirrors and reflectors, hurrying back and forth across the crowded space, his encouraging talk faded like the hushing din of the audience when the house chandelier is dimmed and pulled high, presaging the rise of the curtain.

If she did not tell her mother right away, she would go mad. Today, she resolved, it must be today. She would tell Julie the moment she returned home, and secure the love and support that she needed at this time.

The idea, thought Sarah, that somehow she could wrest from the theater the love that she had lost from the prince now seemed laughable. She had garnered no love from the strangers judging her debut performances. Once onstage, Sarah had felt unprotected, naked. There had been no love in the house, no love on the stage. Her fellow actors despised her pretensions to glory, and upstaged her poorly recited speeches at every opportunity. The audience in the gilded boxes, the front rows filled with bejeweled and white-bosomed matrons, had confronted her with their regal indifference. The very notion that the young girl's declamations could make them forget for a moment the gentlemen in the row behind them, or their rivals in the opposite box, was absurd. No wonder that each debut was worse than the one that preceded it. There was nothing to look foward to but more of the same: indifference, contempt, jealousy onstage, boredom from the house. Mme.

Guérard—who had purchased a seat in the stalls for her two previous performances—could barely convince her to return to the theater for her concluding debut when the prince had already left Paris.

Julie had finally returned from the country, and Aunt Rosine had come back from her late-summer peregrinations at the gambling spas; and together with the little widow, unescorted by any male, they had taken a stage box to share in Sarah's "triumph" in Molière. She had not dared spoil her mother's plans, expose Julie to so grave a disappointment.

It was before this performance that the roses sent in the Prince's name had arrived, and with them his ridiculous letter. Sarah would "inspire" him all his life, he wrote. There was certainly "greatness in her soul." He wished that he possessed the "courage that was her natural life's blood," that he had the "strength to defy his family, and to throw their threats of disinheritance back in their faces."

After she had crushed the life out of his flowers, she could find no way to bring herself back into the role of the young and charming Henriette in Molière's *Les Femmes savantes*. Henriette was desired in marriage by two men, and Sarah was, for the moment, desired by no one. When the curtain rose, her silvery voice was shrill, her every gesture warlike. Backstage, between the acts, the always kind Samson, her professor at the Conservatoire and fellow actor at the Français, could barely look at her. There was nothing to say, no way to improve a performance so removed from the life of the character in the play.

In Francisque Sarcey's review in the next day's *L'Opinion,* the august critic finally lost patience with the new actress. Not only did he ridicule her attempt at Molière, but he went back to her two earlier debuts and insisted that he had been far too kind. Even this was not enough. "That Mlle. Bernhardt should turn out to be an actress without talent is not unusual," he wrote. "She is a *pensionnaire,* and among these trial members of the national company of France, there are bound to be a few without hope of talent. Worse than this is that the regular members of the company were only a trifle better than the *débutante.* Either Mlle. Bernhardt has dragged the veteran members down to her level of mediocrity, or, as seems more likely, the company is in dire need of serious work.

The fact that the Comédie Française has chosen her at all indicates just how badly their thinking is in these sad days for the theater. It is no wonder that without the presence of Rachel, attendance has become so poor. No one wishes to pay money to be bored."

Francisque Sarcey had spoken. She would be lucky to be trusted with silent parts, dressed in maid's costume, serving tea and holding open doors for the Comédie's experienced actors. With Sarcey's venom in print, it appeared impossible they would allow her another chance; her *pensionnaire*'s one-year contract would almost certainly not be renewed.

Poor Mme. Guérard had been so devastated by Sarah's public humiliation that she swore she would never read another theatrical review again. Aunt Rosine, who had seen the same performance and had read the same review, remained sublimely indifferent. She had been much more concerned whether Alexandre Dumas *fils*'s flirtatious wink had been directed at her or at her sister; all she knew for certain was that Alexandre Dumas *père* had looked over his son's shoulder with an aging rival's dismay. As for the Duke of Morny, Sarah's erstwhile promoter, Julie's new emerald necklace proved to be a parting gift to his much-shared mistress. If he would not be back to enjoy Julie's bed, it was unlikely he would return to support her daughter's theatrical career.

Only Julie's reaction to her acting, to Sarcey's terrible critique, to her overpowering sense of despair had finally mattered to Sarah. Once again, she could believe that her mother loved her. "Sarcey's a fool," said Julie the morning after the debut. "Probably he's in love with one of the boys in the cast." She had torn the offending newspaper to shreds in front of Sarah. "You just forget the whole thing. You forget every word. The only thing that counts is that you make a success with the audience."

"Was I really so bad?" Sarah had said.

"No," said Julie. "How can you be so bad if you're my daughter?"

One way to her daughter's success was to be photographed, and photographed by Nadar. Another way was to insist on the proper parts, and if the Comédie Française was too high and mighty to give them to her, well, Julie Bernhardt knew a few men involved with the Théâtre Odéon who—Francisque Sarcey notwithstanding—would be happy to help her daughter achieve the fame that she deserved. Even if she had loathed the idea of being photographed, even if one had been mortified at the notion of meeting influential men who might have gone to bed with her mother, Sarah would have accepted these suggestions at once, because they were gifts from her mother. Certainly these must be symbols of her love.

"Now if you're serious, we'll do a serious photograph," Nadar was saying. "And if you're a smiler, we'll do a funny photograph. If you're a pipe smoker, we can do one with you lighting your tobacco, but I can tell you from experience, it's tough to hold that little match over the pipe bowl without budging for ten good minutes." Nadar pulled his watch out and frowned when he saw the time. "The point is, we can't have you smiling one minute and crying the next, or all we get is a confused exposure, and your voluptuous little mother is going to tell everyone old Nadar's not what he used to be." He came much closer to her and whispered, but not so close as to interfere with her light, "And that's not true, as you can ask my wife, and maybe a few other ladies in this great city. Don't smile, it wasn't a joke."

Sarah didn't smile, remembering the extent of Julie's concern, trying to understand where it had come from, how long it would last. It would not have been out of the ordinary for her mother to have scolded her severely for her poor review or, like Aunt Rosine, to have scarcely been interested in it. She might have used it as a weapon to beat at Sarah's resistance to an arranged, and profitable, marriage. Surely her mother, attentive to the shifting fortunes of fame all her life, understood something of success and failure. It made no sense that Julie Bernhardt was ready to be furious at the Comédie Française even before they had begun to make things difficult for her daughter. It made less sense still that she had praised a performance that even Sarah regarded as hateful.

Sarah knew that Julie, despite her career in the demimonde, was a great believer in hierarchy, authority, prestige. Her mother would presume that if you were accepted by the Comédie Française, you were a good actor. If you were praised in print by L'Opinion, you were worthy of praise. Anyone who failed to win a first prize at the Conservatoire, needed the intervention of the Duke of Morny to get her into the Comédie Française, or who was vilified by *L'Opinion* was never going to have a decent career in the theater.

Yet Julie was suddenly behaving like a dreamer. Her own motto might also have abruptly become "In Spite of Everything." During her summer at Saint-Cloud, she had changed. Julie had suffered for months from the duke's neglect. She had reached an age when she wanted a modicum of respectability, and the duke's hiding her from the eyes of the world made her feel indecent. Back in Paris her clothes and speech were quieter, visits from her hairdresser restricted to but four times a week. Little Regina was brought back downstairs from her exile with Mme. Guérard, and Julie made an effort not to show that Jeanne remained her favorite daughter.

After all, it was not Jeanne who was a member of the Comédie Française. Sarah realized that Julie's love was selfish; for the first time in her thirty-five years, her mother felt threatened by age, and saw in her oldest daughter the chance to live again. Still, Sarah accepted Julie's caresses uncritically. Not once since her return from Saint-Cloud had her mother corrected her for calling her Mama instead of Julie. For a very brief time, they were a little family of women, waited on by Bella and Titine, visited by no men.

"Don't move, my pretty," Nadar was saying from across the room, real desperation in his voice. "No, not after all these precious minutes, don't you dare throw it all away. Do you realize that I have gotten George Sand to sit still for fifteen minutes? We didn't need that many, but I wanted to pay her back for all the times she left me to pay the bill at the Café Momus. You probably don't know the Momus, it's before your time, you ridiculously young creature. Those were the days when it made sense to be a Bohemian, when Baudelaire recited for a tiny audience, provided everyone was at least as drunk as he was. What are you thinking? Are you even thinking about moving?"

She wished he would tell her that enough time had passed, that her image was conclusively preserved, that she could blink her eyes, stretch her arms, and stand up from the tiny stool. What joy it would be to open wide her mouth, to rush to the window and banish the studio's noxious smell of cyanide and nitric acid with fresh air from four stories above the city. The fresh air might clarify intricate problems. Her mother needed her, just when she needed her mother. Her mother was becoming a good bourgeoise, just when she required her to be a freethinker. Her mother wanted her to be a success on the stage, just when Sarah wished she would tell her to stay comfortably home waiting for her baby.

"I have told you and told you, you must not do anything other than keep your pose," said Nadar, his tone resigned to failure. "I can make you immortal, not the Comédie Française. I can make you live forever, but only if you stay still."

"I am sorry," said Sarah. She did not move all at once, indeed, waited a few moments before moving her elbow from the stool, as if this might somehow mollify the photographer.

Of course, the moment she spoke, she had moved her lips, her cheeks, her eyes.

"Are you crazy?" said Nadar. She looked at his red face, under his wild red hair, framed by the red walls. He was across the room, making an adjustment to his equipment.

"Monsieur Nadar, I appreciate how hard you have tried to make this picture—"

"No Monsieur, if you please. I have asked you to call me just Nadar, it is absolutely sufficient, first name and last, and how do you respond? Do you tell me to call you Sarah? No, not you, Mademoiselle Bernhardt. I must call you Sarah all on my own."

"I am sorry that I ruined the photograph," she said in a smaller voice, getting to her feet, clutching the coarse cloak more tightly about her. Curiously, the photographer's angry look was gone, and as he crossed the room to where she stood, he let out a booming, triumphant laugh.

"It will be stunning," said Nadar.

"What?"

"The photograph," said Nadar. "You are a great subject."

"But I moved."

"Not before I finished, my dear," he said.

"So you are not really mad?"

"Only if you don't come back every year for a new portrait."

"I don't think that I—" she began, but Nadar interrupted, full of a fervor that she did not understand.

"You stayed absolutely still, but everything inside your eyes never stopped moving. It will show everything that you've got. Every emotion will be there. You will be a great actress, Sarah. I know. You must not give it up, for any reasons, under any circumstances. No husband, no baby must make you stop. Do you understand?"

"Why do you say baby?"

"It is possible to believe in a child too, Sarah. The way one believes in art. But you must always choose your art. The art must be first. Be selfish, and that way you will give something to the world. No matter what else comes in your way. Rachel had children, but she never left the stage. You will be greater than Rachel."

For a moment Sarah did not know anything. Did he or did he not know she was pregnant? Was this a real man speaking to her, or an apparition giving voice to her dreams?

"I must change into my clothes," said Sarah.

"You are a great actress."

"Stop it," she said, trying to pass his big, sloppy form.

"I saw your debuts, Sarah," he said, taking hold of her like a lover, bringing his large, handsome head close to hers.

"You were at the Français?" she whispered.

His kind eyes smiled at her. "You were terrible, my dear."

"Yes," she said, like confessing a sin and waiting for her penance.

"You were utterly fake. And your arms!" The photographer began to flap his own like a bird trying to take flight.

"I am sorry that you had to suffer through such a performance," said Sarah.

"I didn't suffer," said Nadar. "You did."

She was suddenly so weak that he had to help her to a chair. The photographer poured absinthe into a tiny crystal glass and held it to her lips. He told her to sip, and she did, despite the drink's sickly odor, feeling its sinful texture warm the inside of her heart. "But since I am so bad, why do you say that I am a great actress?"

"Every great artist is terrible at first. Don't you know that? You will probably get worse. You will sink even lower until you will find no one more loathsome than yourself. Then one day you will use every bit of it: the smashed-up pride, the enormous desire, the love and the hate and the madness—"

"I don't want it," snapped Sarah, wiping at her tears, putting down the empty glass. "I only want to go home."

"Yes, you do want it," said Nadar. "Of course you want it. You want it and you need it and you'll never be satisfied until you have it." He was shouting, and his handsome face was distorted by a malevolent energy, an insistent ego. He could see it in her eyes, he claimed. He could see it in her photograph.

Somehow she got to her feet, pushed her way past him to the changing room, and exchanged Nadar's cloak for her own rich clothes. He tried to kiss her, but she pushed at his chest, picked her way past the vases and pillows and crates on the floor, and found the strength to open the door. One of the first elevators in Paris was installed in his building, but Sarah could not wait for the slow rising of the gilded cage. She ran down four steep flights of stairs, and pressed open the heavy door with both hands.

An October grayness had suddenly blown out of the sky, and the fiacres usually waiting on the Boulevard des Capucines were nowhere to be seen. Any Parisian could sense the coming cloudburst, and anyone with fifteen sous in his pocket had waved one down. At the curb groups of women in dark dresses huddled, pointing furled umbrellas into the street at phantom cabmen. Sarah hurried along the fresh pavement, past the old saddler, the new spice shop, the artist's supply shop. She knew what to do, she understood the way to her mother's heart; all she required was a cab.

The rain came as she approached the Place de l'Opéra, where the cornerstone for the new opera house had just been laid. Here, Baron Haussmann had created a vast new square, not simply for the opera house, but as a magnificent central pivot for new boulevards and ancient little streets. Without the opera house, surrounded by old buildings half demolished and new ones half built, the square was forbidding, desolate despite the crush of people around its circumference. Lashed by wind and rain, Sarah braved the boards and sand pits of the various construction sites. She was drenched by the time she had fought her way across the square to Baron Haussmann's Avenue de l'Opéra, which would eventually connect the Opera Square with that of the Théâtre Français. The avenue, like half the city, under construction for nearly eight years, was still a mess of modern roadways, ancient obstacles, and fiacres vying for a break in the traffic toward the First Arrondissement.

I will ask Mama for a name, thought Sarah, smiling against the wind, placing her hand on the emerald necklace about her throat. *I am not an orphan, but a daughter, the child of a mother and a father, the granddaughter of people who were born into the same world as I. I will ask for a name, and then I will explain why I need it.* Her heel broke as she ran through a muddy puddle while crossing the Rue de Casanova. No longer looking for a fiacre, she walked steadily, taking easy breaths, feeling the cold rain slide down her back. She passed the Église St.-Roch, soon caught sight of the top of the Vendôme Column over her right shoulder, then found herself staring into the windows of the familiar shops on the Rue St.-Honoré. Finally, she stood in front of the confectioner's shop on the ground floor of her own building.

Sarah entered, her hair and clothes a disgrace, and silently pointed out the chocolates she wanted to the girl behind the counter. She ate these at once, stuffing them into her mouth before she left the shop, chewing mightily as she ascended the single flight of stairs to her home. Sarah pressed the bell repeatedly until Bella, thoroughly scandalized by Sarah's appearance, ushered her inside. Miraculously, eleven-year-old Jeanne was not clinging to her mother but was busy taunting little Regina in the drawing room.

"What was your father's name, Mama?" said Sarah, finding Julie at her dressing table. She stood behind her, joining her mother's wild stare into the mirror. "What was the name of my grandfather on your side, his first name?"

"Maurits," said Julie, speaking the princely Dutch name without pause. She did not ask why her daughter was soaked to the skin, why a fever seemed to be burning through her pale flesh. There was a terrible pronouncement hanging in the air, only a moment beyond Julie's ken. Sarah repeated her grandfather's name, but the Dutch accent eluded her. Her mother repeated the name properly. "Maurits," she said.

"Is he dead, Mama?"

"Yes."

"Why do you never tell me about your parents?" asked Sarah. "Is your mother still alive?"

"I don't know," she said, though of course she and Sarah both knew why there was no talk of the middle-class Jewish household in Amsterdam from which Julie had fled to live in sin and luxury. She turned around so that she could face Sarah directly. "You see, I ran away when I was very young. Rosine followed a few years later, after my father died. There is other family, but they are not interested in us, and we are not interested in them."

"But you loved your father?"

"Yes."

"In French, Maurits is like Maurice," said Sarah. "It is a good name."

"It is a very good name," said Julie, her voice diminishing in strength. All her energy was abruptly in her eyes. She looked at Sarah as though a whole world might be contained within her daughter's body. Julie stared, and then she whispered: "Why do you ask about my father's name?"

"If I have a son, that is what I shall call him, Mama," said Sarah, pleading with her red eyes, with her wet hair, with her shaking hands.

"Why did you not take a cab from Nadar's studio, my dear?" said Julie. "Certainly I gave you enough money."

"Please listen to me, Mama."

But Julie did not want to listen. "You know that we are not poor, not anymore, never again. There is no necessity for us to live like filthy shopgirls when I own the building that we live in. Imagine—you are the daughter of a Parisian landlady."

"I am going to have a baby, Mama."

"When you are older," insisted Julie, using words to shunt aside any unwelcome facts. She turned her back once again, looking into the mirror with apprehension. She picked up a rouge pot and began to apply the crimson stuff to her lips, as if she were readying herself for an orgiastic night at the Maison d'Or, instead of a domestic evening with her convent-bred children. "When you are ready, when you are suitably married. There is no telling what sort of match we can arrange for you. You are after all a member of the Comédie Française."

"I am pregnant," said Sarah, her green eyes blazing in the dressing-table mirror.

"You are pregnant," said Julie to the glass, so quietly that Sarah had to lean closer to hear. She had been sixteen when Sarah was conceived. Suddenly Sarah was eighteen; nineteen years had passed in the mirror before her eyes.

"If it is a boy, I shall call him Maurice," said Sarah. "After your father."

Julie hesitated before speaking again, tears filling her beautiful blue eyes. She didn't ask who the father was, whether the affair was her first or her tenth, whether it had been celebrated for love or money or fame. All her life, she had given Sarah everything, and Sarah returned her kindnesses with disgrace.

"You will have to leave this house," the grand courtesan said finally. "This is a respectable house, on the Rue Saint-Honoré, and I will have no bastards living here."

Chapter 14

I WON'T
DISAPPOINT YOU

Four years later, in the summer of 1866, Sarah Bernhardt put on a black silk dress, its hemline daringly scalloped to reveal an underskirt of bright yellow; when she walked, her long stride on flimsy high-heeled shoes showed ankles covered by even brighter yellow stockings.

It was a frivolous outfit for such a serious time. Prussian forces were wresting territory from Austria, with whom they had been allied two years before, and alarming Italy, with whom they were allied at the moment. French diplomats engaged in secret agreements to ensure their neutrality; yet Napoleon III was encouraged by his ancestor's name to make a policy as grandiose as his reconstruction of Paris. Supporting the short-lived reign of the Austrian archduke Maximilian as Emperor of Mexico was one short step in the direction of national folly, a childish insistence on humbling the aggressive Prussians. This drive for imperial grandeur would lead, four years later, to a disaster as profound for the French as the Civil War had been for Americans.

The American war had been finished the year before, with the Confederate Army's surrender at Shreveport, Louisiana, in May of 1865. The wounds, nevertheless, remained. An era of banditry, the product of rootless veterans from north and south, began in the West, with outlaws attacking stagecoaches, banks, and trains. The Ku Klux Klan was founded, feeding its poisonous doctrines to the dispossessed and the defeated. The worst wound of all was that President Lincoln, the Great Emancipator, was not there to lead the American Union in peace. He had been murdered in April 1865, six weeks before the Confederate surrender, while sitting in a box at Washington's Ford's Theater during the third act of *Our American Cousin*. Lincoln's murderer was an unaccomplished actor, John Wilkes Booth, who had lived in the shadow of his famous brother, Edwin; tales of Edwin's performance as Hamlet had even crossed the Atlantic. Mme. Guérard had shown Sarah Edwin Booth's picture as the Danish prince, lamenting that the handsome man was not French-speaking. At the moment, however, the actor Booth meant only one man—John Wilkes Booth, dead twelve days after Lincoln—and his notoriety had spawned a wealth of unfortunate jokes in the year following the presidential assassination: Acting was a "murderous" profession; the theater was hazardous to life, particularly third acts; one could live through a play more easily in the stalls than in a box.

"Perhaps another hat, my dear . . . if you don't mind my saying so," suggested Mme. Guérard. "Only because the gentleman in question may prove to be conservative."

"Why should I mind, my dear little lady?" said Sarah. In the badly chipped cheval glass of her dressing room in the too small flat on the Rue Duphot—home not only to Sarah and baby Maurice, but to Sarah's sister Regina, Sarah's maid, Mimi, and Mme. Guérard herself—Sarah adjusted her hat. It was the same bright yellow as her underskirt, made of straw, and trimmed with tiny bells. Whenever she moved her head, the bells jingled. "You know you have earned the right to tell me anything you like, whenever you like."

"Thank you."

"Nonetheless I like this hat, and no power on earth could prevent me from wearing it."

"It is a risk," said Mme. Guérard.

"What sort of risk?" asked Sarah, looking in a drawer for coins for the omnibus ride. In a just world, she could turn left down the Rue Duphot, walk straight into the Rue St.-Honoré, and ask Julie for the loan of her driver. She felt a sharp flash of anger at the memory of her mother's latest carriage, a summer-weight wicker phaeton made in England, which Julie claimed was a mark of her new program of economy—pulled as it was by a single horse. Sarah would have liked to point out the surprising fact that every grand courtesan preening herself in the Bois that summer had the

217

identical phaeton; but she needed her mother's help too much to chance irritating her.

"To be very frank, child, if not for your mother, it is unlikely that the minister of arts would have procured you this very important interview," said Mme. Guérard.

"He was a very good friend of the Duke of Morny."

"Sadly, the duke is no longer with us. And even though your connection to the duke was strong, your mother's was stronger."

"Of course you're right. On my own merits, I am nothing, a nobody," said Sarah. "If I am known at all, it is as a troublemaker."

"You know that you have no supporter greater than I," said the little widow. "I only want you to have the opportunity to exhibit your talents. That is why this interview is so important."

"People are not interested in talent," said Sarah, turning to face her with a violent ringing of the bells on her hat brim. "They are interested in pretty legs." She made a little curtsy, lifting her skirts far more than was necessary to make her point. Sarah Bernhardt's legs were lovely, as anyone who had paid for a seat at the Théâtre Porte St.-Martin in the last six months knew from the evidence of their own eyes.

Sarah's four-year descent from the rarefied atmosphere of the Comédie Française had finally hit bottom in her portrayal of a fairy in *La Biche aux bois* at the Porte St.-Martin. Nothing could be more useless and humiliating, she knew, than to work at such a place while great achievements were being celebrated daily in every field of endeavor. How could Sarah hold her head high while Monet and Dégas and Whistler painted, while Beaudelaire and Verlaine— born the same year as she—published, while Pasteur cured the mysterious silkworm illness, and Lister performed "anti-septic" surgery? While Sarah was shaming herself onstage, the transatlantic cable was finally completed, and a man named Lowe invented an ice-making machine. All about her were marvels and the promise of a world clean and bright and healthful, and in this promise she had no part.

The Théâtre Porte St.-Martin, known for vaudeville entertainments and silly melodramas, was most famous for its "fairy revues." These were no more than an excuse to line up onstage pretty girls in diaphanous costumes and flesh-colored tights. Sarah had taken work as one of a score of winged fairies, skipping, hopping, and prancing about the absurd sets and idiotic story line for the enjoyment of the noisy males in the audience, until the stage manager selected her to go on for the ailing star of the show. While Sarah was not a trained singer, the crowd had not come to hear high notes hit with any precision; and though they loved her tiny waist, her long legs and thin arms, her red-gold hair and green eyes, they loved something else too. There was a plaintiveness about the Conservatoire-trained actress's perfect posture and elegant diction, a regal sweetness about her in Princess Désirée's abbreviated costume. They quieted, they sat forward in their seats, their lips parted in the rapt attention of children.

Unlike the actress playing Princess Désirée whom she had replaced, Sarah was more than a degraded focus of bloodshot, leering eyes. Not simply an actress wearing a scanty costume, she represented a character of noble qualities. The crass audience had been gifted with a taste of the kingdom of art. Surely this was an offering, an achievement. Sarah felt their appreciation. She understood that she had made a hit with these unsophisticated men, and she found in their wild applause a memory of her childish dreams. Perhaps Guérard was right: At twenty-two, life was not yet over.

"You needn't worry, my dear little lady," said Sarah. "Monsieur Duquesnel, as director of the Odéon, will do whatever the minister of arts has told him he must. And if not, then I will do whatever the director of the Odéon tells me *I* must." There was a wince in Sarah's smile as she bent over, hat bells ringing, and kissed Mme. Guérard's cheek. She knew that the little widow disapproved of Sarah's "adventures." She had even mustered the courage to tell Sarah that a loveless affair with a student or a stage manager or a smartly uniformed hussar could not be compared with the first great love of her life, the prince.

"Monsieur Duquesnel, representing the Second Theater of France," said Mme. Guérard, "will surely be a gentleman and a man of principle." Sarah, unlike the other girls in the Porte St.-Martin's troupe of scantily clad fairies, had never looked for lovers among the rich and influential. The daughter of Julie Bernhardt had long since determined never to sell her sexual favors, no matter how grim her circumstances. But the role of Princess Désirée had reawakened her ambition, her pride. Her silvery voice was not meant for doggerel, but for Racine's priceless verse. She knew that the love she had once yearned for from the faceless audience still existed, waiting to be taken into her heart.

Mme. Guérard understood that Sarah's wince indicated just how serious this meeting at the Odéon was: She would make certain that the director of the Odéon desire her as a woman. He would want to add her to his troupe if only to be close to her alluring flesh.

"Don't be absurd, my dear little lady," said Sarah. "If he is such a gentleman, what is he doing running a theater?" She kissed her again, and hurried out into the street without awakening three-year-old Maurice from his nap, or diverting eleven-year-old Regina from the game of cards she was playing by herself on the cold kitchen floor.

Maurice Bernhardt was born in the summer of 1863, in the little flat on the Rue Duphot to which the pregnant Sarah had been exiled. Julie, suddenly too bourgeoise to allow a bastard in her Rue St.-Honoré apartment, had not been completely without the motherly instinct. A new—suitably clandestine—relationship with a rich elderly Russian businessman made it easy to provide a decent stipend to help support the first Bernhardt grandchild.

But this stipend was not granted unconditionally. Regina, Julie's youngest daughter, eleven years Sarah's junior, was her mother's least favorite child. Regina quarreled violently with Jeanne, Julie's great favorite, and was prone to colds; she had disrupted the household with her wild temper, and a nervous, hacking cough. Unlike Sarah, she did not care a fig for Julie's favor, and could not be controlled by small portions of her mother's love. Regina loved only Sarah, who understood her moods, who never criticized her for being too small, or too weak, or too cold. Julie thought it would be a splendid idea for both half sisters to live together in the new flat. Clearly Sarah's career in the theater was finished. She might as well raise Julie's latest bastard along with her own. Jeanne, Julie's second-born and most faithful daughter, would be enough to fill the domestic portion of her life.

Love, and not money, prompted Mme. Guérard to move into the crowded flat. Her one-third share of the rent for the five cluttered rooms was more than kind, since she was the only one besides the overworked Mimi who knew enough to pick up a blouse from the floor or throw out week-old flowers rotting in a crystal vase.

Sarah, hurrying up the street toward the omnibus stop at the Madeleine, grew more sorry by the moment that she had been so brusque with Mme. Guérard. The extra kiss Sarah had given her could hardly compensate for the worry she had caused her by wearing the outrageous hat, by indicating that she would make love to the director of the Odéon if that would get her an appointment at the theater. She owed Mme. Guérard everything. When she was giving birth to Maurice, only Mme. Guérard had joined the doctor at her side. Even little Regina had abandoned Sarah until she heard the baby's screams from the opposite ends of the apartment. She remembered the dear widow's face, drawn and pale, looming over her own as she mopped Sarah's brow. The little woman had exhibited all the pride of a grandmother when she gushed forth the news that her child was fat and healthy and, praise the Lord, a boy.

Sarah would make it up to Mme. Guérard, she thought. She would buy her a cottage in the country. No, not a cottage, but a great house; and she would surround this house with gardens, and then she would add a pond filled with trout, and orchards bearing apples and pears spread out as far as the horizon.

The approach of the omnibus, drawn by four exhausted horses, broke the back of this fantasy. Sarah quickly noted its orange color, remembering that the orange line followed a route that crossed the Seine. For fifteen centimes one sat on top of the bus, exposed to the swift-changing weather of Paris; for thirty centimes one could sit inside as well as get a free transfer to one of the thirty other omnibus lines operating within the city limits.

Or for a franc one could hire a fiacre, she thought, giving the conductor fifteen centimes, and hurrying to climb to the roof of what was really an overgrown, rickety carriage on eight wheels, before the driver could snap his horses forward. "What a nice day to sit outside," she said to no one in particular, pretending that it was perfectly natural for a pale young woman to wish to burn her skin under the summer sun. The half-dozen thirty-centime passengers below and the three fifteen-centime passengers above all stared at the pretty young woman with the ball-adorned hat.

The fifteen-centime savings was an absurd economy for someone without a budget. Sarah had traveled by fiacre and private carriage all her life; she still had visions of herself as a famous actress, rolling in gems. And how was she supposed to budget when one day she was living on the Rue St.-Honoré in a building owned by her mother, the next she was living in a rented little Rue Duphot flat? Sarah's income, dependent on theatrical work and family largesse, was wildly erratic. Her hat was new, and had cost the equivalent of ten trips by fiacre. She had a maid, she had a wealthy mother; and Aunt Rosine, when pressed a bit, always came up with half a dozen big silver five-franc pieces. For Maurice's last birthday, Julie had whimsically added a gold louis—twenty francs—to Sarah's weekly stipend, only because it had fallen accidentally out of her purse.

Still, Sarah had a horror of poverty. As easily as her imagination took her to a glory greater than Rachel's on the French stage, it led her to join the ranks of the broken-down prostitutes, old at twenty-five, bargaining with the fishmongers at the Rochefoucauld Market. Hadn't she already been abandoned by the father of her child? Wasn't it possible that her mother might one day cut off all support? How many more nights would the unwashed patrons of the Théâtre Porte St.-Martin pay to see the same pair of legs in *La Biche aux bois*'s leading role? If she did not get the appointment she sought at the Odéon, who could say how long before fifteen centimes would make the difference whether her child would have enough food to eat or not?

She sat down on a wooden chair bolted to the roof, averting her eyes from any passerby who would surely wonder why someone so well-dressed was on public display.

For ten francs, she thought, one could hire a carriage, complete with driver and footman. Or for ten thousand francs—the monthly sum, according to Aunt Rosine, that the newly "respectable" Julie received from her Russian—one could live as well as Sarah's mother: in capacious rooms on the Rue St.-Honoré, with one winter carriage, one summer carriage, one driver, two footmen, one groom, one maid, one cook, and one butler.

I will make my own ten thousand francs, thought Sarah, ten thousand, and one hundred thousand more. With determination, she pulled out the battered playscript of Marivaux's *Le Jeu de l'amour et du hasard*. The minister of arts had told Julie that the old Marivaux comedy was to be the Odéon's next play. It had none of Racine's poetry or Corneille's tragic grace, but in two days Sarah had committed the part of Silvia to memory.

She had the gift of facile recall. She could conjure up the routes of half the omnibus companies in Paris: yellow, brown, red, blue, and green, their particular destinations designated by an arcane system of letters she had had to learn only in the last few years. The orange line crossed the Seine along the Concorde Bridge, and followed the Boulevard St.-Germain through the Seventh and into the Sixth Arrondissement. It would be no more than a ten-minute walk to the Place Odéon.

As they approached the Concorde Bridge, the wind picked up, and Sarah tried to let go of her anger at Julie. She had disappointed her mother's hopes, after all. It was not right that Julie barely acknowledged Maurice's existence, rarely visited Sarah and Regina, had nothing but an immaculate Dutchwoman's distaste for the slovenly condition of the Rue Duphot flat.

In spite of everything, Sarah would show her. The Odéon would grant her the second chance she needed. Left Bank students and intellectuals who frequented the Second Theater, because they believed it superior to the First Theater—the Comédie Française—would watch her shine in great and small plays. The Odéon was without pretensions, without the crush of society ladies wielding opera glasses to study the stage boxes instead of the stage. They would recognize her talent, they would learn her name, and they would shout it through the streets.

Sarah found herself standing at the edge of the omnibus's roof as they clattered over the bridge, its surface said to be paved from bricks torn from the hated Bastille in 1791. Long ago, Julie's cook, Titine, had walked Sarah over the bridge, telling her how this way the feet of Frenchmen would always step on the tyranny of the Bastille. Sarah had a way of personalizing what belonged to the general public, feeling as though the bricks had been torn from the fortress-prison's walls so that she in particular would have the pleasure of treading on ignominy.

When she squinted down the sun-dazzled Seine toward the twin towers of Notre Dame Cathedral on the Île de la Cité, she thought of how its glory reflected on her life: The first restoration of the twelfth-century church had begun three years before she was born, and ended the year Maurice was brought into the world. She had taken her pampered son to see the restored statuary and stained glass, held him up to gaze through infant's eyes at the newly erected spire and flying buttresses. This made the cathedral part of her legend, subsuming the restoration under the greater subject of her life.

Victor Hugo, still in self-imposed exile on the Isle of Guernsey, had helped spur the restoration with his great novel, *Notre-Dame de Paris*. As the bus stopped for passengers on the Boulevard St.-Germain, Sarah's willful fantasy took this most famous living French writer into her life too. Hadn't she made the discovery that she needed no more than four hours of sleep a night when reading his massive *Les Misérables*? One day Victor Hugo would return to Paris, she imagined, and he would choose Sarah above all others to perform in his great play *Ruy Blas*.

This was not idle wishing, Sarah told herself as a smart Faubourg St.-Germain coach passed the omnibus with speed. Anything was possible, good or bad, swiftly or slowly, in the world of the theater. Perhaps she would have to tell M. Duquesnel, director of the Odéon, with whom he was dealing. She had met Dumas *père* and Dumas *fils;* she had been the protegée of the Duke of Morny, half brother of the emperor, who had died much too young the year before; she had been photographed by the great Nadar, now a balloonist as well as a photographer, the inspiration of Jules Verne's recently published *Cinq semaines en ballon*. If this were not enough, she had given birth to the son of a real-life prince, even if that prince had refused to legitimize—or help support—little Maurice. Fame surrounded her, fame would come to her, fame was her due, she would tell M. Duquesnel. Her name would fill his theater to the ceiling.

"Why is he turning?" said Sarah sharply to one of her fifteen-centime neighbors. "The orange line goes right along the Boulevard Saint-Germain."

"Not since yesterday, Mademoiselle," said the conductor, leering up at her legs from the bottom of the stairwell. Sarah pulled her bright underskirt closer to her body.

"I'm getting off," she said, hurrying down the stairs, and jumped into the street before the driver could bring the omnibus to a full stop. Because of this abrupt alteration of the bus route, she would be late. Sarah was a full block from the Église St.-Germain-Des-Prés, the oldest church in the city. And she had to walk practically as far as the Luxembourg Gardens. She could not very well run on her high heels. And she did not want to be seen perspiring through the thin layer of rice powder that made her pale face paler still. At best, she would be a half hour late. M. Duquesnel would think her lateness a deliberate affront. Now he might remember the calumnies spread about her hasty departure from the Théâtre Gymnase, he would believe the lies about her swift exit from the Comédie Française.

"I'm terribly sorry I'm so late, Monsieur Duquesnel," said Sarah, blinking her eyes and shaking her head at a fat man in a sack suit standing before a desk piled high with playscripts. When she had finally seen the theater standing in the square after her swift, anxious walk through the ancient, narrow streets of the quarter, she raced the last few paces on her toes. Once inside the theater, she had hurried past the reception area to this hot, curtainless, inner office, its windows looking out on a littered courtyard.

"I'm not Duquesnel," said the fat man. "I am De Chilly."

"I am Sarah Bernhardt," she said as sweetly as possible, for she rememberd that Duquesnel shared the responsibilities of managing the Odéon with this man, though De Chilly was supposed to be involved with the business—not the artistic—side of the theater's affairs. "Hello, Monsieur de Chilly. It is very nice to make your acquaintance."

"I told Duquesnel you'd be late. Doesn't surprise me in the least." He left her in the office without pointing her to a chair. Sarah sat, overcome with exhaustion. A framed portrait of Emma Livry was the only decoration on a badly plastered wall. Prince Henri had thought her the most beautiful dancer in the world. In Paris no ballerina was more renowned than Emma, and when Sarah's own figure had begun to swell with her pregnancy, she envied her grace and form. This envy intensified after Sarah quit the Français, and waited for the letters that never came from her prince. Then a catastrophe shocked the ballet world. Like Icarus flying too close to the sun, Emma Livry had ventured too close to an exposed gas jet in the wings of a stage, and had been incurably burned. Somehow Sarah's envy—and subsequent remorse—forever connected her to the ballerina's death.

"He's coming," said De Chilly, coming back into the office and sitting down behind the desk. "I predicted you'd be late. I warned him you'd want to make an entrance."

"I did not mean to be late, Monsieur De Chilly."

"I told him if you quit the Français, you'll quit anything, if it doesn't suit you."

"I object to your extreme rudeness, Monsieur de Chilly," said Sarah. "I am here at the suggestion of the minister of arts, who has known me since I was a pupil at the Conservatoire, and who I believe would appreciate that I be treated with a certain modicum of respect."

De Chilly adjusted a pile of scripts so that his view of Sarah would be unobstructed. A slow smile dawned on his florid face as he examined her with care. "But I suppose the way you quit the Français was one great way to get publicity. I'm all for publicity. You'll never find me saying no to publicity. That's the only reason you're here, as far as I'm concerned. For somebody who's never had a success, lots of people know your name."

There was little truth in the various gossipy versions of how Sarah Bernhardt had left the Comédie Française. She never threw her torn-up *pensionnaire*'s contract into the director's face; she never slapped the pompous *sociétaire* Madame Nathalie during the annual ceremony honoring Molière, the father of the Français; nor did she quarrel with the company's leading tragedienne, Mme. Devoyod, insult M. Davenne, the kindly stage manager, or smash up the makeup kit belonging to Mlle. Coblentz, with whom she shared a barren, top-floor dressing room.

The truth was simpler, and sadder.

She had been given a small role in Molière's first play, *L'Étourdi,* originally performed in 1655. Sarah had found it impossibly dated, silly, and unbelievable. Playing her part was unbearable. That she was growing bigger in the belly was still her secret, but her feelings about the play were common knowledge to stage manager and cast. The director, at the request of some of the company's leading players, had asked Sarah to visit him in his office. When he quietly suggested that she try to be more politic in expressing her feelings about Molière, the founder of the Français, the pregnant eighteen-year-old refused. She hated the play, she hated rehearsals, she hated the bad reviews and the bad feelings directed her way. Prince Henri did not answer her letters, Julie had forced her out of the house, and the director of the Comédie Française had suddenly provided a target for her rage.

"Where is my contract, Monsieur?" she had said, and when he handed it to her, she tore it in half and placed it neatly on his broad mahogany desk. "This will save you the trouble of doing it yourself at year's end," she had added, feeling very free and very proud. She no longer had to worry about sharing the news of her pregnancy with the hostile members of the company.

What she had to worry about was getting a job.

Because of her abrupt departure from the Comédie Française, there was a taint about her name, something that made directors wary of hiring her. This reputation didn't vanish overnight. After giving birth to Maurice and returning to her former thin shape, she took to haunting the offices of the boulevard theaters. Despite her beauty, there were so many other young women around that directors looked for any reason *not* to cast an actress, simply to cut the flood of hopefuls to a more manageable stream; and Sarah's quitting the Comédie Française was such a reason.

Once again, it was Julie's connection to a former admirer that had gotten Sarah an appointment at the Théâtre du Gymnase, famous for being the scene of Rachel's triumphant debut. By Sarah's time, the Gymnase had degenerated to a house for simple-minded contemporary comedies. Sarah left after performing in ten different plays; infant Maurice had taken sick with influenza and she did not want to leave his side.

"I missed your triumph in *Un Mari qui lance sa femme*," said a deep masculine voice, attempting without success to stem the natural sarcasm of his voice. "But I certainly enjoyed *Un Soufflet n'est jamais perdu*," continued Félix Duquesnel as Sarah turned from the portrait of Emma Livry. He met her green eyes with confidence, expecting her to be overawed by his prepossessing image: M. Duquesnel wore a white linen coat over a dandy's red waistcoat. Despite the heat, his bow tie was tightly knotted, his elegant trousers creased along the front and back in the fashion introduced to Europe by the Prince of Wales. He was tall and young, with hungry, arrogant eyes.

Sarah remembered what she had told Mme. Guérard: that she would make him desire her. She sensed that there was little she need do to achieve this. He already wanted what he saw. And more, he believed he could have it, with as much effort as pulling a ripe fruit from a tree.

"Perhaps you have seen my favorite Gymnase performance, Monsieur Duquesnel?" asked Sarah. *"Le Père de la debutante?* Everyone commented on how marvelous it was that I didn't laugh in the middle of all my serious scenes, and didn't cry at what the idiotic playwright meant to be funny."

"I am afraid that I missed that amusing play as well, Mademoiselle Bernhardt," said the handsome young man, coming closer, with a mincing step.

"You don't mean that," said Sarah. "I would prefer if you said what you meant, otherwise I will not know what I am doing in this place."

"I will tell you the absolute truth, Mademoiselle Bernhardt," said Duquesnel lightly, taking her hand and bringing it gallantly to within an inch of his pursed lips. "I found your work at the Gymnase to be first-rate, and I hope to find you a small part at the Odéon so that you may accustom yourself to our company and our theater. And may I say that I absolutely adore your hat?"

"I do not like to be laughed at," said Sarah abruptly. She had not come here for a small part, but she did not withdraw her hand.

"I was not laughing—"

"There was nothing in my work at the Gymnase that one could possibly admire."

"Ask her if that's why she quit," interrupted De Chilly from behind the mahogany desk.

"I left because Racine and Corneille are not done at the Gymnase." Then she added emphatically: "Neither is Marivaux. I have longed to do a play like *Le Jeu de l'amour et du hasard.*"

The elegant Duquesnel reddened, worried that the minister of arts expected more for Sarah than he was willing to offer.

"That is a very old play, and a very interesting one," said Duquesnel stupidly.

His partner was more direct. "I understand you had your chance with the classics at the Comédie Française," said De Chilly, continuing to insult her.

Sarah got to her feet.

"Mademoiselle Bernardt, I hope that you will forgive my friend for his somewhat original sense of humor," said Duquesnel.

Sarah did not answer. She walked to De Chilly's desk and brusquely cleared aside a mess of papers in front of him. She could feel Duquesnel's eyes on her profile as she challenged the fat businessman: "If you are not as great an imbecile as you are a boor, perhaps you will allow me to recite for you."

"That's Duquesnel's department, Mademoiselle Bernhardt," said De Chilly, smiling broadly, enjoying the rudeness his insult had prompted.

"I would be most honored to hear—" began Duquesnel.

Sarah interrupted. There was only one power behind the Odéon; and even if he was poorly dressed and ill-mannered, he was at least capable of making up his mind. "I will recite only if Monsieur de Chilly wants me to recite," she said. "I have learned the part of Silvia in *Le Jeu de l'amour et du hasard.*"

"We have not actually decided to do the play, my dear Mademoiselle Bernhardt," said Duquesnel.

"That part is already cast," snapped De Chilly. "And even if it weren't, you would not be right for it."

"I thought such artistic decisions were Monsieur Duquesnel's department," said Sarah.

"This is not a question of art. Your name is not big enough," said De Chilly. The statement had the air of finality about it, but Sarah was not through. She smiled coldly, and sat down in her chair, crossing her arms in a display of stubbornness: She would stay until they would see things her way.

Duquesnel hesitated, wondering whether to apologize for having said a moment ago that they were not sure whether they were going to do the play. He did not want the actress to complain to the minister of arts. He pulled up a high clerk's stool and sat within inches of her, his eyes momentarily fixed on her ankles in their bright yellow stockings. "The sad truth is, Mademoiselle Bernhardt, that our great theater is also a business. From what I have already seen of you onstage, and even more from what I have seen of you today, you would be perfect for the part of Silvia, but alas, De Chilly is right."

"So you, the artistic genius of the Odéon, allow your theater to be run by the business mind of Monsieur de Chilly?"

"We have the greatest respect for each other," said Duquesnel, patting down an imaginary stray hair in his carefully combed coiffure. "This is a partnership."

"It must be difficult having such a partner about your neck," said Sarah.

"But he *is* an excellent businessman," said Duquesnel.

"I was not talking to you, Monsieur Duquesnel," said Sarah. "I was talking to Monsieur de Chilly about you. And I would appreciate it if you would stop staring at my ankles."

"I am terribly sorry," said Duquesnel. "You are mistaken about where it is that I am looking."

"I am not used to being contradicted by gentlemen on so delicate a subject," said Sarah. She would have gone on, but De Chilly had begun to laugh and shake his head. After a few moments he pulled out a cigar from a case on the desk and stuck it into his mouth.

"I fail to see what is so funny," said Duquesnel to De Chilly.

De Chilly stopped laughing and began to speak to Sarah, emphatically pointing his cigar at Duquesnel.

"He looks at all the actresses, Mademoiselle Bernhardt," said De Chilly. "Up and down. Back and front. In the light, and out of the light. He's a sharp one, my partner."

"Not as sharp as you, Monsieur de Chilly."

The compliment was true, and appreciated. Sarah could feel the considerable weight of the man's expertise play upon her restless features.

"I still do not know what sort of actress you are," he said. This was a return of her own compliment, a recognition that between the gruff manager and spirited actress was a common language.

"You have an idea," said Sarah. "Or you would not be wasting your valuable time."

"You are too skinny," said De Chilly.

"My only appetite is for the theater," said Sarah.

"That's nice," he said.

"Thank you," said Sarah.

"Starving young actress prefers acting to eating," said De Chilly, inventing the line he would give the theater columns, as he examined her face. The businessman picked up a pen and wrote this down. Duquesnel, feeling uncomfortable sitting between his partner and the actress, stood and moved his stool away from where she sat. "Quits the Comédie Française, quits the Gymnase, quits a leading role at the Porte St.-Martin because—"

"Because I need to work," said Sarah.

"Not by the looks of your clothes," said Duquesnel, though neither his partner nor Sarah listened to a word he said.

"Because," insisted De Chilly, "the Odéon is the only place that can appreciate the uniqueness of her talent." He was smiling more broadly than ever. "Publicity," he said as he scratched out a few more notes.

"I want the chance to read the part of Silvia to you," said Sarah. "You need not cast me if I am not correct for the part."

"Well, isn't that nice of her," said Duquesnel, speaking to himself.

"I hope you won't disappoint me," said De Chilly. Without looking up, he added: "We pay one hundred and fifty francs a month."

"To start," said Sarah.

When De Chilly looked up, he found her on her feet, her right hand stretched out across his desk, her green eyes wide with pleasure. He took the hand and shook it as if it were a man's.

"I won't disappoint you," said Sarah, and in her eyes was a radiance glorious to behold.

Chapter 15

FROM THE WINGS
TO THE STAGE

S he was not selfish. Whatever she did was not simply for herself. Maurice was a small child, and Regina was sickly, and who would look after them, and Mme. Guérard too, if not Sarah? She had worked and struggled, but the world of 1869 conspired against her plans, diminishing her successes, leaving her standing on shifting sand.

Sarah was not alone in her insecurity

Prussia made everyone fearful, from the empress Eugénie to the ancient, crippled veterans of the first Napoleon's wars. Defeated by Napoleon I in 1807, this northern German kingdom had never lost its antagonism toward the French; its armies played a principal role in the defeat of Napoleon in 1814, and ever since had looked for opportunities to humble France. With Berlin as its capital, Prussia struggled with Austria for leadership of the movement to unite the separate kingdoms and principalities of Germany. By 1866, the year of Sarah's first performance at the Odéon, this leadership was contested in Austria and Prussia's Seven Weeks' War. Prussia's victory led to the annexation of Schleswig-Holstein, the kingdom of Hanover, Hesse, Nassau, and Frankfurt am Main. Fears that France might be pushed into violent confrontation by Bismarck, the Prussian prime minister, were widespread. Nothing could unite all the Germans, north and south, so well as war with their historic enemy.

"After tonight it will be different, my darling," said Sarah to her only child. She had a vague fancy of a success that would lead to riches; enough money so they could be secure in the coming terrible years. Despite international fears, the collapse of the London stock market, the continuing exodus of Europeans to the promised land of America, fortunes were being made all about her. The empress Eugénie had been given the honor of opening the completed Suez Canal, source of millions of francs to French and British investors. Diamonds, discovered two years earlier in the unlikely land of South Africa, were creating vast new assets. In distant, mountainous Wyoming, a United States territory for only a year, gold had just been discovered by men adventurous enough to brave Indians and wild beasts to stake their claims. Simple actions by people with vision changed their lives, freed their families from want forever.

"After tonight we will be able to go away together," said Sarah. "Just the two of us. We will walk in the woods and pick berries. We will bring home wildflowers for the table."

Maurice kept his pretty lips pursed, his eyes hooded with displeasure. He had heard such promises before and no longer believed them.

"Come on, there's a big boy, give your mama a little kiss," said Sarah. Approaching his seventh birthday, he was small for his age, and overprotected by Mme. Guérard, by Mimi, and by his infrequently available mother. "No one loves you more than your mama, and you know that Mama needs your kiss or I won't be able to have a big success, and if I don't have a big success, we can't go away and be together, just the two of us."

Maurice opened wide his pale blue eyes, and reached out for Sarah's neck with his little hands. He pulled her close with force, and kissed her cheeks and mouth, and rubbed his forehead against hers.

"You will take me away, Mama?" asked Maurice.

"I promise," said Sarah. In her child's powerful love she found a memory of her own for Julie, and wanted, as she did a thousand times a day, to take him into her arms and hold him and caress him until he could believe that she loved him more than anything or anyone else on earth.

But another life beckoned, another love.

This was more than a desire for the financial protection success would bring her family.

She was twenty-five and beautiful, and the students who loved the theater knew her name and adored her. Most were younger than she. They were usually poor, republicans who loathed the aristocratic privileges of the Second Empire that had spawned the great courtesans, that had raised a generation to lust after money and flesh and prestige. These students were different from most men of their time. Their lust was for Art, and Sarah was their High Priestess. Last month, after a superb performance of *Kean,* a dozen of them had unhitched the horses from her rented carriage and pulled her along the Boulevard St.-Germain as far as the Concorde Bridge. Sarah loved them, and wished that they had had the strength to run her across the bridge and onto the Right Bank, to turn right along the quays and left through the Tuileries until they were in the square in front of the Théâtre Français, shouting her name.

On the Right Bank, where most of the rich and the powerful lived, or in the Faubourg St.-Germain, the Left Bank's aristocratic quarter, there were few who had heard of Sarah Bernhardt. The students who pulled her carriage were zealots, filled with the play and too much wine. Their devotion did not make her rich, nor did it make her famous, yet it had given her pride, and it had let her believe in her dreams. This was no small gift, for every artist requires the encouragement of the outside world; indeed, far more than any writer or painter or composer, an actor wants an audience. A writer can retreat into the deepest part of his art by remaining alone with pen and paper, as a painter can with paint and canvas, as a composer never lacks for more than his pencil and score book. Certainly a writer wants readers, a painter hopes for connoisseurs who will appreciate his work, a composer for an orchestra that will bring his dream to life.

But an actor needs to act, and to act one needs an audience, one needs the spirit that comes back from the house to fuel the fire onstage. Sarah could not keep track of all the talented actors she had known to give up the theater in despair, no longer sustained by the speeches they recited against the walls of their miserable flats. Their spirits did not die from lack of fame or fortune, but from lack of a chance to work on a stage, with gaslight in their eyes, with the prompter at their feet, and before them, the huge spread-out gathering of a thousand thinking, feeling fellow beings, eager to join with them in the act of theater.

Sarah was lucky with the Odéon, for the company performed to an audience of Left Bank students and intellectuals and Right Bank adventurers wanting more than a glimpse of Bohemia; they wanted to be renewed by art. They were there for the best of reasons: to suspend the mundane realities of life and believe in the magic before them; to feel with the actors onstage the illuminating moments of joy and sorrow that reminded them of their humanity.

Such an audience is the greatest accomplice of an actor.

Sarah could not dazzle them with tricks of gesticulation or the silvery turns of her voice. She had to reach inside herself for what they demanded. When she felt pain, so did they, and this pain came back to her, redoubling her own; when she was shattered by the horrors of fate, the horror was revealed to them not as a shadow recoiling onstage, but as something inchoate and ineluctable, taking inexplicable charge of their hearts.

And so Sarah searched for every emotion that she needed to play. Unlike the famous actresses of the day, she would not exhibit these emotions from the outside like costumes and makeup, or parade them like advertising placards. The truth must be found within the role she created, a subtle center which would inspire every spoken line. This was what the students noticed. This truth, presented by her startlingly melodic voice, irradiated by her beauty, was what they had come to see. And so every time Sarah faced them, she faced herself, she pushed her talent to its limits, she had the glorious obligation to stretch her wings.

The talent that had been stifled at the tradition-bound Comédie Française had not bloomed in the tawdry glamour of the Gymnase, or in the hothouse atmosphere of the Porte St.-Martin. But at the Odéon, Sarah had been given an opportunity and she took hold of it with all the strength at her command. And beyond this joyous coming into the prime of her talent, she had learned something of grave consequence that many just as talented never learn: That in every great career there is a purpose and a plan.

Not for nothing had she performed Molière and Shakespeare and Racine, pleasing the critics before appearing in a Dumas *père* melodrama that pleased her audience even more. Not for nothing had she waited for the right new play, for the right part, the part that tonight she would create for the first time. Unless she was very wrong, the critics would allow the play to live, and *Le Passant* would be associated forever with Sarah Bernhardt's name.

"Are you ready, dear?" asked Sarah of the ever-faithful, fantastically nervous Mme. Guérard.

"Of course, of course," she said, using an uncharacteristic gruffness—by now a feature of every opening night—to hide the terror that her darling Sarah might fail. "I have been ready for a hundred hours."

"You don't have to accompany me," said Sarah as she always said at this time. Mme. Guérard didn't mind that Sarah would abandon her for the dressing room, leaving her to await the first arrivals in the foyer of the theater, to listen for gossip. Sarah cared a great deal about what would be said: whether the public was there to see Mme. Agar, the beautiful actress playing opposite her, or herself; whether they worried over her health, its fragility greatly exaggerated by De Chilly's endless publicity; whether they acknowledged the importance of this performance for Their Sarah, the Rising Star of the Left Bank.

"It is proper that you be accompanied, my dear," said Mme. Guérard. "Surely that is a little favor that I have within my power to grant."

"You don't have to worry so," said Sarah.

"I am not worrying a bit," she said. Sarah brought her close for a hug, readjusting the ugly heirloom brooch pinned to the little widow's black dress. If she understood anything, thought Sarah, what she was saying to Mme. Guérard, what she had told Maurice was no less than true. Tonight, if the crowd was kind, if the *trac* did not tie her tongue or cripple her walk, if she could open her heart to the simple truth of François Coppée's beautiful little play and let her spirit free to take the shape of her role, she would be famous throughout Paris. "They've put on the play I wanted, they've given me the part I was born to play, and now there is nothing that can go wrong. I shall have a delightful time."

"In spite of everything," said Mme. Guérard, for good luck. Sarah didn't respond to this ritualized intoning of her motto. She was frightened precisely because the performance ahead seemed to promise nothing but applause. There was so much good feeling for her from the playwright, her fellow actress, the managers, the audience that she worried she might disappoint them all. It might have been easier if there were someone she could fight against, someone whom she must overwhelm "in spite of everything."

In the carriage Mme. Guérard tried to instill confidence in both herself and Sarah by recalling each and every one of her productions in the last four years. Suddenly their carriage wheels were quieted by a layer of straw scattered in the street in front of a mansion—a common practice to deaden traffic noise when a party was in progress—and the two women looked out the window. With a start, Sarah recognized the block of houses on which the family of Prince Henri de Luyen had kept an apartment.

"L'Étourdi," said Sarah, remembering the last play she had worked on at the Comédie Française. It had been during the rehearsal of that play when she realized that Prince Henri was gone from her life forever.

"Did you say something, my dear?" said Mme. Guérard.

"Oh, no, just thinking," said Sarah.

She had learned to measure her life by the productions in which she appeared. Each play was a signpost, providing a chronology against which other memories might be placed in time. At the Odéon, where she had worked so hard for nearly four years, there were many signposts: Sarah began an affair with the actor Pierre Berton during the run of Dumas *père*'s *Kean;* she ended an affair with the elegant Count Émile de Keratry while playing a boy in Racine's *Athalie.* Her mother came down with pleurisy during the run of *Le Roi Lear,* the first time that she had attempted Shakespeare, in the role of Cordelia. She transported baby son, little sister, Mme. Guérard, and their maid, Mimi, to her new flat at 16 Rue Auber two days after completing her first short run at the Odéon in *Le Jeu de l'amour et du hasard;* she moved to a far nicer flat on the Rue de Rome a week before her first rehearsal of *Le Passant.*

She appeared in old plays and new, comedies and tragedies and melodramas. Some productions ran for two performances, others for four months. The theater was wild with actors scrambling for rehearsal space day and night, trying to stay out of the way of whatever show was being staged that moment; as many as nine different shows were put on in a single mad week. Rehearsals might be scheduled at dawn or at midnight; the actors who were cast most often were those with the least need for sleep, with the greatest ability to memorize speeches, with the most urgent need to throw themselves out before an audience of strangers.

It was natural that no one worked in more shows than Sarah. When the other actors would take a break from the perennial half-dark of backstage, fleeing for an hour of sun in the adjacent Luxembourg Gardens, Sarah would remain behind, eating up her lines under a single gas jet. Sometimes the exhaustion showed during rehearsal: She would be impatient with the actors' eternal squabbling about where to stand in a scene, and bark out commands that belied her age and the presence of the stage manager.

The others granted her an authority by virtue of her work. Sleeping four hours a night, she sometimes found it necessary to lie down at the edge of the stage, where she had the ability to fall at once into a brief—never more than ten minutes—sleep. The other actors allowed this too, stepping quietly around her pale, thin form wrapped in shroudlike shawls on the hard stage floor. Sarah didn't mind being locked away from the fresh air. She drank in the special odor of the theater—a combination of actors' sweat, cheap perfume, and the glue that held the scenery in place. To her it was like being surrounded by a thicket of blooming lilac bushes.

Certainly she had a life offstage: her baby, Maurice, her little half sister, Regina, the devoted Mme. Guérard, her mother and her aunt, and the various men to whom she turned for love. But it was not as fine, not as romantic and grand as the one she inhabited onstage. And how could it be? The truth that opened her heart to powerful emotions was not expected outside the theater. Sarah enthused about her love for Mme. Guérard, the perfect love she had for her baby, her desperation at poor little Regina's precarious health; and when she was in the presence of these people for whom she cared, her love was real and strong, so real that tears came to her eyes, so strong that she nearly fainted from the action of her heart.

Yet love was stronger on the stage. When she played Cordelia, her filial adoration of King Lear drew on a distant memory of her own father, traveling in China, as handsome as a god. Such a memory was magnified a thousandfold through her art, was blown up larger than anything the real world had to offer. Only here could she wrench from her deepest longings, love and loyalty beyond ordinary human capabilities. When she gently laid these emotions at the feet of her audience, they responded with what she needed to feel: the recognition that what she felt was noticed by them, what she experienced was connected forever to their lives.

"I must go, my dear Guérard," said Sarah when the carriage arrived at the Odéon. She forced herself to turn her eyes from the posters announcing her role opposite the beautiful Marie Léonide Agar in the new one-act play *Le Passant*. "Thank you for accompanying me."

Mme. Guérard kissed her, hugged her hands, breathed more words of nervous encouragement. Sarah, despite the love she had for the little widow, barely noticed. She was already slipping into a deeper part of her soul, a place where she could find her role, and her role's desperate heart.

Duquesnel, standing on the stairs leading up to her dressing room, hardly greeted her. He recognized the look in her eyes, knew she was entering the world of the play that would soon unfold. For Sarah the difficult moment was the first one, when the curtain was up, and the truth she felt must be exposed, expressed to the sea of faces before her. Because her talent was great, her fear was great too. This was neither a fear of stuttering, nor of forgetting lines, nor of being unable to move. Her fear was that she might be untruthful; she dreaded disappointing the audience with a peformance that was not naked, not full.

"Don't you say hello, my dear sir?" asked Sarah as she passed. Duquesnel blushed as she took his hand and pressed it. They had been lovers briefly. Their affair began a day after the close of her first show for the Odéon, and ended just before she had begun rehearsals for the second. She did not encourage the affair as a means of ensuring her new status at Duquesnel's playhouse, any more than because of some sudden infatuation. He was very handsome and was drawn to her with a schoolboy's lust. Sarah took this as a great compliment, as a kind of love that she wished, for a short while, to possess. Between two shows Duquesnel, for all his silly posturing and weaknesses, became terribly cherished. Once rehearsing the new play, she did not forget him, but the attention of her heart was turned elsewhere.

"I didn't want to disturb you, Sarah," said Duquesnel. He had a wife, and told himself and his close friends that his marriage was the reason he and Sarah were no longer lovers. "I know how you get when the critics are in the house."

"Shut up, you idiot," said De Chilly, hurrying down the stairs and planting a kiss on Sarah's forehead. She assumed that the rough, dear man had just left flowers in her dressing room, to "surprise" her. He was nervous, much more so than usual. "We don't mention such beasts on opening night."

"It's only a play," said Sarah. "And a small one at that."

"A trifle," agreed De Chilly. "Hardly worth thinking about." Later she would learn in detail what tricks and cajolery he had performed to bring every critic in the city to the Odéon that night; how he had hinted that the overworked young Bernhardt might collapse from the strain, that the short performance in the little play might be her last forever. Sarah would approve of everything, as she always did where publicity was concerned, for De Chilly's purposes were her own. Even Mme. Guérard couldn't stop her from agreeing to the manager's wildest idea: having her photographed in an elegant coffin. The students loved the picture of their ethereal actress in this fatal pose. In that small group, it made as much of a sensation as Manet's scandalously sexual painting *Olympia* had a few years before.

Deathly subjects had a certain poetic, Bohemian value. Baudelaire, inspired by the morbid realities of life, had just died at the age of forty-six. At twenty-five, Sarah was now the age at which Marie Duplessis, the famous courtesan whom Dumas *fils* had immortalized in *La Dame aux camélias,* had perished. Indeed, the "decline" of poets and artists to the ravages of consumption were so much a part of the popular imagination that an excess of health was considered philistine. Rachel's sad death a decade earlier, like Charlotte Brontë's in England, had epitomized the romantic—and inevitable—demise of a great artist. De Chilly naturally wanted to use Sarah's pallor to good effect. Her public must regard her preoccupation with death as presaging a short, brilliant life—as short and brilliant as the inimitable Rachel's. Sarah complied with more than the coffin photographs. Her death scenes were so unaffectedly natural that she frequently lost consciousness onstage. More than once the first rows of the Odéon's audience were treated to the sight of real blood appearing in a corner of Sarah's white mouth.

"Just a show like any other," said Sarah. "And I don't even have to die in this one." De Chilly hugged her impulsively, an old soldier wishing his favorite warrior well.

Each show was a tiny world in and of itself; with a clear beginning at casting, a middle during rehearsal, and an end in performing. Each play had its particular mood of melancholy or joy, its special moments of triumph or failure that could not be forgotten. Even though most of the actors with whom she worked were part of the Odéon's company, they seemed different, like herself born again in the context of each new play. An actress who had seemed stilted and shallow in Molière proved to be passionate and deep in Shakespeare; an actor whom she barely noticed in Marivaux became an obsessional object of desire once they began rehearsing Racine.

She was blessed—a woman with a thousand lives, myriad countries. Sarah lived as a woman of England, of Rome, of Greece; she was allowed to be noble and base, a harlot and a queen. The world applauded her daydreams, the fantasies she created before their eyes; their approbation somehow made these fantasies real. At home one could not escape the fact that baby Maurice had—like Sarah—no father; one could not pretend that the cheap oil lamps did not leave rings on the drawing-room piano; that little Regina's cough was tubercular, or that Julie's series of illnesses was making the amazingly youthful courtesan suddenly old.

Onstage Sarah escaped this other life.

Every time she began to work on a new character, she felt vastly privileged at this opportunity to live anew. Even if the intensity of her work was selfish, even if it kept her from being intimate with her child, it nurtured her, it gave her a sustenance that made her feel whole. To work onstage was so joyful that it had become intensely difficult to go for too long without a part to play. Offstage she didn't know where she was, where she was going. She didn't know from where she came.

It would have been different had Sarah approached each new role as the company did at the Comédie Française. At the Français, the stage manager retained his time-honored position, conducting rehearsals and occasionally reminding the distinguished actors of the precise gestures and mannerisms employed by the previous generation of *sociétaires* in performing the same roles. It was not at all unusual for a production of a Français classic to go before the public with only a single rehearsal. There were many times when the leading players in a play by Racine or Corneille would show up on opening night, their lines memorized, prepared to meet their cast and their audience together for the first time. Mme. Agar, who had worked in both theaters, said that the *sociétaires* developed their parts like men and women trying on distinguished old coats, heavily laden with medals and ribbon. The Français company worried mostly that their coats be worn with a certain grave dignity. No stage manager dared do more than tactfully direct the traffic onstage and mediate the disputes about who was upstaging whom, which actor was blocking another's light.

The Odéon, as the Second Theater, tried to do everything as differently from the First Theater as possible. Rehearsals were frequent; as many as a dozen for a single classic play, as many as twenty for a new work. The company thought the technique of the Français actors hopelessly outmoded, the stage manager ridiculously trammeled. At the Odéon the stage manager spoke up, and his participation allowed others to have their say: playwright, prompter, even a stagehand. The generally young actors listened to suggestions, and accepted the not very startling premise that a man sitting in the front row of the house might see more of the shape of the play than an actor in the thick of the action onstage.

"Hello, Madame Agar," said Sarah when she saw her fellow actress, already in her stage makeup, her enormous dark eyes as cold and distant as those of a prophetess in communication with her god.

"Dear Sarah," said the much older actress, but though they kissed, though they would soon share intimacies before a crowd of strangers, now they were like distant phantoms, speaking across a void. Without another word, Sarah went into her square little dressing room, personalized by the light green drapes Mme.

Guérard had sewn together from the drawing-room drapes in their Rue Duphot flat. She pulled them back and pressed her face against the small window looking out into the dark courtyard, her forehead chilled by the damp, cold glass. Turning about, she found no flowers from De Chilly, but Duquesnel's bouquet was arranged in a crystal vase with his traditionally double-entendre card of everlasting friendship. Nothing from Julie, who had been ailing, nothing from Aunt Rosine, who remembered only when she had a respite from her admirers. Not even a card from her half sister Jeanne, she noticed, this fact setting off a flash of anger. Even if she was staying home to look after Julie, Jeanne might have taken the trouble to write a note of good wishes. Regina, at fourteen more like a daughter to Sarah than her baby sister, had brought a box of chocolates into Sarah's bedroom that morning, and together, to celebrate the opening of *Le Passant,* they had eaten the entire box in bed. Regina would not be in the audience tonight, even were she not running a higher fever than usual. Because of her poor health, Sarah never let her go out into the wet January air.

A low ceiling, a thick carpet, the burning gas jets on either side of the mirror all contributed to the stupendous heat that Sarah found comforting. Like many actors, Sarah was accustomed to heat and terrified of cold drafts. She liked to stay wrapped up in layers of wool when waiting to enter from the wings, where a breeze from a cracked window sometimes penetrated. Onstage the glow of the gaslights was warm enough for anyone. Even when Sarah— in her days as a winged fairy at the Porte St.-Martin—had had to share a top-floor dressing room with twenty girls, the heat rising from four floors didn't bother her. The close quarters, the harsh burning yellow lanterns, the sweaty dancers washing their armpits before their gentlemen friends came backstage were not stultifying to Sarah. The temperature was never more than pleasant, and all she could smell was the perfume evaporating in the hot air. She liked to tease De Chilly, who could not stand the heat backstage, that only an actor's constitution was able to bear such conditions.

As she changed into a dressing gown and began to apply the greasepaint to her face with a cotton square, she wondered when De Chilly's flowers would arrive.

"Zanetto," she said aloud, for that was the name of her character, a boy troubadour. It was the first time she would play a male part outside of the Conservatoire, but that challenge was not what she relished about the role. It was Zanetto's unrequited love for the impossibly beautiful Sylvia, a love that gives Zanetto's art a depth that it never had before.

"If I may say so, Sarah," François Coppée, the bashful young playwright, had said during the last rehearsal, "what is so good about your part is that you do not get what you want. If I may say so, you are not happy, even though you are a troubadour who will sing more beautifully forever. You are not happy."

Sarah did not like to be told what to think, did not enjoy criticism, no matter how well intentioned. Still, she tried to listen to every word ever said about her performance, as she read every review written about her work. When she was alone, and her rage at being questioned about the truth of her feelings had quieted, she considered these judgments, looking for something beyond envy and wit and hatred in order to improve.

"I am not happy," she said aloud, and in the mirror before her, she could imagine the outlines of Sylvia's face, a faint shadow behind her own image. She dropped the cotton square and picked up a hare's foot to apply the greasepaint more precisely along her high cheekbones. "I want Sylvia, but I do not have her. I do not have her, and I never will."

Le Passant had only two characters, and, though short in length, was being performed, at De Chilly's insistence, alone. The usual background noise of slamming doors, of high-pitched nervous laughter, of tired feet charging up and down the steep staircase, of washbowls clinking and actors reciting, or the callboy's ever more frantic announcements of the impending curtain, was gone. Sarah wasn't aware of the silence until her face was powdered, her lips defined with carmine and her cheeks with rouge, certainly the prettiest boy troubadour in Italy. Suddenly, the unusual quiet broke apart. A sound like an explosion had erupted. Someone was knocking at the metal slide that covered the peephole to her dressing room.

"Yes?" she said, and when there was no response, got angrily to her feet. Naturally the dresser who was to serve both herself and Mme. Agar was nowhere to be found. Of course, there was no maid to attend her. Inevitably the porter was drinking his cheap wine in the lodge under the actors' stairs. "Who is it?" asked Sarah, flinging open the door to a huge bouquet of greenhouse flowers, held in an elegant white-gloved hand.

It was not the porter. Nor was it De Chilly wearing gloves, bringing his slightly belated flowers.

"Like a convent grate," said Prince Henri de Luyen. He had changed dramatically, but for a moment she could not see why. The blond hair, the broad shoulders, the arrogant blue eyes were as she remembered them. That he wore a thick moustache darker than his hair, that his complexion had lost its color were not in themselves reasons to explain why he looked more like a specter than a man. "I scarcely recognize you," he added. His eyes, having barely glanced at her, searched the tiny room. "You're so very sophisticated." Taking care not to slam it, he shut the dressing-room door, touching the peephole's cover with a gloved finger.

"What do you mean?" said Sarah, stepping away from him as he moved closer, the riotous colors of the flowers flashing against the crude light of the gaslamp.

"You know," said the prince. "A convent grate—so the nuns can look in on you when you're sleeping. Make sure you're not up to no good."

She forgot Zanetto, Sylvia, *Le Passant*.

It took a superhuman effort of concentration for her to realize that he was referring to the sliding grate on her dressing-room door. Yes, of course it was like a convent grate, she thought. Only here the callboys looked in to see if you would be in your makeup in time for the rise of the curtain. And the managers were curious to see which gentleman was being entertained after the show.

"Who looks in on you now?" he said. There was something sloppy about his speech, something disreputable about his person beyond the sallowness of his flesh. And something ineffably sad.

"What are you doing here?" she said.

"Congratulations," he said stupidly, thrusting the bouquet forward, like a fencing foil. Forcing herself to examine him, she could see that his eyes were rimmed with red, that when he smiled, his gums looked too weak to hold his teeth. Sarah took the flowers and flung them into the chamber pot against the far wall. But he was not through joking: "Perhaps you should send for the porter. A vase might be preferable."

"I asked what you are doing here?"

"A friend of mine writes for the *Figaro*." He smiled and sidled away from her, taking a seat on the straw-bottomed visitor's chair. Sarah remained standing. "I chose those flowers with great care," he said.

"Henri, your son is seven years old," said Sarah.

"I am sorry, Sarah."

"His name is Maurice, I hope you like it."

"I know what his name is, and I like it quite a lot."

"Not to answer a single letter from a stranger is rude," she said. "Not to answer a dozen and more from me——"

"I was wrong."

She wanted to slap him, but held herself back. The young man she had known was a prince from a fairy tale, a rider of wild horses, a passionate lover, a man with a healthy appetite for life. That young man was dead.

"I never asked for a centime," she said, as much to explain her anger as to castigate him. "But you should have offered. You and your great family! How dare you come here? Who let you in? How did you get backstage at all?"

"I no longer talk to my family," he said, closing his eyes, immensely fatigued. Then suddenly he opened brighter eyes, and began to speak more rapidly with the strange mix of coherence and incomprehension of a man long drunk. "You see, I was wounded. It was long ago, three years, four—a duel. Not a bad wound, but it festered, and it needed a bit of cleaning up. And a doctor injected me with morphine. Nothing like it for the pain, a great discovery. More than just that, of course. Makes you feel better than you have any right to feel, makes you feel—well, I can't explain. Like a god. Like I could do anything. Ingesting it is bad for the stomach, you see. Induces a stupor that way. I was in England. I went to the theater, of course. I should have been an actor. My family—you know, they never allowed it, and I can't do it anymore. It's too late. My wound was here. Little thing." He had taken off his beautiful gloves and dropped them to the floor, and now he pulled back his jacket sleeve and revealed a thick scar marring his pale forearm.

"The injection didn't hurt. British doctors are gentle, and it was they who perfected the syringe after all. Can't get a doctor in France who can handle a syringe like an Englishman. The point is, I'm not very well. Wanted to see you. I'm very happy about this play. My friend from the *Figaro,* he says everyone in the world's here tonight. Just everyone."

Sarah didn't know how long he would have gone on that way before she found the courage to stop him. He was perspiring heavily, and even if that was a product of the backstage heat, it could not explain away the fits and starts of his speech, the way his once ramrod-straight spine curved in a weakling's posture against the rickety chair.

The dressing-room door was flung open peremptorily, ending his speech. De Chilly, his own meager bouquet in his fist, was shouting: "What is going on?"

"It's all right, De Chilly," said Sarah, who could never call him by anything other than his last name. "I know him."

"He pushed the porter down the stairs!"

"I am sorry," said the prince, not moving from his seat, his eyes watering. In the old days he would have struck immediately any man who spoke to him the way De Chilly had. He turned his head to the big manager laboriously. "I only wanted to see Sarah."

"If you don't leave at once, I will call the police."

"I'm not well," said the prince, bending to pick up the gloves he had dropped on the floor. "And as we are very old friends, I thought it might be all right."

De Chilly placed his bouquet on the dressing table and helped the prince to his feet. "I don't know how you had the strength to push anybody anywhere," he said. "But nobody's allowed backstage before a performance."

"Quite right," said the prince. He reached out for Sarah's hand, taking hold of her flesh for the first time in nearly eight years. She allowed him to bring her cold fingers to his bloodless lips. After he took Prince Henri through the door and to the stairs, De Chilly returned and told Sarah to sit.

"I used to know him," she said, looking at her image in the glass.

"Fix your face," said De Chilly.

"I didn't ask him to come." De Chilly handed her the hare's foot, and she brought it to her cheek where the greasepaint had been smudged by tears.

"It is an important night, my dear," he said. "Madame Agar looks very beautiful in her costume. You must dress. You must prepare. I'm sorry if this man upset you, but the curtain will be rising in less than a half hour, and you must be ready to go on."

"He's dying," said Sarah.

"I'm sorry for his trouble," said De Chilly, "but forget it. It is late."

"He's dying and he came to say good-bye," she said. The dresser entered, carrying a small pot of steaming tea. The cup and saucer shook in Sarah's hands. Somehow she found the will to repair the damage done to her makeup, to stand up while the dresser helped her into her troubadour's tunic and tights, while De Chilly carefully arranged the thick red-gold hair tumbling from beneath her tall Renaissance cap.

"That was the green-room bell," said De Chilly, though Sarah had not heard it and did not know whether it was the thirty-minute bell or the five-minute bell. She sat rigid and still at her dressing table until De Chilly, an enormous, friendly shape behind her in the glass, squeezed her shoulders and whispered a single obscenity—for luck. Then he left.

"Zanetto," she said, looking into her own green eyes. She had loved Prince Henri de Luyen, and that love had been in the real world, the world into which Maurice was born. But Maurice was a bastard, and the prince was ill, very ill; and in this world, regardless of having abandoned all responsibility to his lover and his child, he had felt no compunctions about arriving unheralded minutes before the most important performance of her life, exhibiting his fading mortality for her blessing.

"Zanetto," she said again, her eyes wild. "I am Zanetto, and I am not happy." Zanetto loved Sylvia, but Sylvia could never love him, could only give him the gift of love's pain. Sarah had had a surfeit of such gifts. She ran her cold fingers along her brows, along the sides of her nose, adjusted the hair at her temples. Her ankle boots were of soft suede, with flat heels, and when she stood, she felt the troubadour's urge to travel, to sing her songs in distant places. For a moment, when she was hurrying down the stairs to the stage, the prince tried to intrude in her imagination. She was strong enough to banish him.

Mme. Agar was coming out of the green room, a few steps up from the corridor which led to the wings of the stage. Sarah's heart began to pound. Everyone in the world was in the audience tonight, even the prince, even his friend from the *Figaro*. Sarah was suddenly very cold. If only she could go to the green room and warm herself before the fierce coke fire burning in the old-fashioned hearth.

"They've knocked, Mademoiselle Bernhardt," said the callboy, indicating that the audience was finding their seats.

Sarah stood in front of the shut door to the green room, hesitating to finish the walk to the wings. De Chilly was behind her taking hold of her hand in his sweaty fist.

"I am ready," said Sarah. She willed her heartbeat to slow, her anger to cease. The prince had come, the prince had gone, and she was Zanetto, and this was her play. De Chilly said nothing, simply moved his grip to her elbow, and marched her down the stairs to the yellow-walled corridor, lit by a single lantern. Mme. Agar was already out of sight: The play began with Sylvia alone onstage. Sarah removed De Chilly's hand from her elbow and brushed his forehead lightly with her heavily carmined lips. Then she walked down the corridor, each step growing lighter, swifter, as if she were being pulled downhill. Approaching the final four steps that led down to the wings, on the same level of the stage, she slowed. Despite her short suede boots, the bare wooden stairs were noisy, so Sarah took the last steps on her toes. She hated to hear any noise backstage when the audience was already assembled, waiting for the curtain to rise. She detested anything that broke the purity of a world perfectly imagined.

The dresser waited in the wings, holding a heavy shawl for Sarah, but she was no longer cold. Separated from the enormous downward-sloping stage by the upstage right-wing walls—flimsy partitions bolstered by a padding of theatrical posters from the season's offerings—she was flooded by a hot spill of gaslights hanging from battens above the painted scenery of the upstage center wall. She looked through the neat little peephole in the wing wall:

Mme. Agar—Sylvia—glowed in a small cone of limelight, against a backdrop bathed in light filtered through soft blue grass. Who could not love such a vision of loveliness? thought Sarah. She was eager to be with her, to plead Zanetto's hopeless love at her feet. Mme. Agar was completely relaxed, not conscious of waiting for the curtain's rise, not aware of the vast hush of strangers behind the heavy curtain eager to look directly into her heart.

"One minute," whispered the callboy, but this was unnecessary. Sarah could already hear the gaslight man backstage groaning over his frantic task. Sitting before an intricate board of valves and levers, he was turning up the myriad gas jets on the stage and lowering those in the house, even as the stage manager alerted the muscular curtain man on his high stool to be ready to pull up the curtain ropes. Her dresser hurried away from the opening to the stage as the curtain rose to an expectant silence.

Looking enormous through the peephole in the wings, Mme. Agar moved. Sarah imagined how tiny and beautiful the actress must look from the hushed house. She could see the blue-white faces of the first ten rows through the magical glow of the footlights as a force greater than gravity pulled her inescapably from the wings to the stage.

For the last time that night, she thought of the prince, whom she had loved in another world, another time. She let him go, as she let go of that other world to shine only here.

In spite of everything, she thought, this was her moment, this was her place, this was where her feelings emerged in lyrical speech. She was a boy troubadour named Zanetto, hopelessly in love with the beautiful Sylvia. And the pain, the emptiness of unfulfilled longing that led Zanetto to sing would lead Sarah to greatness.

Chapter 16

FOR FRANCE

War came, a stupid war. If the Franco-Prussian conflict had been created as a play, no audience would have believed the plot. Imperial France, jealous of Prussia's new power since its ascendancy over Austria in 1866, felt the need to reassert itself as the strongest force in Europe. The Prussians craved an opportunity to forge the unification of Germany around a great national campaign. "Like nasty schoolboys," said Mme. Guérard. "Children without the sense to stay out of trouble."

In the theater a major incident would have been necessary to motivate these behemoths into action. In reality much less was required to send armies of zealous patriots to their deaths: The throne of Spain was vacant since last year's military rising against Queen Isabella. A constitutional monarch to fill her place was required for the stability of Spain and the balance of power in Europe. Various candidates for kingship were proposed. Prussia had one such proposal, France another. French warmongers made themselves irate over the Prussian choice.

Sarah, like most of her countrymen, did not understand the exigencies of the diplomatic furor. The problems of filling a throne in Madrid appeared to have nothing to do with the life of a young actress and mother. She had trouble finishing the insulting newspaper columns about the Prussian "threat," so obscure were the niceties of this international dispute. Bismarck, the prime minister of a country that had been ruled by a Hohenzollern monarch since

1701, naturally advocated a Hohenzollern for the Spanish throne; yet French militarists insisted on seeing in this a cabal to surround their country by hostile rulers. Even when the Prussians capitulated to French demands to remove their candidate, Napoleon III's empress remained eager to feed the contentious spirit of the times. Empress Eugénie believed that without a war, the French would soon refuse to be governed by an imperial family. She forced her gentle husband into a warlike posture in the name of their son, the prince imperial, who would never rule in a republic.

"It will be like 1848," said Julie. "All the revolutionaries will come out of hiding, and it will be the end of elegance. They will close up the Rue Saint-Honoré, it will finish our rides in the Bois, there will be no more dinners at the Maison d'Or. Paris will close down, and I will lose everything. All because of Eugénie." There was no Prussian threat, Julie insisted. It was simply that the workers in the streets were growing restless with an emperor who existed only for lavish balls and monument building. If the people could not have a glorious emperor like the first Napoleon, they would prefer to rule themselves. So, Eugénie urged her emperor on to folly.

While Eugénie coerced her husband, Bismarck pressed his king, William I. Neither ruler wanted war, but war fever grew hot in both countries. Responding to Prussian "provocation"—Bismarck's publication of an imflammatory version of King William's letter about the crisis—the French declared war on July 19, 1870. Sarah sent Maurice and Regina out of Paris with Julie and Jeanne two days after this declaration. Shops, homes, offices—and all the theaters—were shuttered, and a stream of refugees poured out of the city.

Leaving Paris seemed absurd to Sarah. Most of her fellow actors remained, still unable to believe that the war would touch their lives. The idiotic grievances precipitating this war must surely be resolved around a diplomatic table. Theaters would reopen, and the city would burn with a brighter joy than ever. The French troops marching out of the city in their magnificent uniforms did not seem capable of battle. They were an army famous for their moustaches, for their ability to drink vast quantities of wine. No one would harm such handsome boys.

This insouciance ended when news from the front reached Paris.

Within a week the wounded were drifting back to the city.

The southern German states had joined their Prussian neighbors, and a united Germany, long prepared for attack, crushed France in decisive battles. Napoleon III, forgetting about honor in a sincere desire to stop the carnage, surrendered the main French Army on September 2. The country responded by deposing the emperor. In forty-eight hours, imperial rule was abolished and a French republic proclaimed. This prolonged the bloodshed. The surrender of the emperor did not speak for all the soldiers of France. Troops loyal to the new republic threw themselves against the big German guns, maiming and killing themselves in the name of glory. Two weeks later the Germans began the siege of Paris. Pleasure-loving urbanites, now residents of a republican city, waxed maniacally patriotic. There was no surrender until the end of January 1871 when disease, malnutrition, and fire had eclipsed the reasons for resisting the invader.

This hardly ended the city's suffering. Refugees did not return in droves. The Tuileries Palace had been burned to a blackened shell, and with it half the luxurious mansions of the district. Theaters had been transformed into repositories for the wounded. They were not hospitals, because doctors and medicine were seldom found in the playhouses. Sarah, like many other actresses at the Odéon, had volunteered to look after the defeated, filthy soldiers, crammed onto makeshift pallets on the stage, in dressing rooms, in the boxes, where the plush seats had long since been removed for firewood. She cleaned their wounds with wet rags, helped restore their pride with words of solace. She worked around the clock, going without sleep as she did when rehearsing a play. Here, where she had so often pretended death, men died every day; or worse, they survived without limbs or noses or eyes.

"Forgive me, Mademoiselle," said one gray-eyed soldier, a month after the surrender of the city. "I am sorry to bother you. But is it possible that you are Sarah Bernhardt?"

"How could you know?" said Sarah. His name was Léon. He had seen *Le Passant* three nights in a row, he explained, and then had come back two weeks later and seen it once more. He had just turned eighteen then, and now was nineteen. He had sent her roses after he had seen the play.

"I have never sent flowers to any other woman," he said. Once he was going to study law, but now he knew that he was dying. His older brother, a lieutenant, had perished in the first battle of the war. His best friend, wounded by Prussian mortar, had expired in his arms. He had a little sister, a mother and father, and he wrote to them, dictating to Sarah, that an angel from heaven, a beautiful actress of the Théâtre Odéon, was looking after his wounds. "This is how glorious France rewards its soldiers," he said with no trace of irony.

"You deserve far better than the comfort I provide," said Sarah.

Léon could not help staring at her beauty, yet was shyly reluctant to speak of it in the present. "In the play you were so beautiful," he said. "I wish I could see you one more time onstage."

"I will never act again, my brave friend," said Sarah. "Acting is a useless activity in a world like ours. Utterly without substance or meaning." She cleaned his wounds twice a day, but they never dried. A yellow pus dripped from under the bandages, and every day his pale face became more yellow too. He was weak, yet he insisted on arguing: Their country needed her talents. Victor Hugo, who had been in voluntary exile from France since 1851, when it ceased being a republic, was returning. She must find her strength, Léon begged. Sarah must perform in his plays, so that his republican ideals would shine through her spirit into the hearts of the audience.

"I don't care about republics or republicans, dear friend," said Sarah. "And I don't believe that plays or actors influence anyone. Fools are in charge of the world, men who would not be moved by any play or any actor unless a gun was held to their heads. That is why you are flat on your back, and why this playhouse reeks of misery." Sarah's dreams were dead. Acting was irrelevant. The theater, she decided, was simply a house to shelter actors pretending to be people whom other people paid to watch. Men without arms or legs, women without husbands, mothers whose children were lost to starvation should not interest themselves in fantasy.

And she could not share poor Léon's happiness at the fall of the Second Empire. Sarah had enjoyed living in a magnificent city centered by a royal palace. There was no magnificence in a Paris without sufficient food, water or wine. The republican government that had replaced the emperor was itself attacked by the Communards, who found the new republic insufficiently progressive. Now that the German bombardments had ceased, Frenchmen continued to plunder and burn in the name of liberty. Before they were routed late in May, the Communards managed to destroy the column in the Place Vendôme that Sarah had used as a guiding beacon throughout her adolescence. If this was democracy, she preferred tyranny.

"You must never say such a thing," said Léon. "I do not want to die in vain."

"Then do not die," said Sarah. "Get well. In spite of everything."

"I will try, dear Mademoiselle. But you must believe me that if I die, it will be for France."

"If you die, it will be for lack of trying to live," said Sarah, holding his cold hands. "If you die, it will be for Bismarck and Prussia, not for France. France wants you to live."

"I know that France wants me to live," said Léon, pulling Sarah closer to his broken body with a sudden strength. "But if I die, I know that I will not have died in vain. The emperor is gone, and the republic will be strong enough to fight the Germans one day. We will be revenged. It is why you must go back on the stage," said the dying soldier. "To inspire the people."

It was madness. All they longed for, these boys ruined by war, was another battle, another chance to kill. If not in their time, then in their sons'. Sarah loved her country, but longed for an end to the suffering about her, a finish to the scrabbling in the ruins. Still, surrounded by cripples wanting only the strength to resume the struggle, she could not be oblivious to the humiliating terms of the French surrender, the debilitating millions owed the victors, the tragic loss of Alsace and Lorraine.

"Please kiss me, Mademoiselle Bernhardt," said Léon. "You are an actress, and are surely capable of pretending that you love me, only for a moment. Just to let me imagine what love must be like."

Sarah kissed his eyes and the boyish beard that covered his face. "I am not acting, Léon," she whispered, bringing her lips to his. He shook his head against her protest. Léon did not want the kiss of a lover; he wanted the kiss of an artist. She had been spotlighted onstage, and he had sat spellbound in his seat in the stalls. No moment had ever been sweeter in his young life than this mark of love from an actress who had the power to make any emotion real.

A few weeks later the theaters were being emptied of their war veterans. Soon they would be cleaned and refitted for their primary purpose. There would be no more memory of their hospital function than of old productions whose sets and costumes had been carted away. De Chilly announced that the Odéon would be open for business in October 1871, and he wanted Sarah Bernhardt, the star of *Le Passant,* to take the female lead in Theuriet's *Jean-Marie.*

"It is useless to ask me," said Sarah to De Chilly.

"Please let us not quarrel about the money just yet, darling girl," said De Chilly. "We are all of us bankrupt."

"I no longer plan to go on the stage," said Sarah.

"Why? Have you lost your nerve?"

"There is no point in acting in this miserable world," said Sarah.

"No point?" said De Chilly. "What do you mean? Some do it for art, some for money, some for glory. How many points do you need? Or do you prefer not to eat?" He smiled and squeezed her thin wrists. "There are always wars, darling girl. And there are always plays. What we don't always have are audiences. That is why I want you to appear. You're going to be great. You're going to be bigger than Rachel."

Sarah was not great in *Jean-Marie* when, following De Chilly's schedule, the play opened in October. She remembered her lines and when and where to walk up and down the stage, but her heart was elsewhere. Léon had died in his parents' home outside Fontainebleau two days after leaving the Odéon and Sarah's care. Her family had returned, Maurice sick with a serious head cold and Regina with a hacking cough that would not quit.

And Julie had solemn news from Rosine, who had gotten it from a Belgian count: Prince Henri was dead, one more life gone in this era of wholesale murder, though in his case the murder was at his own hands. He had succumbed finally to morphine, a slow, lugubrious suicide.

The Odéon gave her another chance after the new year of 1872, starring in a new play, *Mademoiselle Aissé.* Sarah was more animated in this play than in her last effort, but with as many stagehands backstage as there were people sitting in the shabby house, Duquesnel and De Chilly began to fear for the life of their theater.

"Sarah cannot draw her Left Bank fanatics anymore," said Duquesnel. "We might have to bring in music-hall players. Or jugglers and magicians. Parisians no longer care about drama."

Sarah, having been cajoled back onstage, had found her stubborn fighter's instinct building in intensity. Even if acting was irrelevant, she would not stand for such treatment from her former admirers. She took the universal disinterest in playgoing personally. The public had forgotten her. At twenty-six, she was an aging ingénue, with one little splash of publicity to her name. Her success in *Le Passant* had occurred in another era, months before the humiliation of France by Germany. Yet, in spite of everything, she would remind them who she was, she would bring them into the theater and get them on their feet shouting her name.

"Victor Hugo," she said, remembering patriotic Léon's advice. "You will get me a Victor Hugo play and you will see the audience come back."

Duquesnel laughed. "Victor Hugo is the last thing we need. The man is an antique. His plays have no emotion. No actress can do a thing with them but fall on her face."

"You are wrong," said Sarah, remembering Léon's courage, his passion. "Victor Hugo is the greatest patriot in the nation."

"If you want to be patriotic," said Duquesnel, "we can wrap you in the flag, put a piano onstage, and sing war songs."

De Chilly was grinning, and not at his partner's wit. "Victor Hugo," said De Chilly. "My God, it's the answer to our prayers. It's a brilliant idea. We'll put on *Ruy Blas,* and Sarah will play the queen." The return of the old, intensely republican writer to France after the fall of imperial rule was one of the few things the public celebrated in those bleak days. The publicity, the good feeling would be overwhelming. Paris had been trying to forget the war, and what better way than to revive Hugo's 1838 poetic drama? It would be like denying that the Second Empire had ever existed, that Napoleon III had ever surrendered to the Prussians.

"What makes you think the old man is going to let us put on his play?" said Duquesnel. "Or put Sarah in the part?"

"It was Sarah's idea," said De Chilly. "I'm certain that she'll get Monsieur Hugo to give her what she wants."

Sarah procured letters of recommendation, sent extravagant bouquets of flowers, introduced herself to Hugo's advisers at cafés and parties and in the Bois. Her persistence was noticed by the poet. He was flattered by the attention of this girl without politics. For a moment he was diverted from the wrenching sadness that overshadowed French politics in the aftermath of France's stunning defeat. Sarah's campaign reminded the old man of other, less deadly intrigues than those of the political arena. He remembered actresses grown old or dead, theaters that could not contain the brawling crowds when his plays had been young, and he had been young. Perhaps his plays might live if Sarah Bernhardt wanted so badly to perform them. He permitted the Odéon to produce *Ruy Blas,* and gave Sarah the role she wanted.

"This play will make us all famous," said De Chilly, counting advance reservations for the first week of performances.

"If you are right," said Duquesnel, "this play might cost us your Sarah."

"Don't be absurd," said De Chilly. He would not admit to Duquesnel what he had always feared: that Sarah's name might become too big for their theater, that the Comédie Française might come over the river and steal her away. "Sarah is nothing if not loyal. She would never go back to those walking corpses."

Yet on opening night, when De Chilly entered her dressing room, he felt as though Sarah were already leaving. She kissed him tenderly, her hands pressing his cheeks in what could have been a gesture of farewell. When he reassured her about the part, about the enthusiasm of the full house, Sarah returned his smile easily. "I must prepare," she said. "I must make you all very proud of me tonight."

Julie Bernhardt was not feeling well enough to attend, and of course Jeanne remained at her side. Except for these two, and Aunt Rosine, busy with an American gentleman in London, the entire opening-night crowd of the Comédie Française had crossed the Seine to the Odéon. Mme. Guérard, from her exalted seat in a stage box, found herself staring into the opposite box at the famous figure of the Prince of Wales.

Victor Hugo waved to the audience from a box hung with the colors of France. This was the writer of *Notre-Dame de Paris,* the author of romantic dramas, voluminous historical novels, poetry that had moved and shaped the French spirit. Refusing to live in a country ruled by an emperor, Hugo had, at the age of sixty, written *Les Misérables,* an indictment of all who allowed those less fortunate to suffer. The play could not start for an hour, so wild and relentless was the cheering for the returned exile, both national poet and hero of freedom. Duquesnel whispered to his partner that it made no difference what Sarah did that night. The audience would love anything with Hugo's name attached to it. They could run this play for a year.

Nevertheless, Sarah did make a difference.

Victor Hugo, on display in the spill of stage light, was forgotten. Sarah, whispering the poetry of her lines, watching her lover die at her feet, demanded their attention, brought them one and all to the world of the play. *Ruy Blas* was not the story of Victor Hugo's coming back to republican France; it was a drama of seventeenth-century Spain, of nobility and pride, of love and duty. When the final curtain came down, Victor Hugo was standing, not in his box but in front of the stalls, shouting her name. Moments later, when Sarah emerged to receive the audience's applause, the great man slowly came onstage to kiss her hand.

"Promise me, Mademoiselle Bernhardt," said Victor Hugo, in full view of the audience yet inaudible to anyone but Sarah, "promise me that you will always follow your art."

"Yes, sir," said Sarah. "Of course."

"Not for self-love, but for a greater love," said the old patriot. "For the love of your country, you understand. For France."

Sarah had never felt better praised. She took his old, capable hands in hers and brought them to her lips, returning his kiss with her own. Léon and not she had been right. She had the ability to inspire, and it would be a crime not to use this talent for the benefit of her countrymen. Sarah missed Léon, and mourned him. The young soldier would have taken intense pleasure at her performance tonight, at her sharing the stage with his hero. In Hugo's iconic presence, a sudden hatred and resentment for the Germans who had ravaged Paris, had killed Léon and thousands like him, swept over her.

The words of France's national anthem, composed eighty years earlier, on the eve of war with Austria, came whispering from her silvery throat into the charged air. The audience remained standing but silenced as Sarah, holding Victor Hugo's hands, recited the seven stanzas of the "Marseillaise." Only when she had recited the poem in its entirety, did they begin to sing the words, joining with the two artists onstage.

"For France!" said Sarah, repeating Hugo's admonition. The crowd would not sit down, did not contemplate leaving. They would not cease beating their hands together, shouting for the honor of their country, the majesty of art.

Chapter 17

I MISSED YOU FOR
A LONG TIME

Two weeks after Sarah's announcement of her move to the Comédie Française, De Chilly died, a victim of sudden heart failure. Sarah had adored the sour-tempered man, so conscious of publicity, of the value of fame. Theirs had been a business relationship, and as he would have been the first to insist, the theater was a business as much as it was an art. If she had told him what the Français had offered, he would probably have decided that he could not match their price. He was overweight, a heavy drinker, a hearty eater. Such men were red-faced, short-breathed, prone to illness. What she had done was not murder. He had not killed himself over her after all.

"I will come right out and say it," Sarah had said to him. "I am breaking my contract." She stood very still before him in his office at the Odéon, with Duquesnel thankfully nowhere to be seen. De Chilly's cigars stank, and he was poorly groomed, too hairy about the neck, too dirty about the collar. When he was angry, his thick lips spat out his words indelicately.

"Go to hell," said De Chilly.

"I am sorry, you know that."

"We'll sue you."

"I would expect that."

"It's going to cost you at least five thousand francs. More, if I can help it."

"Cheap at that price," said Sarah. "I don't think I have to explain why I am doing this. You know that I love you for the

261

chance you gave me." She took a step closer to where he stood behind his desk. "I love you for everything you have done and everything that you are."

"You're an ungrateful bitch," said De Chilly.

"I will never stop being your friend," said Sarah.

De Chilly was not mollified. "Quit looking for absolution. I'm not your confessor. Besides, I'm not nearly through being angry."

"I don't blame you," said Sarah.

Then De Chilly, the man who had given her the chance she had so desperately needed at the Odéon, sat down and buried his face in his arms.

"Oh, darling," said Sarah, hurrying about the desk to place her gloved hands on his thick neck.

De Chilly shook away her touch. He raised his head, pushed back his chair, and stood. "Just go," he said. "I'm not going to tell you not to worry about me, because I don't give a damn about who or what you worry about. You want to leave us, then leave us. Don't expect me to tell you you're a saint for doing it too."

It surprised Sarah that Duquesnel was so mild with her, so gentle. Before the death of his partner he wrote her a note, wishing her well at the Français. After the terrible shock of De Chilly's heart attack, Duquesnel tried to ease her pain, told her again and again that she was not to blame for his death.

Yet, of course she was to blame. She had not wanted more money, but more fame. She had not cared about repaying De Chilly, but about her career. If he were alive, he would be right to hate her, to wish her ill. Dead, his corpse spoke to her, accused her of ingratitude, disloyalty.

It is because of art, Sarah told herself. Only art could make her leave the Odéon. She would not stretch herself if she remained on the Left Bank. The great classic roles awaited her at the Français, and it was for art that she turned her back on friendship.

Julie alone had dared speak her mind about her daughter's quitting the Odéon: If P. T. Barnum—whose American freak show had attracted worldwide attention since opening in Brooklyn, New York, in 1871—paid her enough money, she'd leave the Comédie Française to dance barelegged on a horse's back.

"It is not money, Mama," said Sarah. "And it is not fame that I want. It is the chance to be great."

"Well," said Julie, "that's even worse."

Sarah believed that everyone would see her in a different light once the company gave her a chance. For the moment it was enough that she was center stage.

In the winter of 1874, two years later, she was offered her chance. Émile Perrin, the director of the Comédie Française, told Sarah that he would like her to take the title role in *Phèdre*. Rosélia Rousseil, a popular and respected actress of the company, had rehearsed the role for a month before walking away from it over what she insisted was a dispute with Perrin about money. Sophie Croizette, the director's lover and Sarah's good friend, told Sarah the truth: Mlle. Rousseil had felt insecure in the play, and thought that exposing herself to the critics could destroy her career.

"I will let you know this afternoon," said Sarah.

"Why this afternoon?" said Perrin, trying to smile despite his concern. Sarah would be a last-minute replacement. The part must be learned in four days. He was frantic over the scheduled sets and costumes, the advance sale of tickets based on an actress who would no longer be playing the role. Perrin reminded Sarah that she had performed the part of Aricie in the same play earlier that year, that her silvery voice was destined to recite the poetry of Racine's greatest part. But Sarah needed no reminders of what parts she had played, what new roles she needed to conquer. She knew that her voice and her talent were not what made him need her so desperately. Sarah had become famous, so famous that people were as interested in watching her fail as succeed. That no one else would satisfy the public as a replacement did not mean that she would not be condemned for attempting Rachel's greatest role. She knew too well how the critics delighted in pulling down a career they themselves had helped create. "Why can't you tell me now?" demanded Perrin.

"I must visit my mother," said Sarah. Perrin shook his head in bewilderment at this. "She saw Rachel do the part, and I want her blessing before I agree to do it."

Sarah needed more than Julie's blessing in returning to the Rue

St.-Honoré, her son, Maurice, at her side. The world was pressing in on her, an excessive world of honors and commitments and attention. The rekindling of an old affair with Jean Mounet-Sully, the handsomest actor on the French stage, was not helping the sadness gnawing at Sarah like a festering wound. Her youngest half sister, Regina, was dying, and if the reports from her other half sister, Jeanne, were true, their mother was dying as well. Faced with the most important role of her career, Sarah was suddenly overwhelmed by emptiness. She wanted love, she wanted family, and all she could see was the glare of jealousy, the promise of death, the absence of feeling.

"Hello, Madame Sarah," said Titine, stepping away from the door. "It is a great honor to see you."

"Give me a kiss at once," said Sarah. Julie's plump cook, her black apron as dusted with flour as her brown hair was flecked with gray, hesitated. The Titine whose hand she had once clutched on walks through the Tuileries was immobilized by Sarah's fame. For the moment, the cook stood still, in awe of the actress unbuttoning her white kid gloves in the same entranceway where Titine had received counts and dukes and princes. Few aristocrats received as much attention in the France of 1874 as this dramatic vision in silk and satin. And none had been deified in the limelight of the stage only to come down to earth on the threshold of Julie Bernhardt's faded Rue St.-Honoré flat.

"I must tell Madame that you have arrived," said Titine.

"A kiss, I said," insisted Sarah, looking directly at her with the eyes glorified in the newspaper columns, eyes that were "almond-shaped," that were "tigerish," that were capable of "instant changes in color" to add fire to a scene. For the moment Titine could not discern any changes, could see only what had always been there, little Sarah's green eyes, eager for a touch of kindness from anyone, even a servant. Titine moved closer, her shapeless shoes flopping on the polished wood floor, and kissed the place on Sarah's cheek she indicated with her index finger.

"You smell like Madame," said Titine.

"How is Mama?" said Sarah, twisting about so that the cook could help her out of her white ermine coat. Before the cook could answer, Sarah continued: "Maurice, come say hello to Titine. If you give her a kiss, she will give you a treat."

"I don't want a treat," said Maurice, shrinking behind Sarah in his beautiful velvet-collared topcoat.

"Go on, Titine, give the boy a kiss," said Sarah. "It's the Eau d'Ange," she added. "Mama always wears it, and sometimes I like the smell of it myself."

"Monsieur Maurice is so very big and handsome, Madame Sarah," said Titine, though her eyes barely left Sarah's costume for a moment, taking in the details of her dress that she would later share with her amazed friends. In place of a fashionable long skirt in a bright color, picked up over a bustle in the back, ending in a train, the actress's skirt was white, draping her thin frame like a nightgown. Nearly everything else she wore was white: her scarves, her brocaded jacket, her satin high-heeled shoes. Only over her hair did she wear a hint of color—long purple feathers ran along her flat white velvet hat. And her rings dazzled from every finger, the rubies and emeralds more startling for the paleness of her hands, the whiteness of her attire.

"Let go of me, Maurice," said Sarah. "Take off your coat. Show Titine what a proper gentleman you are."

"I am not a gentleman," said Maurice, removing his topcoat with quick, jerky movements, revealing his English riding habit. He was eleven, dressed like a miniature dandy his mother's age— thirty—and behaving like a large baby. "I am a little boy, a very little boy. You said so yourself." He remained behind Sarah, holding on to his riding crop as though it were a stuffed toy.

"Stop that baby talk," said Sarah, "or you will go sit in the carriage."

"I will not," said Maurice. He suddenly bulled his way around his mother and past Titine, threatening the bric-a-brac with his crop. Sarah didn't stop him as he dropped his topcoat on a chair and hurried toward the drawing room in search of delicate objects to bang together on the floor. Maurice was too shy to intrude on Julie alone, particularly since his grandmother had never shown him the slightest interest.

"How is Mama?" said Sarah for the second time. She selected, then extended one of the gossamer-weight scarves wrapped about her neck to Titine.

"Madame is as well as can be expected, Madame Sarah," said Titine, backing away with the coat and the scarf, apprehensive that Mademoiselle Jeanne might appear.

"Don't put away the scarf with the coat," said Sarah.

"I'm sorry, Madame Sarah," said Titine. "I thought you were giving it to me."

"I *am* giving it to you," said Sarah. "The scarf is for you, Titine. For you to keep. I saw you looking at it. A little gift, that's all, not another word."

Titine burst into tears, and Sarah, taking the ermine coat from her hands and dropping it over Maurice's topcoat on the foyer chair, wrapped the scarf about the cook's thick neck. "Oh, Madame," said Titine. "Oh, Madame Sarah." The cook, either overcome with emotion or simply wanting to express her respect, slowly tried to get down on one knee. Sarah fought this.

"You mustn't," she said, attempting to raise the cook like a queen honoring a zealous knight. "Come, Titine," said Sarah. "You must get up. I never let anyone act so foolishly."

"I am sorry," said Titine, who needed to pull heavily on Sarah's hands to stand.

"You look so smart in that scarf, dear Titine," said Sarah. "So young and fashionable. Do you remember when you used to take me to see the magic tricks of Monsieur Robert-Houdin? Weren't they the most wonderful shows? He's dead, you know, poor man, like so many others."

"So many," agreed Titine, but this hardly stopped her tears. "We must pray for their souls, Madame Sarah. For those who are dead, and those who are sick."

She knew that Titine was too superstitious to voice either Julie's or Regina's name a moment after she had intoned her wishes for the dead. But she remembered how Titine had loved to hold the baby Regina on her broad lap, running her thick fingers through the child's golden curls.

"Regina is comfortable," said Sarah.

"I pray for her, Madame Sarah."

"She has always loved you, Titine."

"I try to make your mother comfortable," said Titine. "We do the best we can, the very best."

"No one can do more for her than that."

"Regina was the most beautiful baby," said Titine, recalling the girl's brief time under her care. Her look and tone were so sad that it was as if Sarah's youngest sister were past struggling, had already crossed to the overcrowded other world. Sarah adjusted the scarf on the cook's neck, and wiped the tears from her red cheeks. Then they hugged, Sarah towering over her, her body as thin and elongated as the cook's was short and stocky. In the embrace, Sarah was safe, imagining that a miracle could stop Regina's slow dying, might reverse Julie's wasting illness, had the power to hold back the inevitability of death itself.

All her life it seemed as though Sarah had been surrounded by the dead and the dying: her absent father, suddenly wiped from her concerns by Julie's decree that he no longer existed; consumptive Regina, thrust into Sarah's household at Julie's whim from the time she was pregnant with Maurice; the great Rachel, whose short career hovered over Sarah's like a pillar of flame, dead at thirty-six, when Sarah was fourteen and dreaming of immuring herself in a convent. Only poor departed De Chilly had ever dared compare Sarah to Rachel favorably. Prince Henri was dead too, never having met his child. Had he lived, perhaps he would have tried to introduce his former lover to his august family, now that Sarah's name traveled the French-speaking world.

She thought of the Duke of Morny, who had introduced her to the idea of acting, who had given her the ivory comb she still wore in her thick hair. He would have so loved to see her fame. And Dumas *père,* who had probably been Rachel's lover as well as Julie Bernhardt's, had died too soon, despite all his zest for life, before reaching his seventieth year. Dumas *père* had lived to see her perform in his *Kean,* but had not been alive to see that on her return to the Français, her first play was his own *Mademoiselle de Belle-Isle.* On opening night she had found a long piece of white cotton thread draped on a prop onstage—a terrific sign of good luck as long as the thread is not discovered (God forbid!) in a dressing room. As superstitious as most actors, Sarah had shut her eyes and dedicated her performance to his friendly ghost.

"Look what your son has broken, Madame Sarah." Her half sister Jeanne's voice broke Sarah and Titine's long embrace. Despite its mean spirit, the voice was as clear and silvery as her own. Maurice was released from his aunt's iron grip and pushed their way. In Jeanne's other hand were two pieces of a painted porcelain dish and Maurice's riding crop.

"It was already broken," said Maurice.

"Hello, sister," said Sarah, using all her acting talent to keep her voice free of complaint.

"How nice of you to grace us with your presence," said Jeanne, turning at once to Titine. "What are you doing with your blubbering? Take the coats and get on with the tea. Mama can't wait forever, you know."

"Look what Madame Sarah has given me, Mademoiselle Jeanne," said Titine, exhibiting the scarf.

"Take it off before you get raspberry jam all over it," said Jeanne. As Titine backed away under her burden of coats and tears, Jeanne added to her sister: "She eats more than our horses."

"Tell Aunt Jeanne to give me my crop," said Maurice.

"You must first tell Aune Jeanne that you are sorry—"

"I am not sorry!" said Maurice. "It was already broken, I didn't do it."

"He was whipping the dish along the bare wood floor," said Jeanne, as though describing the horrors of an execution by guillotine. "He will have to learn to accept the responsibility for his bad behavior."

"I'm not bad," said Maurice.

"Aunt Jeanne does not mean that you—"

"Stop calling me Aunt," said Jeanne. "You may call me simply Jeanne. I don't want to hear that dreadful word, Aunt, ever again."

"Aunt, Aunt, Aunt," said Maurice. "I want my crop, Aunt Jeanne!"

"I am glad to see that the son of Madame Sarah is used to getting what he wants." Sarah, resisting the urge to strike Jeanne, reached out and violently pulled the crop from her hand. She turned to Maurice and handed it to him, then she slowly turned back to her sister.

"If you won't call me Madame, I won't call you Aunt," said Sarah.

"What do you mean? Everyone in the world calls you Madame Sarah. Madame Sarah is an absolute institution these days. I understand that there has been a terrific rise in the rate of suicides among actors. Only by killing themselves can they avoid you on or off the stage. Unless of course you happen to be *related* to Madame Sarah. Then it is entirely possible to miss seeing her or hearing from her for days and weeks and months at a time."

Sarah looked at her golden-haired, diminutive sister, at twenty-three the image of their mother before her illness, and wondered how so much hate could be contained in so lovely and gentle a frame. That she was known familiarly as Madame Sarah, as she was once known as Mademoiselle Sarah, was not the result of a new measure of respect. The reason was simpler: Maurice's existence had become known to the public. One could not call the most famous unwed mother in Paris "Mademoiselle."

"If Mama is awake, I would like to see her," said Sarah. She extended her hand to Maurice, and the boy took hold of it with speed.

"You must think us quite barbaric, having a cook answer the door," said Jeanne, leading her out of the foyer with its empty visiting-card tray, through the large drawing room, where her mother had once entertained the Second Empire's men-about-town in an atmosphere redolent of lust and money. Then there had been a porter to open the door, a porter's wife to help the cook, a footman to help the porter, a handsome coachman in bright blue livery to inspire admiration from the neighbors. Now the neighbors—Julie's former tenants—were gone. The second-floor banker had been killed in battle during the 1870 war, the third-floor retired lawyer had been slaughtered by Communards in the madness that followed the surrender to the Germans. Even the tiny rooms under the roof had different occupants, the servants having given up their rooms to working widows, surviving in genteel poverty by seamstressing or standing all day behind a counter in a shop.

Worst of all for Julie was that she paid her rent to the speculator who had bought the building from her after the war. She was not the only courtesan to lose a fortune in the fall of the Second Empire. But she was the only courtesan to return to the scene of her former glory, the fading opulence of her flat paid for by her famous daughter, a creature of the new Paris.

"You might ask how Regina is," said Sarah, irritated by the way Jeanne ran her finger along the dusty relics in both drawing rooms, emphasizing their inability to keep more than Bella and Titine in service.

"I'm not a great actress, dear sister," said Jeanne. "I am not capable of feigning interest when none exists."

"That is a horrible thing to say about your own sister."

"Regina is not my sister," said Jeanne. "I gave her up long ago, as she gave up Mama and me. She is all yours, and good luck to her."

"I won't have such talk," said Sarah, slowing down in the corridor to the bedrooms. "Just because you hate me is no reason to hate Regina as well. Especially when she is so sick."

"Perhaps she's sick, as Mama believes," said Jeanne. "And perhaps it's only publicity, as I believe." Sarah resisted the urge to strike her pretty face. The famous coffin photographs continued to be mentioned in the columns. A world of "Sarah-watchers" was convinced that she slept in graveyards, that she avoided the light of day as scrupulously as a vampire, that she kept watch over her dying sister with an extra-human hunger.

"Regina is too sick even to get out of bed," said Sarah.

"Then, if she has the bed, I suppose it's true that you have to sleep in the coffin."

"No one sleeps in the coffin."

"Then you use it exclusively for lovemaking? I've always wondered if you closed the lid once you got in."

"The coffin is a prop in a photographer's studio. It is not in my house, and it has nothing to do with myself or Regina." Sarah turned on Jeanne, but did not touch her. "Neither of us has so much family that we can afford to throw them away."

"Mama is all the family I need," said Jeanne. "And before you go in there, may I suggest that you tell her that you are increasing her allowance? It hurts her pride to have to beg for the few francs you give her."

"I am not a millionaire," said Sarah, wondering at the price of Jeanne's blue cashmere dress, its enormous bustle so flattering to her voluptuous figure. "And I do not give her a few francs. The clothes on your back are probably worth more than most actors make in six months."

"And the jewels on your fingers—what are they worth, Madame Sarah?" said Jeanne, wrapping her cold fingers on Sarah's thin wrist, while Maurice stared at the sisters with fascination. Sarah could have named the men who had given her each gift, could have explained that her household expenses exceeded the money she earned at the Français, could have rationalized that the clothes and jewels she wore were not frivolities but necessities for her career. Feeling the hatred running through the thin wall of her flesh, all she could do was pull her wrist free.

"Don't touch me," said Sarah. "If you hate me so much, then don't touch me."

"And what do you think morphine costs these days?" said Jeanne. "Do you think the druggists make it up free of charge, simply as a courtesy to Sarah Bernhardt's mother?"

For a moment Sarah couldn't speak, wondering whether the words were simply another way to attack her. "What do you mean?" she asked finally. "Mama doesn't take morphine."

"How would you know what she takes, when you're never here? How would you know a thing about what Mama needs?"

"But Jeanne, she musn't take morphine, I have seen what it can do—"

"You see what you want to see, you and all the selfish dilettantes you know." Out of the corner of her eye, Sarah watched Maurice lift an ivory figurine of a horse from a low table and drop to the floor with it.

"I won't allow it," said Sarah. "She will not use morphine. Under no circumstances!" Leaving Maurice and Jeanne, she passed through Julie's dressing room, preserved in its familiar state of gleaming bottles and polished boxes of scent and makeup. In its ivory- and silver-handled tools of beauty Sarah saw the vanished years of imperial luxury and waste. Here, in the clouds of Eau d'Ange drifting up from the marble table, it seemed impossible that the Franco-Prussian war had ever been fought, that Paris had been besieged and savaged. It was as if all that had happened since Sarah's first great triumph in *Le Passant* was the simple passing of five years, instead of an entire way of life, instead of a world.

The bedroom was filled with sunlight, filtered through large red and blue stained-glass panes. As she entered, Julie's maid, Bella, dressed in her uniform of faded black silk, scowled at Sarah. That same scowl on that same forbidding face had kept her when she was a little girl from bursting unwanted into Julie's domain. Bella stood up slowly, as if her bones might break. Sarah waited for the maid to leave. They had not spoken when they last saw each other, and they did not speak now. When she was gone, Sarah moved closer, her throat drying up in a familiar fashion, like going onstage with the *trac*. Jeanne remained at the threshold to the bedroom, posing with a martyr's expression that Sarah did not see. Her eyes were on Julie. No gaslight man could have lit Julie better than this stained-glass coloring of natural golds and reds and blues of bright winter light. Her mother's head and shoulders were raised on an elegant jumble of embroidered pillows, propped up to read her gossip columns in the *Figaro* or have a cup of tea with a raspberry tart. Though she wasn't asleep, her eyes were closed, her body was still, vulnerable and sick.

"Hello, Mama," said Sarah. Julie's eyes opened as Sarah bent over and kissed her cheek.

She had not seen Julie in four months. The Comédie Française, after an initial period of slighting Sarah with small roles, now insisted that she take on everything. After creating the role of Berthe de Savigny in Feuillet's *Le Sphinx,* she had gone directly into another new play, Denayrousse's forgettable *La Belle Paule.* This was followed immediately by the title role in Voltaire's monumentally boring *Zaïre.* Apparently, even if the plays and the parts were wrong for her, the Bernhardt name was selling tickets.

"What do you want?" asked Julie.

"I am here to see you, Mama. I have brought Maurice."

"You want something," said Julie. "You always want something or you do not come. Tell me what it is." Sarah stifled the protest rising in her throat. Who paid her mother's rent, who had supported her throughout the war, who bore the burden of poor

Regina if not Sarah? What had she ever wanted from Julie except to see that she was well?

There was a leavening of truth in Julie's statement. As Julie's eyes suddenly grew conspiring, Sarah knew that she always did want something from her mother, even if it would always be denied her: her acknowledgment, her respect, her love. "You must help your sister," said Julie.

Sarah pulled over a figured damask-covered chair to the bed, a huge, elaborately carved rosewood monument to her mother's career. The scent of Eau d'Ange was overpowering. "I'm always happy to help either of my sisters."

"Jeanne, I am talking about Jeanne," snapped Julie. "What is to become of her when I am gone? She is the most beautiful of my daughters, but she has given up everything just to watch over me. You must put her on the stage."

"Mama, I am not a manager of a theater—"

"Don't contradict me!" said Julie. Sarah could sense Jeanne stiffening from across the bedroom. "Jeanne has more talent than you could ever hope for, but she did not have your luck. You owe it to her, as you owe it to me. Put her on the stage."

"How am I supposed to do that?"

"Do you think I know the names of the men you sleep with? The theater is your business, you handle it well. Handle it now for your sister, who has done a daughter's duty all these years. Promise that you will, promise me."

"All right, Mama. I will try to help Jeanne," she said, wondering what talent Jeanne might have beyond her ivory complexion, her bowed lips, and wavy gold hair.

As if in answer to Sarah's thought, Julie said sharply: "Blanche is dead. Blanche d'Antigny."

"I know. I'm sorry, Mama," said Sarah.

"She claimed she was thirty-four," said Julie. "How old do you claim you are?"

"I'm thirty years old, Mama."

"If that's the truth, you'd better start lying about it. Actresses aren't supposed to get old. Like courtesans." What started as a laugh turned into a cough, a violent hacking that shook Julie's emaciated frame. She had been first diagnosed as consumptive, until a German doctor pronounced her a victim of a disease of the lungs he had never seen. There was nothing that could be done. A certain amount of time would pass, and then she would die, as was true of every member of the human race. Julie was uncomfortable, and the veins stood out in the translucent skin of her beautiful face. "Gentlemen liked Blanche," said Julie. "She gave them what they wanted." Blanche d'Antigny had made a sensation at the Théâtre Porte St.-Martin as a "living statue," when she was eighteen. The theater critics rhapsodized over the lines of her face and figure, since she certainly had no lines to speak. From that theatrical foundation rose her courtesan's career. But Blanche always thought of herself as first an actress, next a great lover. In plays at the Folies-Dramatiques, she stopped the show with her tall, lascivious form, her provocative poses in jeweled belts and transparent gowns.

Sarah knew that what Blanche did onstage was neither acting nor art, but she knew also that her mother pretended not to understand the difference between the respect given Sarah and the notoriety afforded Blanche. Five years before, when Sarah's career was finally taking shape during the run of *Le Passant,* Julie spent more time following Blanche's operetta career than that of her daughter. This was partly because Blanche, younger than Julie by a dozen years, had been an intimate part of La Garde, that charmed circle of courtesans as doomed by the fall of the empire as the aristocrats they serviced. But Sarah felt there was more to Julie's interest in Blanche. It was one more way to minimize Sarah's accomplishments, to deny that her life as an actress had any greater value than that of a highly paid whore.

"Actresses are nothing like courtesans, Mama," said Sarah.

"Tell that to your husband," said Julie.

"You know perfectly well that I have no husband, Mama," said Sarah. In the fatigue in her mother's bloodshot eyes, she had a memory of the last time she saw Prince Henri. She wondered for what pain her mother took morphine, for what dreams unfulfilled, what sorrow that could not be banished. "And I do not give myself to strangers in return for gifts."

"I have never been to bed with a stranger!" said Julie. "You act as if you are the daughter of a whore."

"I never said—"

"I am the same mother who gave you every advantage, sent you to convent school, to the Conservatoire, saw to it that you were accepted—despite your inadequacies—at the Comédie Française! You are a miserable, selfish, hateful child!" Julie paused for a moment, very much out of breath. Sarah slowly got out of her chair. When she spoke, she stood at her mother's head, looking down at her in a theatrical pose that might have been that of an angel of vengeance or that of a frightened child waiting for her mother to wake.

"Do not say inadequacies, Mama," said Sarah, beginning softly, letting her audience strain for the words. "I do not have the inadequacies you imagine. It is sad that Blanche d'Antigny has died so young, but it is not a loss to France. Though you do not bother to come to the theater, everyone in this country who cares for the stage knows your daughter Sarah's name. Not Jeanne's name, not Regina's, whom I take care of for you, but Sarah's." Sarah had held back these words all her life; they rushed forth, filled with a spiritual force. "Do not speak of selfishness, Mama. If you sent me to a convent school, it was to get me out of your flat. You never wanted me in your life, and you did everything that you could to shut me out of it. If you sent me to the Conservatoire, it was because I refused to marry the man you had found to buy me. You didn't dream I could become an actress; that was the Duke of Morny, not you."

Julie closed her eyes, but Sarah knew that for once in her life, she had her attention. "As for hateful, who is more full of hate than you? You never thought I would become anything," said Sarah. "And now that I am famous, you hate me more than ever. You hate me because I have succeeded in spite of you. You hate me because I am better than you, because I got what you wanted without selling myself to men."

Sarah was finished, and Julie began. Behind her shut eyes, tears flowed, and sobs began to lift the *point de Venise* lace that covered her chest. Jeanne finally left her post at the door and came up to the bed, gently taking hold of her mother.

"Mama, it's Jeanne," she said. The touch of her favorite's hand could not stop Julie's grief. Wordlessly, she attacked her eldest daughter with cries and sighs and gasps of pain. Her forty-seven-year-old frame shook under its familiar scent, exhibiting the ravaged shape of the body that had carried Sarah into the world. The sobs led to a renewal of the coughing, and each cough wrenched another regret from the deepest part of Julie's heart.

"Stop it, Mama," said Sarah. The sound of her voice only intensified the coughing, brought into sharper relief the sweat on her cold brow, the blood vessels in the tightly drawn skin of her neck and temples. "I'm sorry if I upset you, Mama. Mama, please."

"Leave her alone," said Jeanne. "Mama, it's Jeanne. What do you want? Mama? What do you need?"

With enormous effort, the invalid managed to stop her coughing. "It hurts," said Julie, her shut eyes continuing to repay Sarah for her hateful monologue. "I need help." Jeanne crossed the room, going behind the Japanese screen where Julie used to change her clothes to titillate an admirer already ensconced in her bed.

"What are you doing?" asked Sarah.

"Preparing her medication," said Jeanne.

"What medication?" Sarah asked, but seeing the pain in her mother's pale face, she didn't ask again.

"Jeanne is very good to me," said Julie, whispering the words through clenched teeth. There was a last series of coughs, and then Julie opened her eyes and groped for a glass of water at the bedside. Sarah gave her the glass, and held it to her mother's lips. Julie sipped. She said: "She never leaves me. She's given up her whole life for me." Her mother's great blue eyes, the eyes that Sarah had longed to see hovering above her throughout her lonely childhood, rested on her. For a moment the pain was gone, and a malicious smile danced across Julie's face. "Sarah. You look ridiculous in that costume. Like a scarecrow. Not like a woman at all, but like a boy without breasts or hips. Aren't you ashamed to walk around like that?"

"No, Mama," said Sarah, watching as the pain returned, gripping her mother with invisible talons.

"I am sorry that you hate me," said Julie. Sarah urged her not to talk, but somehow Julie found the strength to snap out each word as Jeanne, her favorite child, prepared the injection. "Perhaps you'll know what I feel when your boy turns on you one day.

When he tells you what little you've done for him. When he forgets completely the tiny fact that you gave birth to him at all."

"I love you, Mama," said Sarah. "And I forget nothing." Jeanne interrupted, bustling back to the bed with a tray in one hand and a hypodermic syringe in the other. For a moment the ground seemed to give way beneath Sarah's feet. During the war when she had dressed the wounds of soldiers, feeding and caring for dying boys like Léon, she could never learn to ease their pain with the morphine needle in Jeanne's hand.

This fear of the drug was strange because Sarah had no fear of blood or corpses. That Prince Henri had died of his addiction did not sufficiently explain her revulsion at all drugs. There was something about the dreamlike quality of the city's opium eaters, the self-celebratory fraternity of absinthe drinkers and smokers of hashish that drove her to a frenzy. It maddened her that the state she entered through her art, they entered through the use of a narcotic. Sarah knew better than anyone how seductive the power of that dreamlike state was, the state of being right, and sure, and without compromise. How could her mother not want to ease her pain with a dream of greatness? But the drug was not a power but a curse, not a palliative but a destroyer of will. With the morphine the dream came from outside instead of from within. It changed no part of one's self. It simply twisted one's perceptions. And all it taught was that one needed more and more, even as it ruined your stomach, loosened your teeth, destroyed your mind.

"Isn't there anything she can take besides that?" said Sarah.

"Nothing as good," said Jeanne. Sarah turned her eyes as Julie inclined her shrunken body toward Jeanne's, like a lover yearning for a last embrace. "Nothing so sure against the pain."

"She is grateful, even if you are not," said Julie. Sarah studied the lacquered blue and white furniture, the bearskin rugs, and the chaise longue upholstered in white stain. There was a sigh as Jeanne injected the medicine, and a moment passed before Julie continued, her words looser, anticipating the pleasure that would soon run through her body. "It is expensive, but Jeanne buys it for me, and I don't need the doctor, because Jeanne knows how to do it. Her touch is so very fine. I hardly feel it, not even a pinch. You were about to tell me what you came here for?"

Sarah turned and looked at Julie, sunk lower in the pillows, a crooked smile on her lips. "To see you," said Sarah softly.

"Tell me what you want, my child," said Julie, a giggle rising incongruously from her chest. Jeanne passed Sarah brusquely, returning behind the Japanese screen with her tray. "You came here because you want something, and I want you to tell me right now what it is."

"I would like Maurice to see his grandmother," said Sarah, looking back at Julie, who was settling into her luxurious pillows with a beatific smile. "If that is all right, Mama."

"No, it's not all right, because you're lying, lying. What do you want? Go on, famous child. Go on, Madame Sarah. What do you want from your old and ugly mother?"

"Leave her alone for a moment, Sarah," said Jeanne, coming from behind the screen. "Let her quiet down." Titine knocked on the open door, then entered the bedroom with a teacart. Jeanne spoke more quietly, excluding Titine from the confidence. "You can see why there is such a need for money. It is not because of my clothes, which Bella makes for me from Mama's old dresses. And Mama, as you can see, requires little in the way of food or clothing. It is fortunate that her line of work provided her with such a stock of bedclothes, after all."

"I am waiting for you to tell me, Sarah," said Julie.

"Mama," said Sarah, going close to the bed against Jeanne's advice. "I do have something to ask you."

"Of course you do. You always do. Even when you had Titine to take you everywhere, what did you want but your filthy old Nurse! You always wanted something, didn't you?"

"I have been given a chance to perform a great role," said Sarah.

"Would you like your tea, Mama?" said Jeanne.

"You and your great roles," said Julie. She lifted herself a bit higher on the pillows, gesturing to Titine to come near. The cook placed a bed tray on Julie's lap, fussing over the pillows to make her more comfortable. The drug had lifted Julie's spirits, returned a measure of youthful arrogance to her pale features. For a moment Julie Bernhardt was wise and powerful, capable of great kindness or great cruelty, of feats of strength and grandeur. "Titine is giving me great tea. And great tarts. I was a great tart myself, wasn't I, Titine?"

"Yes, Madame Julie."

"Phèdre, Mama," said Sarah. "The role is Phèdre."

"I want more sugar," said Julie, tasting her tea. "I want it to be sweet. There is so little left for me in life that is sweet, that at least I shall have sweet tea."

"Do you hear me, Mama?" said Sarah.

"Of course I hear you."

"I have not given the director an answer. It is a difficult part. The most difficult in the repertoire. You asked me what I want. I want you to tell me what you think I should do."

Jeanne came between them and spoke to Sarah: "Why are you bothering Mama with your ridiculous questions? Nobody in this house cares what your next great part is. People who are dying have more pressing concerns."

"What did you say to me?" asked Julie. "What part?" She sipped her tea with a silver spoon, and fixed her eyes on Sarah.

"Phèdre, Mama. I have been asked to perform the role of Phèdre for the Comédie Française."

"You?" said Julie. "So that is what you came here for. Not to show me your little bastard of a son. But to get my help again. I suppose you want to hear how Rachel did it. Phèdre, you say? That's where she loves her stepson? All that raving passion, passion. I saw her, we all did, Tuesday nights at the Français. She got better, if that's what you came here to find out. I saw her in that part, not once, but ten times. Rachel never stopped playing it. Every year she was better."

"Drink your tea, Mama," said Jeanne.

"I have to answer Sarah's question, don't I?" said Julie.

"Not if you're tired," said Jeanne.

"I'll have plenty of time to be tired. This is my daughter and she needs my help."

"Thank you, Mama," said Sarah.

"So you're still trying to stand in Rachel's shoes," said Julie. "That was her part, you know. They didn't want her to play it at all, not at first. She was very thin, and they didn't think that was right for a dignified wife of a hero. And she was young, they said. The part needed an older actress, a bigger actress, a stronger actress. And then she did it the first time, and no one said a word whenever she was onstage. You could see her suffering, and it was real suffering, not something faked on the stage, but suffering that she tried to get rid of, to tear away from her body. But she couldn't. No matter what she did, the suffering picked at her, and stayed with her, and she got whiter and whiter, and her eyes were red, and you could see that the clothes on her back were getting heavier, too heavy for her to wear. That's what you want? You want that part?"

"Do you think I can do it?" said Sarah.

"As well as Rachel?"

"No, Mama." She held her mother's hands, very much warmed by the cup of tea, very much gentled by the drug. "Do you think I can do it? Do you think I can do it at all?"

"It's not true, Sarah," said Julie.

"What isn't, Mama?"

"Take away this tray, Titine," said Julie.

"Mama," said Jeanne. "You must eat something."

"Take it away!" said Julie. "Take it all away and leave me alone with Sarah. Go on, right now! You too, Jeanne." Sarah waited, not helping her sister or the cook return the tray to the cart. When they had left, Julie snapped at her: "Well, close the door." Sarah did as she was told, and then returned to her mother's bedside. "It isn't true," repeated Julie.

"I don't understand what you mean, Mama."

Her mother's smile was no longer crooked. Suddenly it was warm and fresh and new. "I don't hate you," said Julie. Sarah moved her head closer to her mother's, longing for the time when she had been small enough to jump into her bed, to curl up against her side. "I never hated you, child," said Julie. "And certainly now that you're famous, well, I am nothing but proud, nothing but full of praise for your accomplishments. I was famous too, you know."

"I know, Mama."

"When I drove through the Bois, everyone knew my carriage. You've met the emperor, haven't you? He thought me very grand, you know. My manners, he thought them especially fine. Did you know that he was dead? I'll be dead soon. I thought the duke would have done more, somehow. That was not just a little bit of pleasure, you know. There was love there. But he loved many women, I suppose. It is what I told you long ago. Trust no man, trust only yourself. You've gotten prettier, child. You were not a beautiful baby. It was Jeanne who looked the most like me, but that's not your fault, of course. You never knew your father. I will say nothing bad about him. What did you want? Did I help you?"

"Phèdre, Mama. I have been offered the role—"

"Of course you have. Rachel is dead. Long live Sarah, is what I say."

"But do you think I can do it, Mama?"

"Come here, child," said Julie, patting the bed. For a moment Sarah didn't understand. "Hop up, hop in, there's a good girl," she said. "Don't be too grand for your old mother. This bed's held a lot more than what weight we have between us."

Sarah got into the bed, her slender arm around her mother's shoulders. The world was turning wildly in her head as she struggled in vain to remember a time when she had been invited into her mother's bed. "What a big girl I've got," said Julie.

"Mama," said Sarah, wanting to ask her yet again whether she should attempt the great role, but the question died on her lips. Something greater than her vainglorious career had brought her to her mother's flat. She had longed for her mother, and now her mother was with her, and would be with her always. What difference did it make if the drug had eased her anger, her bad temper, her jealousy? A drug could not create a desire, could not fabricate love when no love was there. Her mother would not have invited Sarah into her bed unless the desire had been there.

"Mama," said Sarah. "I missed you for a long time." She held Julie close, surrounded by her mother's flesh, her mother's mortality.

When Julie died later that year, the news that Sarah Bernhardt had lost her mother brought condolences from every part of France. Even death couldn't shatter the bliss of these moments: the memory of her mother asking her to hop into her bed, to cuddle together against a vastness of pillows, in a perfumed atmosphere lit by a golden sun.

Chapter 18

THEY HATED HER

S arah sat stock still and terrified. Her eyes could make little sense of the images before her in the dressing-room glass. In one hour the curtain would rise on her first performance as Phèdre with the Comédie Française. There was a knock, and the door opened before the maid could reach it. Jean Mounet-Sully, the matinee idol of the Comédie Française, entered. He grinned at Sarah's expression in the mirror.

"It is not funny, the *trac,*" said Sarah.

"I am not smiling about stage fright," said Mounet-Sully.

"No?" said Sarah. "What then?" The enormous dressing room was filled with hothouse roses and two dressers—a maid and Mme. Guérard, wearing her dark blue lace-collared opening-night costume. The two actors spoke without reservation before the servant and the faithful old friend.

"I am smiling over your beauty," he said. "It pleases me."

"I know what pleases you, dear Jean," said Sarah sharply. "Feeling superior to everyone else onstage. You are not human, if you would like to know my opinion. You are not human at all."

"Madame Guérard," said Mounet-Sully. "As an impartial observer, tell us please what Madame Sarah looks like tonight."

"She looks beautiful, Monsieur," said Mme. Guérard. "More beautiful than I have ever seen her."

"Thank you, one and all," said Sarah. "But that does not help my throat. If Rachel is a ghost, she is in this room squeezing it dry." She stood up suddenly and looked at Mounet-Sully. "Why are you here?"

"To kiss you," he said. Considerate of her makeup, he brought her hands to his lips.

"It seems every time we start a play we become lovers again, dear Jean."

"Then we must always be starting a play," said Mounet-Sully with histrionic gallantry. He had been cast as Phèdre's stepson, Hippolyte. At Sarah's insistence his name had been printed in letters as large as hers on the numerous bills posted about the city. Neither had wanted to be alone during the hours when they were not rehearsing; and no one else understood the intensity with which each was working. They were friends more than lovers, but in the quiet hours of the night, they were glad of the chance to sleep in each other's arms.

Sarah returned to her seat facing the mirror. "Are you here to take away my *trac*?" she said.

"I am here to tell you my dream," said Mounet-Sully. He was intimately acquainted with her opening-night fears. Tonight was spectacularly ominous: Mme. Bernhardt's debut in Rachel's famous part.

"I dreamed about us last night," he said, putting his powerful hands on her slim shoulders, looking over her red-gold curls into the mirror. "I didn't tell you this morning, because I thought you'd rather hear it now." Both were superstitious and shared a lovers' ritual: Whenever they passed the night together, they started the morning with what they remembered of their dreams.

"Yes," said Sarah. Dreams revealed many truths, good and bad. "Tell me."

"We are onstage, you as Phèdre, and myself as Hippolyte and when you tell me of your passion, the audience hisses. Not at Phèdre, you understand, but at you, Sarah. They hate your acting. They despise your speech, your figure, your gestures. They hate it all."

"You swear that you tell the truth?"

"I swear."

"You dreamed this last night?"

"Yes."

"When I was in your arms?"

"Yes," said Mounet-Sully. She was laughing, getting out of her seat, almost ready to dance out into the hallways. Sarah's *trac* was gone. Every actor knew that the truth in such a dream lay in its opposite, and what could be better than the opposite of being loathed?

"Darling, thank God, you've saved my life," said Sarah. She didn't go so far as to say out loud that she would be brilliant; that would tempt the fates entirely too much. When she walked onstage that night, she was not crippled by fear, and her unique suitability to performing in Racine's greatest play was revealed to a skeptical audience.

Nothing about the Sarah Bernhardt of *Le Passant* or *Ruy Blas* was paraded onstage. This was not a hubristic attack on Rachel's reputation, one star trying to overshadow another's memory. Only Phèdre was onstage. Once again, this play belonged to no one but the playwright. Sarah was naturally thin and pale, a perfect frame to exhibit a death-dealing passion. Her eyes were green, the color of jealousy. She was long-limbed and nimble; her lust was never expressed in an awkward or clumsy pose. What she wanted she took hold of at once, without hesitation.

Phèdre was the second wife of Thésée, and thus an alien in Thésée's court, home, and bed. She desires her husband's son by his first wife, an illicit yearning shocking to the entire structure of society. Rejected by her stepson, understanding that her lust is tabooed, Phèdre still cannot turn back the fact of her passion. Reason cannot stop the wild flow of events of which she is the chief instrument. While she is remorseful at the dire effects her obsession has on her stepson, she is jealous of his love for another. While she is tortured by regrets, she cannot hold back the forces that will lead to the deaths of her confidant, her stepson, and finally herself.

Sarah saw the theme of the play quite clearly: She wanted something that she could not have, a love she would never stop craving; and she must die by her own hand.

She could see why every great dramatic actress wanted and feared the demands of the role. But once Sarah had begun to search inside her heart for what she needed for her characterization, she found everything she needed, and at once. What was Sarah Bernhardt, the illegitimate daughter of a Dutch-Jewish courtesan, performing on the sacred boards of France's national theater if not an alien? Who could know more about passion that was unrequited, love that was hopeless, desires that could never be met?

The ovation that night would not end. The crowd, which had stifled coughs, slowed breathing into a trancelike rhythm, exploded into applause. Many among them had seen Rachel's *Phèdre;* yet, there was no trace of animosity toward the inheritor of the part. They were grateful for what Sarah had given them, and they would not let her go.

"That was quite a dream I had," said Jean Mounet-Sully after the performance, offering his congratulations, his love. "Imagine this crowd hating you, Sarah. Imagine them loathing your acting, your voice, imagine them hissing you off the stage."

It had not been imaginable that night, or the next. Surely Mounet-Sully's dream was true only in its reverse. *Phèdre* had lifted her from a monotonous celebrity based as much on her private life as on her public performances. After *Phèdre,* no one could deny her talent, her preeminent position on the French stage. The demand to see her in this role matched her desire to perform it. She performed it in Paris, in London, in Brussels, in Copenhagen, and every time, the role grew deeper, more intense. When Phèdre wrapped her arms about her stepson, she tried to pull love from his unresponsive body; when she spoke of her passion, the words hissed out like a dangerous serpent, like a warning of all that was to come. When she died, a peace came over her tortured body that nearly stopped the actress's heart.

In six years she made her mark in many other plays, but it was *Phèdre* that tested her, stretched her talents, challenged the limits of her art. Most audiences preferred her in simpler plays, especially Dumas *fils*'s *La Dame aux camélias,* and usually she was glad to give them what they wanted. Yet there were times when the demands of her life coincided with the demands of the play; when there was no joy for her in the world, and her soul yearned for fulfillment. Then she would insist on performing *Phèdre,* feeding her soul with emotions that were denied to her in life.

For the six years since her debut performance in Racine's great play had been filled with unhappiness. Her mother died and Regina died, leaving the words Sarah had never spoken before they were gone sitting heavily on her heart. Jeanne hated her, and Maurice was learning to despise her, and no man desired her for any reason other than to brush against her fame. Worst of all, the terrible dream told to her by Mounet-Sully to calm her stage fright had somehow come true. In slow, terrible stages, she had lost the love of her audience.

The first production of *Phèdre* had contained within it the terrible kernel of the trouble to come, because fellow members of the Comédie Française could not abide the adulation given Sarah. They were jealous of the unanimously ecstatic reviews, which mentioned only Sarah, of bouquets and laurels and endless applause at every curtain that were for her and not the company. The expectant hush before her entrance in *Phèdre*'s second act infuriated the *sociétaires,* who had felt the boredom of the audience waiting for the famous Bernhardt to appear onstage. The public demand for Sarah to appear in other starring roles led to outright hostility from her fellow actors.

It had not seemed possible that the company's envy could lead to the public's distaste, but at a certain indefinable point where praise grows close to a fever pitch, a resentment sometimes sets in, a loathing of the very icon created by an excess of love. Feeling the audience's irritation, she had sought to regain its favor by leaving Paris, hoping that they would miss her. Attempting to restrict her repertoire outside of her native land, she channeled her enormous energies into painting and sculpting.

This proved a miscalculation. The publicity engendered by Sarah's London tour, by her extratheatrical activities as painter and sculptress had brought indignation from those followers of the Français who wanted their star to restrict herself to classics, perform only with the company and certainly only in Paris. For her to act elsewhere was an affront. They were angry that Sarah had need of another audience's love. To see her sell her mediocre artwork, bits of Romantic sculpture, and old-fashioned oil paintings no better than any hobbyist's efforts, marked the actress as crass and commercial. Her love affairs, her bastard son, her all-night revels, her flamboyant dress indicated that she was unworthy of being put on the noble pedestal erected for her by the city's esteem.

She did not understand how to fight slander whose primary purpose was the selling of newspapers. Sarah saw nothing wrong with becoming more famous than she already was. When the London papers wrote that she dressed as a man, that she smoked cigars, that she took boxing lessons with enough enthusiasm to break her instructor's teeth, she never bothered to deny these lies. When the columnists accused Sarah of capitalizing on her renown to sell her sculptures at inflated prices, she agreed with them wholeheartedly, pointing out that her new mansion on the Avenue de Villiers had cost more than any five actors could earn in a lifetime at the Comédie Française. The public did not like such talk from a theatrical idol. They did not want to hear that Victor Hugo had come to dine at her house, that Victorien Sardou and Alexandre Dumas *fils* had promised her great roles over tea. This was not proper behavior for a classical actress. Surely the great Rachel did not chase after playwrights while hawking mementoes and spouting details of her love life to columnists.

"I am not Rachel," she said to the newspapermen who hounded her. "You'll have to wait until I'm dead to make me a saint." She still did not comprehend the extent to which the audience was turning on her. Remembering how her coffin photographs had helped sell tickets to the Odéon, she fancied that publicity, no matter how wild, might once again add to her legend. She had not calculated on the changed circumstances of her fame. Sarah Bernhardt was no longer the goddess of a few students on the Left Bank; she was among the most famous women in France. Notoriety, appropriate for the stars of the boulevard theaters and the international cafés, was inappropriate for the representative of the Comédie Française.

Sarah must be as pure as Joan of Arc. The public wanted their Phèdre to live alone, to dress simply, to wait for each new part with humility and gratitude. When she did not live like a woman of quiet modesty, of high moral ideals, they vilified her, claiming she was not worthy of being a member of the First Theater of France. Unable to bear the animosity of the company, she quit the Français altogether, only to hear herself called a renegade, a traitor to her art. In despair she created her own troupe, reaping honors in England, Belgium, and Denmark; then she was called a traitor to her country.

"I cannot bear it," said Sarah. "I will go to America."

"That is the worst thing you can do," said Félix Duquesnel, who had remained her friend since her early success at the Odéon in *Le Passant.* "If you go to America, they will never forgive you." He explained that every follower of the theater knew that even Rachel had failed to enchant those unlettered, non–French-speaking barbarians. If Bernhardt rushed to America, it would be to disgrace the French stage in a chase for gold.

"Then what am I supposed to do?" said Sarah. "They hate me when I perform in Paris, they call me a traitor when I do a season in England, and you say that if I go to America they will never forgive me at all."

She did not expect an answer. Félix Duquesnel was ready with one nonetheless: "Let's go out of town. Not to America. Just to Lyons. I will manage everything."

He had convinced her at once. Her troupe was put together, the press releases went out, a theater was engaged, and tickets were sold. Suddenly once again it was an hour before she was to go on as Phèdre and she was examining her face in the dressing-room mirror.

There had been so many awful hours like these, so many dressing-room mirrors, so many expectations of performances that might change her life. Now it was 1880 and this was the mirror of the best dressing room in the biggest theater in the city of Lyons. She was thirty-six years old, but no age showed through the greasepaint. She played ingenues and she played crones, and the truth of her portraits created whatever illusion of youth or age was required. Sarah was anxious about the audience, longing to regain their love; trepidation and defiance showed in her eyes, her cheeks, her brow. These feelings had nothing to do with Phèdre's incestuous passion for her stepson, Hippolyte, but Sarah would use them, swallowing every part of the real world until it had been devoured in service to her art.

Her personal problems would only help her perform tonight.

Every misery would soon be ingested, roiled in her flat belly to a useful concentration of pain.

She knew that her sorrows were petty matched against the giant events of the time. The world continued to astonish her with progress that promised universal felicity for mankind: Meat was being frozen in Australia and Argentina and sent across vast oceans to be thawed and eaten by hungry Europeans. The abolition of slavery in America had led to the destruction of the big slave markets in Zanzibar. Everywhere in the world, peasants were being given the chance for an education, their children, an opportunity to share in the wonders of the world. In 1877 an American named Edison had invented a way to record and play back the human voice on a machine called the phonograph; in the same year an Italian named Schiaparelli discovered canals on the planet Mars.

Nevertheless, this was not the planet Mars, it was the city of Lyons. And her task was not to find faint lines in a telescope, but to open her heart to an audience that might have come only to gawk at her disgrace. "Ask them to come in," whispered Sarah to the maid.

Her visitors—Mme. Guérard, Félix Duquesnel, and Jean Mounet-Sully—entered so quickly, it was likely that they had been waiting all this time outside the door.

"All you must do is tell us when to go," said Duquesnel, glancing at his watch.

"Yes, an actress needs to concentrate alone," said Mounet-Sully. "Especially a great actress."

"And your sister Jeanne did say that you would need to give her a moment alone," said Mme. Guérard, settling into a too deep armchair.

"I have no time for Jeanne, and you must none of you go until I say so. Please," said Sarah, turning her queenly head to find the familiar faces in the mirror: Mme. Guérard, bedrock companion, mother substitute, and selfless friend, who had followed her from home to home, from Paris to London, from Belgium to Denmark, and would continue to follow her no matter where she went; Duquesnel, who had arranged this production more out of compasssion for Sarah than for hope of financial gain; and Jean Mounet-Sully, as celebrated for being the former lover of Sarah

Bernhardt as for his interpretation of the classics at the Comédie Française, who had defied his colleagues to attend this performance. "I have a bit of the *trac,* you know, and I do not want to be alone."

"But Jeanne wanted to speak with you," said Mme. Guérard.

"Jeanne, Jeanne, Jeanne! I don't give a damn about Jeanne! Jeanne will want more money, won't she! Jeanne will want to tell me that she is too far downstage, and the actors get in her light! Jeanne can wait, can't she?" said Sarah. No matter how many times the widow witnessed it, Sarah's anger was terrible to behold. Her pale face colored, and her lips tightened into sharp red lines against the heavy makeup on her face. "Just because I hire her to play a part a thousand fools could do better, that does not mean that I will jump to satisfy her every whim."

"Do not be alarmed," said Mounet-Sully, exhibiting his great white teeth to Mme. Guérard. "Sarah is simply warming up for *Phèdre.* You musn't take it to heart."

"I am not," said Mme. Guérard in a lugubrious voice.

"Oh, no," said Sarah, taking a close look at her. "I have insulted you, haven't I, my little lady? Tell me that you forgive me. Oh, please, how could I be such a brute, and always to my little Guérard?"

"I am all right, Sarah," said Mme. Guérard. "I am only sorry that you are so easily agitated these days."

"I am not easily agitated. It is just that they are going to hate me tonight, and I think I would prefer to be dead."

"You are just a tiny bit nervous," said Duquesnel.

"I am not the only one," she said sharply. Then she brought her hand to her lips for an exaggerated stage whisper: "The stage doorman was *whistling.*"

"Oh, no," said Mounet-Sully, like all actors an expert on a hundred superstitions pertaining to the stage. Stagehands used to communicate exclusively by means of an arcane whistling code, and therefore any additional whistling was not appreciated in the theater. There was more than practical wisdom in the prohibition. For anyone else to whistle in the theater was said to bring bad luck. It was a way of inviting the Devil backstage, a sign that the show would have a short run. "Merde, Sarah," he said. This was an even more venerable opening-night superstition: tossing out profanities to keep evil spirits at bay.

"Merde," said Sarah, slapping the dressing table. "Merde, everyone. Merde into the house, into the wings, into the gaslights. Merde!"

"Merde," said Duquesnel, the exhaustion from preparing this production showing in his red-rimmed eyes.

"Merde!" shouted Mounet-Sully.

"And good luck," said Mme. Guérard, getting to her feet with a feeble smile.

" 'Merde,' my little Guérard," said Sarah. "I have not heard the word pass your lips."

"You say such frightful things, Sarah," said Mme. Guérard. "Just because I am a lover of the theater, does not make me a woman of the theater."

"Nonetheless, you must say the terrible word," she said, turning from the mirror to beg this favor of the little widow with dramatic force. They all watched as she raised her famous face, outlined with broad strokes of paint, as she opened wide her thin arms, ringed with a queen's bracelets, toward Mme. Guérard. "You must," said Sarah, and the words were not mocking or comic, but hard. Mme. Guérard, intimate with every one of Sarah's thousand moods, knew that terror lurked within the actress tonight, a terror that explained her backstage bursts of temper, that would not end until it would be devoured onstage.

"Merde," said Mme. Guérard as quietly as possible.

"You mumble like an amateur," said Sarah, turning back to the mirror.

"Leave her alone, darling," said Mounet-Sully. "Madame Guérard is quite right. Civilians should not be required to participate in our superstitions. Besides, there is nothing to worry about tonight. I have brought you a little something from the Français." The handsome actor ran an index finger through his moustache and winked. "The magic words are fame and fortune," he said, reaching inside the sleeve of his double-breasted dinner coat and pulling out a silk shawl of very bright blue, its many sequins dazzling in the harsh light of the dressing-mirror's gas jets.

"It's not really," said Sarah to Mounet-Sullet, tears threatening her makeup.

"The same," said the actor. "Not exactly a prop, but there it was in the prop room, under Hippolyte's dagger. I am now guilty not only of acting in plays, but stealing from them."

The shawl satisfied two more superstitions: the good luck of bringing a prop or a costume from a previously successful production into the one in which you were about to perform, and the good luck associated with the color blue. Sarah, who favored all-white outfits, frequently added a feather or scarf of blue or purple to her opening-night finery. She would howl if anyone showed up in her dressing room in yellow or black (except for the dressers in their old black silk dresses) or green. Every actor knew that yellow—the color of the Devil's costume in medieval mystery plays—lent disaster to opening nights; that black, the color of death, presaged a quick death for any show; that green, which turned to an unappealing brown under gaslight, was the fairies' favorite color, and any actor wearing it risked their jealous wrath.

With great care, Mounet-Sully placed the shawl about her head and shoulders, framing her face in coruscating folds of blue. This was the Phèdre they had all seen at the Comédie Française six years before, the Phèdre who had crossed the Channel and electrified the British, the Phèdre whose star had grown too bright for the company of which she had been a part.

"Darling," said Sarah, turning about to embrace him, shutting her eyes against grateful tears. "It is such a beautiful gift you have brought me. Such a wonderful gift."

"And my mother always told me to bring flowers to a lady!" said Mounet-Sully.

"They hate me so much," she whispered, holding him with a demonic grip, wishing to draw the strength of his love into her yearning heart. "You don't know how much I go through, darling. You who are loved so much, and always have been."

"You exaggerate. There are many who love you."

Sarah let go her hold of Mounet-Sully, caressing the shawl about her neck as if it were alive. "I have lost their love."

"I can quote back more than a few critics who hated my Hippolyte and loved your Phèdre in the same breath."

"Here's another critic," said Sarah, reaching under a rosewood box for a thin sheet of cheap stationery. "The sort of critic I am attracting these days." She watched in the mirror as Mounet-Sully took hold of the paper, holding it up to a gas jet in the small and dingy space.

" 'Dear Skeleton,' " said Mounet-Sully, reading aloud from the sheet of paper, his theatrical voice booming about the little room like a great beast confined to a tiny cage. " 'You will do well to keep your horrible Jewish nose outside the city of Paris.' " The actor stopped reading and raised his black eyes in a look of anger that could have been seen across fifty yards. "This is hardly a critic," he said.

"Go on, darling," said Sarah. "I have already read it. Now you must read it too."

"Why must you torture yourself with a lunatic's ravings?"

"Go on," insisted Sarah. "I want you all to understand why I am so anxious to begin an American tour."

Mounet-Sully continued reading: " 'If you dare attempt to filthy our national stage with your foreign body, you will find potatoes and tomatoes waiting for you in the gallery. Even though you are so old and bony, your nose is an easy target, and I can promise that it will not be missed.' " Once again the actor stopped reading. "I refuse to go on," he said, beginning to crumple the sheet.

"Don't," said Sarah. "I want to keep it."

"Let him show his face to me," said Mounet-Sully. "The great courage of these letter writers."

"You have courage, darling," said Sarah.

"What courage?"

"The courage to see a former colleague. A colleague ostracized by the others."

"You are not ostracized."

"I was always politely hated and resented. I used to imagine it was because of my talent. Apparently I am hated for my race as well."

"You know that actors have no race prejudices. We only hate one thing—bad notices," said Mounet-Sully. "Besides, I bring greetings from Sophie Croizette and Marie Lloyd."

"They have not come to see me."

"Lyons is not like crossing the river to the Odéon."

"Nor do they visit me in Paris," she said, remembering her student days with Marie Lloyd at the Conservatoire, her shared intimacies with Sophie Croizette in a corner of the green room at the Théâtre Français. "And neither sent a card." Sarah's eyes were wild, registering her hurt and the anger she would guard within forever. "Only you. I am glad you are here." Carefully, Sarah flattened the crumpled sheet of stationery with the side of her elegant hand.

"You should not keep such garbage," said Mme. Guérard. "She wants everything saved. Every vile review, every column attacking her."

"I don't mind the part about the nose," said Sarah, adding a touch of rouge to her cheeks. "It's that idiocy about my age."

She had begun to lie about her age. There were much younger women in the troupe she had gathered around herself after leaving the Comédie Française. Her sister Jeanne, younger by seven years, looked less than twenty-nine, so Sarah insisted that Jeanne lie too: Therefore, Jeanne was pretending to be twenty-two, and Sarah twenty-nine. But how old was Maurice, and when was he born? She couldn't very well ask a boy of seventeen to announce that he was really ten. And by honoring her dying mother's request and placing Jeanne in her troupe, their mutual agreement to keep each other eternally young frequently confused Sarah about her real age.

She was now, at thirty-six, exactly the age Rachel was when she died, her career and her legend assured forever. If Sarah were to die at that moment, she wondered if she would be forgotten in a year. For what had she done except make herself hated by everyone in Paris? Rachel had quit the Français too, had undergone a trip to uncivilized America, had outraged society with her lovers. And Rachel had not only been born Jewish, but had all her life remained a Jew. Sarah, who had been baptized as a child, who loved the Catholic Church as she honored the fact of her Jewish birth, was called a dirty Jew. But Rachel was beloved. Rachel had died a martyr to her art.

"If you take such things seriously, you are mad," said Duquesnel.

"How is the house?" said Sarah.

"Full," said Duquesnel.

"Perhaps full with every Jew hater in Lyons."

"You may be surprised to know that the men and women of Lyons do not read the Paris theatrical columns," said Duquesnel.

"Sarah," said the little widow. "I stood at the box-office window for half an hour, just as you asked. And what did I tell you? They love you, every ticket buyer."

"I don't remember."

"You don't believe," said Duquesnel. Maurice, Sarah's narrow-shouldered and parochial son, once asked her why she didn't marry the manager. Maurice hated the booming voices and extravagant manners of actors as much as he loathed their immoral customs, and thought Duquesnel elegant and proper, with all the outer lineaments appropriate for a father. She didn't bother to explain that Duquesnel was already married, or that no man could love her because she presented nothing to love but a vacant self, waiting to be filled by a part. Sarah had wanted Maurice to feel proud of his mother and happy about the family of which he was a part. So she had explained that she had loved only one man, Maurice's real father, a prince whose greatest sorrow was that he could not raise his son. "It is only in Paris that they are angry about your leaving the Français," said Duquesnel. "Everywhere else they are thrilled that you are here, that you can travel, that you are not chained to those old fools of the Comédie." The manager nodded apologetically to Mounet-Sully at this.

"Worse than fools," said Mounet-Sully. "And you will play Paris again. Even the Comédie Française if you want it."

"It is not fair that they hate me so much," said Sarah. "I never did anything to be so hated." They could not know that she had a sudden image of Julie, not as she looked on her deathbed, but as she had looked before the war when her figure was full, and the waves of her golden hair shone. Julie had told her so many lies. How Sarah's father was in China, how no one loved her so well as her mother. "I did not do anything," repeated Sarah, remembering how her mother's face used to twist with distaste. She blinked into the mirror, and there she saw Julie, smelling of rice powder and Eau d'Ange, looking at her child's head of unruly hair. Julie was finding fault with her temper, her accent, the dirtiness of her hands.

"They find fault with my accent, accusing me of foreign birth," said Sarah. "They talk about my temper as if I go around attacking the audience with my umbrella."

"The public has a very short memory," said Mounet-Sully. "Every career goes up a little, down a little, sideways too. They loved you once, they will love you again."

But Nurse had loved her, and then had gone away forever. Julie wouldn't let her write to or send for Nurse. Nurse couldn't read or write, though she had pretended to, simply to make Sarah feel good, to allow Sarah the fantasy that Julie wrote to her, that she thought of her constantly, that her mother's greatest regret was that she could not be by her side.

"Come on, Sarah," said Mme. Guérard. "In spite of everything." She held her from behind, and Sarah felt reassured, loved. The vision in the mirror was replaced with one in her mind: a childhood memory of Nurse's broad face and stolid body, the copious lap and coarse hands, surrounding her, above and below her. The image seemed to drift, like one of the hot-air balloons launched from the Paris Exhibition of 1878, riding silently over Paris like a reminder of distant heavens.

"I don't think they will ever love me again," said Sarah sadly. "Not in Paris."

"Listen," said Mounet-Sully. "As one actor to another. To hell with Paris. We're in Lyons, and the house is sold out." Once more Sarah embraced Mounet-Sully, gave her hand to Duquesnel to brush with his lips, and lowered her head for dear Mme. Guérard to fuss with her hair.

"Good luck, my dear," said the little widow but the two men of the theater quickly canceled out this civilian's remark."

"Merde," said Mounet-Sully. "Bad luck to you."

"Merde," agreed Sarah.

"Forget your lines," added Mounet-Sully.

"And break your legs," said Duquesnel.

"I cannot listen to this," said Mme. Guérard politely, opening the door.

"May the audience shower you with tomatoes," said Mounet-Sully. "On your Jewish nose. Your dear, beautiful Jewish nose."

"My Jewish nose," said Sarah, when they had followed the widow out the door, and left her alone.

The quiet, the isolation were instantly shocking. At home there were Maurice and his tutor, Titine, who now cooked for her, her two maids, her butler and his wife, her houseboy, Émile, her kitchen maid, her steward, her footman, her dogs. The antipathy of the Parisian audiences hadn't left her poor; foreign tours had left her richer than ever. Mme. Guérard lived with her, and she had recently hired a fiercely loyal Negro page. There was no reason to be alone. Breakfast with Guérard, luncheon parties with a dozen celebrated guests, afternoon teas with columnists, dinner parties that would go on into the small hours. Needing little sleep, she read indefatigably, but preferred to do this in the presence of her dogs, or even sitting in the kitchen while a girl cleaned the silver.

But she resisted the urge to ring for her dresser. Mounet-Sully was right: An actress needed to concentrate alone. Quickly, she brought her head close to the mirror. Mounet-Sully was even more right about something else. *To hell with Paris, she was in Lyons.*

She smoothed her eyebrows, she touched a powder puff to her forehead, she remembered that she was a queen, married to Thésée, the ruler of Troezen. Thésée's son by his former wife, the Amazon Antiope, was a beautiful as a god. She had not created his beauty; the gods had created him in order for her to desire him. Fate decreed Hippolyte to love another, because such love ensured the gods' plan. It was spun into the thread of life that passion would destroy them both.

The callboy had to help her up from her dressing table, so intense was her concentration. Standing in the wings, she forgot the year, the city in which she played, the friends who would be there after the performance. There were only the beckoning gaslight, the steps to be taken, the words to be discovered at the moment of truth. Onstage her voice was clear, the poetry limned in ferocious lines of passion.

She was very good that night, though the audience did not know it. Mounet-Sully, who knew Racine as well as anyone in the country, had never seen a better Phèdre. Yet the audience could not be moved. The Parisians, more sophisticated than they, had told them what to expect: an opportunist, a charlatan, a charmless actress who lived without morals. Between the acts of the play, she stood in the wings, wrapped in furs against a chill that no one but she could feel. They hated her. Still, when she walked out onstage no cold came from her, there was nothing but fire in her frame. Her lust burned to the highest seat in the gallery, for she was Phèdre, consuming herself in hopeless love.

Chapter 19

MARRIED

Notwithstanding the hatred that Sarah felt, the audiences, fascinated, kept coming. In Lyons, Duquesnel convinced her to prolong her engagement. Before it was over, he had cajoled her into a provincial tour: twenty-two cities in twenty-eight days. Returning to Paris, Sarah found little joy at her return. Critics of her visits to foreign capitals did not praise her provincial appearances; everything Bernhardt did, they pronounced, was not for Art but for Mammon. Incensed by the constant vilification, she announced her first American tour: one hundred and fifty-seven performances in fifty-one cities. When she returned, she declared to the hostile press, she would be the richest performer in the world.

"It is easy to understand why you are so hated," said Jeanne to her sister, in the celebrated drawing room of Sarah's Avenue de Villiers home. Sarah had taken care to be polite, to sit up straight on the divan immortalized in Clairin's famous 1876 portrait in which her lascivious, half-reclining pose had suggested an attitude of sophistication that would be emulated by half the women of Europe. "You are the most selfish woman in the world."

"If I am selfish because I do not wish to meet the man who has been hanging on to you like a leech throughout our tour—"

"That man has a name."

"You're right. I have no wish to meet Jacques Damala. Not because I am selfish. Because he encourages you to drink."

"Who besides the Divine Sarah does not drink a glass of wine with dinner?"

"I drink—"

"Certainly you drink," said Jeanne. "A sip from a sparkling glass of fine champagne, a touch of foie gras on a silver platter—everyone in the world knows the diet of Madame Sarah."

"My drinking does not make me forget my lines."

"The only time I miss a line is when I cannot hear a cue," said Jeanne.

"I can always hear Hippolyte quite clearly, even backstage."

"If you would cast the correct actor for the part of Hippolyte—"

"I have cast the correct actor. And I am not worried about casting. I am only worried about you."

"For once you might believe me, and not stupid gutter talk."

"You are my sister," said Sarah. "And if I hear that a man has you drinking absinthe all night—"

"I loathe absinthe," said Jeanne. "I am asking you a favor: Meet Jacques—"

"No."

"I want you to offer him a part in the troupe." Damala was one of a long line of Jeanne's lovers. Like most of them, he was dark, handsome, and full of ambition to meet Jeanne Bernhardt's sister.

"He's not even an actor," said Sarah.

"Jacques has been studying, and if you would only please see him, even for a moment. I want him to come to America—"

A commotion at the double doors to the drawing room quieted Jeanne. Sarah's houseboy, Émile, was trying to hold on to the broad shoulder of a man forcing his way into Sarah's inner sanctum.

"Shall I send for the police, Madame?" asked Émile, stepping away from the stranger.

"It is all right," said Jeanne. "He is with me."

"Monsieur Damala, I presume," said Sarah, sardonically echoing Stanley's famous line upon meeting the explorer Livingstone at Ujiji, on the eastern shore of Lake Tanganyika, ten years before.

Damala raised hat and gloves, clutched together in his right fist, in a gesture of greeting. The man's lapels were velvet, and his fingers were long and elegant. He looked at Sarah without speaking, studying her with as little self-consciousness as if she were a statue in a forgotten, isolated corner of a garden. No man, none of her lovers, not even Prince Henri, had ever looked at her with such perfect indifference. She wanted to tell him something clever and acerbic—that he was handsome, but not so handsome as he imagined—but abruptly she didn't trust herself to wit.

"I would like to introduce Monsieur Jacques Damala," said Jeanne with grave formality.

"I am glad of the opportunity to meet you, sir," said Sarah. "Let us come right to the point. My American troupe is cast, and there is no room for another soul even if—" Sarah stopped speaking, appalled at the diamond-studded cigarette case in the man's hands. Without asking her permission, he was beginning to remove a cigarette.

Finally, he broke his silence. "Apparently you are not a smoker, Madame Bernhardt," he said.

"I consider it a filthy habit," said Sarah, stiffening. "I do not permit it in my presence in a public place. And I consider it an outrage to smoke without asking a lady for liberty to do so."

"Stop playing the grand actress with us," said Jeanne. "I told you, it's like visiting the queen."

"I am afraid I must ask you to leave, sir."

"You surely don't want me to leave," said Damala. He spoke with a foreign accent that she could not place, but his tone was all too familiar: He was as contemptuous as Jeanne. "You have not even attempted to get to know me." With infinite care, he removed a cigarette from the case and put it to his full, bowed lips.

"I want you both to leave," said Sarah. "I want you both to leave at once."

"And if we don't?" said Damala. He lit a match, and the flame was like a crude explosion in the rich room. "If we don't leave, you will recite one of your great speeches, I suppose. You will strike terror in our hearts with the purity of your phrasing, you will force us to flee from the power of your immortal acting." Sarah watched as he lit the cigarette, inhaled deeply, and then let the smoke out through flaring, sensual nostrils. Smiling, as if he had won a great battle, he pulled out an upholstered chair and sat on it, his face, and the smoke, inches from her divan.

Jeanne watched, waiting for Sarah. The silence built until it was thicker than the smoke, until it seemed endless, a permanent condition of this enclosed space, of these entwined lives. Yet it was only a moment before Damala brought the cigarette to his lips for the second time, and drew on it.

It was at that instant that Sarah stood up and slapped him with her right hand. There were rings on four fingers, her bracelets were heavy gold, and Sarah hit him with all her force. She wanted nothing less than to break all the bones of his insolent face. Her first slap wrenched the cigarette from his lips, the second scratched his beardless upper cheek, the third bloodied his nose.

Then, exhausted and frightened by her effort, she ran for Émile. "Get out," said Sarah.

Damala didn't move. He had allowed the slaps, had not tried to move out of the way or defend himself. And he had exhibited neither pain nor surprise. After a moment he brought a silk handkerchief to his nose. The bleeding stopped at once.

"Let's go, Jacques," said Jeanne.

"There is something you should know, Madame Bernhardt," said Damala in an easy, conversational voice. "Your sister and I are dear friends, and that is all. We are not lovers."

"What we are to each other is none of her business," said Jeanne.

"That is not completely true," said Damala, getting out of his chair. "I am looking for a position in your sister's troupe, and as my potential employer, she has the right to know that my character is not as black as some like to paint it." He bent low at the waist, retrieved the lit cigarette and crushed it into a porcelain dish.

Sarah moved away from him, her hands finding and gripping an exquisite glass vase. The door opened before she decided to hurl it. It was Émile, and behind him were the butler and Titine, carrying a rolling pin.

"Get him out of here," said Sarah.

"Please, Jacques," said Jeanne, her usual petty contempt suddenly dwindling to a childish fear.

"I suppose I'll just have to wait a bit," said Damala. "Until after your American tour. I shall study my acting very hard while you're away, Madame Bernhardt. Perhaps we could read a scene together then."

"I'll read a scene with you in hell," said Sarah. She watched him leave, the servants stepping out of his way, an arrogant exit worthy of applause.

The encounter with Jacques Damala plagued her throughout her six months in America. She understood that no matter what transpired in the time away from him, he would be waiting for her in Paris. What she did not comprehend was why his image, which should logically be detestable, was distinctly the reverse. His rudeness was inexcusable, because he detested the way other men venerated her. His ambition was laudable, because he did not pretend that it did not exist. And he was handsome. His hands were long and elegant; they grasped his hat and gloves with tenacious strength. A man's hands contained within them the clue to his passion. She remembered the way they opened his cigarette case, the careless fashion in which they held the offensive object to his lips. Sarah knew that she would not refuse to see him. And some part of her would be destroyed.

Before and after the theater, she avoided Jeanne, unable to look at the hurt in her eyes. Jeanne's pupils closed into tiny points when the stage was bright, and though she seldom forgot her lines, she was frequently inaudible. Backstage gossips whispered that Damala had introduced Jeanne to morphine, and that she pined for the drug as much as the man. Sarah did not believe this. Surely she recognized her sister's affliction: Jeanne wanted love and knew that love would be denied her.

The truth was more sordid. Damala had first met Jeanne at a disreputable party at which he was one of the hosts. Morphine and opium were as available to the guests as champagne and absinthe. Jeanne's familiarity with morphine—through her sorry experience of giving it to her dying mother—had impressed Damala more than her beauty, far more than her famous last name. He had already tried the drug on several occasions, but it was Jeanne who showed him how best to enjoy it: heating the mixture of powdered morphine sulfate with distilled water until it dissolved, and injecting it while still warm into the inner side of the arm. Jeanne had at first taken to the drug only to keep him company; to share the dangerous thrill with him was something like sharing love.

Yet there was never any love for her from Damala, and when his restless womanizing made her sick with jealousy, she used the drug to ease her pain. Even before she joined the American trip, Jeanne had the beginnings of a morphine habit. Twice during the tour, Sarah had been forced to replace her at the last moment when she was too ill to perform. Sarah hadn't understood the reasons for Jeanne's collapses. When Sarah asked what was wrong, Jeanne laughed in her face. "You've always hated me," said Jeanne. "Don't pretend you give a damn now."

Nevertheless, the American circuit was a personal triumph for Sarah. She was a sensation, where years before Rachel had been a failure. Americans who could not understand a word of Rachel's eloquently phrased poetry were mesmerized by Sarah's sinuous motion onstage. They did not have to understand Sarah's words to know that she was in love, or in a rage or in the throes of miserable death; and doing so for their entertainment and enlightenment was a great compliment.

Nothing succeeded so well with the Americans as her theatrical demises near the apron of the stage. Sarah quickly limited her repertoire to eight plays: *Phèdre* and *Hernani,* the serious dramas of Racine and Hugo, and six melodramas, *La Dame aux camélias, Adrienne Lecouvreur, Froufrou, Le Sphinx, La Princesse Georges,* and *L'Étrangère.* In every one of these plays save the last, Sarah died. French culture was suddenly popular in the savage reaches of the American continent. Every American who aspired to be among the elite had to go to the theater at least once when Sarah Bernhardt perished. Newspapers explained that no actress in the world could die so well, and they wanted to be able to tell their grandchildren that they had seen the great Frenchwoman crumple with exquisite grace to the stage floor. It was no wonder death, as well as Damala, haunted her dreams.

Long before she returned home, she began to understand that the overwhelming success of a Frenchwoman's tour of fifty-one American cities would have ramifications beyond the world of the theater. Even though she was excluded from the Comédie Française, the United States had made her bigger than the national theater of France. In spite of everything, she had made herself more than the most prominent French actress in the world. The traveling that left her too exhausted to know whether she was in a hotel in Philadelphia or Boston or Montreal had paid handsome returns beyond the huge sums of gold-backed dollars she earned for performing. She had become an ambassador. Wherever she went, the "Marseillaise" was played, citizens of French descent appeared, shouting her name, the keys to the cities she visited were placed in her pale hands as symbols of Franco-American friendship. French flags flew, French songs were sung, French books were translated into American English. Women copied her French clothes, cooks attempted her French cuisine, politicians tried to understand the French point of view.

Indisputably the United States had redeemed her value with the French audience. Sarah had become the living symbol of her country. To hate Sarah Bernhardt was to hate France itself.

Returning from America, she found her countrymen cheering at the dock. Offers awaited her from every leading manager in Paris. She could choose any play, hand pick her cast, demand any price.

"No one sees me anymore," said Sarah to Mme. Guérard, watching the actress finish breakfast in bed.

"What do you mean, child? Everyone in the world sees you. You can't walk ten feet without being recognized."

"They don't see me. Only my fame," said Sarah. Mme. Guérard had little patience with this grievance. Sarah had been home for two weeks, and instead of relishing the joy at being welcomed in her native city, she complained at being too famous.

"And Jacques Damala," said Mme. Guérard. "I suppose you imagine that *he* sees you?"

Sarah did not answer. She was convinced that Damala was able to see something in her that no one else could: She was emotionally hungry. The insulting young Greek who six months before had invaded her drawing room was not intimidated by her renown; he had hardly blinked when she slapped his face.

When she returned from her triumphant travels in the spring of 1881, he reappeared in her house, a lit cigarette in his scornful mouth, and demanded a role in her company. It was impossible for Sarah to act offended. Nor was she able, for all her training, to feign disinterest.

"Sometimes I think I am dying," said Sarah to Mme. Guérard.

Sarah took a tiny bite of a baked apple and then pushed away her breakfast tray.

"Stop talking nonsense," said Mme. Guérard. "You're as healthy as a horse."

"Then why do I look consumptive?"

"Because you play consumptives. Because you don't eat. Because you put on too much rice powder." As Mme. Guérard spoke, the sun emerged from behind a cloud. The morning light was unkind to her face and hands. Sarah had always thought the widow's hands lovely, and was disturbed to notice how crooked they had become with rheumatism, how marked with age spots. "It's your repertoire," continued Mme. Guérard. "You are acting in your sleep, my dear child. Most of all, it's because you wait for that Greek person to call on you."

Indeed, she dreamed about death. Death was darkness, obscuring the white light about her. Death was cold, like the blasts of icy air that penetrated the wings of overheated theaters. Death was silence, blanketing every breath, every tiny human movement with absolute silence. Sarah wanted life.

"My dear Guérard," she said carefully. "I will ask you to please do me a favor. Do not say anything more about Monsieur Damala, if all you have to say about him is negative."

All he wanted from Sarah was a job. Damala showed no interest in making love to her. The most famous woman in France was intrigued by his indifference. Damala was not well read, but he understood frustration. He was not a sympathetic soul, but it was obvious to him that her need for love would never be met by the men who worshiped her. Jacques did not worship her. He made it clear that he found many other women more beautiful, that she was far too old for his taste, that her acting onstage did not merit applause, and that her life offstage was a shambles.

Jeanne no longer championed the man. He was a drunkard, she said, a womanizer, and worst of all, a man who had used her to inject him with morphine.

Sarah did not want to believe any of this.

She did not understand that the man was working a spell on her. Jacques Damala had been born into an aristocratic Greek family, but all his adult life he had lived on his wits, his proper manners, his good looks. He had been a diplomat, a banker, an investor, and to all these fields he had brought one special skill: the ability to project a seriousness, a sobriety that was completely foreign to his soul. Jeanne Bernhardt had first given Damala the notion that his mellifluous voice and noble bearing were particularly suited to the acting profession. The man discerned the great benefits concomitant with such a career, one in which he could romance an endless supply of actresses, and which would give him a passport to the demimonde he found so irresistible.

"I am sorry that you and Monsieur Damala are no longer friends, Jeanne," said Sarah. "But that is no reason for slander." She refused to believe that a man so robust and clear-eyed as Damala could ever have tried morphine.

"That's because he's even younger than I am, dear sister," Jeanne said. "He should really be having tea with Maurice and his friends, and not with you and yours."

Sarah did not invite Damala to tea.

She made every effort to keep the appearance of a gulf between them. Her interest in him, she claimed, was strictly professional. To Maurice, she mocked the man's accent and foppish clothing; to Mme. Guérard, she pretended that she found his looks too pretty for a man. Instead of inviting Damala to tea, she invited his acting coach.

Yet when Damala's acting coach visited her, she tried to convince him of his pupil's genius. Later she would tell Mme. Guérard that despite Damala's inexperience, his teacher believed him to be potentially one of the greatest actors on the French stage. As for Jeanne, surely her opinion was not to be trusted. She had loved the man, and he had wanted no more from her than friendship. If he drank to excess, it was because he was unfulfilled in his career. If he ran after women, he did so to search for love. If he had gone so far as to try morphine—which seemed impossible—it must be an expression of the pain and dissatisfaction he suffered in life.

"You're completely mad, dear child," Mme. Guérard said as the weeks of infatuation grew into months of bewitchment. "It would be better to cut your throat than to fall in love with this man."

"Oh, I don't love him," Sarah said. "I don't even like him."

She hired him for her European tour, an acting student without any professional experience.

Sarah made up a hundred excuses why she had taken this chance, insisting that his audition speech had brought tears to her eyes, that his Greek accent added a leavening of welcome gravity to his speeches, that his beauty would sell tickets. She cast him in small roles as they toured England, the French provinces, and Italy. In his native Greece, she imagined that he was something of a local celebrity. Sarah gave him larger roles, and placed him at her side when she met the Greek press. She ignored the grumbling of the experienced actors he had replaced. This was not favoritism, she said, but business.

Any talk of Sarah having taken another lover under her wing was quashed by Damala's obvious lack of interest in the star, and by her brutal criticism of his work.

After every show, she castigated him in front of the company for the inadequacy of his performance. When the troupe left Greece, he was returned to tiny parts, standing in dim light downstage, holding spears and announcing entrances. In Hungary and Switzerland, he threatened to quit. In Belgium and Holland, not a day went by without Sarah threatening to tear up his contract.

Every time Damala sat down to dinner at a restaurant, she would walk in, an overperfumed, overstated vision in silk and sable, clutching the arm of Philippe Garnier, the handsome actor who had most of the male leading roles on her tours. Sarah would hardly deign to greet Damala. And he, usually drinking heavily with one or another pretty actress from the troupe, or with a local girl young enough to be Sarah's daughter, would barely acknowledge the great actress's presence.

By the time they began their tour of Russia, in St. Petersburg, Damala had had enough. He walked into her dressing room and demanded a starring role.

"Absolutely no," Sarah said, posing her queenly head as if she were standing center stage, lit by limelight, and he were on his feet in the last row of the stalls.

Damala took the burning cigarette out of his mouth and dropped it into a flower vase. Then he moved close to her, took hold of her painted face by the chin, and with the heel of his free hand, removed the paint from her lips with violence.

Then he kissed her.

This kiss was tender. He crushed her slender body to his powerful chest, but his lips were soft, barely parted. It was her lips that opened wide, her tongue that reached inside his mouth, her teeth that were hungry for his lips, his beard, his neck.

Even then Sarah did not know how infatuated she was with this man twelve years her junior.

Damala knew; he had always known. He was the kind of man who assumes that all women want him, who never needs to plan further than one step at a time.

He pushed her away, and held her at arm's length.

"I want Garnier's part," he said. "Or else I am going."

He could not have been any clearer. If she wanted him, she must pay for him. In his eyes, she was old, and without her paint, an ordinary woman. Her fame meant nothing to him, she was sure, and suddenly she felt absolutely naked, gloriously stripped of her rank, her privileges. Not since Prince Henri had she taken a lover who made love to her without also making love to her name. Sarah moved away from him, her slender body shaking with desire. She locked the door to her dressing room, came up to him, and took hold of the cravat about his throat.

"We have an hour," she said.

He smiled at the pressure of her hands on his powerful neck. Then he removed her grip, and ripped off his cravat. He dropped his jacket to the carpeted floor. Sarah took hold of the waistband of his trousers, but he pushed her away.

"Take off your robe," he said.

Sarah did as she was told, standing before him in her embroidered drawers, in her fragile camisole of silk and lace. Damala looked at her as if she were a whore on a street corner and he was deciding whether to buy. She had a vague memory of her mother in her dressing room, dressed in the courtesan's working costume: a cambric dressing jacket trimmed with lace, worn over nothing but pale scented skin. Damala roughly unbuttoned the camisole and, more roughly still, pulled open the pretty drawers at the waist. None of her lovers had ever treated her this way. She thought of her first love, Prince Henri, of gentle Mounet-Sully and quiet Duquesnel, of her current, anxious lover, Garnier—all of them had been eager to please Madame Sarah. Surely every one of them thought of the others who had shared her bed, every one of them wondered what she would think of his prowess.

"I want you naked," said Damala.

Sarah pulled the camisole over her head, and stepped out of her drawers. She knew that she was painfully thin, that her breasts were too small, her hips and thighs without a morsel of fat. Damala kicked off his shoe boots, and removed his trousers with care. There was an armchair as wide as a bed and a sofa of inviting softness. But Damala, not commenting on the translucent loveliness of her skin, or exclaiming at her baby-soft skin, took hold of her red-gold hair at the nape of her neck and pulled her to the floor. Sarah placed her hands on his cheeks and began to kiss him, her teeth and lips forcing wide his mouth and threatening to swallow his tongue.

Abruptly Damala was through with kissing. Having this much control over the most famous actress in the world excited him. He pinned her shoulders to the floor, he straddled her as if she were contesting him in a wrestling match, and entered her with no more thought of pleasing her than if he were the sultan and she his lowliest slave.

But Sarah was made for pleasure.

She was as excited as he, as eager to pull him inside as he was to penetrate her body. And if he took no care to discover her needs, it made no difference. She would take what she wanted from this man.

Her shoulders pressed to the floor, she pushed her knees up against the small of his back, driving her fingernails along his muscular thighs. He tried to move his penis inside her, but her muscles squeezed with unbearable sweetness about him, so that tears of pleasure came to his eyes. The young man's wild pace slowed, and as he moved inside her, he felt the world turn ecstatically around him.

So wonderful were these moments that Damala nearly spoke her name, nearly mumbled an endearment. Suddenly she had begun to ease the pressure on his penis, to rotate her pelvis even as she pulled the weight of his torso closer with her powerful legs.

Unexpectedly he wanted tenderness, and now her mouth was shut, her wet forehead against his, her breath coming in short, quick bursts. Now that he had learned to be slow, Sarah was quick, and sure, and insistent. Needing to delay the moment of fulfillment, to hold it back until the darkness behind his shut eyes would explode into a whirlpool of light, she would not wait an instant more.

Sarah's body trembled slightly, then began to shake wildly, even as her genital muscles let go of Damala, let go of his pent-up pleasure, allowed him to explode inside her, along with her; their open mouths met voraciously, not kissing but breathing in the world.

They waited until a half hour before curtain, until the dresser had given up knocking, the callboy had called for the manager, and Mme. Guérard herself had come to the locked door to ask if Sarah was well enough to go on.

"You mustn't go," Sarah had said to him finally. "You must not leave."

"Then give me Garnier's part," he said.

Shortly it was common knowledge that they had begun their affair in St. Petersburg, where Damala took Philippe Garnier's part in *Froufrou,* and Philippe Garnier returned to Paris with the scandal fresh on his lips.

Soon after, Damala was playing Armand Duval to her Marguerite Gauthier in *La Dame aux camélias.* The star parts had a fascination for the man, and for a while he was content to be Sarah's lover on and offstage. This happy time passed. Damala learned to envy her talent. If she attempted to show him a different way to read a line or direct him in a gesture, he blew up at her. The critics who routinely praised Sarah just as routinely found his acting mediocre. They implied that he had not gotten his roles by virtue of his talent as an actor. Damala took her every attempt at tutoring as an endorsement of his treatment at the hands of the critics.

Never again was their lovemaking as good as that first time. Even Sarah could not draw love from a stone, could not stir passion in her loins when Damala accused her of using "all the bed tricks of the whores she came from."

Damala's vanity needed to be comforted, and he found this

comfort in flaunting his affairs before his leading lady. Sarah's response was to buy him clothes, horses, jewels, to give him every part he wanted. Spiting her, Damala sold her presents to pawnbrokers, squandered the money on gambling and whores. Determined to spit in the face of critics, he managed to forget most of his lines. Sarah defended him to the press, to her company; yet Damala remained unmoved by her efforts.

In March of 1882, Jeanne Bernhardt quit the company. Her addiction to morphine was now common knowledge. Sarah refused to let anyone from the company mention the drug in her presence. Jeanne's absence was due to an "illness" that must never be named. After deliberating with Jeanne and Mme. Guérard, Sarah agreed to send her sister to a sanatorium in Switzerland. The doctors there promised to wean her from the drug in six months. Sarah begged her to try to get better, told her that she was all she had left in the world.

"You have Maurice, you have Guérard, you have your fame," said Jeanne in the minutes before she had to leave the hotel to catch her train.

"I want my sister too," said Sarah. "I want my sister to be well."

A flicker of affection appeared in Jeanne's cold blue eyes, so that her face twisted into the image of Julie's that continued to visit Sarah's dreams. "You're such a fool, Sarah," said Jeanne. "Spread your legs for anybody, won't you?"

"You must not be angry if I am in love with a man you once knew," said Sarah.

"Is that any way for a queen to talk?" The affection was gone from Jeanne's beautiful face. "If I were you I'd take what I wanted too. Even if it belonged to my sister. You really should do anything to get a little love in your miserable life."

Sarah knew that because her sister had abstained from the drug for half the day, her mood was ugly. At any moment she could turn completely despondent. She might turn over a chair, or recoil at a hallucination of Damala sneering over a cigarette in the sitting room of Sarah's suite. But suddenly Jeanne quieted. She took hold of Sarah's hands and pressed them with great force. "If you marry him," Jeanne warned, "he will destroy your life."

Sarah didn't heed this warning. Her infatuation had become like a wound that would not heal. Every logical part of her knew that her wild desire to possess him was mad. She told Mme. Guérard that she didn't truly love him, and this was true. She could not explain to the widow any more than she could to herself why she wanted him so obsessively. Sarah knew only that her madness would snap, would leave her free the moment they became man and wife.

The little widow reminded Sarah that she was thirty-eight and Damala was twenty-six. Mme. Guérard told her that he would take her money, drag her name through the mud, ruin her relationship with Maurice. Sarah would not be stopped. It was she who proposed the marriage, but Damala quickly agreed. Marriage to Sarah would legitimize his ambition and give him an international status, a fame that he had never known. In April of 1882, after a disastrous performance of *La Dame aux camélias* in Nice, where an unruly press had called him "La Damala aux camélias," she made up her mind. Sarah and her young lover fled to London and were married.

Chapter 20

IN SPITE OF
EVERYTHING

Contrary to Jeanne's prediction, the marriage did not destroy Sarah's life. Instead, Sarah slowly and irrevocably was broken of her infatuation. As lovers, they had not lived together; but as man and wife, particularly on tour, they were closeted in the same houses, the same rooms. Up close, Jacques Damala was petty and vain and cruel. He laughed at her family pictures, called the story that Maurice was the son of a prince a lie, claimed that all her talent was in taking curtain calls that lasted as long as any five-act play. As a daily dose, his indifference was nothing more than a childish pose, his contempt the mark of a man who loathed nothing more than himself.

And Jeanne's assertion that Damala was a user of morphine was proven within a week of their marital vows: He sent Sarah's servants to purchase morphine sulfate and distilled water, he laid out his extensive paraphernalia of syringes and needles and cleaning wires for all the world to see.

Jeanne's sorry example meant nothing to him; he was eager to prove that his need for morphine was the fault of his famous wife. The world had laughed when she married him, a handsome rake twelve years her junior. She was rich and he was poor; he was an actor without a reputation and she was the most celebrated actress in the world. He did not realize that this laughter was directed as much at Sarah as at him, that it pained her as much as it pained him. All he could see was that marrying this woman had not met his expectations. By giving her what she wanted, he had made a fool of himself.

"I am a laughingstock because of you," he said. After they were married, they performed together in *La Dame aux camélias,* first in Paris, then in London, and the critics applauded Sarah for being able to shine in the presence of such a dim star as her husband. "If not for you, they would take me seriously," said Damala. "If not for you they would not call me a nonentity, they would not imagine that I am incapable of supporting myself."

Married in April, by May they were sleeping in separate bedrooms. Damala did not like the way his room was furnished. He said that it had the look and smell of a whorehouse. "It is too bad to see how much of your mother's taste has passed down to you."

"If it smells like a whorehouse, it is an appropriate place for you to stick yourself with your filthy needles," said Sarah.

"I must do something to occupy my free time as Monsieur Bernhardt," he said.

"It is not my fault that you are a drug addict," said Sarah.

"I'm not an addict, you fool," he laughed. "An addict takes at least eight grains a day. I barely take a grain, and never more than once a week."

"But you are not sick," said Sarah. "You have no need to stop the pain of some terrible disease."

Damala's superior smile vanished. "I have to stop the pain of being married to an old and ugly Jewess."

How could she slap a man who had just injected morphine into his groin? As she watched the euphoria quickly soften the lines of his beautiful face, she only blamed herself for his presence in her home. No one had forced her to hire him, no one had held a gun to her head when she responded to his first kiss, no one had predicted anything but disaster for their marriage.

"You'd like this, Sarah," he said, suddenly much friendlier, as he reclined on the chaise longue in his bedroom. He shivered slightly, as though from an excess of ecstasy. She could see a pair of abscesses on his left forearm, where the skin had become irritated and inflamed from too many injections by the thick needles. There were many more ugly lesions in the soft skin under his left arm, his favorite place for injecting the drug. In a moment his lips closed about a smile, his breathing slowed, and he went to sleep on the red velvet of the chair.

Sarah had no desire to fight him.

The truth was that their marriage had revealed him as a monstrous stranger, a loathsome alien in body and soul, and she wanted nothing more than to be rid of him: out of her bed, her home, her life. Playwrights and producers were wary of offering her a project if it meant including her husband. Maurice, nearing his twentieth birthday, had not talked to her since her surprise wedding. He had taken an extended trip to a school friend's château the day before the newlyweds came to Paris and made it clear he would not enter the house as long as "La Damala" was there. Mme. Guérard, the soul of gentleness and consideration, walked around the great house like a lioness in a cage.

"Throw him out," she said to Sarah. "Just call Émile and the footmen, and have him tossed into the gutter."

"He's my husband."

"You don't have a husband," said Mme. Guérard sharply. "Sarah Bernhardt is too important for such a useless thing."

Instead of following the widow's advice, she imported a doctor to live in her house while she performed the title role in Sardou's *Fédora*. Once again, Sarah had taken a part where she could die onstage. This death was suicide by poison; every time she went into her famous, drawn-out agonies before a full house of Bernhardt watchers, she could feel the morphine slowly killing Damala, could feel the terrible guilt at being unable to wish anything better for him than his demise.

The part of Fédora, played before a critical Parisian audience, was a great success for Sarah. Occasionally during the run of the play, she was able to strip away the outer walls of her public personage, letting her spirit move into the body of Fédora, allowing everything to vanish but her fellow actors in the stage light. Sometimes magic happened, and it was not till she had begun her death scene that she remembered Damala, sensed the breathless audience. Then she would happily prolong her death agonies, drawing more and more sympathy from the audience.

"Sarah! Sarah! Sarah!" they shouted, getting to their feet, needing to express their love as much as she needed to accept it. They tossed bouquets, they brought up laurels; when the curtain attempted to hide her from view, they beat their hands until the insistent rhythm brought her back. Slowly she bowed from the waist, so slowly and so deeply that she seemed more like a young ballerina than a mature actress. Always there were tears and an astonishing modesty in her green eyes. Neither tears nor modesty was fabricated. It was one thing to know in advance that the audience was predisposed to worship her at whatever theater she graced with her presence. It was another to experience that love directly, to stand before the audience without the armor of her role, and watch the house explode in wild, spontaneous approbation.

Her leading man—in *Fédora,* it was Pierre Berton—would stand in the corner so that she might have someone to lean on and to help her offstage. If she had committed all her talent to the performance, she would have barely enough strength to take a simple bow, much less twenty curtain calls. But she would continue to come out from behind the curtain as long as the house applauded. Only the applause could rid her mind of a thousand problems and projects— a planned tour to South America, a wild notion to take the part of Hamlet in a new French translation, attempts to buy an estate in Brittany, not far from where Nurse had taught her to walk and talk and dream. Only when she was surrendering herself to the audience could she forget that Damala awaited her in her own house, either drunk or in a morphine-induced stupor.

But by the end of the first run of *Fédora* late in 1882, Damala had deserted her. This was a mixed blessing for Sarah, for the world still considered them man and wife, and there was always the chance that he would return. Sarah found it difficult to deny him a bed or cash or a part in a play; over the next six and one half years, he would come back for these things, for a month, or a week, or two days. A legal separation was arranged, yet a separation was not a divorce. Sarah Bernhardt still signed her legal documents with Damala's name. And because "Mme. Damala" was Sarah Bernhardt, the press never tired of his escapades. Every time he ran off with another pretty young thing, he took the opportunity to heap scorn on his famous wife, to ridicule her achievements, to add five years to her age.

But Sarah left him behind, lost him in a storm of applause. It was not just the pain caused by Damala that she needed to wash away, but the pain caused by what he had been unable to provide.

She toured America again and again, becoming so popular that dresses and chocolate drinks and perfumes were named after her. Still, this did not mean that she was loved, but that she was an object of mystery, someone who must be seen, must be touched. That she knew the Prince of Wales or had corresponded with Queen Victoria provided fodder for press releases, but not true love or solace. She was surrounded by famous acquaintances who were not her friends. Her closest, truest friend was an elderly widow who disapproved of her loveless affairs, and of all her extravagances. As Mme. Guérard grew older, she was not afraid to claim that after her death, Sarah would be utterly alone with her money and her fame and her sycophants. Though there was always an actor willing to share her bed, often as young as and always more gracious than her husband, Sarah usually slept alone. In public she might rattle off famous speeches in her silvery voice, she might titillate the press with statements about her lovers, but in private she was quiet, she was sad. That the British public was even more enthusiastic about her than the American, that young girls made holy relics out of her playbills and press clippings did not fill the void in her heart. Nothing satisfied like applause, like the live moment when the curtain lifted and she saw the raised faces, honoring her with their rapt attention, waiting for the cue to begin signaling their love.

With every year came new plays, new tours to mark the passage of her empty life. Jeanne's addiction ruined her health, and Mme. Guérard aged, and her cook, Titine, died in the crash of a provincial train; and Sarah armored her heart with *Fédora,* learned the part of Ophelia to play opposite Philippe Garnier's Hamlet. When her grief became insupportable, she bought something that she could not afford: a house for Jeanne that she would never use, a cottage for a retiring teacher from the Conservatoire, a diamond bracelet for the little widow. Then she would have to tour to pay for it all; to perform at eight and be on the train all night, to rehearse all afternoon. It was a luxury to have ten minutes for tea before the call: "Half hour, Madame Sarah."

The great success of *Fédora* led her to add the play to her repertoire, because every year she wanted more and more to ensure the pleasure of her audiences. In the sad year when Jeanne, unable to break her morphine habit, died of influenza, which her weakened body couldn't fight, Sarah triumphed in another Sardou play, *Théodora.* She had lost two sisters, but the audience would not let her leave the stage until two dozen curtain calls had reduced Sarah to uncontrollable tears. When Victor Hugo, to whom she was always grateful for having given her the role of the queen in *Ruy Blas,* died a year later, Sarah did a sentimental revival of one of his plays. Not knowing how to cry in private, she dedicated the audience's applause to him, raising her bouquets to the gallery and shouting his name. In 1887, when her aunt Rosine finally finished killing herself with drink, a week before Sarah created the title role in another Sardou success, *La Tosca,* the opening-night audience had the subdued grace of a congregation of mourners.

It was not till she accepted their applause with her famous open-armed gesture, a frail, ageless beauty gathering their love to her exhausted spirit, that she understood how much even her aloof aunt Rosine's death meant in her circumscribed world. With Rosine gone, and poor Jeanne too, and dear Regina long ago, only Maurice was connected to her by blood. And Maurice, her most frequent visitor, hated that blood. A social-climbing dilettante, he was as humiliated by his grandmother's profession as by her Jewish ancestry.

But she would let no one, not even the son she indulged in everything, say a word against Julie.

Sarah found herself missing her beautiful mother more than anyone. She had loved Julie with the hopeless devotion that can take root only in childhood, and to give up this love would be tantamount to cutting out her heart. Not a day went by when she did not mention to Mme. Guérard how sorry she was that Julie had never had a chance to be proud of her, that her premature death had prevented her from seeing Sarah's greatest roles. Mme. Guérard never failed to contradict the actress: Julie had seen *Le Passant,* had been alive during five years of theatrical columns filled with Sarah's name.

"But she was not really proud of me," Sarah said on a bleak January day in 1889. "She never thought I would last."

"You are wrong, absolutely wrong, dear child," Mme. Guérard said. Ignoring that Sarah, at forty-five, was well into middle age, Mme. Guérard pulled her into her motherly arms. "Your mother was proud of you, so full of pride that she could not speak." Sarah tried to believe this, tried to bury under a memory of sweet scent and golden hair the fact of her mother's contempt. She could never quite forget the perfect shame of being the child whose hair was too wild and face too plain, the unwanted baby who made her mother feel old at seventeen. If only Julie could have forgiven her while she was still alive, if only she could have actually told her that she was glad that she had been born, Sarah would have been able to believe in the pride and the love that Mme. Guérard promised were always there.

But Julie had not forgiven her.

Every time Sarah faced the audience, Julie's presence was out there somewhere, sitting cross-armed in the back of a pretty stage box, waiting for her to prove herself. It was no wonder that Sarah had to bring the crowd to their feet, force them to love her, to shout her name so loud that even the ghost of her mother must acknowledge her worth.

This did not endear her to her fellow actors. Indeed, the ties that are supposed to bind stronger than those of blood among the members of her profession often proved weaker than water. Actors kissed her hands and her cheeks, and behind her back accused her of filling her casts with second-raters so that she alone would shine. Playwrights made love to her to get her to read their new plays, and if she gently refused to take a part, would gossip about town that they had rejected her in favor of a younger actress. Directors, indebted to her for their jobs at a time when most stars refused to be directed by anyone other than themselves, accused her of ruining their productions with show-stopping bows to the audience.

But always the audience was a tonic for her grief.

When the emotional emptiness of her life grew overwhelming, Sarah threw herself into a killing schedule of work, into monumental tasks that would enrich her more than any actor of her time.

"Perhaps you won't have to build that extension at Belle-Isle after all," said Mme. Guérard, who had a more urgent topic to broach than Sarah's regrets about Julie. She was referring to Sarah's estate in Brittany, though her expression was suddenly too grave to have anything to do with real estate. Maurice, though still unemployed and forever at his mother's heels, had gotten married, and his new bride was expecting a child. Sarah was consulting with architects and artists to add a "Maurice wing" to the seventeenth-century fortress she had already converted into a comfortable country home. "You'll have something else to squander your money on," continued Mme. Guérard. "Unless you have finally come to your senses." She paused, in an approximation of Sarah's theatrical manner. "Your husband is back."

"I have no husband," said Sarah.

"Then tell that to his doctor," said Mme. Guérard. She stood up and opened the drawing-room doors to admit a red-faced Émile.

"I asked Madame Guérard to mention it first, Madame Sarah," said Émile. Once her houseboy in the mansion on the Avenue de Villiers, presently her butler at her new house on the Boulevard Péreire, Émile brought in a visiting card as if it were something that had been touched by the plague.

"Mention what?"

"That the doctor has news of Monsieur Damala."

"What doctor?" asked Sarah. "Oh, never mind. You treat me like a fool. Bring him in."

"You are Sarah Bernhardt," said Mme. Guérard softly. "You have paid more than he's worth, and many times over. And you have never loved him."

"That is why I will see the doctor, my dear little lady," said Sarah. "And if you don't mind, I will be more comfortable doing this on my own." Mme. Guérard nearly collided with the anxious visitor brought in by Émile, but she edged away, avoiding contact with him. She threw Sarah a sharp glance, as if to say that this was the doctor that Jacques Damala deserved.

"You won't recognize him, Madame Bernhardt," the doctor said. His name was Munzer, and his clothes and the fingers clutching his leather bag were not clean. The black collar of his suit was flecked with dandruff, and his shirt cuffs exhibited dark spots. Sarah wondered whether they were the marks of grease or sweat or blood.

"What do you want, Doctor?" Sarah asked, sitting up straight on her divan. She knew immediately that he had brought bad news of his patient, and that his patient was as disreputable as he. "I am very busy today. If you would please state your business at once—"

"It is about your husband, Madame Bernhardt," the doctor said.

"Obviously."

"I understand that you are legally separated."

"What are you, Monsieur, a doctor or a lawyer? Will you kindly state your business."

"I am not here for any legal reasons, Madame, but only out of Christian charity."

"And I have no funds at my disposal. He will only inject more poison into his body. I will not give him a franc, I will not allow him in my house, and I am not even interested in hearing his name."

"I am sorry to hear you say that, Madame Bernhardt, as I am the only doctor treating your husband, and he is absolutely destitute. Without my help he will certainly die." Dr. Munzer paused, taking the time to look past the famous face at the drawing room's red damask-covered walls, at the jungle of potted plants and cut flowers, at the birds in gilded cages, the bronze and marble busts of Victor Hugo, Alexandre Dumas *père,* Julie Bernhardt. Everywhere were busts and portraits of Sarah as Phèdre, as Théodora, as Floria Tosca, as *La Dame aux camélias'* Marguerite Gauthier. There were many photographs as well, but all of them were of Maurice, vying for attention in ostentatious frames of heavy silver. The doctor finished his quick inventory, remembering that the newspapers claimed she had poured half a million francs into furnishing this house after her 1887 South American tour. "Have you ever heard the expression delirium tremens?" he asked in his most doleful voice.

"Give me the address, Doctor," Sarah said suddenly, ringing for Émile. "And then you may please leave."

The doctor did not appreciate the import of Sarah's request. To ask for Damala's address meant that she would fly in the face of Mme. Guérard's disapproval, would defy any reasonable interpretation of her past. If he was dying, she would comfort him, she would provide for him, she would let him leave the world lying on clean sheets, with a semblance of human dignity.

"You needn't be afraid of the term. Morphine addiction is curable under the proper medical conditions."

"I know all about morphine, thank you," Sarah said.

But the doctor, after briefly examining a collection of theatrical weapons hanging from the wall, would not stop. "Believe me, Madame, there is no sin in not understanding such a complex medical subject. There was a time when I was first practicing that morphine was all the rage, the cure-all for pains great and small. Quite natural after the war, thousands of dying soldiers getting such relief. Who would have thought how much it could hurt the living? Now everyone's terrified of it, but we doctors know that it is still very appropriate for all kinds of disease. Everything from cholera to convulsions to epilepsy to—if you'll pardon me—incontinence of urine, to laryngismus stridulus, to—I beg your pardon once again—nymphomania."

Émile entered noisily and crossed his broad arms, like a powerful eunuch in the sultan's harem. "Madame Sarah?"

"Go and get this man one hundred francs," she said.

"At once, Madame Sarah."

When the butler left, the doctor swallowed the minor embarrassment at being rewarded so well, so quickly, and continued: "I was called upon by your husband's neighbors. They found him howling like a madman, his bed overturned, stark naked and raving. Not knowing who he was, I came to his aid, never expecting such generosity as you exhibit, Madame."

"My generosity is stupid," Sarah said. "But this is the end of it."

The doctor smiled, patted his greasy hair, and returned to his subject as if mining for ore. "To a professional the abscesses all over his body are clear evidence—"

"Stop," Sarah said. "I don't want to hear it."

"I believe it my duty to tell you that I spent three days with him, Madame. He was delirious and wild and I helped him during his hallucinations, and when he could take it no more, I injected him with a small dose of morphine, enough to calm him. A half grain at first, and a few minutes later, another half grain. He must have a fourteen-, fifteen-grain-a-day habit. Quite formidable. The problem with these addicts is that they have no skill at injection, and they do not know how to keep their needles clean."

"Émile will be here with your money in a moment."

"I have not come here for the money, you understand," the doctor said. He gave her the address, and she wrote it down on the back of his dirty visiting card. "If you like, I can procure for you, at reasonable cost, hypodermic syringes made of silver, hard rubber, and glass. The needles must always be of stainless steel. I would never sell you the gold or the gold-plated, as they are much more painful. The essential things really are the rimmers. They are the only things with which you can clean the needles properly, and if the needles aren't clean, then it's only a matter of time before the infections, the abscesses, tetanus too. I have an excellent rimmer right here in my bag to show you." Dr. Munzer extracted an evil-looking instrument, tapered and sharp at the end; she would have liked to plunge it into his heart.

Émile returned with more noise than before, no mean feat on the thick carpets. "Give him the money, and see that he leaves."

"This is very kind of you, Madame Bernhardt. I am sure that your husband will be very happy to see you. If you have further need of me, you have my card." He closed his bag, and walked to the drawing-room door before turning to the famous actress one last time. "This has been a privilege meeting you, Madame. Something to tell my grandchildren."

Then finally he was gone. Sarah got up from the divan, and for a moment stood quite still, unable to move. He would tell his grandchildren that he had met Sarah Bernhardt, but what could he possibly say? That she lived in a house filled with gaudy treasures? That her golden hair was no longer natural, that the youth displayed under the stage lights was as artificial as the props and the scenery in her plays? That her success had driven her husband to drug addiction? She wanted to stop the doctor, stop up his lips from telling any tales to his grandchildren, in this year of 1889 or in any year to come. What could he know of Sarah Bernhardt from seeing her at home, when all that must be knowable about her was on the stage?

She felt old, too old to walk, too old to plan, too old to rage. Jacques Damala was back in Paris. She had his address in her hand. There had been other addresses for Jacques. This time it was the Rue d'Antin in the Second Arrondissement. There was no thought of bringing a friend, a police officer, a doctor who specialized in morphine addiction. She would not ask Mme. Guérard for advice, would not bring along her secretary or her maid, would not even take her own carriage.

She simply hurried past Émile, pulling open the massive house doors before he understood that she was leaving. He ran after her, asking if she would like the carriage, if he could get her a fiacre, if she wanted him to call for Mme. Guérard.

"I am best doing it this way," said Sarah. "Alone." The butler, sent emphatically back to the house, watched as she made her way to the street, limping slightly because of the pain in her right knee, and hailed a fiacre on the boulevard.

The knee had been injured during her South American tour. She had tripped over a prop improperly placed by a young actress playing the part of Nichette in *La Dame aux camélias*. Nichette had been one of Jeanne's favorite parts, and as bad as she was, she never placed a stool in the wrong place so that her hated older sister might fall into the hard wood floor of the stage. The forty-three-year-old knee had been permanently damaged.

Of course, the show had gone on. The girl playing Nichette had not even been replaced. Two years later, Sarah limped, more noticeably offstage than on. If it would not look so weak, she would walk with a cane. But how would she ever convince a producer or her public to let her appear as a vigorous Prince Hamlet or as a nineteen-year-old Joan of Arc if they knew the pain she suffered in hurrying for a cab?

The driver recognized her at once, just as he recognized her famous house. He would have known her frail, golden-haired figure, wrapped in a dozen white silk scarves, anywhere in Paris. He bowed and he blinked and he jumped out of his seat to open the door. Before she got in, she said: "I would like you to drive slowly, go through the Parc Monceau, and make your way without any haste toward the Boulevard Haussmann. Then turn right into the Boulevard de Malesherbes, go around the Madeleine, along the Rue Saint-Honoré, turn around at the Comédie Française, and go up the Avenue de l'Opéra until the Rue d'Antin."

If anyone else had dared instruct a thirty-year veteran of the Paris fiacre wars in so minute a fashion, he would have dropped his horse's fodder bag into the passenger's lap. But this was Sarah Bernhardt, lovely to behold and a creature outside the pale of ordinary standards of behavior.

"That is the long way, Madame Sarah," the driver simply said, "but it's lovely to hear you sound out all those streets and parks and avenues."

One sharp look from the actress hurried him into the driver's seat, and to his quick snapping of the reins.

Abruptly the voice that had toured North and South America, astonished theatergoers throughout Europe, penetrated the vast reaches of imperial Russia, reached out to the driver once again. It was as melodious as a love song, as loud as a stevedore's chant. "Slowly, I said! I want to take time!"

But the driver, like time. itself, would not go slowly.

Almost immediately they were approaching the Parc Monceau, passing the imposing gray house at the corner of the Rue Cardinet and the Avenue de Villiers, which Julie had once pointed out as the home of a courtesan with a single rich client. Clearly, Julie had implied, that was a sensible way to make a living instead of frittering away one's youth on the stage. But Sarah had not followed in her mother's footsteps, no matter what malicious tongues said. Her money was her own, hard-earned in the theaters of three continents and not flat on her back in a brothel, or a boudoir, or a private room at the Café Anglais.

Already the cab was flying along the Boulevard Haussmann, its new cafés more fashionable than those demimonde favorites of the Boulevard des Italiens: the Café de Paris, Tortoni's, the Maison d'Or, the Café Riche. She had been to every one of them, had eaten ice cream and oysters and foie gras and champagne. It no longer mattered if she never again stepped foot into any of those places, eating their food, clinking their glasses, bathing in their gaslight.

Once she had been young, and had believed in love, and had wanted to be the greatest actress in the world. But the world had changed. Love was something for the young, something to be gotten over with the maturing wisdom of experience. Acting, like poetry, like music and art, was very nice, but the world had more important things to think about in the final years of the nineteenth century.

Dinochau's Café, that happy haunt of the Bohemians, had died along with M. Dinochau at the end of the Franco-Prussian War. There Sarah had first heard about where the world was headed, there the Bohemians had sworn that science was made only to discover new ways to inflict destruction on man. Yet the optimism of the masses disregarded the guns and bombs of greater power, preferring the dream of universal light and cleanliness and plenty to the dire vision of unwashed poets. Sometimes it seemed that the entire demimonde was still dying the slow death that had begun at the fall of the Second Empire, and accelerated with each new technological wonder of this quick-moving age.

The sun had begun to set behind the Madeleine, and down the darkening avenues, the bright spots of street gaslamps were interspersed with the raucous self-advertisements of electric-lit cafés. In the nine years that had gone by since Jeanne first brought Jacques Damala into her dressing room in Lyons, Sarah had seen London and New York begin to be lit by electricity, had witnessed Chicago's newly constructed ten-story "skyscraper," had seen traffic crawl over the amazing length of the elegant Brooklyn Bridge. Every week there were more articles promising the advent of the horseless carriage, the creation of an international language, a drug that would prolong life to a hundred years and more.

Who would want to live to be so old? she thought. At forty-five she already felt too old to draw the desire of strange men, too weak to ride wild horses over the rocky coast near her country home. Listening to the tributes of critics, she wished that they had come earlier, when she had wanted to hand them on a platter to her mother, to her prince, to her infant son. How good would a drug be that let her live far into the future, if she couldn't perform onstage? And even if she could perform, how good would it be if the world no longer wanted to watch? How could *Phèdre* compete with pneumatic tires on carriages driven by magic engines, how could a stage lit by limelight compete with ships sailing to the moon? The only drug that Sarah was familiar with was morphine, the drug that had made her mother's death easy, killed Prince Henri de Luyen, hastened the death of her sister Jeanne, and was shortening the life of Jacques Damala. Wasn't that a drug that all four had eagerly wanted, that had come blissfully into its own with the new-age hypodermic needle, a drug that, in its capacity to destroy reality, was made for their time?

No, living into the next century would have no purpose if she had no one to love, and no one to love her. The incredible life detailed in the gossip columns, filled with the names of famous people and distant cities, with rumors of lovers in high and low places, with rich houses and carriages and clothes and jewels, was shadowy and insubstantial compared to the memory of sitting on Nurse's broad lap, waiting for her mother to come. There had been no love given her as good as Nurse's, no love she had ever felt as strong as her childish yearning for Julie. She had given birth to a son to whom she was devoted, but sometimes it seemed the love she'd given Maurice had soured in his selfish heart, repaying her with poison. She had loved the father of her child, and been infatuated with her husband, but neither man in her life had penetrated to the deepest part of her heart, the part that she strove to find onstage. Her life thus far, thought Sarah, had been as meaningless as a tourist's swift visits to a round of monuments.

The fiacre driver had already passed Julie's old house on the Rue St.-Honoré, had barely slowed going around the Comédie Française, and now, in the final stretch up the Avenue de l'Opéra, he was weaving in and out of the horse-drawn wagons and omnibuses as if chased by the Devil in a burning chariot.

"Driver," said Sarah. "Slow down, or I will make you drive the same route all over again, and I will not give you a tip."

"But we are here, Madame Sarah," said the driver, turning about to face his passenger, showing a full mouth of yellow teeth. Sarah looked at the address in her hand, and then at the address on the squat little building compressed between two new brick-faced five-story edifices. She had a sudden vision of the back room her husband must have let on a month-by-month basis, the iron bedpost, the dirty sheets, the cracked windows looking over a courtyard strewn with garbage. "Shall I help you down, Madame?" said the driver, getting down from his seat. "I'm sorry if we were too quick, but the horse, she knows her own pace."

"I'm all right," said Sarah, though she was suddenly incapable of moving from her seat. There was no hurry to go in; her heart told her everything. Even if she had not loved him, Jacques had played opposite her, had shared her bed, had been her husband. In this age of miracles they were making better needles, so that addicts would be less plagued with horrible abscesses, but the last time she had seen the handsome, still young man, his skin was hideous with pockmarks and scabs and scars. She knew that in the room there would be a litter of coffee cups, because addicts believed that coffee would help the natural flow of urine that the drug inhibited. There would be dozens of empty bottles, wine and absinthe and whiskey, for her husband, like poor Jeanne before him, would have nobly tried the time-honored custom of easing his drug intake by drinking himself into oblivion. There would be needles and syringes and rimmers, but no morphine; he would have used it all up the moment he got his hands on the drug, even if he'd had to inject it into his belly or breast or neck.

And she knew, with absolute certainty, that he would be dead.

"I'm happy to help you down, Madame Sarah," said the driver, cap in hand, standing at the curb with his free hand extended like a gentleman's. "It would be an honor."

"Have you ever seen me perform?" asked Sarah suddenly.

"Of course, naturally," said the driver, stepping back and looking up at the celebrity determined to keep her seat in his passenger compartment. He was a bit stoop-shouldered, but his forearms were heavily muscled. "I've seen you more than once, and you were good."

"Thank you."

"Listen to me telling you what I think." The driver laughed. He was becoming more and more concerned. The day was growing rapidly darker, his wife would be preparing his evening meal, and she would hardly believe that it was Sarah Bernhardt, on the verge of tears in his fiacre, who had made him late. "I'm always in the gallery, but I've got very good eyes. I don't miss a thing, even from up there." The driver turned to face the shabby door of the house, so close to the Vendôme Column and the richest homes in the city. "Do you want me to tell someone you're here?"

"Yes, thank you. I'll wait," said Sarah. She handed him the card with the address and Jacques Damala's name, and asked him to find the concierge. Later she would remember that she wanted to offer him a stage box for her next performance, and ask that he come backstage after the show to have a glass of champagne. But like so many of her good intentions, this one would never be carried out, lost in that day's wild rush of feelings.

The driver did as he was told. He was gone for a full five minutes, and when he came back, he was accompanied by the concierge. The driver's weather-beaten face was deathly pale. Jacques Damala was dead, an empty hypodermic needle stuck into the flesh under the breastbone, but Sarah wouldn't let them offer condolences. "Take me home," she said. "And drive as fast as you can."

Every moment she was more and more alone.

She never knew her father, she couldn't hold on to her mother, she had survived her sisters, her first lover, her husband. Everyone was dead or dying, but not Sarah. Soon Mme. Guérard would leave her, eventually Maurice and his bride and child would go off into their own little world, and she would be forced to live a life alone and without meaning.

She compelled herself to think about what the driver had said: that his horse knew her own pace. Perhaps the same thing was true of every living thing, of every age. Once, she had known her pace, understood what she had wanted, had gone after it with all her life. Faced with a loveless world, she had created love where none existed, had found in the expression of her art a comfort and a joy.

Yet there was no longer any risk in her work, no attempt to push her art further than it had ever gone before. When she came out from the wings, she vanquished her *trac* not with an open heart, not with reaching for some truth she had never known, but with a simple memory of a thousand audiences paying tribute to her, a hundred thousand people beating their palms together for what they were about to see. They were not there to experience a play, but to be in the presence of Sarah Bernhardt. It seemed a hundred years ago that she had poured her spirit into the simple verses of *Le Passant* at the Odéon, that she had first exposed her heart by performing *Phèdre* for the sophisticated audience at the Français. She had wanted the audience to pay attention to her, to love and respect her, but she had not expected that respect to solidify, to become like the automatic response of churchgoers to the prayers of their priest.

Long ago, she had been young and the world had refused to love her, to let her into its heart; Sarah had made the world notice, she had forced them to want her. Falling back against the splitting leather cushions of the cab, she tried to slow the wild beating of her heart, tried to remember, like a long forgotten melody, the rhythm of life she once knew.

She was alive, and she was determined to stay alive. As soon as a theater could be rented, she would again do *La Dame aux camélias,* a great production dedicated to Damala's memory. They would cry for her dead husband, while she died for them under the gaslights. Certainly a sentimental, sympathetic crowd would throng the theater, yet Sarah realized that this audience could turn against her as they had once before. To be a monument would be to disappoint them. She swore to herself to be better than she had ever been, to give them everything she possessed as an artist. She needed them to want her always, never to leave her. Even when her skin turned to folds of crepe, her bones creaking louder than rusty hinges, her following must fill the house. Sarah vowed to be faithful to them, to belong to them. In spite of everything, she would endure, she would embrace life in the fullness of their love.

A CHILD CRIES

E
nter, my dear, enter," said the silvery voice, a voice which reached every corner of the dim, very hot room. The bright winter sun was blocked by embroidered tulle curtains, so that at first the young visitor could hardly discern the face and form of the most famous actress in the world. Drawing close to the vague outlines of an enormous bed, she could discern the pampered tufts and swirls of golden hair. This would be one old lady whose coiffure would be flawless, whose clothes would be fresh, whose cheeks would have been rouged by an artist's practiced hands. "Did you close the door, my pretty one?" asked Sarah Bernhardt. "There's a fearful draft, and this room is cold enough already. Come, come, I won't bite. I want to see who and what you are."

"It is a great honor to be allowed to come into your presence, Madame Bernhardt," said the young woman in excellent French. She was English, straight-backed and beautiful. In slightly shaking hands she held out a gift like the offering of a priestess to her god.

"Anyone can come into my presence. They need only buy a ticket, and there I am. Now you will please tell me your Christian name."

"Appollonie," she said, in perfect awe of Sarah, propped up on a mountain of gold and silver pillows. The name elicited a shiver from the old woman. Sarah had known another Appollonie, one of an unremitting series of names and faces and speeches that had visited her since her last illness, whispers of childhood calling to her in old age. How many times in the last week had she, expecting Titine, been surprised to find an unfamiliar servant carrying the breakfast tray? Trying to read through the Hachette translation of Dickens's *Little Dorrit* on her night table, she had found her eyes forming images on the closely printed pages: Nurse, Aunt Rosine, little Regina. And though the windows of the bedroom shut out the noise of the street, she would hear, like a golden bell, her mother's laughter, high-pitched, girlish, once again receiving the extravagant compliment of an admiring gentleman. If life was a circle, she was not remembering the past, but returning to it.

On her last trip to America she had met the great magician Houdini, and asked him whether he was related to Robert-Houdin. He was not; Houdini was a stage name deliberately taken from the old conjurer's name. Houdini was touched to meet someone who had actually seen his mentor's show. And Sarah was moved by the fact that Houdini had changed his name in homage to a showman dead three years before he was born. She wondered if anyone would want to appropriate her name, if the performances seen by so many thousands would vanish from the world along with their mortal audiences, if in a hundred years anyone would have known who and what she had been.

"I know my name's not very English," the girl continued. "My mother is French, and though we live in London, I study mostly French plays."

"Yes, of course," said Sarah. "Appollonie. The English girl with the French name. You want to be an actress, and you have brought me a gift from dear Mrs. Pat. I had her letter only last week, and my secretary told me not a minute ago. You see what my memory is like." The great actress narrowed her green eyes, as if to close the door on false modesty. "Not of course when I must *go on*. I have never forgotten my lines. I was just reading when you came in. I must learn Cleopatra in *Rodogune*. Do you know that this was Corneille's favorite play?"

The young woman's eyes had become accustomed to the bad light. She could see the pain in Sarah's crabbed hands, the wrinkles through the thick makeup over her pale skin. How could anyone, even a heroine, rise under the weight of such tired flesh, walk downstage, and find one's light? Appollonie did not mention last year's disappointment when illness had forced Sarah to drop out of the new Sacha Guitry play. As she extended the gift package, she tried not to stare at the old lady, her eyes made up as if she were indeed about to go on as Cleopatra, her lips as red as a caricature of a whore.

Sarah still did not take the gift. "I knew a girl named Appollonie," she explained. "A very dear girl. In school. It's about a million years ago. Dinosaurs ruled the earth." Sarah, mistaking the girl's unease for distaste at her physical appearance, did not take offense. She remembered that at twenty it was natural to be revolted by an image of what one might live to look like. As though she were onstage, Sarah ran a vain finger through her thin hair, forced a coquette's smile through her lips and cheeks and eyes. "You've seen me before?"

"Yes, Madame Bernhardt."

"Where was it? Before the Great War? In London?"

"Yes. Yes, it was actually," said the young woman. "The first time."

Appollonie had been ten years old, and because she had been raised by a French governess, she understood the language. The play was *La Dame aux camélias,* and though Sarah had been a woman in her sixties, Appollonie hadn't doubted for a moment that Sarah Bernhardt was young, beautiful, and doomed. Sarah's right knee had been so bad that she urged the set designer to place the furniture in strategic lines so that she could lean on it and push herself across the stage. Once the play had begun, no one thought of Sarah Bernhardt's physical troubles. Onstage the actress was radiant, in her first blush of youth, and when she died in the arms of her lover, it was as if all the light had gone from the world. From the moment the dead Marguerite Gauthier rose from the dead to take a dozen curtain calls, Appollonie had been in love.

Appollonie had become one of the theater-mad legions of English schoolgirls who took the twisted "facts" of Sarah's life and converted them into a gospel of art and beauty and truth. Over the years she collected Mucha's flamboyant idealized posters of her idol as Phèdre and Théodora, she bought a dozen reproductions of early photographs of the actress by Nadar, she joyfully inherited a huge scrapbook of Bernhardt clippings from her mother. Like any goddess, Sarah was ageless, not defined by her sex, exempt from any natural laws. This was the woman who at fifty-five had played Hamlet, at fifty-six had played Napoleon's twenty-year-old son, and at sixty-five had played the nineteen-year-old Joan of Arc.

If some elements of the press dared insinuate that these roles were little more than stunts, fueled by nostalgia and respect for an actress long past her prime, Sarah's adulating fans shouted them down. This was no invalid begging for sympathy who in her late fifties had taken a lease on her own theater, and proceeded to perform in forty productions in fifteen years. The same columnists who found fault with her for daring what no one else would pointed to a hundred scandalous liaisons. Lou Tellegen, the handsome matinee idol, had been in one of Sarah's fifty-city American tours; he was thirty-one and she sixty-six, but that did not stop the press from imagining a torrid affair, hinting that the old actress had purchased the young man's body with the promise of a leading role. If the columnists had softened to her somewhat in recent years, it was not out of respect for her age but out of deference to her heroism. An additional injury to the knee that had troubled her for two decades led to the amputation of her right leg in 1915. The operation in February on the seventy-one-year-old Bernhardt had been bigger news than the raging European war. By October she was back on the Paris stage in a one-act patriotic monologue; a few months later, borne on a litter like a Roman empress, she took her monologue through the war-torn countryside to cheer battling French troops in impromptu open-air theaters.

There had been little talk of stunts after that.

She had continued to perform after the war, when there was no longer a pressing national emergency, when there was no special need to bring the national symbol of France to the men dying to protect her borders. The need was her own. Appollonie had read with a fanatic's approving zeal Sarah's statement that she would perform as long as she lived, even if the director might have to "nail her to the scenery."

Sarah chose short pieces in which she could remain seated, her amputation hidden by a lap robe. Each performance had within it the kernel of a farewell. Though her spirit soared, her body was sick and growing sicker. The audience approached her every appearance with veneration. Sarah was larger than life, she was a vision of what men and women aspired to be. There was something she understood that they did not, something in her heart that they wanted to feel before she was gone from their world.

Appollonie saw her perform in Paris in 1920, in an abbreviated presentation of scenes from Racine's *Athalie*. Once the curtain was raised, the facts of her age, her amputation, her mortality were obliterated under the magic of the stage lights. In the role of the murderous widow of King Jehoram of Judah, Sarah had not only been a believable force of danger to the House of David. She illuminated the play so that one could understand the rage and frustration of the impious Baal-worshiper in a land ruled by the invisible god. Without reinventing or reinterpreting the piece, she brought the forgotten poetry into the light, took hold of the audience's attention with sufficient force to fill their hearts with the joyful satiety of art. Sarah had also been so beautiful, so full of grace that at any moment she seemed capable of leaping from her throne.

"You must not cry, my dear girl," said Sarah, seeing the tears in Appollonie's wide eyes. "It's not at all proper for an Englishwoman to cry under any circumstances, but particularly in my house. I'll think myself a bad hostess, I'll imagine that you're crying for lack of a good cup of tea."

"I'm sorry, Madame Bernhardt," said Appollonie. "It's that I'm so happy. I saw you in *Athalie*. I came to Paris, and I had a letter of introduction with me then, but I wasn't ready to go backstage. You were so magnificent that I was just afraid."

No matter what the young woman said, Sarah saw only pity in her wide eyes. "Everyone is more beautiful onstage. Even you will be, my dear," said Sarah. "Now enough nonsense. Let me see my present."

The young woman wiped her eyes and tried to smile. Sarah was mistaken. Appollonie felt no pity, but only a fanatical admiration. The proximity to her idol was making her faint. The blazing fire in the huge marble fireplace had heated the room to a temperature higher than a hothouse, and the invalid's perfume was more overpowering than the heat. Yet she took a step closer through the stale scented air. A cashmere blanket covered Sarah's lower extremities.

Sarah tilted her head, flaring her nostrils and fixing Appollonie with her intelligent eyes. Appollonie returned the gaze; their eyes would have kept locked together for an eternity if Sarah had not finally understood and spoken.

"You want to be an actress," said Sarah.

"More than anything in the world, Madame Bernhardt."

Appollonie dropped the package into Sarah's lap, looking in horror as it pressed the blanket flat where her right leg should have been. Though she had not been asked to sit, she found herself sitting down hard on the armchair at the foot of the bed. The gift was from Mrs. Patrick Campbell, a friend of Appollonie's family, the star of George Bernard Shaw's *Pygmalion.* Sarah opened the package, recognizing at once Gustave Doré's 1853 illustrated edition of Rabelais. Poor Doré had died so long ago, at the age of fifty. Sarah had been in her thirties, and thought the artist too young to die, although certainly not in his first youth. Now she was seventy-nine, and fifty seemed a lifetime ago.

Like so many old people, she had buried most of her generation. Paul Verlaine, born the same year as Sarah, died at fifty-two. Mme. Guérard, whom she missed most of all, had died a year later, leaving Sarah motherless a second time at fifty-three. In those distant days, time had crept along, hour by hour, week by week. Patience was a virtue. Once, one had to wait for a chance to audition, an opportunity to perform, a new year when a part might be offered that would change her life. Today, it seemed every instant was a new season; every time she blinked, the leaves were beginning to fall from the trees, the cold winds of winter were once again being replaced by a gentle summer breeze.

"This is very beautiful, my dear," said Sarah, bringing the tooled leather binding of the Doré book close to her face. "Will you see Mrs. Pat?"

"Yes," said Appollonie.

"Will you please tell her that I love her with all my heart, and that she is the truest friend in all the world?" Sarah could feel pleasure rising in the young woman, the sort of pleasure she felt in the audience when they were responding to the deep spaces between the words of a speech.

"I will tell her, Madame Bernhardt."

"Why do you smile?"

"I never thought I would be with you, not like this. Close enough to touch." Appollonie moved to the edge of her chair. For the first time, Sarah saw her clearly. Her hair was arranged in two no-nonsense auburn plaits, and in her blue eyes was the wild fire of ambition. "And I am so happy that I will see you act once again onstage," said Appollonie.

"Did you ever think they would stop me from going back on?" said Sarah.

"Even when I first walked in, I didn't think it was possible, Madame Bernhardt. But now I know that it is. 'In spite of everything,' " she added Sarah's famous motto as if it were her own.

Sarah didn't mind the borrowing.

Suddenly she remembered the letter from Mrs. Pat in its entirety, like a speech recalled from a play memorized long ago. "Tell me why you are here," said Sarah.

"I believe you know, Madame Bernhardt."

"I want to hear it from you."

Appollonie paused. Her young blue eyes narrowed with a hunger familiar to anyone who had spent a life in the theater. "I want you to tell me if I'm good enough."

"And if I tell you that you're not?" asked Sarah.

Appollonie paused, gathering courage and energy. When she spoke, the tone of her voice grew fervent. "I will forget about acting. I will quit studying. I will get married, I will have children, I will live a conventional life. When I go to the theater it will be to sit in a box." Appollonie got up from the chair, towering above Sarah. She made an effort to speak more calmly. "But if you tell me that I have something, anything, I will do whatever you tell me to be better. I will dedicate my life to following your teaching."

There was a long pause, while the young woman stood perfectly still, raising her eyes where the curtains shut out the sunlight.

Finally, Sarah spoke: "You perform beautifully."

This was not yet what the young woman hoped to hear. "I have not performed for you, Madame Bernhardt," she said, uncertain whether the actress had just insulted her. "I would like to recite for you. I have prepared speeches from *Phèdre*, from *L'Aiglon*, and from *La Dame aux camélias*. It would be an honor."

"You have ambition and you are beautiful," said Sarah. "That is good, my dear." She raised a single crooked finger to her lips, and gestured imperiously to the armchair. Appollonie hesitated only a moment. Then she sat. "You have a lovely speaking voice; that is good too. But what is most important in a speech, in any speech, is that you assimilate all the emotions of the character you play. I am not a modern teacher, you understand. I am not advising you to cut your personality in half, put half of you onstage and half of you off. I am telling you to do something more difficult. When you are playing your character, you must turn yourself inside out, you cannot do it by half. You must empty yourself completely, and then fill what is empty with the character that you play. Do you understand what I am saying?"

"Yes, Madame Bernhardt," said Appollonie, who had read every one of Sarah's interviews printed in England in the past ten years.

Sarah smiled. "I am glad. That is what I thought. When you are onstage you must believe what you say utterly, even if it is only that you will do with your life whatever Sarah Bernhardt tells you to do."

"I hope that you will not take offense—"

"Tell me truthfully, my dear," said Sarah. "Is there anything in the world, myself included, that could prevent you from trying to be an actress, a great actress?"

"There is nothing in the world," said Appollonie in flat tones. "It is because of what I have seen of you, but you are right of course. Even you could not stop me."

"Even if I were to tell you that you have no talent?"

"No one could stop me," said Appollonie with vehemence.

"I know," said Sarah.

"I did not mean to be impolite," said Appollonie.

"That's fine, my dear," said Sarah. "No one can stop you. In spite of everything." Appollonie got up and took hold of Sarah's hands. She had no idea how much Sarah wanted her kiss, and when she brought the cold hands to her lips, she was surprised at the sigh that shook the old woman's frame.

Sarah leaned back on her pillows, and rang the bell for tea. "I am so very glad that you are here," she said. "I am so very glad that you want to go on the stage." Later that day she asked the girl to bring from across the room the battered volume of La Fontaine's

Fables, from which she used to read to Mme. Guérard. In a moment Sarah found her favorite fable, "The Wolf, the Mother, and the Child." It was this fable that Sarah asked Appollonie to recite, closing her eyes in childish joy when she came to the fabulist warning at the end: "Wolves: Do not believe everything told you by a mother when her child cries!"

"Thank you," said Sarah. "You are a very good actress. And you can learn to be as great as anyone."

Sarah died less than three months later, in March of 1923, never again getting a chance to perform onstage. Appollonie would grow to understand that she could never approach the magic that was Sarah's birthright, could never claim the talent and the will and the pain that made up her genius. But all her life Appollonie remembered their afternoon together, remembered her teaching, and, with her aspiration, returned Sarah Bernhardt's love.